AVRIL MARIA SERENE

AUNT TIK'S: THE KILLER APP

A DEBRA ANN WYNN MYSTERY

AMS Media

AMS Media
1646 East North Street #1H
Springfield, Missouri 65803-4357

First printing, June 2025

https://AvrilMSerene.com

AMS MEDIA is a registered trademark of AMS Media, LLC.

Printed in the United States of America

10 9 8 7 6 5 4 3 2 1

ISBN (paperback) for Amazon: 979-8-2857919-6-6

ISBN (paperback) for everyone else: 979-8-9928602-8-3

To Miriam and her search for peace

Her ending was a silent choice, so I would choose to be her voice.

And in her story, I could see her pain in its totality.... - AMS

*"We do not see people as they are, but as they appear to us.
And these appearances are usually misleading."*

- Robert Greene

PROLOGUE

Jessica was nervous.

Awarded her first real challenge since she'd passed her dismembering initiation, she wanted to be sure she did everything exactly right.

But she didn't know quite what to do with the grocery receipt.

The notification of her challenge award came with the location of a Luggage Hero in San Diego's Little Italy and a home address on Kettner Boulevard. The next day, she'd received a snail-mail package containing a note, two locker numbers, and two keys.

The first Luggage Hero locker held a large, empty, cushioned mailer emblazoned with a smiley yellow arrow. Alongside was an Amazon Prime T-shirt, sized medium. The second bin contained a family-sized box of Fruity Cheerios. Stuck to the back with static electricity was a Vons Supermarket receipt.

Jessica's part was simple. She was to place the Cheerios in the cushioned envelope, seal the package, don the T-shirt, and deliver the mailer to the residence address provided in the decrypted instructions.

But those instructions didn't mention the receipt. Jessica tossed it in the package along with the box of cereal. Maybe whoever got the Cheerios would know what to do with it.

———

A bright-yellow New Holland W130C end loader sat gleaming in the afternoon sun under a clear azure sky. The machine waited patiently on the level-graded top of a steep rock-strewn hill, precisely as Sean's decrypted Signal instructions described it.

"Nice equipment for this one," he murmured, searching the ground around the tractor. His eyes landed on a softball-sized rock distinct from the others. Unclipping the measuring tape from his belt, he placed the stone eight feet ahead of the left front tire of the end loader.

He chewed his lower lip as he realized his marker was just three feet away from the unreinforced end of the turf at the cliff's edge.

Man, that's not leaving me any extra room.

The bucket stuck out another six feet from the front wheel. That would put the load out in space three feet past the cliff when he got the machine to the mark. Once he dumped the bucket, the contents wouldn't hit the side of the scarp until halfway down it. That might be okay for the load, but it wouldn't be great for him or the tractor if they went over the edge with it.

With one boot, Sean slammed the top of his rock marker with all his weight. He began stomping around the stone with both feet in a semicircle, trying to read how stable the hard-packed soil was, watching the weeds at the edge for any motion. Satisfied that the ground beneath him wasn't likely to suddenly collapse, his confidence grew that he'd have time to get off and away from the end loader if it *did* flip.

Pulling on his rawhide work gloves, Sean climbed into the cab. He'd picked up the key from the storage locker downtown that morning, and it turned effortlessly in the ignition. With a small puff of blue smoke from its upright exhaust stack, the machine roared and rattled to life, settling into a raspy growl.

Sean chose this task because it seemed a natural fit. He was comfortable around large equipment — he'd worked construction several years ago to pay his freshman college tuition. The challenge was simple: he had to raise the bucket a couple of feet off the ground, pull forward to his marker, and dump its load right at six p.m.

The tractor was brand-new, fitted with a high-capacity front bucket that could hold almost twenty cubic yards of material weighing up to four and a half tons. Someone overflowed the bucket with big chunks of concrete — Sean assumed as part of a previous challenge.

As he pulled the handle to lift the bucket, the pitch of the hydraulic pump's squeal and the stiffness of the lever told Sean the strain on the machine was testing its limits. The rear-mounted engine acted as a counterweight, but even so, the vehicle bounced and rocked with each bucket move.

"Smooth and slow now," Sean cautioned himself under his breath.

Raising the bottom of the bucket two feet off the ground, he feather-pedaled the clutch to bring the end loader forward, careful not to jerk the tractor any more than necessary. Sean paused to monitor the minute hand on his watch once the front wheel reached the stone marker he'd placed, the bucket suspended well out past the cliff's edge.

When it reached twelve, he pushed the dump handle forward.

Concrete and rebar tumbled into the air with a creak and scraping rumble.

The rock and mortar dropped one hundred and fifty feet before sliding and bounding onto the nearly vertical hillside, raising plumes of grayish-white dust and causing a landslide that cascaded down the hill.

Suddenly, a piercing shriek knifed through the air above the rumbling rocks.

Its intensity lingered in Sean's ear, then subsided into the jumble of noises following the raw, broken rubble fanning out onto the street.

Ah, a drama queen among the observers, he thought, even as he was pleased by the shock and surprise the stunt generated.

The fine, acrid dust wafting up from the cliffside burned his nostrils and obscured Sean's view of the street below. Still, he didn't want anyone seeing him peering over the edge of the precipice too long — the game inflicted severe penalties for getting caught.

So, with the challenge that made up his part of the punk completed, Sean shut the tractor down.

Leaving the key in it, he quickly climbed off the seat. Walking at a fast clip, he headed for his tan Ford F-150 parked, per instructions, three blocks away down a dirt path.

✦

A paved street ran below the cliff where the yellow tractor was perched. Parked on the far curb a hundred feet south of the rockslide, still rolling onto the pavement, a lone male observer sat in the shadows of his idling Jeep. As Sean jogged to his pickup on the pathway above, the onlooker scrunched deep into the SUV's seat to avoid notice.

The falling rubble and sliding dirt slowed its descent and spread out as it neared the bottom of the cliffside. Its hidden witness captured every moment on his cell phone in high definition. He didn't want to miss a single detail — save one.

The videographer kept the light-blue Ford Fiesta out of the image frame, now buried under concrete chunks and nearly unrecognizable.

He was pleased he'd had the forethought to turn off the microphone before he began recording. The shrill screaming when the rocks smashed the car wouldn't do, nor would the gradually subsiding moans that followed.

He'd wanted the video to have a more upbeat spin for his audience.

CHAPTER 1

Paul and I were cleaning up in the kitchen and getting Tommy, our three-year-old, ready for his new Montessori class. We'd just finished our breakfasts of French toast and eggs; the smell of maple syrup and turkey sausage lingered in the air.

"See, Debra Ann, I *told* you I can cook!" Paul grinned. "As the only member of this family who's not redheaded, I feel compelled to show I can do my bit for the team."

"I've gotta admit, you know your way around a stove."

I nodded appreciatively, marveling that I was still learning more of Paul's talents three and a half years into our marriage. "But you know this means you'll get more opportunities to cook — a *lot* more. And next time, I expect eggs Benedict with homemade hollandaise sauce."

"Oh, no…." Paul's mouth was open, and alarm showed in his dark eyes — the effect came off a little *too* pronounced.

"I broke the cardinal rule of marital bliss. Guys gotta keep the bar low — let their lovely wives think their husbands can't do anything right. Mission: Incompetence. 'Do what she asks but mess it up when you do' is much better for the marriage and the man's health than saying 'I don't wanna....'"

Tommy was listening.

"Daddy, I know what a cardinal is. It's a red bird with a point on its head. With a mask. I saw pictures. But what's 'in com-', 'in-com-pent-,' 'in…' — that word you said?'"

"Don't worry about that yet, Sprout," Paul answered. "When you find somebody to love who loves you back, and you want to be together forever, I'll tell you *all* about it."

I snorted at Paul's promise, giving him the side-eye.

The cryptic reply didn't satisfy Tommy, scrunching up his freckled nose. "But I have you and Mommy forever, so tell me now!"

Paul looked at me for support, but I could only shrug my shoulders.

Picking him up from his booster seat so he could climb down, I realized how much our son had grown. I try to hit the gym regularly, but at five-nine and almost forty years old, lifting him was awkward enough that I felt a little twinge in my back. Keeping it to myself, I put a hand on Tommy's copper-colored curls and said, "Why don't you go find the boys?"

Suddenly, a burst of raucous laughter resounded from the other end of the house. Marci Robbins's sons — Matt, sixteen, and Mike, fifteen — were watching videos in the den on Paul's old laptop.

Marci, one of my closest friends for over ten years, had dropped her boys off last night. Now into her third year as a Homicide unit detective, she'd gotten an unexpected request from her lieutenant to come into the precinct for a late shift. He needed help on her night off; the department had received reports of three seemingly unrelated murders over the previous twenty-four hours.

"Aunt Deb, come here, check this out!" Matt called from the room we used as a home office.

Mike's howling followed immediately, "Oh, my God, he's gonna *kill* that guy!"

That got my attention. Tommy trailed after me, and as I entered the room, we caught Mike laughing so hard that tears streamed from his eyes.

"Wait, Mike! I gotta rewind this for Aunt Deb!" Matt was excitedly clicking the mouse as he bounced in his seat, his long, curly black hair flying.

Seeing the two, you'd take them for twins. They were skinny and hyperactive — when both got going, they became a party unto themselves. I leaned in and squeezed between them, trying not to catch an accidental elbow to the face.

The laptop screen displayed a video of a home, shot from across the street, likely taken with a cell phone camera.

An older but well-cared-for silver BMW 325i sat parked in the driveway of a two-story, tan brick house. An attractive, short brunette in her mid-thirties, dressed in black yoga pants and a green sweatshirt, walked out of the home's front door. She skirted the nose of the sedan, getting in on the driver's side.

A tall, slender man in a white polo shirt and jeans, roughly the same age as the woman, stepped out of the residence, accompanied by a full-grown Irish setter. Pulling the door shut, he headed to the car's passenger side, letting the dog into the back seat and taking his place up front. The car's reverse lights flashed as it backed out of the drive.

When the car shifted to pull forward, the image went out of focus momentarily. I briefly saw snippets of the interior of another vehicle, as though the person filming was ducking down to hide from the passing BMW.

As things came back into focus, the BMW was further down the street, the camera now shooting through the photographer's windshield. An engine accelerated in the background as the image followed the silver sedan, hanging back when the BMW slowed approaching a stop sign.

A bottled-water truck had stalled in the intersection, the traffic on the cross street edging its way around the big diesel.

"Look, look!" Matt urged me. "Watch this."

As the BMW waited for the truck to clear its path forward, a raggedy man carrying a bucket and squeegee stopped at the passenger side of the German hardtop and began swiping away at its windshield. A hoodie obscured his face as he leaned into his work, leaving a trail of greasy streaks on the glass with the sleeve of his Army jacket.

The car's driver rolled down her window and yelled at the vagrant to stop, her partner chiming in.

The setter began barking loudly, its claws clicking and scraping on the inside of the window glass, trying to get at the squeegee guy.

The driver deployed the windshield washer, but instead of washer fluid, what looked like used black motor oil sprayed out of the jets onto the glass.

The wipers smeared the mess over the entire windshield.

"Can you believe it?" Mike howled.

A red Mustang pulled up next to the driver's door of the BMW, blocking the oncoming lane.

A heavyset man jumped out, carrying a paper grocery sack.

"I got this!" he yelled.

Plopping the bag on the hood of the silver car with a loud thump, he pulled out a bottle of dishwashing soap and a roll of paper towels. As he squirted the dish detergent all over the windshield as far as he could reach, his belt buckle dug into the paint on the BMW's fender, prompting a yelp from the front seat.

Ignoring the complaint, he yanked a wad of towels off the roll. He swabbed at the green and black goo, timing his swipes between each wave of the wiper blades, his buckle ripping horizontal scrapes across the car's sheet metal.

By this time, the male passenger had both palms in the air, bellowing, "What the *fuck?*" out his window. I cringed, confident Marci would've preferred her boys didn't hear that.

A graying woman left the sidewalk and hobbled to the passenger side of the BMW, crying out, "Here, you need water!"

She dumped several liter bottles onto the hood, then furiously flailed her forearms across it to keep them from rolling off. The water she shook from the bottles added to the glop on the windshield.

The churning of the wipers generated a rapidly expanding brown foam, now cascading down the car's hood and fenders.

Amid the scraping, screaming, and barking, the parade of "helpers" grew. One activated a fire extinguisher to blow off the goop; another dumped an industrial-sized sack of Tidy Cats kitty litter on top of everything to dry up the stubborn foam remaining.

When the speeding wipers hit the piles of clay, one broke off and flew over the side of the car, nearly hitting a teenager in the gathering crowd.

The end of the other blade shot straight up, away from the windshield, twisting uselessly in the wind with every attempted swipe.

Even against the background noise, the crunching and grinding of clay granules working their way into the gears of the wiper mechanism was audible.

Although they'd already seen this at least once, Marci's boys couldn't stop giggling. When the wiper blade sailed away, they yowled in laughter.

There was a jump in the video — the BMW driver had exited the car during the break. She was crying, sitting on the grass of the parking strip alongside her partner and the excited dog, now straining at its leash.

The video cut again to a later scene: a tow truck hauled the car off by its rear wheels — its front end looked like one TV news crews like to show in the aftermath of a vicious tornado.

The recording broke away once more. The BMW and observers were gone; the tangled mass of cars had freed itself and moved on. The silver car's driver and her man were still in the grass off the curb. She cried softly into his shoulder as he patted her back with his free hand. Their dog, spent, lay on the ground beside them.

Out of view of the camera, a smattering of applause rose in the distance and grew louder as another tow truck turned toward the pair from the cross street. This one pulled behind it a brand-new, deep royal blue BMW 330e xDrive sedan, the dealer stickers still on the windshield, and a large red bow affixed on top.

The man said something to the woman and pointed at the tow vehicle. She turned to look over her shoulder, her eyes wide and mascara running. It gradually dawned on her what had just happened. The man held up a key fob. She turned toward him, grabbed it, and began beating her balled-up fists on his upper chest, once again shrieking — but this time in joy.

"Wow, that was *some* video!" I exclaimed.

Matt beamed at me, almost as though he'd created it.

"Talk about bait and switch. Where in the world did you find the link?"

"Mike and I joined a free website — they call it 'Aunt Tik's.' They do punks — you know, play jokes on people, like Ashton Kutcher used to do on TV before he got old. When you join, you can volunteer to do parts of the punks they play on people."

I'm not much younger than Kutcher; hearing him called "old" stung. But I understood what Matt was trying to say.

"So, all those people in the video were plants?"

Matt and Mike both nodded with wide grins.

The credits were rolling, but the names weren't real. They looked more like account usernames typical of social media platforms.

I had to admit it was a great concept — it had me a little freaked out until I saw how it ended; still, I wouldn't forget the video anytime soon. Belatedly, my motherly instincts kicked in on behalf of my obligation to look after Marci's interests.

"Okay, that *was* awesome," I conceded, "but *please* tell me you boys didn't join this website to do anything like that to anyone. Nice surprise, yeah. But only if she doesn't have a heart attack first."

"Nah, Aunt Deb," Matt replied. "You have to pay and be eighteen to become a member. We just wanted to see what everybody else did."

While I was grateful that I could relay that information to Marci, I couldn't help but note real disappointment in his answer.

The good news was that Matt wouldn't turn eighteen for two more years … I could only hope, for Marci's sake, that the two would grow out of their fascination by then.

CHAPTER 2

Paul was on his cell when I returned to the kitchen to tell him what the boys were up to.

"It's Louis," Paul mouthed at me silently and then spoke into the phone. "Hi, Lieutenant. You caught us finishing breakfast. I'm getting Tommy ready for school, and Debra Ann wants to say hi. Okay if I put you on speakerphone?"

"Sure, I'll use my nice words." Lieutenant Louis Harbin chuckled as Paul hit the button and set his phone on the table.

"Listen, I need to ask a favor. I hoped I'd catch you before you started your morning rounds at the Forensics lab."

"Hi, Louis, what's up?" I announced myself.

"Hey, Debra Ann — if you can spare a few minutes, I'd like your input, too. It's personal, but I need your professional opinions, maybe more. It's a little between the lines — someone asking me for help. I don't want to talk about it over the phone. I know you just ate, but how would you feel about getting together for coffee?"

"Works for me," Paul answered. "Honey, don't you have something going this morning…?"

"I do … We've got the UPI meet-and-greet to discuss adding us to their aggregated news-and-analysis providers. But Doug can handle it. He's done some of these outreaches from the wire and newsfeed services. I can drop in on the meeting later and make it work. Marci should be picking up her boys any minute now."

"The Denny's restaurant on Rosecrans, then?" Louis asked.

Paul looked at me, and I nodded.

"Works for us — give us thirty minutes," Paul replied, and we signed off.

"Doubling up on breakfast shouldn't hurt my diet, right?" Paul lifted his eyebrows, seeking my support for the idea.

My crooked smile was less than sympathetic as I picked up my cell to call Doug Stein. An old friend, he's now my partner in our six-month-old newsgathering startup. Our new business was why, after talking it over with Paul, I still used my maiden name, "Wynn," professionally rather than "Castro," Paul's last name. Using my birth name helped tie the old to the new. That continuity allowed our fledgling enterprise to tap into the reputation and relationships I'd built as an investigative journalist.

Paul and I had lived together for a year in college. We'd reunited when he came to San Diego as a U.S. Navy officer serving with NCIS a little over five years ago.

Paul took a civilian position with the California Bureau of Forensic Services shortly after we began dating again. The higher income and location stability helped while he cared for his daughter Cindy, who passed following a torturous battle with cancer.

The state later lent Paul's services to the San Diego Police Department when they formed the Joint Terrorism Task Force. That position became long-term, working exclusively with SDPD to help close high-profile cases. Paul also applied his skills and training to reassess evidence in a backlog of cold cases. He focused primarily on homicides, exempt from California statutes of limitation.

As his alliance with SDPD became semipermanent, Paul worked closely with Lt. Harbin, whose rank with the police department was roughly equivalent. They partnered well despite an eleven-year age difference. It wasn't long before their relationship spilled into our personal lives, making the three of us fast friends.

I didn't usually join the two for their working get-togethers, so this morning's invitation piqued my interest — and a slight change in my routine wouldn't hurt anything. After Doug and I finished our conversation, I dialed our babysitter.

Sophia Ferguson, "Fia" to Tommy, had been our sitter for the past year. She lived with her mom just three doors down, on the other side of the street, and she and Tommy got along famously. An eighteen-year-old senior in high school, Sophia was always looking for an excuse to drive, so we'd given her a child's convertible car seat to keep in the back of her little Mazda, ready to go.

Sophia was heading out the door when I called, and she agreed to run Tommy to his preschool before leaving for her classes. Once Marci picked up her boys, we'd be free to meet Louis.

Paul and I got to the restaurant first, taking a corner booth. I scooted over on the bench seat, my husband seating his six-two frame beside me. A few moments later, Louis arrived, and Paul waved him over. Where Paul was tall and fit, Louis stood a few inches shorter and sported a paunch he'd developed over the years on a cop's diet. Idly, I wondered whether Paul's black nest of curls would one day give way to Louis's brush of brown hair, skimming his shirt collar, a circle of scalp on top, and the sides heavily grayed.

"Good morning, Debra Ann. Thanks for coming," Louis offered, grunting as he lowered himself into the booth opposite us.

Paul jumped right in. "I heard you're going to get your twenty-year brass next week! You could have mentioned it, you know. I would've hated to miss the festivities."

Louis feigned irritation. "Oh, yeah, it's great when they make a big deal telling the whole world you're older than dirt."

"That's okay." Paul laughed. "The gossip mill has already spread that around pretty much everywhere."

When not on the clock, the men were close comrades and equals. Officially, however, Louis had taken over as commander of SDPD's

Homicide Unit eighteen months before, with Paul becoming his primary liaison with Forensics. Although Louis's advancement subtly changed their work dynamic, it didn't impact our social lives as longtime friends.

Louis's wife, Jenny, a schoolteacher for over a decade, was pursuing her master's in child psychology. I asked him how she was doing, and he gave us an update before pivoting.

"What's up with the news business, Debra Ann?" I knew Louis intended his question as more conversational than probing.

I'd been an investigative journalist now for seventeen years. After earning my journalism master's at USC Annenberg, I spent the next nine years with the *Union-Tribune*, at the time a real newspaper, San Diego's major daily. That was where I met Doug Stein. A little older than I was, he'd taken me under his wing, and we shared dozens of bylines. A few years after I'd left the paper, Dad joined my mother and little brother Eddie in our family plot at the memorial gardens. In his will, my father had left me a generous trust that opened up my career options.

Doug received his MBA a year later, earning it in his off hours while working at the paper. Not long after, he became the latest victim of the *Union-Tribune's* extended death throes. In the meantime, I'd been working as a stringer doing freelance work. My articles included those on the James and Theresa Seaver cases and the Hodin cabal exposé. They'd burnished my résumé and reputation in the field, making my work marketable to a broader audience.

After some lengthy dinner conversations once the paper let Doug go, he'd convinced me we should open a modern, high-tech online news bureau together. The early going had been rough, but we could see brighter lights on the horizon.

While telling Louis about the stories I was developing, I kept it brief. Despite his polite question, I could sense that he wanted to get to whatever was on his mind.

Paul had the same thought.

"So, boss, you called this meeting. What's going on?"

"Our neighbor requested my help this weekend. I think you've met Tracy Nielsen several times; she was at the barbecue last Fourth of July … ?"

"Yes, the single mom in the Dutch Colonial south of you," I recalled. "She seemed nice … not the outgoing life-of-the-party type, but she comes off like a good person who cares about her kids. In pharmaceutical sales, if I remember correctly. What did she need?"

The waitress brought our coffee, left the pot, and took our breakfast orders. Louis went for the Lumberjack Slam this morning, appeasing the cholesterol addiction he blames whenever he's up for his annual physical. I stuck with coffee, and Paul opted for a Danish with his caffeine.

"So," Louis began, "Tracy's oldest, Steve, got caught up in something serious. A traffic stop turned into weapons charges, federal. The good news is, it's a first offense, so hopefully, he'll get his hands slapped — best case, maybe some probation that they'll expunge once he completes it. Tracy wants me to look into it from a detective's point of view and give her some guidance.

"But now that I'm the unit commander, I have to consider appearances, and doing personal favors becomes, well, awkward. I want to help her and her son, so I thought maybe I'd abuse *your* free time — ask if the two of you could be my eyes and ears. Just to check some things out."

If Louis felt it necessary to ask, he knew only too well we'd do whatever we could to help. Paul intentionally blew past his politeness.

"Since you're helping them, I assume Steve's a decent kid?"

"When he was younger, he'd mow our yard, walk the dog, that kind of thing, for extra money. Steve worked hard and did a good job. When he became a teenager, Jenny and I always felt we could trust him to babysit the twins. I appreciated that Steve was honest. He'd tell us when, say, a dish got broken. Never tried to hide it."

To me, it seemed quite a leap from that to gun charges.

"So, when did Steve change? Or did he?"

Louis pursed his lips.

"Jury's still out. Tracy told me that Steve stole her credit card a couple of months ago to buy a gallon of paint stripper and two dozen cans of fluorescent orange and gloss-black paint. He refused to acknowledge the theft or explain the reason."

I'd left the coffeepot lid open, and the waitress leaned in to swap it out.

"I sympathize with her," Louis continued. "It's tough to tell at that age what you should and shouldn't worry about. I can see positives and negatives as mine move out of their tweens. But I've got Jenny to help me figure it all out. Tracy doesn't have anyone."

Something's missing, I thought.

"Earlier, you said 'serious.' You wouldn't say that about a swiped card or an offense punishable with a 'hand slap.' I'm guessing there's more to this. An honest kid stealing is a big change in itself. And then there's the question, 'how'd he get from taking a credit card to something involving illegal weapons?' and maybe more you haven't mentioned yet … So, just out of curiosity, *how* serious are we talking here?"

Louis sighed, his expression wry.

"A lot more than I'd want any of *my* kids caught up in. Mind you, I'm getting this thirdhand, so don't hold me to the finer points. If you're willing to dig into this, you'll want to talk to Tracy and get it straight from her."

Louis exhaled through his teeth as he eyed me.

"He's tangled up somehow with an online group that issues what he called 'challenges.' And that's all he'd tell her. She doesn't have enough information to know *who* they are. But she *does* know that one little task Steve performed for this group got him charged with — get this — transporting a loaded AR-15."

Paul and I exchanged surprised glances in near lockstep.

"An assault rifle? *Loaded?*" Paul pulled his head back, his face showing concern mixed with disbelief.

"And … the weapon was on a tripod, mounted to the car's floorboards — rigged up to trigger remotely from any location on the planet, using the Internet."

"Whoa, are you *kidding?* That's full-on ATF territory!" Paul exclaimed, not prepared for the sudden jump in the level of criminality.

"Not done *yet*," Louis continued. "Given a choice of anywhere in the world, he planned to park that junker with the ready-to-fire AR-15 in the worst possible spot."

"And where might *that* be?" Caught up in the story, I'd become impatient.

"Why, across the street from a magistrate's house, of course."

CHAPTER 3

lthough I couldn't have anticipated Louis's response, it *did* explain why we were here.

A dozen questions popped into my mind.

"You said he 'planned' to park there. We wouldn't be discussing this if things didn't backfire on him. How? Before or after he'd made it to the judge's house?"

Louis explained that the heretofore-rebellious teenager feared getting busted for driving too fast. So, he cruised the old beater and its contraband down Interstate 5 at fifteen miles per hour below the speed of other traffic — during the tail end of rush hour. Only a fraction of the way to his destination, the boy had a half-mile of pissed-off drivers behind him, honking and flashing their high beams. To register their displeasure, they began pulling around him and then intentionally cutting back in way too close to his front bumper.

The vehicle had one rear window completely blacked out and factory tint on the others, so it drew attention anyway. Sure enough, a CHiP officer saw all this and pulled Steve over under suspicion of impaired driving.

Then he saw that assault rifle in the back seat.

The cop called for backup, and three patrol units joined his bike and the car Steve was driving on the side of the freeway.

I asked Louis how Steve explained his cargo. He said the kid refused to give the police any straight answers.

"Their watch commander, thinking, 'old car, young kid, assault rifle,' called the Gangs Intervention Unit to the site.

"Meanwhile, Steve's cell phone is on the passenger seat, running Google Maps. Instead of an address, the destination window had a GPS location. The gang unit lieutenant arrived and checked the coordinates. They pinpointed a spot right across the street from the private residence of San Diego County Superior Court Judge Silvia Wasserman."

"*Oh, my God…,*" was all I could say. I knew the judge was a single mother with several young daughters.

Louis ran his hand over his head. "So, an officer asks Steve if there are any other weapons in the car they should know about. Steve replies, 'Yeah, I left my suicide vest in the trunk.'"

Paul and I were stunned.

"*Holy shit,*" Paul exclaimed. "What was that kid smoking?"

"I can only guess he thought that biting sarcasm would make these people leave him alone.

"As you might imagine, now everybody freezes in place or backs off this vehicle until the bomb squad arrives. Those guys go over that old car with tweezers and a magnifying glass, looking for explosives. That simple traffic stop turned into a four-hour ordeal for everyone on that stretch of highway."

Louis propped his elbows up on the table and dropped his chin between his wrists, his cheekbones resting on the heels of his hands. He stared at the salt and pepper shakers, drew a deep breath, and sat back up.

"Tracy retained a good lawyer, so that'll help. The only off-ramp for Steve is full disclosure. But Steve wants to play it close to his chest. He insists the incident was just part of some game he was involved in."

"Game? Like online, maybe fantasy role-playing? Something like *Dungeons and Dragons?*" I struggled to make the pieces fit.

"Tracy didn't know. He kept telling her, 'Everybody plays it, it's no big deal.' He goes into his shell and shuts down when anyone else asks about it."

"Not a game anymore once someone introduces a loaded gun into the contest," Paul scoffed. "Then it becomes, at some level, a matter of life and death."

"So, Tracy's asking me to investigate the group Steve's involved with. It needs to be off the clock. Get their story and learn what they're trying to accomplish. She especially needs to know whatever it is they're holding over Steve.

"That part gets a little trickier since it's a federal investigation. We're out of the loop. A local jurisdiction homicide unit asking the feds to keep them apprised when there's no deceased raises eyebrows. Usually, I'd call in favors from friends at Quantico in circumstances like these.

"But my role heading the unit escalates things — people attach more importance to my requests, which is not what I want in this situation."

Paul understood Louis's predicament.

"No problem, boss. I've got your back. You and I know some of the same people; I'll make those requests in my name. Forensics' purview includes various types of crimes, and our responsibilities include running down the weaponry used. They'd expect us to stay abreast of the skills, methods, and technologies employed to discharge assault rifles remotely on our turf. I'll approach them from that angle."

Louis smiled his thanks, paused, and then went on.

"I need to be clear because, officially, you report to me, Paul. I don't want to pressure you to do anything outside the normal workflow. Jenny would kill me, and then I'd have to answer to Debra Ann."

He smiled at me, then turned back to Paul.

"If you want to stay out of it, you'll get no complaint from me; it's all cool. That goes for you, too, Debra Ann."

Paul looked at me. His right hand rested on the table, and I put my left hand on his.

"Of course, we're both in," Paul said.

"Marci will want in, too," I offered. "If I ask her as a friend outside the department, no one will think she's doing off-the-books work at your instruction. But I'll tell her exactly as you told us — she's under no obligation. She'd know what the street says about anything else this group is involved in."

Marci passed the exam for her gold shield three years ago after climbing through the trenches amid many personal challenges. She moved to Homicide from Major Case early last year. Marci thrived in her role, and her superiors assigned her as the lead detective for several recent murders. Having her as a dear friend for all these years meant I was biased, but Paul and Louis had both worked with Marci, enjoyed the experience, and respected her.

"Thanks," Louis responded, "I'd greatly appreciate that. Ethically, I'm crowding the line here and need to be up-front with anyone who tries to help."

"Tracy might welcome contact from someone who's not law enforcement," I suggested. "Why don't I call her to understand better where she's at and what we can do for her? Assuming we're good to go, I'll talk to Steve and see if I can establish a rapport with him."

"The court hasn't set bail," Louis informed me. "The feds are still contracting with Western Regional Detention Facility, the privatized county jail, for pretrial detention. You'd have to see him there until he bonds out."

"That's okay." I knew the setting could provide leverage if Steve proved uncooperative. "A glimpse of freedom on the other side of a partition in the jail's visitor area might provide some incentive. Talking to someone who's neither a criminal nor armed could be a welcome change; maybe he'll open up."

"While you're interviewing Steve," Louis added, "I'll visit Mondo. You're welcome to join us, Paul."

Captain Edmond "Mondo" Cranston, recently promoted as the department's new Vice unit commander, was one of the finest officers on the force, someone the three of us considered an ally.

"I'd like to tag along," Paul replied. "Mondo always has an interesting take."

"He's up to speed on most things involving the Internet and digital crime," Louis agreed. "Let's see if he's heard anything about a new criminal group in the area. One that's recruiting young kids in middle-class neighborhoods to commit major felonies, maybe through online games."

A sardonic grin crossed Louis's face.

"I paid a high price for stumbling around the web by myself. Most of what I retrieved was unrelated garbage, primarily references to play-by-post role-playing games. Now my browser cookies tell Google I'm a failure-to-launch, living in my mother's basement. Whenever I open my computer, I get hit with ads for online games."

Paul tried to stifle a laugh.

"Mondo has sophisticated search filter tools. Maybe we can get him to donate his time to do a deep dive for us and chase down anything he finds."

<hr>

Several hours later, after we'd all returned to our regular routines, I got a text from Paul: "So, how'd you like to hobnob with the rich and famous? :)"

I texted him back: "Why? Are you one of those now? ROTFLMFAO."

He phoned me a few minutes later.

"Hi, sweetheart. I'm sorry to report I'm still groveling for nickels. The government has to take half of them away from us to give to wealthy people so they can pay for their orange spray tans...."

"Awww … I had such high hopes the day would turn out nice," I said with a chuckle.

"…but I've got a new coworker with deep pockets. It might be a better career path to suck up to somebody like that. He's offering his fellow detectives free tickets to Saturday night's Rady Children's Hospital charity ball. Louis is passing his on to us. Getting a little taste of the rarefied atmosphere could be enlightening. Afterward, we could come home, get drunk on cheap wine, and bemoan our poor choices in life. What do you think?"

"Sounds like a hoot — why not?"

"Okay, I'll let Louis know we'll take them off his hands."

"Wait, how'd you end up working with a flush detective in the first place?"

"Louis touched base with Mondo to set up a meeting about Tracy's situation with Steve. Mondo's got a new second-in-command, a Lieutenant Strickland — Bob, if I remember correctly. He comes to us from the vice unit in San José, but I understand he's originally from here.

"Anyway, Strickland's in with the high-society crowd. He inherited a big chunk of change from a relative, or so I'm told. His family is one of the sponsors of Saturday's charity ball."

"You don't see that too often," I had to admit. "Usually, when someone in law enforcement trips over a bunch of money, they can't wait to give up their badge. Of course, that might be because there's something fishy about how they stumbled across the cash. Your Mr. Strickland is the first I've heard of anyone in the trenches coming into a lot of family money."

"Mondo suggested the charity ball as a good way for Strickland to meet everyone socially," Paul explained, "so anyone with a city badge gets in on Strickland's dime. I'm technically an employee of the state, so I didn't get an invite.

"You know Louis isn't one for society affairs anyway, and going by himself was a deal-breaker. Jenny has a night class at SDSU and couldn't take the time away. So, he begged off.

"Louis sent his tickets to my inbox with a note that he thought we might enjoy going to a hoity-toity soiree. It's at six-thirty, Hotel Del. Black tie, dinner, and dancing until midnight. Can you check with Sophia to see if she can babysit Tommy? She wouldn't have to go to school the next day, but I don't know if her mother will let her stay out of the house that late...."

"For a night at the Hotel Del, I'll turn on all the persuasion I can muster! Maybe we'll see some celebs."

"Maybe," Paul acknowledged the possibility. "But I'll take my date over any of them."

Oh, nicely played!

And Paul knew it — I could hear the grin in his voice.

Chapter 4

I wanted to talk to Tracy in person while Louis's words were still fresh in my mind. When I called the number Louis gave me, a woman picked up on the third ring, seeming hesitant at first.

Once I'd announced myself and verified it was Tracy, I explained, "You may not remember, but my husband Paul and I were both at the July 4th picnic last year — I'm a friend of your neighbor, Louis Harbin."

"Yes, Debra Ann, I remember — I enjoyed talking with both you and Paul. He won the karaoke contest hands down."

"You have a good memory! I'm an investigative journalist, and I'm calling in semi-work mode. Louis shared some details about Steve's situation. He asked if I could help — as a reporter, but off the record. Do you have a few moments for a conversation?"

"Yes, I do. Louis told me you might be calling. Steve's still in custody, and I've taken some personal time off work. I appreciate that you're willing to help us. I imagine you have some questions for me?"

"Good; yes, I do. Has there been a bail hearing yet?"

"No, the lawyer tells me he's filed some motions, and the hearing should be the first of next week."

"So, we don't know yet when Steve will be released. I'd prefer to talk to him sooner rather than later to see if he'll open up to me. Would you object to me visiting him before they let him out?"

Tracy seemed pleased with the prospect, and her tone was welcoming.

"Oh, not at all. I think it would be a good thing."

"Louis tells me Steve's been a pretty good kid in the past, works hard, does a good job, honest. *Something's* different for all this to have happened. Still, no one changes completely overnight. Can you give me some idea where Steve's head might be now? Any twists and turns he took to get there?"

"You know … when Steve was younger, as a single mother, I couldn't imagine raising a better child. He was smart, always eager to help, earned good grades, and got along well with most people."

There was pride in Tracy's voice; then, her tone became less upbeat. "But shortly before he turned nineteen, Steve's behavior deteriorated — about a year ago. He started missing classes at UCSD and hiding his grades. When I did see them, they were pretty bad.

"He'd stay up until all hours of the night and just disappear with no warning. He'd come for breakfast the next day without explanation, as though nothing had happened that he needed to tell anyone."

I'd heard the same complaints from friends, and I could sympathize.

"There's always that difficult period parents hate when their teenager wants to be independent while still living under Mom and Dad's roof."

Tracy agreed.

"Girls, cars, drugs, alcohol… I expected I'd have to navigate some of those things. You know, *new* things to deal with. I never thought about changes to what we already had.

"Then, one day, he took my credit card without permission to buy some paint. First, he denied it, and then, when I wanted to take what he bought back for a refund, he wouldn't tell me what happened to the paint.

"In the past, when he did something he knew was wrong, he'd 'fess up and take his lumps. I never thought he'd lie to my face."

Tracy let out a long sigh.

"But that's not why he's in trouble now. How did this all start? I mean, the specific thing they arrested him for…."

"He wouldn't tell me much," Tracy confided. "But it began with a simple job he signed up for, something he calls a 'challenge.' He was supposed to drive this old car from one location to another. He's adamant that's all it was, nothing more. He did say they warned him not to check out the car. Don't look; just drive."

"But it's a car with an *AR-15* mounted in it…."

"He says that wasn't obvious at first." Her tone had tightened.

"Being a typical teenager, he *has* to look around. Someone modified the back seat. He pulls aside a tarp and sees an automatic rifle with a banana clip and a webcam sight clamped on it. The gun barrel's pointed straight at the rear driver-side window. The whole thing's hooked up to circuit boards, gears, and wires and mounted on a tripod bolted to the floor. He says a car battery on the other side of the center hump made everything go.

"I asked him why someone would build something like that. He guessed it was so somebody could fire the gun remotely. I was terrified when I realized what Steve had gotten himself into."

No wonder, I thought. Tracy's description made the hairs on my neck bristle, but I kept my voice even.

"This sounds like a sophisticated setup. Is this real, or a teenager's idea of things from a graphic novel he read?"

"It's funny you'd ask where this is coming from. Maybe not comic books, but a couple of weeks ago, I heard Steve and his friends discussing an online website. They called it 'antics' … or something like that. I think it's some kind of online club — I googled it but couldn't find anything.

"All he'll say is that it's a social media thing for playing games. They require members to do certain things to belong, all very secretive. But when his friends were over that day, I swear they talked about cutting somebody up. I hope I misunderstood. You know, kids and their slang…."

I turned this information over in my mind.

"Worst case, something satanic, maybe with blood rituals?" I mused. "Still, you'd see obvious signs of something like that. Clothes, posters on the wall, weird artifacts lying around. Cults proselytize, and secrecy wouldn't help. Or it could be a subversive group. Political, as opposed to religious."

Tracy ran with that thought.

"Our attorney wants to know — if he can't negotiate a deal for Steve, he only gets one crack at a defense. He needs to know who else has a hand in it and their motivations."

It made a difference if the results couldn't have harmed anyone because this was a slap-dash thing thrown together by people who didn't know what they were doing. Intent would still be a serious issue, but insincere or sloppy follow-through would help dial down the threat level.

"How much effort did this group put into setting up that gun? Is Steve filling in the blanks with assumptions or an overactive imagination?"

"I had my doubts, too. Then Steve told me he took pictures of the setup with his cell phone. The feds confiscated the phone and impounded the car, but Steve has Google Cloud to back up his mobile phone photos. So, I found the pictures and copied them. Let me text you a couple of them."

That just worsened the puzzle.

"If he was aware enough to take snapshots, why on Earth didn't he just walk away? Leave the car there and make up an excuse, like maybe he got the date wrong?"

"Believe me," Tracy replied, "I've asked myself that question. I tried to bring it up with Steve, but he won't answer me."

I'm not technical, but I learned some things from my dad's construction crew, especially their fascination with working on cars. My stomach knotted up as I saw the wired connections in Steve's photos. Whoever built this thing didn't just twist the wires together; they'd soldered, wire-nutted, and taped them. There were other signs of professionalism – insulating standoffs under the circuit boards, the cuts in the metal straight and clean, bolts and nuts instead of screws. So much for my wishful thinking that the builders might be amateurs or at least careless.

It's plausible the kid knew just enough about guns and technology to realize too late that this was a lot more serious than he'd anticipated. He probably thought he was in deep doo-doo no matter what because he wasn't supposed to check out the car.

"From what I pieced together," Tracy said, "he was afraid of what would happen if he didn't complete his instructions. Something in the 'antics' membership rules."

It suddenly struck me how all this must have impacted her life, dumped in her lap in the few days since answering a phone call from the arresting officer.

I felt for her.

"I'm sorry you've had to deal with this alone."

"It *has* been a wake-up call. I was so spoiled. My son never caused trouble when he was younger, so I managed just fine.

"I can't say I've been totally by myself; a few people have tried to step up, but it hasn't been helpful — this is as new to them as it is to me. Before Steve got arrested, I mentioned the credit card incident to my ex, but Jerry thought it was a phase that wouldn't amount to much. He didn't have to see or deal with it every day, so, out of sight, out of mind.

"Now, Jerry wants to go in, guns blazing, and take on everybody to save the day. But my lawyer says that's the last thing we need — it sends the wrong message."

I steered the conversation to positive ground.

"Let's talk about how Louis and I can help. He tells me you understand that because this is a federal case, we can't intervene directly with the specific charges or their process."

"Oh, I wouldn't want anyone to interfere with whatever the law requires."

Tracy's voice was firm.

"I just need the investigators to know all the facts and see the whole picture. I *want* Steve to pay his dues for anything he's done wrong. Hopefully, the process will help him clean up his act.

"But I think he's caught in the middle of something and taking the fall for other people. Steve made a mistake, but I don't believe he intended to commit a crime. If it was just an error in judgment, it shouldn't permanently derail his future. The federal investigators don't seem to take this 'antics' thing seriously, so I asked Louis for help."

Her worry was obvious even over the phone.

"That's right up our alley, something we *can* do," I reassured her. "If federal agents choose not to investigate problems local to us, nothing stops us from seeing what's there, though we'll need to tread lightly. Louis's position as commander of the homicide unit and the two of you being neighbors means anyone on the force must be professional – they can't do anything differently than they would for anyone else. So, their asking around has to be unofficial until they find something to latch onto. That's where I come in."

"I understand and appreciate their situation."

Tracy paused.

"I believe that once all the facts are known, Steve will get through this okay and do what he should. I trust the system. If I'm right — that he didn't mean to do what they've accused him of — the truth will eventually come out. It just needs to happen before they ruin Steve's life."

"I don't have enough facts yet," I replied, "but I'd agree with you based on what Louis told me."

"The federal investigators keep asking me questions, insinuating Steve isn't giving them the whole story. I'm concerned Steve doesn't even *know* 'the whole story.' They want blood from a turnip. They've threatened him and me that if they can't get it, they'll lay it all on him.

"The worst possibility is that maybe he does know something, but he doesn't want to — what do they call it? — 'rat somebody out.' Steve's not stupid. And yes, I know he's done some things that make people doubt that. Still, if he could safely expose this cult, or whatever it is, he would."

"Let's take this one step at a time — we'll see what Steve shares if he's willing to trust me and where we can go from there. It would help to know his bond situation. If prosecutors aren't blocking reasonable bail, they may at least *suspect* that Steve's not the heavyweight in this thing."

"Our attorney thinks they'll let him bond out. If it's not too crazy, I've got equity in the house I can put up, and my ex has resources he'll contribute."

"Good. I've got a better idea of where to start and the work I must do. Thank you for your time — I'll keep in touch as things progress."

"Thanks again, Debra Ann. You don't know how much we appreciate what you're doing."

"Don't thank me until it's resolved. But I'm glad I can help."

I promised to stop by after talking with her son.

I'd shown Tracy confidence ahead of the conversation I planned with Steve because she needed that from me. However, Steve was a teenager at the stage where having independence in his personal affairs was a big deal. That's especially true for someone demonstrating their masculinity, which I suspected played a role in Steve doing whatever he'd done.

Honestly, I wasn't yet sure how to approach her son. I wouldn't be until I saw how he accepted my involvement. From there, I'd have to wing it. I had no tricks up my sleeve to prepare me for a sympathetic interview of a suburban teenager accused of significant felonies — someone who'd just spent a week incarcerated for the first time in his life.

THE WRITINGS OF
AVRIL MARIA SERENE

CHAPTER 5

Lead Detective Marci Robbins and her partner, Detective Eve Byrne, pulled up in separate unmarked vehicles. Their crime scene was alongside the eastbound lanes of State Highway 52 just west of Interstate 5. A CHiP patrol unit sat fifty yards west of the victim's vehicle; the incoming detectives parked on the shoulder further west of the car to avoid contaminating the scene.

Checking her watch, Robbins scratched "3:37 a.m." across the top of her notepad. As she stepped out onto the cracked asphalt, she felt the crisp chill of the very early morning. Her long, blonde hair was loose in its bun; re-pinning it, she was suddenly aware she needed coffee.

The Forensics van drove off the road onto the grassy area alongside Robbins's vehicle. It wheeled around to shine its headlights on the front of the murdered man's automobile. Robbins approached the CHiP officer who'd been the first on-scene. His wiry frame and good-natured demeanor were familiar — Robbins had known him since they'd been teammates in the intrasquad softball league a few years earlier.

"Officer Harris," she said. "I see we're in capable hands."

"Det. Robbins, of all people!" Harris exclaimed. "Sorry they dragged you out of bed, but glad to see you again. I don't think we've worked together since you made detective. Now they tell me you're taking the lead on this. You must have, what, fifteen years in the department by now?"

"Time flies, right?" Robbins answered with a sideways grin.

"Good morning, Marci." Byrne was rubbing her eyes as she walked up between them. Shorter and stockier than either of her co-workers, Det. Byrne created a first impression that, even when sleepy, projected a confident, let's-get-down-to-business attitude.

"Harris, meet my partner," Robbins announced, "Det. Eve Byrne."

"Good to meet you, Officer." Byrne politely smiled as she crossed her arms against the cool early breeze.

Harris responded with a nod and a grin, saying, "I caught one of the rookies on his way in. He's bringing us some Starbucks."

"*That* would be awesome," Byrne said with a little laugh, pulling her coat tighter around her muscled frame.

Robbins bobbed her head in agreement.

"I understand you happened onto this scene while making traffic stops," she said. "The call said 'homicide,' which means we'll be taking this out of your hands. Can you fill us in with what you know?"

Harris switched to a professional tone as he consulted his notes and continued.

"Shortly before three o'clock, a citizen phoned in, asking for a health and welfare check on the occupants of a blue 2024 Audi A7e on the roadside, its lights and engine off."

"Did the caller say anything specific about the driver's condition or indicate they stopped to check out the Audi?" Robbins asked.

"No, only that the vehicle was dangerously close to the traveled portion of the road. When I arrived, the driver's window was rolled all the way down. The occupant was dead, slumped over on his right side, with no pulse.

"There's spatter and pools of blood on the center console and front passenger seat. The passenger window was blown out, with shattered glass on the inside and outside of the vehicle. I haven't touched anything except to check the victim for signs of life; everything you see is exactly as it was.

Plates and VIN come back to a James Robert Marshall III, clean, no wants or warrants."

"No vehicle alarm you had to shut off?" Robbins peered into the vehicle.

"I assume you requested a bus?"

"No alarm, Detective, and yes, I called for an ambulance as soon as I saw the body. The EMTs should be here any minute; they'll notify the medical examiner."

"Alright, Harris, good job." Robbins nodded. "We'll take it from here."

"Oh, and one weird thing," Harris added. "Dispatch says the 911 caller described the car as 'Triton Blue.' Either they really know their Audis or knew this one fairly well. People on the street don't normally describe cars using the manufacturer's name for the paint color."

"Thanks, Harris, interesting to know. Did dispatch mention whether the caller was male or female?"

Harris shook his head no. He smiled and tipped his hat to Byrne in parting, turning back toward his patrol bike.

Byrne had walked a wide circle around the Audi, returning to Robbins's right side.

"Did you get all of that, Eve?" Robbins asked.

"Got it. I also located the 911 dispatcher and got everything she could give us on the original call-in."

Robbins and Byrne had partnered for more than a year now. They'd developed a system of calling out their notes to one another at a crime scene whenever one of them wasn't talking to someone else. Two sets of notes helped when one caught something the other had missed. There wasn't much that slipped past both detectives.

"Perfect. Let me copy what the dispatcher gave you."

Byrne handed over her notepad, saying, "I see the coffee's here — I'm going to grab a cup. Would you like me to bring you back one?"

"Please!" Her partner responded enthusiastically, and Byrne headed for the rookie's patrol cruiser.

As she turned away, Robbins spotted her old friend, Paul Castro, leading the Forensics team. He was a supervisor, so she didn't often see him in a white bunny suit, but today, he was working the trenches. At six-two and 190 pounds, he cut quite a figure in the protective coveralls, even with the comical drawstring hood.

"Hey, Paul, I thought you might have stayed home for this one. Debra Ann tells me Tommy's not feeling well, and you might keep him out of Montessori today."

"Good morning, Marci. You're the Homicide lead for this?"

Robbins nodded.

"Good. Yeah, Tommy will be fine — she's working from home, just in case. I'll tell them you said hi."

"Could you let me know once you've gotten footprints and tire impressions from around and under the Audi? Eve and I need to do a run-through — nothing invasive, won't be adding anything to the scene."

"No problem," Castro replied. "We won't be much longer. The tech will be over to let you know when they're ready. I'll touch base with you again before we leave the scene."

He gave Robbins a two-finger wave as he headed back toward the Forensics van.

By the time Robbins had transcribed Byrne's 911 dispatcher notes, the junior detective had returned. As Robbins chugged half the cup Byrne handed her, a forensic technician approached, letting the detectives know they could look at the car.

"Dry pavement and asphalt, not much here," the tech explained. "We took photos and soil samples beyond the shoulder, that's about it. Do me a favor, though — use the Tyvek shoe protectors and tread lightly. The asphalt's rough off the traveled portion, and the cheap covers rip. I'll want to look again at the ground surfaces when we get some daylight. We can't dust or go over the vehicle for trace until the ME removes the body, so you know the drill. Otherwise, she's all yours, detectives."

"We need ten minutes or so to get the lay of the land," Robbins said. "Then you can have her right back."

The tech nodded at Byrne and waved an acknowledgment to Robbins as she turned toward her team surrounding the Forensics van.

Robbins and Byrne gloved up. Robbins went to the Audi's driver's door, and Byrne scanned the exterior with a flashlight.

"Black male victim, early to mid-thirties," Robbins announced into her handheld recorder loudly enough that Byrne could hear.

"No shell casings means a revolver or the shooter policed their brass; no apparent damage to the driver's door or glass. Blood spatter on the inside of the door panel, so it was likely closed during the incident. A driver's license and what appears to be an insurance document on the front passenger floorboard. Drops of blood and shards of what looks like tempered glass randomly distributed on top of them, so the driver dropped them there before or as the perp fired the first shot."

Robbins turned toward the passenger side of the vehicle in Byrne's direction.

"We'll let Forensics finish doing their thing before we disturb anything in the passenger footwell. The key fob's in the center console cupholder. Harris said 911 dispatch reported the vehicle as 'engine not running.' We need to double-check that Harris didn't turn off the ignition himself.

"If the doer shut it off, maybe Forensics can get some clean latents off the Start button."

Byrne called back, "Exterior from the rear driver's-side door around the trunk to the rear passenger-side door looks clean. Likely not a bump-and-rob. All four tires have air.

"Checking inside the rear passenger area — the rear seat and floorboards are clean, except for some directional blood drops in the rear passenger footwell. They're coming from the area of the driver's seat — could be cast off from the victim's head going backward and to the right."

"Copy that," Robbins said.

She leaned in to smell the area around the victim's mouth.

"The deceased last consumed something with garlic and onions. Slight smell of alcohol."

Robbins used two fingers to raise the right wrist of the body slightly.

"Right hand's resting on the center console; rigor's just starting. The victim's fingers are curled around a partially open brown trifold wallet. Maybe three hundred dollars inside. So, not a robbery. At least two gunshot wounds I can see. Both to the left side below the hairline."

She tilted her head, squinting at the wounds illuminated by her flashlight.

"Entry wounds are sizable, larger round, maybe .40 caliber. Stippling and gunshot residue visible on the deceased's skin indicate both shots were at close range. One round entered the ear canal. The other struck the head in the temple area. Trajectory suggests the shooter was just outside the center of the driver's door."

"No obvious damage or marks on the exterior driver's side sheet metal, front trim, or hood," Byrne responded. "We'll cross our fingers that Forensics can pull prints or DNA from the driver's door area. Let me see what we have on the passenger side."

Robbins called out, "The driver's window was down when they shot him. There's blowback spatter on the top edge of the glass inside the door.

"I see a bullet hole in the interior front passenger door panel. While you're over there, can you tell if the round went through? We know one bullet impacted the glass. It'd be nice to find at least one slug for matching."

"I've got an outward bulge in the exterior door skin," Byrne replied, "about six inches below the bottom of what would have been the glass, but no exit opening. The round should still be in the door.

"The sun's coming up. Maybe Forensics will find the other projectile close by. Other than that, no obvious damage to the door."

Gingerly unlatching the door and swinging it wide, she squatted inside the opening, keeping her body from contacting anything. She leaned over with her left hand to carefully open the glovebox.

"Let's see — no weapons in the glove compartment; no obvious drugs, paraphernalia, or cash."

Robbins popped the trunk open using the driver's seat side lever. Both detectives examined the trunk's interior, but it contained little more than an open box of oily rags and a loose roll of paper towels. Nothing struck either of them as unusual or obviously out of place.

As the pair stepped away from the Audi to assess what they'd observed, Robbins gave the Forensics tech the okay sign to let her know the detectives had finished their work.

"The body's slightly warm, and most of the blood's still wet," Robbins said. "We didn't miss our murderer by much. The comment about the Audi's paint color makes me wonder if our killer knew this car, maybe the victim, too, and called it in themselves.

"High-end casual clothing suggests he went out for the evening; cell phone's in his pocket. Either our driver wasn't aware he needed to call anyone for help, or he couldn't. He's ingested some alcohol but not so impaired he couldn't pull off the road in an orderly fashion."

Byrne took over the summation. "No exterior marks or recent damage other than the passenger-side window and that bump in the sheet metal. No tire marks from braking, parked normally; not a road rage incident. Money's still in the wallet, so it's not a robbery. Our guy's not armed; I doubt he was looking for a confrontation. We've got a vehicle interior that's neat and clean, except for the immediate results of the homicide itself."

Robbins spread the legs of her tweezers wide. To avoid disturbing any prints, she used the tweezers to push on the outermost edges of the Start button. She turned the car on but didn't start the engine. She waited a moment for the dash lights to come to life.

"No instrument-panel indications of a mechanical issue."

Robbins turned the vehicle off.

"Driver's window rolled down. Victim's wallet open, the cash still there. Driver's license and proof of insurance out for inspection. What does all that together say to you, Detective?"

"Traffic stop?" Byrne replied.

Robbins nodded, her lips pursed, and the detectives' eyes met.

Both understood *that* answer could throw a monkey wrench into their case.

THE WRITINGS OF
AVRIL MARIA SERENE

CHAPTER 6

Though she doubted they'd be so lucky, Robbins needed to know if there was an official record of a stop.

"Can you get on the radio?" she asked Byrne. "Check with ChiP, San Diego police, and county traffic control dispatchers. See if they had any cruisers or motor units with reported incidents in this area between, say, midnight and three-thirty."

As Byrne headed to her car, the Forensics tech called Robbins over to review the contents of the victim's wallet.

Robbins and Byrne met back at the Audi a few moments later.

"No highway patrol or traffic control units assigned to or reported in the immediate area," Byrne announced.

"His ID matches the vehicle registration, James Marshall," Robbins said. "For now, let's go with a straight-up officer-impersonation traffic-stop assassination. The victim dutifully pulls over in response to a command, sirens, or lights. He extracts his driver's license and insurance papers. Takes two rounds to the head before handing anything over or putting it back. What does your gut tell you? Anything you see that says differently?"

Byrne furrowed her brow.

"I can't see an amateur putting together the equipment for the stop. Unfortunately, as a young black male driving a pricey vehicle, our victim has likely been stopped before and knows the procedure. Whoever pulled him over was convincing enough in appearance and demeanor that the deceased complied. There's no sign he tried to react to anything he saw as a threat.

"I'd expect smaller rounds at close range from, like, a mob hitter. If they're .40 caliber — and I hate to say this — that's the standard police issue. We might have an ex-officer or somebody with a badge freelancing. Because this happened before the driver put his ID back in its place, I'd say the doer wanted to kill him right from the start. Otherwise, something went way south early in the incident, and the perpetrator lost it."

Robbins lowered her voice and leaned closer. "I hear you on the 'one of our own' thing, but it's too early to open *that* can of worms. Let's keep that to ourselves until we see how this plays out, okay? I'd like you to hang back and track the Forensics team. See what you can pick up. Marshall's name seems vaguely familiar. So, while you're doing that, I'll grab my laptop and see what pops up on the Internet for him. Say, twenty minutes, and then we'll compare notes back here."

<hr>

After thirty minutes of googling, Robbins knew she'd need to talk with Byrne before they did anything else. There was an aspect of this homicide that changed how they'd conduct the investigation — the victim wasn't just any citizen.

Robbins set her open laptop on the hood of her vehicle as the two investigators reconnected. But before discussing her Web research, she wanted to check with Byrne to see what else had developed in the past half hour.

"Did Forensics turn up anything promising?"

"As soon as you left," Byrne began, reading from her notes, "the ME took the body, and the Forensics squad began working the Audi's interior for fingerprints, DNA, and trace evidence. Once there was enough light, two techs and another with a metal detector started a ground search. They're covering a fifty-yard radius around the Audi, looking for the usual — spent rounds, fragments or casings, cigarettes, chewing gum, anything that might tie back to the perp.

"They pulled the interior panel from the passenger front door and recovered a .40 caliber slug. The lands and grooves should be suitable for ballistics matching once we have a weapon for comparison.

"The prints pulled from the exterior didn't look promising, but they'll know more when they get the lab results back. They swabbed the roof above and the sheet metal below the driver's window glass. The tech says they get lucky sometimes and find expectoration when the perp's that close.

"They're readying the Audi for flatbed transport. Once they've got it in the shop, they'll look at it under multiple light sources for other evidence. What did you learn about our victim?"

"I turned up several images of the deceased on the Internet. He's a political research consultant for a prominent national election campaign management firm."

"Explains the nice car. So the guy's connected, but then you have to ask, how well?"

"*That's* a good question." Robbins smiled. "But you're getting ahead of me. Looking deeper into the Google results showed Marshall as a magna cum laude graduate at Howard University. If you're unfamiliar, it's one of the better HBCUs in the country. He went on to get a master's degree in political science.

"Marshall's prominently featured on their alumni page, in black-tie, at sporting events, and on stage for awards ceremonies. They credit him with sizeable donations to the school's scholarship fund. Facebook and Instagram posts show quite a social life, at least up until about three years ago, always accompanied by one or more lady friends."

"If this was a red state," Byrne mused, "I'd have to wonder if being a successful black man and not hiding it put him on somebody's radar."

"Good point," Robbins acknowledged. "Unfortunately, that can apply anywhere these days. Hold onto that thought — it's something we may have to chase. Before Marshall turned up here four years ago, he racked up points working in Philadelphia for PoliTech. The *Wall Street Journal* says it's a respected nationwide political consultancy.

"He started as a neighborhood organizer and polling analyst, working his way up within PoliTech's offices in Philly. He managed several local election campaigns there. They did well, so there shouldn't be any hate for him. But even for the losers, four years is an entire major election cycle — a long time to hold a grudge.

"Either way, he came to Southern California to take a more responsible role in PoliTech's management."

"Probably more money and fun doing that here," Byrne guessed. "So, he's an up-and-comer in politics at a time when there's real hatred between the partisans. Any political ambitions of his own? Maybe he wanted to run for office?"

Byrne was thinking about motive. Robbins knew it was where their focus needed to be; that and identifying a suspect were their remaining tasks since means and opportunity were obvious.

"Another good question we can't answer just yet, one you'll want to add to your notes. One other thing: Marshall wasn't just a corporate lackey. His LinkedIn profile says he's something of a computer nerd. He's active on a social media gaming website. He describes it as 'a bunch of kids playing practical jokes on people,' and says it's pretty popular."

"Do you have the name of the gaming website?" Byrne was scratching away at her notepad.

"The bio didn't give the actual name. LinkedIn's more for professional networking; he may not have wanted to mix business and hobbies. Some employers restrict their staff from giving out free publicity or advertising. Marshall also has accounts on Facebook, X, and Instagram. We can get one of the guys in the Computer Forensics lab or Information Services to run down the gaming website."

"Do you think someone would go to the trouble to impersonate an officer and kill him over an online game?"

"I don't know. It seems like a big leap," Robbins conceded.

"On the other hand, these gamers can get very intense, and it only takes one going over the edge...." Byrne's voice trailed off.

"I'll give you that. We'll circle back around to it if we need to. This social media game had a local branch in Philadelphia. The national organization franchises it to individual communities. As the website expanded — 'exponentially' is the word he used in his profile — Marshall dived in, learning the ins and outs of running this thing." Robbins flashed air quotes. "'In a viral growth environment.' Again, his words."

"So, from what we know so far," Byrne summarized, "that website was a franchise tied to Philadelphia and belonged to someone else. Once his main gig got him promoted with the location change, he would've left all that behind when he came here, right? Didn't you say four years ago?"

"You'd think. Except when Marshall arrived in San Diego — and yes, four years ago — he started a local branch of that website from scratch. He's 'quickly become well-regarded in local circles as its founder, promoter, and chief enthusiast.' I got that last bit from a society-page article in the *Union-Tribune*. Several online references mention his job title and this hobby, though in general terms.

"I didn't spend much time looking, but I didn't find any online dissing of Marshall. I saw on his Facebook page that Marshall's nickname changed after he arrived here. In high school and college, they knew him as 'Urkel,' but in San Diego, they called him 'the Czar.' Maybe a sign of respect or maturity, or just that nobody remembers who Steve Urkel was."

"We have things we can chase down for the victimology. A good place to start."

"Well, yes and no. Maybe." Robbins bobbed her head side-to-side. "The problem is, it won't be James Marshall's stellar and impressive academic, career, or hobby achievements that'll impact our homicide case the most. It'll be that he was the longtime, soon-to-be-married fiancé of City Councilman Harrison Scott's daughter Elyssa, who happens to be a beauty with quite a brain in her own right."

"Uh-oh, I think I know where this is going…." Byrne grimaced. "This is a celebrity situation."

"Yeah, well." Robbins sighed and continued, "The papers say Marshall and Scott's daughter were inseparable. Let me quote the *Union-Tribune's* society page: '…their public romance fashionable, even wholesome; our local version of a royal couple.' Yeesh — wanna sprinkle some sugar on your cotton candy? You get the drift. It wasn't hard to find information on the Internet about these two. Councilman Scott's campaign *did* hire

Marshall's employer for the last election. However, Marshall and Elyssa met before that — at Comic-Con three years ago."

Byrne grinned. "Comic-Con? That's different, but it'd work for me."

Robbins paused, thinking.

"Debra Ann's tuned into San Diego celebrities and all this local society stuff. She'll be up by now." She glanced over at the Forensics team. "I see Paul's still here — let's check with him and see if he's okay with calling her.

"Maybe she can educate us … she might have ideas about what this guy did to put him in a killer's crosshairs."

CHAPTER 7

Tommy was having a miserable time with a nasty head cold. He'd slept fitfully all night and wound himself up after the department called Paul to a crime scene early. Tommy couldn't sleep anymore, even though he was too sick and irritable to do anything else. I finally got him to eat a bowl of cereal. I curated some of his favorite *Bluey* and *Peppa Pig* episodes into a playlist to keep him busy. He settled down long enough that I hoped I could answer some messages for my news bureau.

I'd just opened my e-mail client when my phone vibrated, and I saw it was Paul's department-issued cell number.

"Hi, honey. I just got Tommy over his latest round of the fidgets. He's watching his videos. You don't usually call me from a crime scene … Is everything okay?"

"Good morning, sweetheart. Everything's alright. I hope Tommy gets to feeling better. He needs to be doing something he's really into and burning off some excess energy.

"Listen, Marci's here with me, and so is Eve — you're on speakerphone. We need some background for the case we're working. Marci suggested tapping into your knowledge of the comings and goings in San Diego's glamor scene."

"Hi, Marci! Eve, you should bring Elsie over for coffee; it's been too long."

I turned my attention to Paul's request.

"I'm no expert on the high and mighty, but I *do* try to keep up. One of the requirements of my job."

Realizing the three were at a murder scene, I grew more serious.

"So, what's up?"

"We caught a case where the deceased may be from that crowd," Paul replied, "a James Robert Marshall III. We understand he was engaged to Councilman Scott's daughter, Elyssa. We're trying to get up to speed on them so we know what to look for at the crime scene."

"Oh, no!" I exclaimed. "Oh, that is so *sad...*"

I went silent for a few seconds as I absorbed the news.

"I have *so* many questions, but they can wait until you get home. I know Elyssa was at Comic-Con three years ago, drawing attention. As I recall, the society pages gave her rave reviews for cosplaying Hela from *Thor: Ragnarok*. James was looking to add to his first-edition classic comics collection. They met at a vegan diner when they both needed a break. It was, as they say, love at first bite.

"They're popular, prominent regulars of the social circuit. Local paparazzi frequently publish photos of them together at area nightspots and entertainment venues. They set the date, in June, of course. The *Union-Tribune*'s style and society page and local media influencers talk about the upcoming wedding as 'the social event of the season in San Diego.'"

"Oh, boy, paparazzi, high society, and influencers — this won't go down easily." There was just a touch of cynicism in Byrne's voice.

"Anything negative in the rumor mill?" Paul asked. "We're trying to understand why anyone would want him dead."

I racked my brain, but nothing shook out.

"I haven't heard so much as a whiff of scandal, certainly not anything on that level."

"You've given us exactly what we needed to know," Paul said. "We're on the clock, so I have to run. Call me later and let me know how Tommy's doing — once we catch up here, I can take a babysitting shift if you need a break."

While I appreciated the offer, it sounded like their team had their hands full.

"Thanks, hon. I'll keep you posted. Good luck with your case. From what I know, James Marshall was one of the good guys. I hope you can nail his killer soon."

⁂

After Castro hung up and Robbins thanked him, she turned to Byrne.

"Could you ride back to the squad room with me? We can discuss how this impacts our case on our way in."

The highlighted ends of Byrne's short, black hair turned up as she ran her hand over her head.

"I'll get one of the uniforms to drive my car to the station."

She walked over to the officer who'd brought the morning coffee. Robbins checked in with the forensic technicians working the scene, but they hadn't found anything new.

As they rolled to the precinct in Robbins's unmarked, the detectives resumed their conversation. Aware Byrne had passed her detectives' exam less than a year ago, Robbins explained, "I'm guessing you know, but a perp's or victim's social standing isn't a trivial matter in a homicide inquiry. VIPs mean this murder requires more than an investigation. Managing a political, social, and publicity spectacle requires unique skills and resources. That's why these things go to the Escalation Management team."

Robbins turned toward Byrne. "We've never worked one of these together. Did you ever run across a situation like this when you were in the patrol unit?"

"Not really. We've picked up celebrities speeding or under the influence and handled several of their domestic disputes. But other than squawking about who they were, their notoriety didn't affect the arrest. Those things usually went squirrely after — when the booking photos hit the media. It never came back on the street cop. Bragging rights for the arresting officer, mostly, a story to tell their friends and families."

"You'll want to buckle up for this, then. Let me walk you through the terrain. Most of the larger metropolitan police departments in California have investigative teams that specialize in high-profile cases involving celebrities. Their departments train them in the issues raised by cases with unusually high public visibility. Things like near-daily press conferences and controlling the politicians and other celebrities who take advantage of the heightened publicity.

"These teams aren't always official. San Diego has one of the formal ones, though they avoid acknowledging it. It's dicey — you don't want the public to know some citizens get special treatment, but certain people come with so much crap you *have* to carve them out."

Robbins pulled into the department's parking garage.

"We know the unit as the Escalation Management team. Mostly, they're a bunch of pretty faces, talking heads, and glory hounds chasing the cameras."

"They're outside our regular chain of command, right?" Byrne asked as they wended their way to the garage's third floor.

"Do our orders come from Escalation Management, or do they take the case from us?"

She seemed nervous about the changes in protocol.

Robbins pulled into an open slot across from the garage elevators, and the two detectives finished their discussion in the car.

"With possible officer involvement *and* a celebrity, they'll pull the entire investigation into their unit," Robbins answered.

"Otherwise, they don't like to get their hands dirty, meaning we do all the grunt work and hand over the dog-and-pony-show aspects to them so they can take credit.

"But in this case, we've also got blood and gore, the Internet, young lovers with good looks, politics, and the social scene — there'll be cameras and attention all over this. Trust me, they'll take the whole thing off our hands. But until then, we still have our jobs to do, and we'll need to work it as best we can."

"Okay. I'll follow up with victimology until Forensics sends us their report."

"Perfect. I'll text Lt. Harbin. We'll brief him after morning roll call; see where he wants us to go with it."

<hr>

Robbins texted Lt. Harbin from her desk to fill him in on the high-profile aspects of their new case. She'd had two of these celebrity cases before. One was a drive-by shooting, the other a domestic dispute that resulted in a fatality. Honestly, she hated dealing with them.

She was crossing her fingers that the lieutenant would let her pass the case to him, and he'd take it from there. He'd done that for other detectives when a celebrity was the homicide victim. She knew he had a good relationship with one of the Escalation Management guys, Lt. Ezra Brooks, who'd recently taken over their unit.

Unfortunately for her, Lt. Harbin was tied up with the captain for the morning. Given the urgency of getting ahead of the press, he asked Robbins to drop the case file off with Lt. Brooks.

As she rode the elevator up two floors to Brooks's office, Robbins worked herself into a positive mindset, mulling over her lieutenant's words.

"I know their unit has a bad rep, but we can work with Brooks," Lt. Harbin said. "He's got some real investigative chops. He worked his way through the ranks before they put him in Escalation Management — a pretty savvy guy. I partnered with him on several cases back in the day, and we became tight. I respect the man, and he's never shown anything but the same toward me."

As Robbins tapped on the frame of his open door, she saw that Lt. Brooks was a tall, middle-aged man, skinny as a pencil. The narrow face, large protruding ears, bushy eyebrows, and pronounced cleft in his chin made him look nothing like the TV weatherman-slash-used-car-salesman she was expecting.

"C'mon in, take a seat, Detective. Your lieutenant told me you had a hot one for us. Oh, good, I see you brought the case file. He mentioned the deceased is an up-and-coming political operative engaged to a councilman's daughter?"

"Sorry, Lieutenant, there's not much here." Robbins handed over the manila folder. "We just picked it up a few hours ago. That's why Lt. Harbin wanted me to drop it by personally and give you a pass-down."

As Robbins communicated what she knew, she was impressed with Lt. Brooks's demeanor and that his questions went straight to the point. Heading downstairs after they'd finished, Robbins was satisfied that they were in good hands with the situation being what it was.

Two weeks after being handed the Marshall homicide, Lt. Brooks reviewed the latest Forensics reports. There wasn't much he didn't already know, making anything new stand out. That included an e-mail James Marshall sent himself from his cell phone three days before his death. Brooks assumed he meant it as a reminder about something important. It was a trick some investigators used to keep from forgetting one thing while concentrating on another. The first line of the e-mail itself read, "Set meet with blotto_bill — tractor." Under that, Marshall had typed, "***ASSHOLE!***"

Any expression of strong emotion so close to a victim's death is critical to a homicide investigation. Still, the message didn't give them much to work with. The "blotto_bill" snippet looked like a username, maybe an e-mail address missing the domain name.

The domain appended to Marshall's e-mail account, the one he'd used to send and receive the terse message, was "@politech.com." Brooks attached the same domain to the end of "blotto_bill" as the intended recipient of a new message, using one of the department's anonymous e-mail accounts as the sender. He gave his message a generic "Wassup?" subject and body and hit the Send button.

Seconds later, Brooks got a "Could not resolve address" notification from his e-mail client. He googled the same e-mail address to see if it was once valid but got no hits.

The message would have to go to their Computer Forensics department to see what its technicians could do with "blotto_bill." In the meantime, Brooks contacted Det. Robbins. He wanted to see if that name or the "tractor" message meant anything to her or her partner — maybe something that hadn't made it into their reports?

"Good afternoon, Detective. Ezra Brooks. I have a quick question about something that came up from the forensic examination of James Marshall's laptop. He was the driver in the roadside homicide case you caught a couple of weeks ago."

"Yes, Lieutenant, the case we thought might be an officer impersonation assassination," Robbins replied. "How can I help?"

"He sent himself an e-mail three days before his murder. Let me forward it to you."

"Got it," Robbins said a moment later. "Hmmm, obviously, the man was upset about something. But 'blotto_bill' and 'tractor' mean nothing to me. I'll print it out and tack it to my corkboard. I can pass it around; maybe someone else knows what it means. I'll get in touch if I come up with something."

"Thanks. We're still trying to get somewhere with this case, so I'd appreciate whatever you turn up."

As Brooks ended the call, he had a sinking feeling that he was in for a long slog with this investigation. It didn't bode well that he would have to pin his hopes for a better outcome on the nerds in the Computer Forensics department.

THE WRITINGS OF
AVRIL MARIA SERENE

CHAPTER 8

The night of the charity ball was a welcome respite from our work and daily routines. With Tommy safely committed to Sophia's care, Paul and I had dressed to the nines and given ourselves up to our illusions of elegance. Paul never looked more handsome, even in the full-dress uniform he wore to the Navy's on-campus events back in college.

The Hotel del Coronado, or Hotel Del as affectionately known among San Diegans, is a local icon. It hosts several prestigious events throughout the year, from extravagant weddings to the annual Rady Children's Hospital ball, which starts off the summer social season. Paul and I had the valet park our car, making our way with the rest of the crowd to the ballroom as a resplendent sunset spread out over the ocean horizon.

The ballroom was a sight to behold. Six massive crystal chandeliers hung from the domed ceiling. A semicircular stage enshrouded in gold lamé curtains sat opposite the main entrance. The dance floor, emblazoned with the children's hospital logo, was surrounded by tableclothed round tops, each seating between eight and twelve people. Indirect pastel lighting illuminated the lower tier of the dome. As we took it all in, the maître d' accepted our tickets and directed us to our table.

There, we saw Mondo, his wife, Teri, and Capt. Jerrod Jarvis, whose spouse, Jill, was on the children's hospital fundraising committee. Capt. Jarvis was the head of Investigations II, the division that included Homicide. Two high-ranking officers I knew only in passing, along with their significant others, were standing with the Captain. The men wore tuxes; the women dripped diamonds.

Before Paul and I reached the group, we crossed paths with a stocky, athletic-looking man in his early forties, slightly shorter than Paul. The tailoring of his tux was so precise it looked glued on; the graying at the temples of his otherwise dark brown hair seemed professionally rendered as if by a makeup artist.

"Paul Castro?"

The stranger stuck out his right hand and clapped Paul's shoulder with his left. The man introduced himself as they shook.

"I'm Bob Strickland. Nice to see you could make it. I've heard so much about you."

"Thanks. I understand you made our being here possible," Paul replied. "This is my better half, Debra Ann — we're both looking forward to the evening's events."

Strickland gave me a curt smile.

"I'm sorry to have to run, but my date checked her purse with her wrap, and I promised I'd get it for her. I'll come join you in a few minutes."

And with that, Strickland was gone. Paul and I were left looking at one another, feeling like we'd just experienced a drive-by. Shaking my head, I could only assume that Strickland was naturally brusque, or perhaps his date was one very demanding woman.

Paul had a stronger opinion.

"When I'm with you," he whispered into my ear, "I'm accustomed to gentlemen addressing you first as a matter of politeness. But Strickland seemed almost rude, considering you're the hottest lady in the place. That's okay — the man has a clammy handshake anyway."

I had to hide a smirk at his observations.

Mondo spotted Paul and me as we approached, gesturing toward the table as he greeted us.

"Paul, Debra Ann, two of my favorite people!"

I nearly did a double-take when I saw Mondo. He wore a boutonnière and a bowtie instead of his captain's bars. His usual haphazard, salt-and-pepper mullet was gone, replaced with hair-gel styling. He'd completely transformed himself for the evening.

Still, classic Mondo, he bent into a chivalrous bow, kissing my fingers as I curtsied and offered my hand, something we'd been doing since we first met five years ago.

Mondo grinned and shook Paul's hand.

"Paul, I am so glad you could come. Debra Ann, you look positively radiant, but then again, I've never seen you otherwise."

I batted my baby blues — well, greens — at him, and he gave me a mischievous smile. I winked at Teri, who rolled her eyes even as she chuckled. I was happy to see Marci and Danny approaching the table from the opposite side. Her dress, like mine, was black and formal. While I wore a simple sheath with a halter top, hers was off-the-shoulder, highlighting the gentle waves of loose, long blonde hair usually coiled into a work bun.

Nearly her date's height in three-inch heels, Marci was beyond gorgeous, which wasn't surprising. Danny's metamorphosis, however, was shocking. In all the times I'd seen him in public, he'd worn either cowboy boots and jeans or his firefighting gear. Tonight, he was casting a definite Daniel Craig vibe in his tux, and it was easy to visualize him in the James Bond role. Marci and I hugged, and the men shook hands.

The dining staff had set the round table for twelve, large enough to seat our entire party. Strickland returned and joined his date, an attractive, younger Hispanic woman, in conversation with a waiter just behind the table.

Mondo glanced in their direction, saying, "Let me introduce you to the man who was kind enough to invite us as his guests, Lt. Robert Strickland, and his beautiful companion, Christina."

Paul nodded at the couple with a polite smile. I grinned and said to Mondo, "Yes, we met briefly earlier."

Turning to Strickland and his date, I added, "I assume you succeeded in finding the purse. It is nice to meet you, Christina."

The petite, raven-haired Christina smiled shyly and dipped her head at us.

"Bob's my new second-in-command," Mondo continued. "He comes to us by way of the San José Police Department. I need to quit introducing you as a newbie, Bob. Hard to believe, but you've been with us almost a year."

Mondo finished introductions all around, and we found our seats.

Strickland and Christina were seated on the same side of the table as Paul and me, with Mondo and Teri between us. Strickland turned to Paul and said, "I've heard great things about your work. I understand you're Lt. Harbin's go-to Forensics guy in Homicide. I'm sorry he couldn't make it — the man's quite the legend.

"But I'm grateful you could. I can personally relate to your role there in Homicide. I feel fortunate that Mondo selected me as his wingman in Vice. I understand there were any number of fine officers he could have chosen."

I had to make a real effort not to spit up my drink. Louis, Mondo, and Paul were close friends. We knew that Mondo's longtime deputy, Jeff Bennett, had been the Vice unit's second-in-command for a year before a new arrival pushed Bennett aside. We didn't know his name then, but Strickland was that added officer.

Because Bennett had been happy in his role, he hadn't been aggressive about taking the lieutenant's exam. That, in turn, meant Strickland, as a recently promoted lieutenant, took over second chair when Strickland transferred to the department. Mondo had been sick about the whole thing, even though he and Bennett did their best to take the situation in stride. Bennett was the quiet, still-waters-run-deep type, and if Jeff harbored any strong resentments, the man held them close to his chest. I wouldn't have blamed him if he felt dissed.

Regardless, that situation was a hell of a long way removed from "Mondo selected me as his wingman." I glanced over at Mondo, who was engaged in another conversation behind the back of Paul's chair and hadn't heard the comment.

Strickland didn't seem to catch my discomfort. He plowed on ahead, turning now to Marci. "You and your partner caught the James Marshall case before it went to the Escalation Management team, right?"

"Yes. That lit up the newswires," Marci answered. "I imagine a lot of the people here were affected. I know he was active in these kinds of events."

"Truly unfortunate," Strickland said. "He was a good man to this community. But let me apologize to your companion for talking shop — Danny, if I recall, you're with the fire department. Is that right?"

Danny nodded and was about to say something when Strickland abruptly turned back to me, leaving Danny with his mouth open.

"It was so nice for you to have come, Debra Ann. I hope you and Paul truly enjoy your evening. Oh, and you should try the mackerel. It is excellent. But don't order a white wine simply because it's fish — try a rosé of pinot noir instead. You'll find it a much better pairing."

The mansplaining — *that* Mondo did hear.

To take the edge off the arrogance of Strickland's suggestion that either Paul or I wouldn't know wine selection, Mondo offered, "Bob is quite the connoisseur of fine foods and very particular about these things. See if he'll invite you to his home and have his housekeeper whip something up. Quite the experience, but it'll cost you. You'll be on SlimFast shakes for a week afterward."

Paul and I both laughed politely. I made a mental note — along with Paul, I'm sure — that Strickland was a condescending jerk.

Still, we'd had a wonderful evening. The food and beverages, the music and dancing — all were magnificent. I was especially happy for Marci. Since her surgeries, she hadn't been one to seek out attention. But when it came her way, she reveled in it. Danny looked on approvingly and generously took turns sharing Marci's graceful moves with the other gentlemen who came asking — she was our table's most popular dance partner. But she did save the last, not just one, but three dances for her date.

Danny and Paul had started a running commentary surreptitiously via text, including candid remarks about their female companions. Wanting Marci to know what he thought of her, Danny forwarded her snippets of the exchange. In her turn, Marci thought I might want to know how our men felt about us. She sent me a cutout from their texting after Danny had waxed effusive about Marci's looks and the quality of her dancing.

In it, Danny hinted that he was working on plans to make Marci an honest woman. Paul admonished him not to wait too long, expressing remorse that he hadn't asked for my hand back in college.

I texted Marci, "Awww, gee … & I didn't think they'd had that much to drink! :)"

Neither Paul nor I wanted the evening to end. Still, when it did, we'd have plenty of amazing things to talk about well into the wee hours of the morning in the comfort of our home.

When we arrived at our door, Sophia was lying on the couch, binge-watching *The Crown*.

"Tommy had fun tonight," Sophia said. "We put up the tent in the backyard and dressed up the dogs. He wanted to pretend we were in Africa on safari. If you wonder why we were in the den, we had to get the antlers from the Christmas decorations. I put him to bed at nine, and he only got up twice before he fell asleep for good."

"Thank you *so* much, Sophia! We had such a good time and couldn't have gone if you hadn't watched Tommy. It's awfully late. Would you like Paul to walk you home?"

"No, I'll be fine. Mom's waiting up for me. Come to our car wash tomorrow if you can. It's at the high school from ten 'til five. We're raising money so the drama club can enter the Broadway San Diego Awards competition."

"Okay, I'll be there. I promise," I said as I flicked on the porch light for Sophia. Paul watched from the window to see that she'd made her way home safely.

I sighed as I reminisced about our evening. Though I'd thoroughly enjoyed it, some of my feelings were mixed.

For one thing, Paul and I had always been open with each other about everything. Paul made it a point not to withhold anything from me, apart from the more unpleasant details of his work, and I'd done the same. But I didn't want to draw attention to the rare imperfections of our night, so there was one thing I would not confide to him now. I chose not to share how much I didn't care for Robert Strickland.

I didn't know where the dislike came from, and making a big deal of it served no purpose. My feelings might be rooted in the two high school summers I'd spent with Dad as he went on the road. He was supervising projects for his growing construction business after Tropical Storm Allison.

I was at an impressionable age when I spent those six months in small towns in the Deep South.

Strickland's attitude reminded me too much of a condescending elder inviting unwashed heathens into the church to "save" them. Even as a teenager, the clergyman's arrogant assumption that the invitee wanted or needed saving had put me off. The sole purpose of the exercise seemed to be demonstrating the evangelist's presumed merciful and charitable nature — traits they were sure to point out as akin to "godliness."

I'm sure many of the ball's other attendees knew that the police officers who were present, except Strickland and perhaps Captain Jarvis, didn't travel in the upper-crust social circles they did. But we'd been accepted graciously for that night. Only Bob Strickland, with one foot on department turf and the other on gilded ground, made me overtly conscious that the men in blue didn't belong.

On that score, the upside was that Strickland worked for a different unit than Paul's. And, invitations for Paul and me to participate in the events to which Strickland's wealth entitled him were rare.

Still, while the evening may not have been perfect, it *had* been grand; I had to admit I wouldn't mind invites to more affairs like this one. And oh, what I wouldn't give to, just once, be at the center of it all.

Would Columbia University consider moving the Pulitzer Prize award ceremonies to the Hotel Del?

THE WRITINGS OF
AVRIL MARIA SERENE

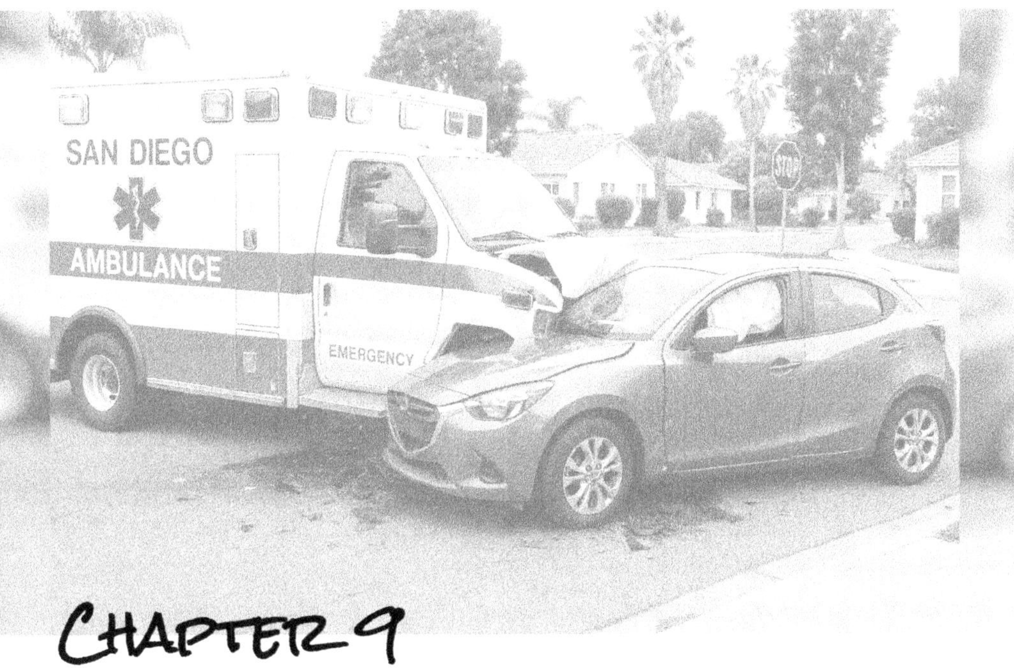

CHAPTER 9

Carla Littman was standing, immersed in rereading for the umpteenth time the presentation spread over her kitchen table as she poured the milk into her bowl. In her head, she ran through the delivery tweaks she wanted to try, looking to give it more *oomph*.

Carla experimented, emphasizing each critical word in its turn, adding a pause here and there. Her eyes fixated on the second paragraph of the first page, she absentmindedly pulled out the chair, sat, and began eating.

Carla's first warning came from a sensation she couldn't swallow, as if she'd suddenly developed a sore throat.

She coughed and began wheezing — she could feel the rapid swelling of her throat and tongue.

Now unable to breathe and her throat too constricted to scream, Carla struggled to rise from her chair.

Her heart was racing and beginning to pound.

She recognized the symptoms of anaphylaxis — she had to get to the EpiPen in the drawer next to the sink.

As Carla grabbed the table edge for support, it tilted with the sudden weight and threw her off-balance, flinging milk and cereal to the floor.

Her papers slid from the smooth surface, wafting in the daylight that streamed through the open window, a light breeze lifting them into the air.

Carla's bare feet slipped from under her on the spilled milk, and she crashed to the floor.

Her hips caught the edge of the chair seat on her way down. The chair flipped onto its side and away from her, slamming her head and shoulder into the table.

Panicked, desperate, and disoriented, she tried to push herself up.

She had a brief sense of detachment, mind from body, as she processed what was happening to her.

Carla felt herself rising above her circumstances, as though watching someone else on the floor … just before her brain released the thought and collapsed mercifully into unconsciousness.

⁂

Paul and I stayed in bed late the following day, awakened by Tommy crawling in with us. We'd re-shared the details of our magical night deep into the early hours until we fell asleep.

Our Sunday began uneventfully enough. But things took a horrific turn with an unexpected and jarring phone call shortly after noon. It was Kimberly, Sophia's mother — her trembling voice instantly told me something was terribly wrong.

"I'm calling from the hospital." Kimberly's tone was distraught to the point of incoherence.

"It's Sophia — she passed away two hours ago."

"What? I'm sorry, I didn't hear you — Kimberly, what did you say?"

"They couldn't save her. She was hurt in too many places; there wasn't enough time."

"*Oh, no! Oh, my God,*" Stunned, I sat down hard on the kitchen chair. Then, a perversely cold logic kicked in.

"Kimberly, that can't be … Sophia was here, lying on our living room sofa, just last night."

"She was in a traffic accident," Kimberly said in a broken voice.

"She didn't make it. She … was running late to pick up Karla for the cheerleading car wash. It was their last chance to raise funds for the state competition in Pasadena."

Kimberly was sobbing in short bursts, and it took a moment to choke out the words.

"An ambulance ran into her."

My brain wasn't accepting the information; it was coming at me too fast — I needed to slow things down.

"An ambulance? Didn't it have its lights and siren on?" I was trying to rationalize the news in my head

"It did," Kimberly replied. "They were taking a woman to the hospital. The police said Sophia had her earbuds in and didn't hear the siren."

It took me several more moments to process what she was telling me. I understood the words, but the reality and finality weren't sinking in. It just didn't make sense.

Why would a beautiful young life end that way?

I thought the accident must have been in the neighborhood, and I was confused about why we hadn't heard about it. My denial insisted it couldn't be true if we didn't already know.

"How could that *happen*? Where did this take place? We haven't heard anything…"

"She was at Salizar and Auburndale," Kimberly replied, sniffling.

"I don't understand why she went that way … it's not how she usually goes. She must have thought the intersection was a four-way stop.

"But there aren't any stop signs for the cross street, and the cars come down those hills too fast. They said Sophia slowed down for the sign on her side, then pulled out right in front of the ambulance like she never saw it. Her little Mazda didn't stand a chance."

"Oh, Kimberly, I am *so* sorry," I said weakly. "Oh, my… She's a wonderful girl. She's so good with Tommy and the dogs, so nice to be around."

Even if I accepted what had occurred, the why would take longer.

Because she was late for a car wash?

I wanted desperately to find the right things to say. Worse, a guilty thought suddenly overcame me — *did staying up late babysitting Tommy contribute to her accident?*

I'd have to deal with that later. We needed to be there for Sophia's mother now, and my heart went out to her.

"Do you have someone with you? Is there anything we can do to help?"

"Yes, her father's here. And my parents are on the way," Kimberly answered. "But thank you for offering. I just wanted you to know what happened — you and Paul have been so good to her, and she always looked forward to sitting for Tommy."

"I'll let Paul know. He'll be devastated. I wish I knew what to do or say … But if you need anything, want company, or to talk, please call. I'm so sorry, Kimberly — this is just heartbreaking."

Deep in my soul, I felt Kimberly's pain alongside my emptiness and loss over Sophia's death. Adding to my emotions, knowing there was very little I could do for either of them left me with a frustrating sense of helplessness.

And so, I glanced with some trepidation at my ringing phone a few hours later when I saw Kimberly's number displayed.

"Oh, Kimberly, I've been thinking about Sophia all afternoon," I said as I answered, none of the traditional greetings seeming appropriate.

"I don't know what to say when Tommy asks about his Fia."

I nearly broke into tears, focusing on Kimberly to maintain control.

She must need something to be calling back so soon. Let me open that door for her.

"But this is so hard for you … Is there something we can do to help?"

"Darin is beyond upset, and he feels like he needs some answers," Kimberly said of her husband.

"You know how he can get. Sophia is his daughter, and it's hitting him awfully hard."

Darin was Kimberly's second husband; her ex was the father of her eldest, Kathy.

"Darin wants me to ask if you could use your contacts in the police department to find out if anything was off with that ambulance. Like, was the driver drinking or doing drugs, or maybe something else that messed with his concentration? Or could something be mechanically wrong with the ambulance, you know?"

I'd admit to having similar thoughts, though part of me also understood the desire to place blame.

"Debra Ann, I hate to ask, but if you wouldn't mind, anything you find out … maybe it would be easier for Darin to hear it from you."

I'd seen enough anger and transference in my career and personal life to understand what was happening. Still, it's different when you're in the middle with people you care for and know well. Everyone progresses through the grief stages differently, in varying orders, and in the unique ways they express themselves.

I couldn't be sure Kimberly wasn't presenting Darin's feelings as proxies for her thoughts. But either way, what she was asking was simple enough and allowed me an opportunity to do something for them in their time of need.

"Tell Darin I'll look into it. I can't promise how soon I can get back to you. It depends on what the police learn during their investigation. I hate to bring this up now, but there are things they can't know until after the autopsy."

There was a brief pause on Kimberly's end; when she spoke, I heard the tears in her voice.

"I understand. There are so many things we'll have to learn to deal with. But thank you, Debra Ann. It helps to know somebody we trust is looking into what happened."

* * *

As had become my habit when I needed information about department activities, my first call went out to Marci. Even for situations that didn't involve Homicide, I could count on her to know what was happening within SDPD. She kept her finger on the pulse of the department through her friends and working relationships among the less-noticed officers quietly doing their jobs.

"Hi, Marci. I need to ask you a personal favor," I said after she'd picked up.

"*Again?*" Marci quickly gave up her overblown protest with a laugh. "Okay, Debra Ann, I'll bite. And I mean that. You're going to have to buy me breakfast. So, what can I do for you?"

"There was a young woman killed this morning in a traffic accident with an ambulance in a residential area, Salizar and Auburndale...."

"Oh, yes, one of those truly tragic things. Which one are you calling about?"

"'Which one?' I'm sorry, but you've lost me...."

"There were *two* young women killed — the homicide victim and the accident fatality," Marci replied.

"I was thinking of the girl who died in the crash, checking if anything looked wrong to you about the accident. There was a homicide victim?"

"The accident was just one of those unfortunate things — a young, distracted driver who rolled through a stop sign at an intersection with a bad reputation. The ambulance had 360-degree video, pretty clear-cut. I feel so sorry for the Mazda driver; the best I can offer is that I don't think she realized her mistake or suffered — it was over so fast.

"But yes, the homicide victim was *in* the ambulance. With everything that happened, given the accident, the paramedics couldn't save her. Honestly, her chances were slim before the wreck."

"Who was she? What happened to her?"

"Her name was Carla Littman. She was the victim of a poisoning and died from her allergies. She ate a bowl of breakfast cereal laced with raw peanut oil. She went into anaphylactic shock. Plus, someone tampered with her EpiPen — nothing but saline in it. She never got to it, but it wouldn't have helped her if she had."

Oh, no ... as if Sophia's death wasn't bad enough.

What could I tell Kimberly that wouldn't make her feel worse? That Sophia died as an unintended consequence of murder?

Four days later, on the afternoon of Sophia's funeral, the skies were cobalt blue with the occasional fluffy white cumulous cloud scudding by — a beautiful setting for remembrances.

The family had opted for cremation, with Sophia in repose for the funeral services in an open casket. Given what had happened to her, the mortician's efforts showed skill and compassion.

Videos of Sophia's life were displayed on flat screens on either side of the church's vestibule, along with still photos on the walls and among the flowers near the casket. In each of them, Sophia had been caught in the motions inherent to an active young life — cheerleading, volleyball, helping at a bake sale, and playing with family, her friends, and her pets. The images only heightened the shock felt by those of us who knew her upon seeing her body, once so vibrant, energetic, and engaged in life, lying there cold and still.

I hadn't slept the two nights before, wrestling with what to say to Kimberly and her family about whose fault it was for Sophia's death.

In the end, I'd tell Kimberly that as tragic as Sophia's accident was, there was no one else to blame. I decided not to mention Carla Littman, the murder victim in the ambulance, in part because Ms. Littman had people who loved her, too. I didn't think it fair to entangle the two families' losses or to complicate for the police what was an ongoing homicide investigation.

I promised myself I'd keep tabs on the Littman case. Once Sophia's loved ones had their time to grieve and the circumstances and perpetrator of the murder were known, I'd inform Kimberly of the connection in case it might help her in some way.

Paul and I would sorely miss having Sophia in our lives. Tommy wouldn't know she was gone until he became a teenager in his own right.

But his world would be a little darker without the light Fia had brought to ours.

THE WRITINGS OF
AVRIL MARIA SERENE

CHAPTER 10

The no-nonsense posting on the tan-painted block wall next to the jail's main entry door read, "NON-LAW-ENFORCEMENT VISITORS MUST PREARRANGE PRISONER'S VISITS WITH THE JAILERS BY TELEPHONING AHEAD FOR AN APPOINTMENT."

Another sign mounted to the wall just inside the entryway repeated the wording. Forewarned by Marci about what to expect, I'd called ahead. The security officer found my name on his list, signing me in as a visitor for Steve Nielsen, Tracy's son. After I'd completed the paperwork, he waved me toward the security conveyors.

Once I'd navigated the inspection apparatus, gathered my things from the plastic tub, and put my shoes back on, another officer apprised me of what to expect.

"You'll be called by first initial and last name over the loudspeaker when the prisoner's available. There's an electronic tote board on the wall listing the last several visitors we've paged." The officer directed me to the black-and-gray vinyl shell chairs in the waiting area.

The light-gray-over-dark-gray paint on the cinderblock walls made the large main room of the jail's visitor center seem dreary, smaller than it was. The air smelled of damp basement. A long, four-foot-wide steel table painted a neutral gray divided the room lengthwise. Three-quarter-inch-thick Plexiglas ran from the ceiling down to the top of the table. A steel plate welded underneath and running down to the floor completed the separation of prisoners from their visitors.

Sturdy three-foot-wide Plexiglas partitions on either side of the central acrylic glass wall formed small booths for prisoners and visitors. Corded beige wall phones mounted on the left partition of each booth permitted communications between visitors and inmates.

Armed guards on either side of the room directed the prisoners and their guests to their assigned numbered seats across from one another. The officers would then return to their positions, overseeing conversations. Several large, circular convex mirrors aided them; each was mounted at an angle in a corner or between the ceiling and the outer wall. Video cameras hung at regular intervals from the ceiling recorded the activity.

When the speaker announced my name, I sat at the booth indicated by the guard. The painted surface of the table and lower portions of the partition had been etched and inked with various names, sets of initials, and vulgarities, along with descriptions and crude drawings of genitalia. They included explicit instructions in three languages for intercourse, with and without a partner. As I awaited Steve, I wondered what archeologists unearthing all this some thousands of years hence would conclude about us.

When Steve arrived in handcuffs and leg shackles, he wasn't the same cocky smartass I knew from the summer barbecue. He was taller than I remembered, easily five-ten, and lanky. Steve was at that age where young men slouch into chairs more than they sit in them. He was defeated and frightened. His face was that of an abused and cornered puppy; I could see faint salt traces from wiped-away tears in the outer corners of his eyes, which he quickly cast downward.

This kid's scared out of his mind, floundering in water way over his head.

He looked like he hadn't a friend in the world — though I felt guilt over the thought, that was good for me. If I could get Steve to see I was there to help, most of his barriers would likely come down.

I picked up the phone on my side of the Plexiglas, and Steve did the same.

"Hi, Steve. I'm Debra Ann Wynn. Your neighbor, Louis Harbin, and I've been close a long time; he asked me to speak with you and your mom. You and I met at the July 4th picnic last summer, but I don't expect you to remember me. I'm here to help as a friend."

Steve's sullen response was, "Yeah, everybody wants to be my BFF now. All I gotta do is tell them everything they want to know. Fuck that shit. So, what's *your* angle?"

He might be terrified, but he chooses to play the tough guy and tries not to show fear. Good luck with that. But it means I've got my work cut out for me.

"I'm an investigative reporter, Steve, but that's not what this is about. I'm here because my job means I can check some things out unofficially without making waves. I can go places and see things Louis can't because he must follow certain rules as a police officer. The rules I follow aren't as strict."

"If there's supposed to be rules, why am I *here?*" Steve complained, dropping his banger façade enough to play the victim.

"I didn't do anything — why aren't they following the rule, 'innocent until proven guilty?' Why doesn't anyone care about the rules that are on *my* side?"

"Look, Steve, I see why you'd think that. I get that you didn't *intend* to hurt anyone. I even get that you were just doing what somebody else told you to do. But you saw there was a gun — a *loaded assault rifle, Steve* — in the back seat of that car. And you drove it anyway."

"Why's that such a big deal? Nobody got hurt, so why does it matter?"

"Because your part in this ended up scaring the living crap out of a mom and three little girls. *That's* why it matters. They have rights, too, Steve. You say you don't deserve what's happening to you, and you might be correct for some parts of it. That's why I'm here.

"But the judge and her family didn't deserve this either. Everyone acts like a judge is powerful, but she's just a single mom with a job trying to care for her kids. Just like *your* mother. They were, and still *are*, being hurt by this."

"How? It's not like they got shot or anything…," Steve protested.

"They're so frightened they can't stay in their own house. If you learned someone pointed an assault rifle at your bedroom, wouldn't *you* be scared to death, even if they didn't shoot you? Her youngest daughter's eight. Can you imagine how you'd feel if you were eight years old and they said you could get killed just for being in your room?"

He blinked at me, softening but trying not to show it.

"They didn't tell me she had kids. Besides, if the police didn't tell them, they'd never know, nothing to worry about." He was still trying to rationalize his way out of this.

"Interesting thought, Steve." I gave him my *I think you know better* look. "Let's say they didn't have the right to know about crimes threatening their lives — not telling them can only work if you lied about the involvement of other people.

"Think about it. If the police believe your story that somebody else set this up, that's even worse for the judge and her kids — it means someone is still out there wanting to kill them. Not only are they frightened by the part *you* did, they're *still* in grave danger of being murdered."

Steve was silent for a moment.

"So, what, they don't even have to care what *really* happened? I'm some lowlife piece of shit now, and they can just ruin my life?"

Now, Steve's fears were expressing themselves as indignation at a perceived injustice, which was unsurprising for someone who had no understanding of the system. Still, that he'd listened enough to change his approach signaled progress.

"No, Steve. People care — it's why I'm here. Louis is working on this from his end, and your mom is sacrificing everything to get you out of here.

"But you must understand that before law enforcement can let you back onto the street, they must protect the public. That protection requires an answer to a question, one they can believe. That question is this: Did you make a simple mistake in judgment? Or are you part of something bigger, something intentional that could easily have killed someone? *Or still might?*"

"They *know* I didn't do anything on purpose. They only stopped me because I was being too careful to make sure nothing bad happened."

"Steve, I believe you. But how do you expect the police to know the difference between somebody being careful and that person just trying not to get caught? What they can see looks the same to them either way."

He wrestled with his expression, unwilling to yield to what he could see made sense.

"Look, I think you made a mistake, and that's not nearly as bad. Still, it's not *nothing*, and you're going to have to own whatever you did."

"I'm trying to do that, but they don't believe me," Steve complained.

"I'm going to see if I can help you fix that. I have to ask you some questions. I need answers that will even up the playing field between the facts they have and what you're telling them."

Steve spoke with a pained and exasperated look on his face.

"I keep telling them I don't have anything to give them. And they act like they know everything, anyway."

"Right now, you're not answering to them, Steve; you're talking to *me*. As a reporter, my sources are confidential. Our next step is to discuss things while your lawyer's in the room, somewhere we can have some privacy; the jailers record these telephone conversations. If I can get what I'm looking for, I'll tell your story for you, backed up with facts they can't ignore.

"All I'm asking today is for your promise that if I make those arrangements, you'll talk to me honestly about everything you know. *Please.*"

It took Steve a few moments to process what I wanted from him, but I could see his demeanor changing. The tension left his frame, and his brow furrowed as he considered my request. Finally, he nodded his head slowly.

"Okay, I can do that. How long will it take to make it happen?"

I caught a touch of eagerness in his tone that confirmed his attitude had shifted. He still had hope for something positive out of all this.

A stolen car, an assault rifle, a judge and her three little girls, and a geeky teenager fresh out of suburbia certainly made for an engrossing backdrop.

I was genuinely curious how much I'd learn from this kid in our follow-up conversation, away from the prying eyes and attentive ears of armed guards.

CHAPTER 11

Three days after I last spoke to Steve, Richard Gardner, the attorney Tracy retained to replace Steve's court-appointed lawyers, agreed to meet me.

He stood as I entered the small interview room provided by the county for its inmates and their counsel. Portly and of average height, Gardner appeared to be in his early forties with a friendly disposition. His brown hair was receding, prematurely graying at his temples. We shook hands across the small wooden table, and Steve and I exchanged nods.

"Richard Gardner, of Shaeffer and Gardner, Ms. Wynn. It's a pleasure to meet you finally. I've read many of your writings over the years; they're impressive."

"Thank you, Mr. Gardner. Please call me Debra Ann. I understand you'll see Steve's situation through to its conclusion?"

"'Richard' works for me. And yes, I'm going to help Steve navigate these waters."

As I turned slightly to address Steve, he placed his hands on the table, and I noticed jailers had uncuffed him. I'd done several interviews in rooms like these and found that unusual. Still, I was glad for his sake.

"Steve, it's good to see you again, though I wish it could be under other circumstances. I notice they've taken off your restraints. That's an improvement."

"They've treated me better since Mr. Gardner talked to them, so yeah…. But I just want to go home."

Steve sounded more tired than angry. I couldn't fault him for his complaint, and despite it, his body language told me his attitude was more positive than the first time I'd seen him. It was a welcome change that would make my task more straightforward.

"Ordinarily, I wouldn't permit a client in Steve's circumstances to interview with a journalist," Richard intervened. "I want to clarify you're here as a friend of the family rather than professionally."

"Yes, Richard, this is all off the record. I may use the information Steve provides to help me in my investigation and reporting as it relates to others. Still, he won't be one of my subjects."

"With that addressed, I'll let the two of you converse. I'll remain here to protect privilege, but I'll try not to interrupt unless you have questions of a legal nature. If so, feel free to ask."

"Thank you, Richard." I turned to Steve.

"I've been thinking since we last talked, and here's what I believe I can do for you. You told your mom you were merely following instructions, driving this car from one location to another."

Steve nodded.

"My husband, Paul, who works for the state as a criminalist supervisor, has volunteered to help. We've all talked about your situation — me, Paul, your mom, and Lt. Harbin — and we all agree that the only answer is to nail down the people who gave you those instructions. The police are leaning on you to give them up and aren't doing much else. Until you do, they're happy leaving it all up to you to prove your version of the incident.

"Showing law enforcement who's responsible for the bigger part of this will stop them from accusing you of more than you did. To that end, I need to learn everything you know. It won't leave this room unless it helps you."

"I understand you're on my side," Steve replied, trying not to offend me — again, progress.

"And I want to help you, I *do*. But nobody *gets* it. I'm here because of all the things I *didn't* know. When I accepted this challenge, I didn't know about the gun, where those GPS coordinates were, or who lived there. I didn't *know* they stole the car. If I'd known any of that shit, I wouldn't have bid on the challenge."

"Truthfully, we *do* get all that, Steve. The little bit you *did* know only made things worse. If you hadn't looked under the hood covering the gun, you wouldn't have been driving like a grandma going to church on the busiest highway in San Diego, and you wouldn't have gotten pulled over. Even today, you still wouldn't know you'd done anything wrong.

"The problem is, none of that helps us. What *would* help us is to give law enforcement some other targets to worry about. Without those, they'll keep banging on you until they get the answers they want."

"You're right," Richard interjected. "The indication I'm getting from the DA is that they know this is bigger than what Steve could have pulled off alone, even if he'd wanted to. Giving them some alternate theories for their case wouldn't hurt anything. They seem to be looking for an off-ramp."

"Good. The door's open a crack," I replied. "Steve, let's start with what I think I already know. Your mom tells me you're in some club called 'antics' or something like that. The club has strict rules about what you can and can't do. I'm assuming one of those rules is that you can't rat out the club or its members, or they'll do some pretty bad things to you. Am I on track so far?"

"Yeah. But it's a website, social media," Steve answered. "'Aunt Tik's.' For screwing around with outsiders."

Belatedly, the light bulb went off in my head.

"Oh, wait! I've *heard* of this. Not *antics,* but *Aunt Tik's* — as in, your mother's sister. 'A-u-n-t-space-T-i-k-apostrophe-s.' Where you play jokes on people — they call them 'punks.' My friend's kids like to watch the videos. But the idea is just goofing around, punking your buddies, right?"

"The actual name is 'Aunt Tik's Jape Juice and Dido Dispensary,'" Steve offered. "But yeah, it's supposed to be for fun. Sometimes, to embarrass somebody, like Borat did to Giuliani. I never heard about anything terrible happening — nothing like what they did to me. That's why when the cops pulled me over, I didn't take it seriously. I thought *they* were punking *me*."

I sat back in my chair, astounded. *That* explains why a decent and reasonably intelligent kid like Steve would lip off to police officers, I thought. Some of this was starting to fall into place.

But I needed more clarity.

"'Jape?' 'Dido?' Not familiar — are those terms the website invented?"

"The opposite, really," Steve informed me. "Ancient history, like in the 1800s. 'Japing' means making fun of something. A 'dido' is a practical joke; now everyone calls it a 'punk.'"

"Ah, got it," I said, inwardly smiling as I realized Steve was comfortable explaining things he knew that I didn't — a good thing for this interview.

"You didn't answer the question about flipping on other members of Aunt Tik's," I pressed him. "So, I'll assume that giving up this 'Aunt Tik's' thing doesn't work for you right now."

"You've got it all wrong. *Everybody's* got it all wrong. That's not it. Like I keep telling the police, there's nothing to give up. I don't know anything. Aunt Tik's is all about secrecy. The members all have made-up names; the messages are all encrypted."

Steve flashed a little anger.

"*Jesus*, man, how they operate is out in the open. It's all online. The cops can look it up and see I'm not lying."

Though I heard him clearly, I decided to blow past his outburst. Something else had just clicked — when Marci's boys watched the video trashing the older BMW, I recalled that the credits roll didn't use real names. *Steve's telling the truth*. But still....

"You had some way to decrypt your instructions so you'd know what to do."

I needed to find a way past this roadblock.

"Couldn't you just do that again and give it to the investigators?"

"The messages disappear a few minutes after you download them. If I go online under my user account to get those messages again so I can decrypt them for the cops, Aunt Tik's will know. My challenge is already over. What reason do I have now to get my instructions again? They probably dismembered me, which means they're coming after me and won't let me get anything from my account anyway."

'Dismembered?' That must have been what Tracy overheard that freaked her out.

Steve's concerns made sense to me; more of the puzzle pieces were fitting.

"I take it 'dismembered' doesn't mean someone taking your body apart. It means getting kicked out of Aunt Tik's, like 'unfriending' someone, right?"

That got a smile and a nod from Steve, one that seemed *friendly.* Progress…

"I'm starting to get it, at least parts of it.

"The investigators think you know more than you do, and they couldn't care less what Aunt Tik's does to you after they get what *they* want. They know you're in trouble with the website — your mother told them she overheard something about Aunt Tik's causing you harm if you failed your task or didn't follow the rules. She thought she was protecting you. But the investigators took it instead as confirmation that you know something you won't tell them for fear of reprisals. They're fine with the extra pressure on you — hey, maybe you'll crack."

Seeing my dawning understanding made Steve visibly more relaxed.

"I can't even defend myself from Aunt Tik's in jail."

He began to open up.

"And the detectives are such assholes. I wish they'd make up their minds. One minute, they treat me like a little kid, then the next, I'm a mastermind serial killer."

"Good cop, bad cop. It's their thing. And because you're young and not a hardened criminal, I'm guessing they're laying it on thick. I'm starting to see your problem more clearly, Steve. Aunt Tik's and law enforcement are both making your life miserable, even though all you've done is what Aunt Tik's told you to. Except for looking under that gun cover. Seems like you're taking a lot of heat just for *that.*"

I wanted to give Steve a little support — an inside look at how they make the sausage, a positive thought he could take back to his cell.

"Here's something I probably shouldn't be telling you: no matter what they say or how they say it, they *know* you didn't steal that car. And they know that's not your gun for the same reasons *I* do."

He sat up straighter in his chair, his eyes widened with renewed interest.

"C'mon, Steve, you've never done anything like this before. But suddenly, you're putting together a customized professional weapon meant just for assassinating someone? Someone with whom you've never had any interaction? Your mom says you've got a grand total of $27.39 in your bank account, so it's not like anyone's paying you.

"And you can't drive for crap because you're so afraid of this gun you supposedly made yourself? And then, what? You wrote yourself a note on the computer because you're so forgetful that you couldn't remember this scary thing you told yourself to do? Trust me, we all know that's horse manure you weigh by the ton.

"The agents will never *tell* you, but they know. If you've never played poker, how they're acting toward you is called a 'bluff.' They'll keep trying to make you believe they think all of this is on you. It's their easiest path to closing this case."

Steve scowled. "They act like I'm John Dillinger come back to life."

Good, I can work with that.

"Pretending they can nail you with terrible crimes is their only leverage. Without information from you, figuring all this out would take a lot of work, which they'd rather avoid if they could.

"Here's something for you to consider. It doesn't matter what I think or what those detectives believe. It matters how that judge and her family feel about it. Trying to hang all this on a nineteen-year-old kid with no criminal history might work for the agents — and if it does, shame on them — but it's not going to make that judge or her kids sleep better at night. The investigators have no choice but to come up with answers that the family finds believable. We just need to keep you from becoming collateral damage until they figure it out."

Steve was hanging on my words, searching for some shred of hope.

"I get that, I guess. But I still don't see how to do what the agents want."

I leaned toward him.

"One thing we could give them that will help me get them off your back without losing any leverage is information about that gun. They'll already know what the builder intended the thing for. But describing to them how building it would be broken up as separate tasks among other people you don't know makes you seem cooperative. It's also a solid working example of what you've been trying to tell them, and you've shown me you know how to explain things.

"Your mom told Louis that they rigged the gun up for remote firing somehow. She says you're good with electronics and mechanical things. For my edification, can you tell me how they put it together and how it worked?"

He gave me a sideways glance.

"That's complicated, and I don't think I can last that long."

THE WRITINGS OF
AVRIL MARIA SERENE

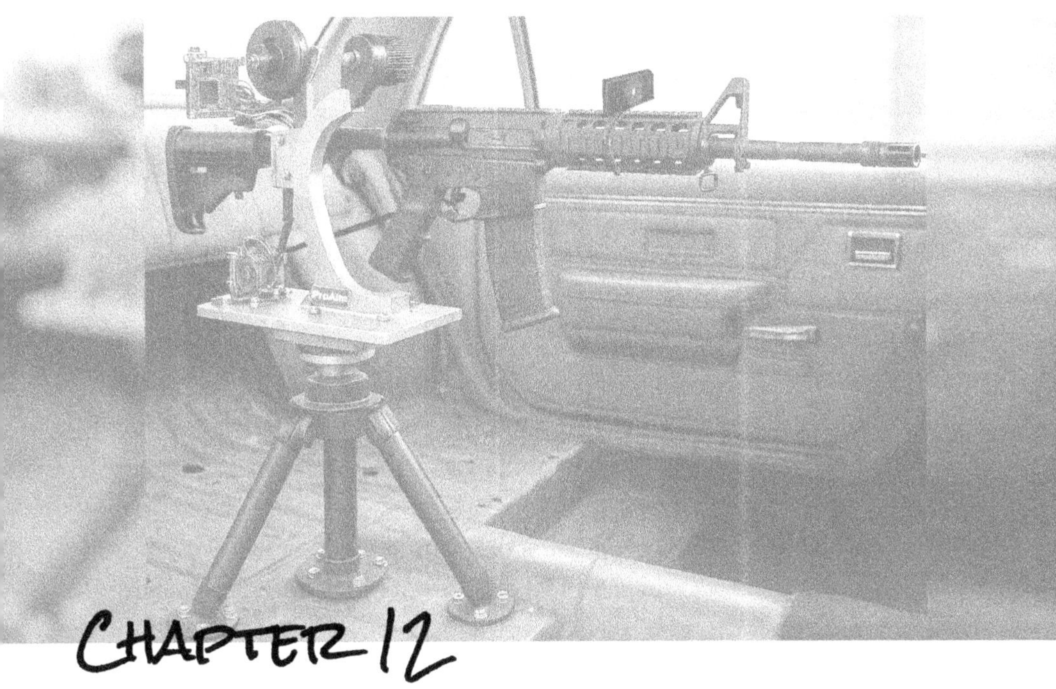

CHAPTER 12

Before Steve could answer, he needed to take a bathroom break. He wasn't sure how to get permission — a reminder of how little control inmates had over their lives.

I sensed I hadn't fully gained Steve's trust, but when he and Richard returned, I saw the young man's demeanor *had* brightened.

"You were going to teach me about how that gun worked," I reminded Steve, giving him the knowledge advantage.

He seemed to welcome discussing something that didn't directly threaten him.

"Sure. Some of us play around with drones a little. We can't afford the expensive brands, so we buy the kind you get at CVS for under a hundred bucks. We trick them out. There's stuff on the Internet, and we figure out the rest."

"You lost me. Was the gun mounted to a drone?"

"No, but they adapted drone parts and technology to control the gun."

"Oh, I get it. By the way, that's the perfect approach to take. Let them see why you know about that gun in theory but without having explicit knowledge about weapons. Just explain it like you're doing now."

"Okay. The punk rules say nobody is supposed to do anything illegal. So, no way I thought anyone stole the car I picked up. It was just a junker, anyway. Same with the gun — even after I saw it sitting there, I didn't think it could hurt anyone. The punk description said it was a paintball gun made to look like a real gun. You know, to scare somebody."

Now we were getting somewhere. I nodded and made a mental note to ask Steve later about what a 'punk' represented in Aunt Tik's world, as opposed to what I understood from Ashton Kutcher's old TV show. I'd also need to know where they posted the punk rules.

"Again, good." I wanted to build up Steve's confidence and show that I was on his team, but now he *was* going about this exactly the right way. His attitude was more positive, and I could see that the technical realm de-stressed him and allowed him to engage. Knowing that could be useful if I needed to guide him back to his comfort zone in the presence of others later.

"When I got the car, I looked in the back. The rear bench seat was missing. I saw some metal — the feet of this heavy-duty tripod bolted to the floor. Right away, when I took the hood off the whole thing, I could see the gun fastened to it.

"There was an aluminum plate bolted to the tripod's top instead of a camera mount. Screwed onto the middle of the plate was this metal stand bent like a letter *J*. U-bolts clamped the gun to the stand, and a big red sticker on one side said, 'Proaim Senior.' I guess that was to point the gun.

"Next to the gun was this motor and wheel fastened to the stand, with a brace from the stand to the gun's handle end. The top plate also had a little Raspberry Pi and some electronics mounted to it."

"Not 'raspberry pie,' like the dessert?" I was confused.

"'Pi,' like the radius of a circle. It's the name of a compact Linux computer you can play around with, and it's perfect for writing and running Python programs. People have been experimenting with them for years. It has USB, video, and controller ports. It's a complete computer, just small and cheap. You can do a bunch of cool things with one.

"So, I could see that they hooked the Pi up to the guts of a FlytNow remote-controller setup, plus some parts from a Mavic 2 drone. The Mavic isn't the cheapest; it's a nice drone."

"What's FlytNow?"

"It's a preconfigured communications system that uses the Internet so you can control your drone from anywhere. The commands go from your app to their server on the cloud, then from there to the FlytNow controller that runs your drone. You pay for the service on a subscription, like VoIP for drones."

"Voice over I/P?" I wanted to verify the acronym.

"Yes, but just for drones and commands instead of words."

"Interesting, but chilling in this context. Sorry, go on with what you saw on the gun. This is useful stuff."

I didn't need Steve's level of detail, but he was clearly in his element now. Since the discussion wasn't broken, I wasn't about to fix it.

"On top of the barrel part — where the bullet comes out, right above where you put your hand to steady it for pointing — there was a quality 4K Logitech Brio webcam instead of the stock Mavic 2 camera. Metal bracing around the camera locked it into a fixed position with the gun's barrel. Somebody painted a little crosshairs on the plastic lens."

"Like with nail polish or model paint?"

"Yeah, like that. The Brio's all plastic, though, so if the gun got hot and all that metal conducted the heat, it would melt after a while. I guess it was just to use one time. They wired the whole thing to a 12-volt car battery on the floorboard. I think that was so the car's ignition wouldn't have to be on when they fired the gun."

"Okay, you *really* got into this."

The nerd in Steve was exposed for me to see.

"Yeah, how they used the drone parts made me curious," he admitted, almost bashfully.

I doubt whoever's behind this ever considered the inquisitive mind of a teenager, especially a techie one, I thought — big mistake.

"I assume, seeing all this effort, you thought that gun might be real?"

Richard spoke up. "I need to protect my client here. Steve's never owned a gun, had never before seen a real AR-15, never served in the military, and has never fired such a weapon. Steve was in no position to say whether or not the gun was real.

"I'll let him speak to whether it made him nervous driving it around. But I don't want anything in your notes that says Steve drove the vehicle believing the gun could kill anyone. I'm sure you can appreciate the implications for defending him if he *knew* that was a working assault rifle."

"I do understand your concerns," I conceded. "Let me ask it a different way, then. Did the appearance of that gun and the way they set it up make you worry it might *accidentally* harm you or someone else?"

Richard nodded at Steve, acknowledging this form of the question was acceptable.

"Yes, it did. More because I was afraid that whoever was doing that part of the punk hadn't finished yet. Like I said before, it was supposed to be a paintball gun. I didn't think it would be like I saw it whenever the punk went down."

"Okay, that makes sense. What else can you tell me about the setup?"

"Wires were going into that rear door, and I think that was so they could roll down the electric window in front of the gun without starting the car.

"I don't know much about guns, but I could see that they were using relays to take the signal from the Pi and use it to run this motor. It's like maybe a windshield wiper motor geared down to drive a wheel. They hooked a pull rod to an offset hole drilled into the wheel. That rod would pull the trigger when the wheel went around."

"It would fire then, once it got the right command," I summarized. "I don't suppose you know enough about the AR-15 to know if they'd set it in single-shot, semi-auto, or automatic mode?"

Richard leaned forward to reiterate his earlier concern, but Steve answered before the lawyer spoke.

"No idea, sorry. The FlytNow with the Raspberry Pi meant you could run the whole thing remotely from anywhere you had an Internet connection. Maybe hack the WiFi from one of the houses nearby. They could've used a cell phone instead, but this way, they wouldn't need a SIM card that somebody could track from the cell tower."

I'd understood that the Internet connection and the mounting apparatus meant they could aim and fire the gun from anywhere. Still, until he mentioned cell phones, I'd forgotten the rig could also *see* the target over the Web. "Wait — this wasn't a line-of-sight thing, like the old-school radio-controlled model aircraft from when I was a kid. With this rig, nobody would have to be anywhere close to the car as long as they had an Internet connection. The camera on the gun would be their eyes. Assuming the car was in position, which was *your* job.

"Wow."

Steve was getting wound up, fidgeting in his chair and shifting his eyes from one side to another. Fear showed in his features. He was upset, which was, in a way, a positive thing. It spoke to his sincerity.

But I'd have to tamp it down at some point, for his sake.

"It was supposed to be a punk," Steve insisted, "and I know my lawyer doesn't want me to say this, but the gun looked real to me. Maybe this one had blanks or something; I don't know. But a real gun? One of the kids in our school killed himself with the wadding from a blank when he was just goofing around. I didn't plan on there being any real guns. So, I was like, 'Holy crap, what should I do?'"

Now, the frustration of being faced with a lousy choice came through in his expression and tone of voice.

"But, shit, if I didn't do my challenge, were they going to shoot *me?* How was I supposed to know? *Fuck,* man."

THE WRITINGS OF
AVRIL MARIA SERENE

CHAPTER 13

I had no answer for Steve about what Aunt Tik's might do, so I took the subject back to the paintball gun to let him calm down.

"You've said several times that when you agreed to do this punk, you expected a paintball gun and that putting it in the car was somebody else's responsibility."

Steve nodded.

"So, what was there didn't match what you were expecting. I need to understand clearly how that could happen. Can you go back a few steps? When you say 'punk,' what do you mean exactly?"

"A punk is like a practical joke," Steve replied. "Aunt Tik's breaks the punk up into little pieces so that a bunch of different people can each do a part of it — they call one of the parts a 'challenge.' Driving the car to where it was supposed to go was my challenge."

"Getting all these people together to play a joke on someone, then, that's what it's about? Aunt Tik's, I mean — kind of a competition or game for bragging rights playing tricks on people?"

"Basically, yeah. It's a little more complicated, but that's the idea."

"Okay, that squares with what I thought. But you were worried about someone possibly shooting you? Targeting outsiders is bad enough, but members, too? Seems pretty extreme for a game."

"I mean, I don't think they would, but they could, I guess. They're serious about it if you mess up, and they have to kick you out of Aunt Tik's. Not completing your challenge is one of the ways you can screw up. That wrecks the whole thing for everybody else."

I had to leave soon to pick up Tommy from Montessori, so I decided not to pursue that.

"I understand they found a note when they stopped you. I presume it was the instructions where you were supposed to pick up the car and where you were to drive it. You got the keys to it from a bus locker?"

"Luggage Hero. Some challenges use that; some use storage units."

"I take it you've done these things before for them?"

Steve slid around in his seat and didn't answer immediately.

"That's okay. We'll save that question for another time. I assume you copied the instructions they found on you from something you downloaded? Investigators will go through your cell phone and any computers you use at home or school. If you got it electronically, they're going to find it anyway. With guns potentially shooting at judges, the feds can secure any search warrants they want. If I can get ahead of what they learn, I'll know better how to help you."

Steve's brow furrowed, his lips pursed. His eyes focused on the table's edge as he processed that last bit. Finally, he said, "We use the Signal app, encrypted messages, and sometimes encrypted attachments for Outlook or Gmail. I just decrypted the notice from the punk master and wrote down what I needed before it disappeared."

"Who's the 'punk master?'"

"The person who manages the punk for Aunt Tik's."

"So no one else's prints are on the paper, then. Did you touch that car's gun, battery, or wires?"

"Well, I removed the hood over the gun and the tripod and put that back, but I don't think I touched anything else. I just gave it a good look. As soon as I saw it was a real gun, I didn't want to do anything. If I messed with it, Aunt Tik's might know I didn't follow the instructions, and I was afraid it would go off."

"'They' meaning Aunt Tik's? The instructions being not to examine the car?"

Steve nodded.

"How did you get your Signal account? And how did you decrypt the encrypted e-mail messages?"

"You get a Signal account using your Aunt Tik's handle once they accept your membership application."

"'Aunt Tik's handle'?"

"Your account name on Aunt Tik's website. And you get a little standalone app, just for Aunt Tik's, with a built-in encryption and decryption utility for e-mail attachments. They also give you a mobile app for iPhone or Android, which ties everything together. If you sign in with the phone app, your Signal account will automatically activate when you want to send a message. Encrypting and decrypting happen by default when you're in the phone app."

"Is there any way I can get a copy of the Android app?"

"It's easy; even a free member can download everything. But the app can't do anything until you log in to your Aunt Tik's account. The login tells the app if you are free, premium, a cell captain, or the czar. Downloading the app any time you want, like when you get a new phone, means you don't have to call support, which is cool."

Cell captain? The czar? Hmmm, good questions to ask later.

"If I get a free Aunt Tik's account and download and install the Android app, I can just sign in as someone with a different account, and I'm good to go as that person?"

"Sure. It's two-factor authentication, but I put it on my mom's phone once when I couldn't get my battery to charge anymore."

"Any chance it's still on your mom's phone?"

"No, I erased it. Mom would have asked what it was."

"Fair enough. Are you still a member of Aunt Tik's?"

"I don't know. I haven't been on it since I've been here. I didn't quit, but Aunt Tik's might've kicked me out."

"I need to ask you a big favor, then. You can say no, of course, and I'll respect that.

"But if you're willing to let me have your login information, it would help us check out Aunt Tik's. We wouldn't do anything when logged in — I assume the site monitors everything. But we could look at what's happening and not worry about encryption. I know it's a big ask, but we're trying to expedite everything possible to get you out of here."

Steve thought about it, his facial expressions changing as the gears turned in his head.

"Sure, okay," he finally said, as if still trying to convince himself.

"I guess it doesn't matter. Mr. Gardner told us I can't be on Aunt Tik's anymore — we have to promise the court to get bail. But you can't tell Aunt Tik's I'm letting you use my account, or they'll come after me for that, too."

I looked Steve in the eye and nodded my agreement.

"The website is 'AuntTiks dot com.'" Steve spelled it out. "All one word, capitals don't matter."

"Got it. That helps."

Steve gave me his handle and password, then told me his mother's maiden name, first pet, and grade school for the verification questions.

"It's dual authentication, so the app will ask if you want to validate with an e-mail, text phone number, or verification question. Choose 'verification question' and use the answers I gave you. If that doesn't work, you'll have to use my cell phone at home for the secondary authentication. Ask Mom to get it for you. Here's my PIN for my phone."

After taking careful notes, I finished up, not wanting to push any harder during this session.

"Okay, Steve, that's great for now. You've helped me a lot. Let me see what I can do with what you've told me, and I'll come back the day after tomorrow if you're still here. Hopefully, your mother will have you bailed out by then. Let the jailers or Richard know if you think of anything else that might help me help you. They'll get a message to me."

"I'll do that." He added softly and hesitantly, "Thanks."

"You're welcome, Steve," I replied as I signaled with a nod to Richard that I was ready to leave.

"We'll get this worked out. Remember what I said: the agents know you didn't do this. Don't say that to their face; try to get along with them as best you can until we get you out of here. Answer the questions you feel you can, like you did here with me, and you'll be fine."

He flashed a half smile as he turned back to his lawyer. We made good progress this session. Still, I'd have felt better had a reminder not suddenly flitted across my mind. We were, after all, here because Steve couldn't follow instructions on not looking under the hood.

Or resist the temptation to make a snide remark about a suicide vest.

THE WRITINGS OF
AVRIL MARIA SERENE

CHAPTER 14

On my way home, I stopped by a Walmart and paid cash for two TracPhones and a hundred-dollar preloaded debit card to go with each.

The burner phones would host the Aunt Tik's apps I downloaded. I'd use one to log onto Steve's Aunt Tik's account and the other to create a new premium account under my control. Nothing about the accounts, devices, or debit cards would tie back to me. I'd use the debit cards to buy TracPhone minutes online and to pay for membership fees or services once I could access a premium Aunt Tik's account separate from Steve's.

I briefly stopped by Tracy's house to tell her how her son was doing. While there, I picked up Steve's cell phone in case I needed it to log into his Aunt Tik's account.

Just as Steve said, the free Aunt Tik's membership application on the burner phone was straightforward. After downloading the Aunt Tik's app from Google Play, I installed it onto the burner, logging in as "FlyNHigh," Steve's member handle. When the authentication message went to his cell phone, I copied the six-letter code into the Aunt Tik's login window on the burner phone. I changed the phone number in the app's account settings to match the burner's.

When I shut down and restarted everything to test my access to Steve's account, the two-factor authentication message went to the burner instead. I logged into Steve's account, getting a "Welcome" splash window as my reward.

Checking out the punk result videos window, I could see several pages containing video links I hadn't seen as a public user. It seemed Steve's membership was still active.

Next, I used the second burner to download a copy of the app and sign onto a premium Aunt Tik's account of my own — that, too, went as expected. However, a notice appeared that an established member must vouch for me to attain full access.

To resolve that issue, I logged back into Steve's account on the other burner, walking through Aunt Tik's menu to find the option for validating new members. Once there, I located my application and approved it as Steve. After a few moments, my new Aunt Tik's account went active, and I could explore at will. Although there were some differences between the two accounts based on Steve's past activity, they seemed to have equal access.

Waiting until she was off-duty, I called Marci to fill her in on my conversations with Steve.

"Hey, Marci. Sorry to call you at home, but I wanted to discuss the Steve Nielsen case."

"Your timing works out great," Marci replied, "I needed to talk to you about that, anyway. I'm still investigating the James Marshall homicide. Even though it went to Escalation Management, I'm still on the hook as the lead detective. It's taking up all my time.

"But with their team picking up the rest of the work, Eve's freed up. I talked to Louis, and he agreed to let her help you with Steve's situation off the clock. Let's see if she's home yet; maybe we can conference her. Give me a second…"

I briefly heard the voice of Elsie Gonzalez, Eve's wife, as she picked up the phone and let Eve know she had a call.

"Hi, boss, *¿qué pasa?*"

"Hey, Eve, I know you just got home, and I hate to interrupt your supper, but something's come up — Debra Ann's on the line. I wanted to see if you'd be okay with helping us out. It's a personal favor, so feel free to say no — it's all good."

"Hi, Debra Ann. Sure, I'll help if I can. What's going on?"

"Debra Ann's been doing some digging around for our boss. The lieutenant's neighbor's boy got into trouble that blew up into something way out of the kid's league. Debra Ann, Paul, and I have been looking into it outside official channels. One of those things where Lt. Harbin can't get directly involved because it would look bad."

"That thing with the assault rifle pointed at Judge Wasserman's house?"

"You know about that?" Marci was surprised.

"That's how it is around the squad room — people talk. Nobody thinks a teenager came up with all that on his own."

Marci took the opportunity to dispel any inaccurate rumors Eve may have heard and fill her in on the details she didn't already know.

"I'd be glad to help out," Eve volunteered. "Louis asked me to look through the cold cases if I had time. He wants to clear any low-hanging fruit that no one else has claimed as a pet project. Getting him a list of those was going to be my next task.

"The good thing is that I won't have anyone looking over my shoulder asking me to account for my time."

That gave me an opening to tell Eve, as Marci listened in, about my conversations with Steve at the federal detention facility.

"We first thought Aunt Tik's could be a cult, and we didn't know how truthful Steve might be," I explained. "In talking with him, he's pretty convincing. Something's definitely off with this Aunt Tik's thing."

"You're confident Steve didn't intend to harm anyone?" Marci asked.

"I had to cut through some attitude and the reactions you'd expect from a 19-year-old. Still, I'm convinced Steve wanted no part of this once he knew what it was, but by then, it was too late, in his mind, to get out of the situation. I think all he's guilty of is immaturity and poor judgment. If those were jailable offenses when I was a kid, I'd *still* be locked up."

"Is Aunt Tik's part in this specific just to what Steve was supposed to do, or is something bigger going on?" Eve asked.

"No clue yet. Aunt Tik's is all about screwing with people, so there's that. Could be a punk within a punk, maybe, where freaking people out with an assault rifle instead of a paintball gun was supposed to be part of the joke? Or causing him real trouble was somebody's idea of getting back at Steve for something? It's possible one of the punk participants ahead of Steve screwed up or misunderstood what they were supposed to do.

"Those are the innocent options, things that possibly got out of hand. But if somebody manipulated the circumstances *intending* to kill someone, this could be a much bigger problem."

The line went silent for a moment.

"How much time would you need from me?" Eve asked.

Marci stepped in.

"The only things we can do have to be off-the-books since we don't have an official case and don't want to be stepping on the feds' turf. Maybe a couple of hours a week?"

"That I can do. I have several questions already, but maybe we can get together after I've familiarized myself with the basics."

"Thanks, Eve; I hoped you'd come on board." I was pleased — she was a solid investigator. "I have questions, too. Aunt Tik's is new to all of us, so it won't take long to get you up to speed with what we know.

"Steve gave us his premium Aunt Tik's membership login info, and I set up a burner phone to access his account. I installed the app onto another burner with a new premium Aunt Tik's account that you can use. We can switch the phones between us if we need to. That'll keep Aunt Tik's from detecting multiple simultaneous logins on the same account or using a recognizable department device."

"Good," Eve said. "Makes it easier to work on this between other things."

"I'll dig around Aunt Tik's website some more. As I told Steve, we can't *do* anything with his account, like accepting challenges or asking questions on the message forums, because we don't know if Aunt Tik's is monitoring that account. His lawyer promised the judge that Steve would stay off Aunt Tik's, so we should tread lightly."

"But we'll be able to see anything visible to Steve on that website, right?" Marci asked.

"For now," I replied. "By getting caught, Steve failed his challenge and thought he'd get kicked out of Aunt Tik's. I understand that's a scary thing, or at least Steve believes it is. His access as a premium member could go away at any time.

"'But then again, Aunt Tik's might be holding off because it's become a police case, not drawing attention to themselves by immediately going after Steve. When and if they do, we'll have to rely on my new member account."

"How can I help?" Eve asked.

"The website has videos and comments about past punks. It also has lists of what they call punk challenges that members can perform. Challenges are the pieces of a punk stitched together to make the thing happen. Members can bid on the right to perform one of those challenges and get points for doing them. I'm unclear on the bidding process, but maybe we can figure it out from previous punks. We should also see what things are on the new challenges list."

"What should I be searching for?"

"Let's put your experience and memory to work, Eve. On the one hand, we need to know what parts of these punks might be crossing the line legally, in your opinion. On the other, we want to tap into what you know about the department's current and past cases. Have any elements of these challenges or punks shown up in investigations or citizen complaints? Or might they be related to filed cases in some way? It would be nice to know if law enforcement has previously encountered a situation like this, and if so, how common it is."

"Now I get where you're going — should be right up my alley, no problem."

"Once we know whether this thing goes beyond Steve's circumstances, we need to see all those challenge descriptions. Maybe we can piece together some of the new punks they might be doing.

"If you or Elsie are going to be home, I can drop the burner off to you tonight. Or I can leave it with Marci, and she can pass it to you at work. I'll text you the new Aunt Tik's member account info so you can log in."

"Bring it over. We planned on staying in this evening, so we'll be here. I'll play with the app tonight and during my breaks tomorrow to see what I can learn. I'll have to run through the cold cases first and make up the status report Louis requested. Then I should have some time."

"By the way, I know the lieutenant's been getting calls from Tracy," Marci said. "I'm sure she doesn't *mean* to helicopter, but if I were in her shoes, I'd be doing the same thing."

"Oh, of course," I replied. "Thanks for the heads-up. The lieutenant would probably appreciate an update.

"Paul's more likely to run into him than I am. I'll see if I can get him to fill Louis in on what we're doing."

CHAPTER 15

The czar was seated in a warm robe in the comfort of his spacious and well-appointed home office, silhouetted by the glow of his open laptop. He stared at it, knowing he had a problem, albeit one he'd anticipated. The issue wasn't the challenge he'd awarded Jessica — that had gone as intended, and she'd done everything he'd wanted her to do.

Nor was the snag that the punk target, Carla Littman, had passed away due to anaphylactic shock from her severe peanut allergy. That, after all, was the whole point.

But Littman had spent her final moments dying in an ambulance. The complication was that he'd need to fake different results to show the game players. After all, the punk description had said the goal was to trick the target into taking multiple doses of Dulcolax and Ex-Lax. It said nothing about killing anyone.

He owed the punk participants a video that they could point to with pride yet satisfied Aunt Tik's prohibition against performing criminal acts.

He'd prepared in advance a couple of alternatives for resolving this situation. He chose the cell phone video he'd made surreptitiously several weeks before. After spiking a friend's breakfast in the morning with a heavy dose of laxatives, he'd later taken her to the Olive Garden for a lunch of all-you-can-eat pasta.

"*Lessee….*" He opened the files and folders app on his notebook, scrolling through the listings. "Where'd I put that video of Carmen wearing out the carpet to the ladies' room? Ahhh, here we go… Okay, let's speed 'er up."

After making a working copy, he used PowerDirector to clip out the irrelevant table conversations between her frequent trips to powder her nose, blurring her face where necessary. He then sped up the resulting mashup of the overweight woman repeatedly excusing herself. Dressed in a skirt too tight and heels too high, she'd half-run, half-walk to the restroom, arms extended for balance and hands flopping at the wrists as the camera followed her.

"That'll work!" he proclaimed to his invisible audience. The result had exactly that old *Benny Hill* vibe he was looking for. He congratulated himself as he uploaded the video to Aunt Tik's punk results web page, tagging it with the header information from the original punk and challenges.

While he'd solved *that* problem, he wanted to rescan his digital environment to see if any other "gotchas" were awaiting him, in keeping with long years of training in the criminal arts.

Okay, who should I be today? So many choices, so little time … it's good to be the top dog.

Fortunately for his purposes, the czar had many contacts within the San Diego Police Department. Some were also members of Aunt Tik's, whose complete membership information and activities only he could see. He ran through the computer system logins displayed in his Excel spreadsheet.

"You'd think cops would know better," he marveled as he scrolled down through the records of all the officers who used the same passwords and handles in their Aunt Tik's accounts that they used at work. "But, if they want to make it this easy, I'll accommodate them…."

Choosing an account with the level of access he wanted, the czar used it to sign into the department's databases.

He'd kept a finger on the pulse of the follow-up investigation through the electronically filed records and digital evidence. He'd watched as detectives traced the cause of death to the contents of a box of breakfast cereal. He'd read the digital report indicating the Cheerios had been liberally sprayed with unrefined peanut oil and then dried. He'd smiled as he learned that the recipient had discarded the Amazon soft-pack envelope in which the cereal arrived long before the forensics team discovered the contamination.

"Let's see if anything new has turned up in the Forensics reports," he muttered. Then his eyes fell upon the line he was searching for: "No viable prints or trace evidence recoverable from the cereal box."

That's good, he thought.

There was a scanned image of a handwritten note that was helpful: "Because peanut oil is a natural substance," it declared, "there's no practical way within the department's budget to trace the origins of a sample without a candidate batch to match it to — no national comparison database exists for raw peanut oil."

I could have told them that.

He smiled to himself.

"Awww, so sad. Seems the homicide investigation has stalled." His voice dripped with derision.

There were no other complaints of product tampering to law enforcement or the retailer responsible for the delivery. Nor were there reports of similar illnesses or injuries in the area. There was no basis for detectives to widen their investigation. The authorities wouldn't panic the community with a recall over just one known instance of food poisoning, and they didn't want to provide free publicity to glorify the attacker or inspire copycats.

This thing's going to the cold-case files. Good riddance — that's it for me.

With his work done, he shut down the laptop and began his daily routine.

Detectives often say that a homicide team's primary role is to provide a voice for the deceased through the collected evidence. Yet just one man hiding in plain sight had seen to it that calls, pleas, and prayers made by Carla Littman's family asking law enforcement to speak for her through their investigation were effectively on hold.

He, therefore, was off the hook — and, by extension, free to focus on the next irritant he wanted to eliminate.

———————

Mike was in his Subaru Forester, cruising west on Mission Hill Ridge past the early-morning joggers running against the traffic. The two-lane, tree-lined street meandered east and west for five miles through a middle-class suburban neighborhood, passing an occasional strip mall or school.

As he crossed into a residential area, his watch chirped out the 6:55 a.m. alarm he'd set. Mostly two-story family homes, the front yards were littered with toys for kids and pets. Yard signs for service companies suggested many had pools in the back, and he rolled past several RVs in the driveways and on the curbs.

The street spawned cul-de-sacs and branch avenues to the left and right, including Heartvine Circle, the one Mike sought. According to Google Maps, Heartvine Circle was a loop — it teed into Mission Hill Ridge from the south in two three-way intersections half a city block apart. Heartvine Circle climbed a steady southerly grade from each intersection for nearly a mile before joining to form an elongated letter U on the slowly rising side of a mountain.

Mike parked his car on Mission Hill Ridge, pointed away from the rising sun, a hundred yards west of its westernmost intersection with Heartvine Circle.

He'd deciphered the punk master's simple instructions and copied them onto his phone for the challenge. He quickly reviewed them, just to be sure.

"Okay, Panzer, let's do this thing," Mike muttered to his year-old black Labrador retriever.

He clipped the leash onto the dog's collar and opened the door. Wearing a ball cap, shades, and a nondescript navy blue jacket and jeans, Mike trudged up the long hill with his Lab leading the way. They slowed a few dozen yards from where Heartvine Circle started its bend to join its eastern leg.

Mike did a quick double-take as he noticed a Ford F-250 flatbed parked at the curb on the opposite side of the street. The truck's cab looked like someone had painted it black with a spray can.

Confused, Mike pulled his phone back out of his jacket pocket and carefully reread the Aunt Tik's message. No, the flatbed he was looking for was supposed to be on the *eastern* leg of Heartvine Circle, and it was described as an F-350 dually. The F-250 Mike was looking at had a single-wheel back axle. Now uncertain, he continued up around the loop of Heartvine Circle behind Panzer.

As he rounded the bend, he saw another truck parked curbside, a decades-old Ford F-350 dually flatbed with a brush-painted black cab — precisely as described in the message.

Mike tied Panzer's leash to the parking sign pole next to the truck. Kneeling to pet the dog and partially shielded by the vehicle, Mike looked around for any observers.

Not seeing anyone, he pulled on a pair of blue nitrile gloves, then stood up, opened the passenger door of the flatbed, and leaned in.

Mike grabbed the truck's gearshift and put it in Neutral. Then he softly closed the door and returned his attention to Panzer.

He scratched the Lab's neck, waiting until his watch read 7:15 a.m.

Then, Mike opened the driver's door and climbed in.

He kicked off the truck's emergency brake, and as the flatbed began to move, he jumped out of the cab, pushing the driver's door closed in the same motion.

He strolled around the rear of the truck as it rolled away, untied Panzer's leash, and casually walked the Lab back the way they'd first come, uphill around the loop that connected the circle with its western section.

A few moments later, the noise of a horrendous crash below reverberated throughout the valley.

Mike steadfastly continued around the bend back down the hill, taking great care not to look at the source of the explosion's echoes, per the warning in his instructions.

As he trekked the downward slope, he spotted the other flatbed. He shook his head slightly, asking Panzer, "What are the odds there'd be two of those junkers in the same neighborhood?"

Once he and his dog were back in his Subaru, Mike carefully drove off, trying not to draw attention to himself and avoiding the temptation to look into his rearview mirrors.

Junior found his parking space several hundred feet east of Heartvine Circle's eastmost T-intersection with Mission Hill Ridge. While downing the last of this morning's thermos of coffee, he reviewed the instructions printed from his computer.

At 7:10 a.m., he exited his three-year-old Camaro and climbed the hill up Heartvine Circle.

As he reached the halfway point, an old black flatbed Ford passed on the street beside him, gathering speed as it rolled down the hill. It caught his eye because it was nearly identical to the vehicle described in his Aunt Tik's challenge. As it cruised by, Junior saw no driver, and the engine wasn't running.

Warned by his decrypted Aunt Tik's message to ignore distractions, he mentally put his blinders on and continued his jaunt.

It didn't keep him from nearly jumping out of his boots when Junior heard the enormous bang and clatter of a vehicle-on-vehicle collision down the hill behind him.

Reminding himself why he was here, he refocused and resumed his journey.

Seeing someone walking a dog fifty yards ahead, Junior slowed his pace. He wanted no interactions with anyone until he completed his challenge.

Junior wondered if he'd misunderstood what he was supposed to do — the truck he'd just seen looked like the twin of the one described in his challenge. But he was relieved when he came around the bend and found the Ford F-250 sitting against the curb, pointed down the hill. The flatbed pickup was as described, down to the cracked windshield.

Junior scanned the landscape to see if anyone else was around.

Satisfied there wasn't, he followed his challenge instructions to the letter. He put on the work gloves he'd tucked into his back pocket, climbed into the cab, and shifted the transmission out of gear.

At exactly 7:30 a.m., he released the handbrake, then stepped out of the cab, closing the driver's door.

The truck began rolling, and Junior skipped around the back as it went by.

Retracing his steps back up the hill, he'd follow the loop around to the east, then downhill at a steady gait, keeping his face forward.

Suddenly, the banging, screeching, and clattering collision of the flatbed truck he'd released bounced back at him from the hillsides.

The vehicle had hit the intersecting curb and flipped, eliciting screams and gasps from an audience gathered before him.

As he approached the intersection with Mission Hill Ridge, the growing crowd of onlookers murmured and pointed at the commotion and activity generated by the crash he'd just heard.

A patrol unit had pulled up, lights flashing. Both officers in it were hurrying to a tan-colored sedan on the far curb. A different flatbed truck, probably the lookalike Junior saw earlier, had T-boned the car. Excited chattering accompanied the group's shift to the west as it tried to get closer to the second crash.

Putting his head down and focusing on the sidewalk, Junior skirted outside the crowd and quietly broke away in the opposite direction.

Once he reached his Camaro, he slid into the driver's seat and drove slowly east, reflecting on what he'd just done, seen, and heard.

CHAPTER 16

Officer Gary Tilman, a seven-year veteran of the traffic unit, and his rookie partner, Joey Legato, got the call at 7:24 a.m. — a two-vehicle collision, with a possible fatality, on Mission Hill Ridge. He switched on the cruiser's sirens and lights and headed to the scene. The 911 dispatcher had already sent an ambulance; the paramedics would meet them there.

As Tilman pulled up, he saw two dozen neighbors congregating on the south side of the street. On the north side, a large flatbed truck had smashed into a light brown sedan at center mass. The impact had been so severe that both ends of the car were accordion-folded, like paper fans.

The officers scrambled out of their vehicle and ran to the crash scene, taking the north sidewalk nearest the curb where the wrecks now sat. As they did, a middle-aged woman in a blue dress and flowered apron came running out of the home immediately north of the accident scene, hysterically crying and screaming in Spanish.

"Legato, keep her away!" Tilman shouted as he waved his partner over to intercept the female.

"Call in for backup; I'll check out the sedan!"

Tilman could see massive blood spatter radiating away from the point of impact on what remained of both the car and the truck. There was no obvious indication of a human torso visible where the two had violently collided.

Tilman lowered himself into a pushup position on the sidewalk — he wanted a better view underneath the area where the victim may have been between the car and the truck. His eyes searched for any evidence of a victim's lower extremities where the vehicles had met.

Suddenly, another collision exploded eighty yards ahead, commandeering his field of view.

He couldn't believe his eyes — a different runaway truck had come rampaging down the hill at the next intersection.

Tilman reflexively went into a defensive crouch as he raised himself off the sidewalk. Both hands out in front of him, palms outward, he squinted between them at the unfolding scene.

With an empty bed and a driverless cab, the truck had bounced off the corner curb at the intersection.

It went into a roll, shearing off a stop sign and clipping a light pole before sliding on its driver's door into a house on the north side of the street.

As the flatbed impacted the home's exterior, the cab swung around, scraping and bouncing along until it lodged between that residence and the next one to the east.

As a cloud of dust rose along the truck's path, then gradually dispersed, Tilman rapidly scanned the scene for any other approaching threats.

Seeing nothing else coming, he tried to maintain a professional façade, but his heart was racing.

He called into his shoulder mike, "Dispatch, we've got another accident, two hundred fifty feet directly west of our position. Get us fire rescue with jaws of life ASAP to extract a possible victim here. "

"We'll need a HAZMAT crew to contain fluids and a water tank unit for fire control and washdown at both scenes. Send two additional patrol units and three tow trucks, heavy-duty flatbeds with winches, for vehicle removal."

Tilman's radio transmission had walked all over an incoming 911 dispatch call, rendering it unintelligible, and he received no acknowledgment. He repeated his radio request in full.

He could hear the loud garble from his cruiser's radio as a burst of chatter erupted from both 911 and central dispatch's attempts to navigate a flood of citizen call-ins.

"Housekeeper says we have a potential victim," Legato shouted. "Female, early fifties. The subject was standing on the driver's side of the sedan at the time of the collision."

Peering through the crushed car's shattered passenger windows, Tilman could see more signs of extensive blood loss. Scattered bits of human flesh were evident in the collapsed cabin of the vehicle.

"I've got significant blood and tissue inside the sedan, which appears to originate on the outside of the vehicle," he called into his shoulder mike. "There's no body evident in the interior. No access available to the remains until they remove the truck."

Tilman could also see that he could realistically do nothing for the victim.

Two patrol cruisers pulled up, one behind Tilman's squad car and the other just beyond the crash scene to the west. Tilman directed the two officers from the patrol unit nearest him toward Legato for coordination and a status sync-up.

In the meantime, he returned to his vehicle for an intense exchange with dispatch to sort out the confusion between two similar incidents near and within moments of each other.

***

The cell czar had ordered a venti-sized Blonde Roast classic coffee with two shots of espresso — the most caffeine he could get in a single container at Starbucks. As he sipped from it in a stolen ten-year-old, pewter-gray Buick Lacrosse, he watched the sun climb the eastern sky.

He wanted to be sharp today. The czar had elected himself punk master for two nearly simultaneous punks and personally handcrafted all the challenges. He didn't want to pat himself on the back prematurely, but this was one of his most audacious and elaborate stagings yet.

He knew he was pushing the boundaries of what he could get away with. Aunt Tik's members trusted that their challenges wouldn't ask them to do anything illegal, or at least not *too* far out of bounds. He wasn't about to tell the participants, but he'd have to bend that rule for these two punks to work. He'd substitute plausible deniability for criminal liability, relying on human nature and a lesson from the annals of justice to do the rest.

Back in the day, when executions were still performed by firing squads, each shooter was made aware that at least one of the rifles contained blanks. There was always a risk that one or more of the executioners might have misgivings or an attack of conscience after the fact. In that case, they could always convince themselves that they'd drawn the impotent weapon and bore no responsibility for the outcome.

That idea proved helpful in these circumstances. The cell czar would need to hide the actual results of these punks from Aunt Tik's members, as he'd done frequently.

He'd record only the second punk's spectacular finish to serve as the conclusion video for both punks. Using similar props and timing them within moments of each other, the participants in either punk would accept that video as showing *their* outcome. Given the way Aunt Tik's worked, and in keeping with the game's rules, the challenge actors had no way to compare the results of their punk to someone else's. The first punk's players would never know they were seeing the same finale shown to the actors in the second.

The cell czar would ensure that the view of the runaway truck video posted for public downloading was only generically labeled with the date, that it was morning, and that it happened on Mission Hill Ridge. Each group of challenge participants could privately claim credit for their part in that video, and no one would be the wiser.

The only remaining problem was that the intended target of one of the two punks was an influential local figure. The victim's demise was likely to draw significant real-world media attention. There was a sizeable risk here that any of the members performing the critical challenges for these punks might put two and two together and realize they'd been part of a murder. Though the secrecy within Aunt Tik's would protect the punk master from having his role discovered for a while, he wasn't sure how long that protection would last if a member flipped.

To resolve *that* problem, he'd need each punk challenge participant to convince themselves they'd drawn the rifle with the blanks and weren't answerable for anything that happened. He'd make sure each of the final challenge performers would see another, nearly identical truck on the scene by crisscrossing the paths they would walk. Confusion and not wanting to get involved in confrontation should keep anyone from reporting anything. He'd rely on natural procrastination, the rationalization that authorities in time would figure it out without outside intervention.

The czar would let the strength of Aunt Tik's dismemberment rules and the fear of being accused themselves if they went to the authorities do the rest for him. Few members knew the real identities of any other Aunt Tik's subscribers, and he'd picked players he was sure were unrelated. None of the performers would know which other members he'd chosen for these punks' challenges. In short, no one else could corroborate what another might say. With all that, he was willing to bet on human nature to keep his secrets.

He had, after all, the advantage of higher intellect. These weren't rocket scientists he was dealing with, and he was confident he could figure a way around any problem they might pose. And it wasn't like the geniuses in the police department would be able to sort any of this out on their own.

But the complicated scenario meant he had to be on the scene early and blend into the background. He must play his uncredited role with precision. The trick would be to switch tasks quickly. First, he'd finish guiding the first truck to its intended destination with the RC controller. He'd then get into position quickly with his cell phone to film the journey of the second truck downhill as he followed slowly behind. If he pulled it off, the rewards were huge — none of the participants for either of the two punks would ever know they'd helped him kill his ex-wife's attorney.

The czar had parked facing uphill on the eastern leg of Heartvine Circle, a little ahead of the flatbed truck on the opposite curb.

At a few minutes past seven, he saw the first challenge participant and his dog cresting the hill. He watched as the pair walked on down toward their designated derelict truck. The cell czar scrunched down in his seat and flipped on the toggle switch for the RC controller.

Let's do this!

He dialed his intended victim's cell number from his burner phone.

Once she answered, he played the helpful tow truck driver role, luring her to the driver's door of her disabled Honda.

Playing his part to perfection, he walked her through several useless exercises with ignition button presses and dash display screen selections.

Meanwhile, he guided the speeding truck straight at her with the RC controller.

As the vehicle bore down upon her, he could feel his pulse racing and his anticipation accelerating along with the flatbed.

The moment of actual impact was orgasmic; he felt years of pent-up anger and resentment releasing in a single flash.

He couldn't help but take a few seconds to admire his handiwork; his only regret was that the truck itself was obscuring his view of her crushed and lifeless body.

It's time to get moving.

The czar slowly drove the Buick up around the curve of Heartvine Circle and parked. His vehicle was now headed downhill on the wrong curb, two car lengths behind where the other flatbed sat on the opposite side.

He kept the engine idling and scrunched in his seat as he saw the next challenge participant approaching the second flatbed truck.

The czar readied himself, pulling up the camera app on his cell phone.

The second punk player released the emergency brake on this flatbed, and it began rolling forward.

Waiting until the man was out of sight of his rearview mirrors, the czar pulled out slowly behind the rolling flatbed.

He captured the truck's downhill journey with his phone's camera as it reached its final resting place.

The czar then calmly wheeled the Buick into a left turn onto Mission Hill Ridge, smiling at all the carnage and activity he saw choking off the street to the east.

In hindsight, for all their complexities and all their parts, he had very little invested in these two punks. He'd removed a chain from a construction company's yard gate to access the first truck and paid cash to purchase the second from a junkyard.

It had taken a few taps on a keyboard to pass instructions to ten or so of Aunt Tik's members. There was the sign maker, someone to place and remove the placards, two people to paint the vehicles, the remote steering mechanic, the tow truck drivers who would move the two flatbeds, and two men to release the truck emergency brakes. His only other skin in this game was his slow drive up and down Heartvine Circle. It was almost too easy.

Time for some breakfast to celebrate the successes of this excellent morning!

After all, how many other people on the planet could have pulled all this off with such perfect precision? Like maybe … *zero?* They should give out golden statuettes for this kind of thing.

He'd have a closet full of them.

THE WRITINGS OF
AVRIL MARIA SERENE

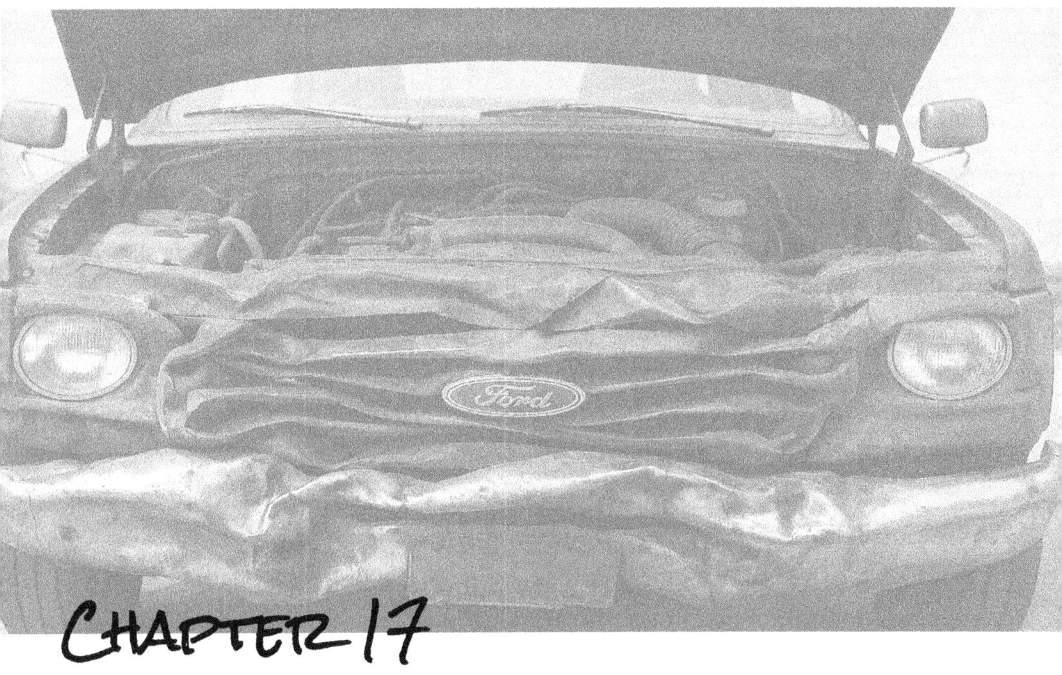

CHAPTER 17

etective Corrine Braxton and her team members wouldn't get a clear view of all that transpired until nearly ten a.m.

It was, by then, an hour and a half after Braxton declared the area a crime scene, with Homicide detectives taking control of the investigation. They'd had to wait until after the rush of emergency responders to both scenes, the arrival of senior officers, the eventual dispersal of much of the curious crowd, and the beginnings of the forensic investigation. And Braxton, whose fast-twitch muscles and considerable skills on the basketball court had won her tryouts in the WNBA, wasn't one to be patient.

But the detectives had found their stride and were actively interviewing witnesses and exchanging notes. As patrol officers Tilman and Legato approached, Braxton was scribbling on her old-school yellow legal pad and clipboard.

"Hey, Detective," Tilman said, "we wanted to let you know they're calling us back to the streets so we can protect citizens from each other. Anything more we can do for you?"

"Thanks, guys," Braxton replied. Her high ebony cheekbones, tight fade, and stern angular features contrasted with a normally pleasant disposition, and with the increased activity on her team, she was settling into her element.

"Nice job on the front lines, gentlemen, but we're good for now. If we need anything more, we'll be in touch."

"Anything you can share? Like, what the hell is all this about?" Tilman asked.

"No problem, a good excuse to organize my thoughts," Braxton replied. "In the first incident, we've got JoAnne Mabry as our murder victim. She was a longtime divorce lawyer and a brand-new partner at Lithgow and Marnes, a pricey downtown law firm.

"One of our Spanish-speaking officers talked to her very distraught housekeeper. She speaks English, but not well when she's that upset.

"She didn't witness the collision. She couldn't see the intersecting street because of those trees bracketing the front door — they block the headlights of cars coming down that hill from entering the residence's front windows at night. She did see the immediate aftermath, unfortunately. Once our interpreter got her calmed down enough to understand, she said Mabry's car wouldn't start, so Mabry called the dealer.

"Their doors weren't open yet, so they sent their after-hours contract tow service. The tow truck driver called, wanting her to try some things from the driver's seat while waiting for his arrival to get her back on the road faster. She was relaying that to the housekeeper across the yard, facing away from Heartvine Circle, when the first truck careened down the hill and T-boned the car.

"Killed her instantly; she never saw it coming.

"By the time the tow truck driver showed up, she was dead. We asked him why he had her standing out there, and he claimed he didn't know what we were talking about. He said he got the call from the dealership and didn't speak to the victim."

"So, what's the story with the second truck?" Legato asked.

"We don't know much more than what you saw. Another flatbed, nobody in it, flew down the other hill at high speed. That street runs parallel to the one Mabry's truck was on. You saw what happened once it hit Mission Hill Ridge; ended up stuck between the two houses across from that intersection. The good news is that no one got hurt in either residence."

"Thanks, Detective," Tilman said. "Not something you see every day."

"Stay safe out there, boys." Braxton turned back to her notes.

Tilman and Legato pulled away in their patrol unit as another uniformed officer approached, walking from across the street.

"Detective, we've got one more witness you might want to interview yourself, Susan Bell. She says she saw another car up that second hill — the driver was taking pictures with a cell phone. Over there."

He pointed to a heavyset, short-haired blonde woman. The witness was several feet removed from a group of onlookers across from the smashed Honda, now being prepared for hauling.

After thanking the officer, Braxton approached the woman.

"Hello, Ms. Bell, I'm Detective Braxton. I understand you saw a person with a cell phone camera taking pictures of one of these accidents?"

The eyewitness seemed both nervous and flattered by the attention.

"Yes, Detective. I live here, the corner lot, and I was getting my paper when I heard — well, *saw* — I mean, I heard it first, then I saw it…"

"Take your time, Ms. Bell. You can relax. I need to ask some routine questions, and then you can return to what you were doing. Did you know the deceased?"

"You can call me Susan." She smiled shyly. "No, not really. That poor woman. She seemed nice, but she'd only been in the house for about a year. I see her now and then in the mornings and wave, but she must be busy because she's not around much later in the day."

"You said you heard the first crash, probably pretty loud, right?"

Braxton raised her eyes from her notes as Susan nodded.

"And then you saw the damage it did? What happened next?"

"Yes, it made so much noise I thought I'd have a heart attack. There wasn't any warning, I mean, no engine revving or squealing tires. Just a huge bang, all of a sudden.

"Well, as soon as it happened, I ran to the sidewalk for a better look."

She was blurting everything out in a rush now.

"I couldn't see the lady or the driver either. At first, I didn't think anyone got hurt.

"My friend lives on the next street, west Heartvine Circle, so I looked over there, wondering whether she was up. If she'd seen the accident, I thought she might come here, and I wanted to talk to her.

"She didn't show up, but that second truck flew by right about then. And behind it, going slow, was this other car. The driver, a man, was taking pictures with his phone.

"Then, there was the second crash, and I looked down there to see what was happening. I forgot all about the guy taking pictures. But the officer asked if anyone had witnessed anything unusual, and that's when I remembered."

"That's a big help, and the department appreciates you coming forward, Susan. Do you remember anything about that vehicle that stands out?"

"It was gray or silver, like a four-door car, not an SUV or a pickup."

"A sedan, then? Was it big, like, say, a Cadillac? Or smaller?"

"In between. It looked like the smashed car, except old and gray."

"What did the vehicle do after you first saw it?"

"I took my eyes off him when I heard the crash. When I looked back, he was turning left onto Mission Hill Ridge. Then he was gone."

"That would be to the west, then?" Braxton asked, and her witness nodded. "Good, Susan. Can you tell me about the man taking pictures? Was he Caucasian, Black, Asian, or Hispanic?"

"He wore sunglasses and a blue hat, so there wasn't much showing. But I think he was just a regular white guy, medium height, no mustache or beard, maybe middle-aged. He had square shoulders, like in the military or worked out. He had on a dark blue T-shirt.

"The sun was in his face, and he had his window rolled down to take the pictures and everything, I guess. But he *was* kind of far away."

"That's great, Susan. Could you describe his face if we put you together with a sketch artist?"

"Yeah, sure. I mean, I can try. I've never done that before, but okay."

"Good, we've got an artist who's fabulous with people. He'll walk you through it. If you could wait a few minutes, one of the uniformed officers will get with you to set up a time and give you the information you'll need. Thanks, Susan. You've been a great help."

Braxton turned to go, dreading what was sure to become a long day, as Susan smiled and gave the departing detective a shy wave.

The area was a crime scene as well as a crash site, requiring both respect for the deceased and an awareness of the lingering spectators. That meant it took well past noon to separate the Honda and the flatbed and extract the body.

Preliminary findings from the Forensics team were informative but not as helpful as Braxton had hoped. It was about two p.m. when the coroner's wagon left with the victim's remains. Braxton pulled investigators together in the front yard of the Mabry residence for an informal meeting.

She turned to Sam Kelley, the lead Forensics investigator, a stocky, white-bearded, balding man with a prominent nose.

"Sam, what do you have from your Forensics team so far?"

"We've made progress but are limited in what we can do here. The prints we pulled — and there were dozens of them — were all partials and overlapped, mostly in and around the engine compartment of the first truck, none of which will be usable for matching, even for elimination. Nothing in the cab of either truck jumps out forensically.

"We'll take both flatbeds into the shop, go at them with different wavelengths of light, and do the hair, fiber, trace, and DNA analysis there. Hopefully, that'll lead us in a good direction."

He motioned toward a tall, rangy redhead in his mid-thirties wearing a lab coat.

"Rick's our forensic mechanic, and he found something interesting. Rick, want to tell us what you discovered?"

"Thanks, Sam. The collision mangled the truck's front end, but in the contest with the Honda, it came out the winner. That it's not as torn up helps us see what's going on, and a couple of obvious items popped up.

"One was that the engine wasn't running — rusted up solid, no oil in the pan. Gravity was its only source of power. That means not just that somebody had to set it in motion down that hill, but they also had to tow it here.

"The big news is the factory steering for that truck had been disconnected and replaced with a servo motor rigged for remote control, likely with a handheld controller, maybe from a model car or plane…."

"Wait, you're saying they drove that old truck from a distance?" Braxton interrupted.

"I'll know more when it's back in the shop, but yes. No other way that truck could have stayed between the curbs for the distance it would have taken to get up to a fairly high speed."

"Why the hell would somebody do all the work to remote-control a junker like that just to wreck it?" Braxton frowned.

"Never mind; that's rhetorical. Go ahead, Rick."

"I need a clean environment to disassemble it, as there's a good chance of DNA, prints, or fibers left from when they put it together. The great thing about grease is that it helps retain all those things. That's it for the first truck."

Braxton sighed.

"This wasn't going to be a straightforward case anyway, but it gets more complicated every minute. What do we know about the second flatbed?"

"The other truck had serious maintenance issues with its engine. It wasn't running, either, when it came down that hill. Having no keys in it would have locked the steering wheel — it could only go in the direction they turned the tires when they parked it.

"There's no sign of any mechanical modifications. Still, like the first truck, somebody had to have done something to get it suddenly moving from a parked situation. Again, there's the dependency on towing to get it where it started from.

"For these two vehicles to leave the launchpad this close together couldn't have been a mechanical failure or accident."

"Do me a favor when you return to your facilities?" Braxton asked.

"We're assuming these trucks are related, but it would be nice to have evidence. The cabs of both trucks have recently been hand-painted black. Can you check for chemical similarities between the paints used on each? If we end up without usable prints or DNA, that could give us a concrete link. Thanks."

"Will do. That brings us to the Honda. I pulled the last error code from the Honda's computer module, which indicated the module wasn't receiving primary power, even though there was no indication of battery failure. These things have lithium battery backups for the electronics. My gut tells me the vehicle was intentionally disabled.

"The liquids present weren't from the Honda — mainly rusty coolant from the truck radiator — so not a severed fuel line. Given the car's condition, finding where someone cut or disconnected a wire will take a while. But if it's there, we'll find it. We'll get our reports to everyone as soon as we have them."

"Good job under difficult circumstances, Rick, Sam," Braxton said.

"I suspect victimology is going to be vital to sorting out who wanted this woman dead. She was an expensive divorce attorney, hard-nosed enough to break through the glass ceiling to partner in a prestigious law firm. Influential people, maybe clients, might have hated her.

"Either way, it's time we wrapped up both scenes here. Go ahead and take down the crime scene tape and pull the cruisers back so people can access these intersections. See you over at the precinct. Do stay safe out there."

And watch out for runaway trucks. They seem to be a thing.

THE WRITINGS OF
AVRIL MARIA SERENE

CHAPTER 18

Walking into the bullpen after spending the early evening canvassing the residents of Heartvine Circle, Detective Jon Masters saw that the under-counter lights in Detective Braxton's cubicle were on. It was 9:15, not unreasonably late, so he took an indirect path to his desk to see if she was in. He tapped a forefinger on the metal frame of the cubicle wall to draw her attention without startling her.

"Corrine, what are you doing here at this hour? Sam told me you were at the runaway truck scene at eight this morning. Makes for a long day."

"Hi, Jon. You're here kind of late yourself. The brass tells us good things come to those who don't sleep, but I think they exaggerate." Braxton smiled.

"This truck thing is driving me nuts. If you're back here now, you must have done some after-hours canvassing of the neighbors. Did you come up with anything?"

"That's why I'm glad I caught you. Couldn't get anything specific on the doers themselves, but I did learn more about *what* they were doing. I came back to write it up. If you've got a few minutes, I can give you a rundown."

"Absolutely. I'd rather head home knowing a *little* more than I've learned so far."

She slapped the file she was reading on the desk, and Masters sensed she was exasperated.

"According to the residents, someone staged the entire scene on Heartvine Circle beforehand. Two days ago, whoever brought those trucks waited until everyone went to work, freeing up the parking spaces they wanted alongside the curbs. Once the trucks were in position, someone placed orange cones and official-looking signboards to clear out any vehicles in front of them down to Mission Ridge. A small white pickup gathered the signs and cones just before the flatbeds rolled down their hills."

"Anything to tell us who these people were? One person, several different people?" Braxton asked.

"No, sorry — poor lighting, nobody paying attention, doers wearing hats, sunglasses, and clothing that didn't stand out. Not the kinds of activities that would register with anyone."

Braxton sat forward, head tilted, her lips pursed. "That tells us somebody's put a lot more time and effort into this than I thought, even beyond the remote-control steering, which is quite a bit of work on its own. And it tells us that whoever did this is no idiot.

"Good job sticking with it, Jon. You've put any questions to rest about whether these two runaway trucks are related or if their presence was coincidental.

"This set of events was a highly coordinated thing — either a lot of people involved or one guy scrambling around, busting his ass. The quality of the trucks made me think we were dealing with low-rent amateurs. Instead, someone put considerable time, resources, and thought into this. Very organized. I'm not sure what we can do with that. But at least we're headed in a better direction."

Braxton paused in reflection.

"Seems a crazy way to go about it when the only thing anyone gains out of all this is the death of that attorney."

The forensic technician finished his reports around 10:15 a.m. and called Det. Braxton to advise her of their progress.

"Good morning, Detective; this is Rick Denman, the Forensics garage engineer. We met yesterday afternoon at the Mabry homicide scene."

"Of course, Rick. What do you have for me?"

"I just finished my report on the first flatbed truck, the one we're treating as the murder weapon. Sam said you were putting in some long hours on this case, and I thought I'd call to summarize what I discovered."

"I hope your morning was productive. What have you learned?"

"They fitted that truck with line-of-sight remote-controlled steering. That means someone was within a one-mile radius of the flatbed, steering the vehicle as it rolled down the hill into the victim's Accord. That places our subject on or near the scene during the collision.

"For profiling purposes, you'll want to know that our doer, possibly a team, has impressive technical capabilities. The steering modifications show automotive expertise. The RC controller indicates electronics knowledge. The step-down circuitry for controlling amperage and voltage was custom work. Knowing how and where to access the Honda to keep it from running shows particular skill."

"Interesting." Braxton paused. "I thought they meant all this indirection to keep the killer out of the picture. But what you're telling me says they had to be there to pull the trigger, in effect. So, they had a hidden RC controller of some kind. None of the witness reports describe visible electronic devices. I assume they'd have to keep it pointed at the truck."

"That's true for most RC transmitters."

"Hmmm. So far, we only have one guy reported in a vehicle; the man caught filming the second crash left the scene in a gray sedan. The radio control unit might've been inside that car, and no one would've seen it. Anything else for me?"

"Yes, three things. The Accord itself had been intentionally disabled before the incident, which explains why a quality vehicle in good condition wouldn't start. Several wires to the ignition module were severed, probably with a pair of wire cutters. We preserved the ends of the wires on either side of the cut for tool mark comparison. If you find the wire cutter, we can match it."

"Good, more proof of intent for the homicide case. And, hopefully, we'll find what we need to make that match. You mentioned 'three things'?"

"Sam asked me to pass along some information related to those trucks. As to the ownership of the two attack vehicles, the first flatbed, the F-350, had been down for repairs. We confirmed the engine was not in running condition when a construction company reported it stolen from their gated yard last month. Easy target, no security around for a broken-down old truck on the Sunday it disappeared. The thief cut the gate chain with bolt cutters, hooked it up, and took off.

"They would've had to tow the truck from the construction company to wherever they modified it for driverless steering. The flatbed needed towing again to the top of that hill on Heartvine Circle.

"The second vehicle was sold for parts, cash, three months ago. DMV shows its title as junked. The recycling yard that bought it turned around and resold it as-is. However, the copy of the receipt had only the word 'CASH' for the name — no address or other identifying information. The junkyard employees couldn't recall anything remarkable about the purchaser. That's about it for now."

"I'm trying to understand why someone would steal a broken-down old truck or buy a junker that didn't run for this," Braxton mused. "Why not just steal newer trucks that they could drive?"

"Javon and I talked about that because, at first, it didn't make sense to us, either. But we think they chose older, low-value, high-mass vehicles for good reasons. Possibly because no one guards a broken-down truck particularly well or gets too upset when one turns up missing. Those flatbeds don't have onboard alarms or electronics like computers and key fobs to mess with. Dispatchers and patrol units wouldn't put the trucks on their be-on-the-lookout advisories if the stolen vehicles didn't run.

"Driving stolen trucks around would have required current plates, registrations, smog inspections, and insurance — too much risk of being pulled over. What they did makes sense if all you want is crushing weight rolling downhill at low risk and cost. And here's the kicker: with no engine, there's very little noise. Nothing to warn the intended victim if she's not looking in that direction."

Braxton twirled her pen as she considered Denman's passdown. "Thanks for the updates, Rick. That'll help us with the bigger picture. If you can e-mail me a copy of your report and ask Sam to send me his, that'd be great. Good job — I hope the rest of your day is as fruitful."

After Braxton got off the phone with Denman, she added the new information to the case elements before her, writing them out as a list. When she finished, it was longer than she expected:

- Steal truck A using a tow truck;
- Purchase truck B;
- Tow truck A to a hidden work location;
- Modify truck A's steering for remote control;
- Tow truck A to the crime scene;
- Tow truck B to its launch point one street over;
- Create and place signs to clear room for both trucks to roll;
- Study the victim's habits to know exactly where she'd be and what she'd do that morning;
- Clip the wires on the Accord so it wouldn't start between the time it was parked the evening before and 7:00 a.m. the following day;
- Remove the street repair signage;
- Induce the victim to put herself into the proper position;
- Release the emergency brake on truck A;
- Steer truck A via remote control to the crash point;
- Release the emergency brake on truck B; and
- Follow and record truck B as it rolls down the hill.

Her list raised another question: Could they have done it all without being seen by anyone except *maybe* when they left the scene? She supposed it was technically possible, but they'd have to be the fastest, most skilled, and luckiest person she'd *never* met. Her instincts told her no.

Okay, so not just one person.

How and why, then, did multiple people, all these resources, and all this planning go into the murder of a woman they could have just shot dead in a drive-by? That implied somebody was going to an *awful* lot of trouble to confuse any ties between themselves and this homicide. Yet they couldn't keep themselves away from monitoring the results. And obviously, they truly hated this woman.

Braxton had a detective running the victimology. That meant walking through all the attorney's cases — assessing the lawyer's opponents, disgruntled clients, relationships with other attorneys, and any connections to organized crime. However, the attorney had thousands of these contacts over her two decades of work, almost always in the context of conflict. Investigators would prioritize these by recency and severity. Still, the latter was subjective — what a police officer might consider benign could be a trigger to a psychopath.

Braxton turned her thoughts from the victim to the doer. The range of skills displayed — mechanical understanding, crawling under a vehicle to clip wires, vehicle theft, remote-control electronics knowledge, driving a tow truck — suggested one or more fit males. The witness *did* see a man photographing the second truck collision. Still, that could have been pure coincidence; perhaps a gawker who was quick to his cell phone camera app while driving to work. If not, why record the truck that *didn't* kill anyone?

Two male passersby were in the neighborhood, but being on a sidewalk wasn't probable cause. And nothing ruled out a woman. Was the killer intelligent and organized? Obviously. Obsessive-compulsive? Possibly. Or maybe they got off on the nuances of reasonable doubt and plausible deniability, perhaps themselves practitioners of the legal arts? The degree of complexity and obfuscation alone *would* make this difficult to explain to a jury without generating reasonable doubt.

She didn't feel any closer to knowing the who, or the why, or quite a bit of the how, even though she knew most of the details as to the method by which they committed the murder itself. It had been a good day thus far, but much more work was needed.

First things first — *some* person or group was motivated in the extreme to kill this woman, and graphically. Something very intense, at least from the murderers' perspective, connected the victim and her killer or killers. And the payback was something the doers had planned very carefully over a long time, suggesting that whatever set them off may have occurred a while ago.

The answer was *somewhere* in that victimology. Braxton needed her team to concentrate on finding one or more persons with whom Mabry had significant negative interactions, likely in her not-so-recent past. They'd have access to substantial resources and a comprehensive understanding of the physical world or links to others who did. Tomorrow, she'd add another detective to examine Mabry's cases going further back in time. The investigator would look for significant losses or outcomes that led to perceived injuries downstream.

What could this woman have possibly done to justify so much planning, effort, and sheer determination toward exacting revenge?

THE WRITINGS OF
AVRIL MARIA SERENE

CHAPTER 19

Two days after Debra Ann told him of her three-way phone conversation with Marci and Eve, Paul Castro spotted Lt. Harbin at his desk. Paul had promised Debra Ann he'd update Louis with what she'd learned about Steve Nielsen and Aunt Tik's. The lieutenant would want to know Steve's motivations for driving that loaded AR-15 through the city. Paul headed to Louis's office to share the results of Debra Ann's jailhouse visit with Steve.

"Hey, boss, got a minute?" Paul leaned in through the door, still in his white lab coat after his rounds inspecting the forensic techs' work.

Louis looked up and smiled. "Come on in. I've got a meeting in twenty minutes, but I'm all yours until then."

"Debra Ann talked to Tracy's son, Steve, and says she agrees with your initial assessment. This kid got caught up in something, and he had no intentions or idea that it could go as far as it did."

Louis nodded. "I'd never seen him under stress, so I wasn't sure."

"I talked to Debra Ann again last night," Paul explained. "She believes Steve's just a puppet in whatever's going on here. He's sharp, though. He won't say the words out loud, but you can tell he wants to do the right thing if we show him a path forward. And he's savvy enough about technology to give us a pretty good feel for that car's setup. Do we know yet if the rounds in the AR-15 were live or blanks?"

"Steve's charging documents say that not only were they live, but a round was chambered."

"So, whoever's pulling the strings has bad intentions." Paul raised an eyebrow.

"Debra Ann tells me that whoever rigged that gun knew what they were doing. Given that it had live rounds and that they meant to park it across from a likely and high-visibility victim, it was for one purpose only. I know we need to keep our distance from the feds on this, but is there any way we can tune into what they were able to lift from that gun? It'd be nice to know where they stand in working this."

"I'm way ahead of you there," Louis answered. "I have a friend in the FBI, an agent who trained at Quantico with one of the profilers working this case, and he's keeping her in the loop. He told her the AR-15 itself is from a gun show sale out of Wyoming, so no paperwork links it to anyone."

"Unfortunate, but no surprise. I was half expecting it to be a ghost gun. Does the assault rifle itself tell the agents anything?"

"There were no prints on the weapon proper, but they lifted partials from the cartridges and circuit board. They found palm prints on the battery and the inside of the door panel. Nothing that brings up a match yet. Someone stole the car from a Stop 'N Go three weeks ago. All kinds of prints and DNA in and on the car itself. The FBI's forensics team says it'll take a week to do all the elimination printing from past owners and known passengers."

"Was there anything in Steve's instructions they could use?"

"The only evidence on the note was Steve's fingerprints and DNA, which makes sense since he generated it from his phone. Speaking of which, they're now decrypting the messages and files on that cell. They expect to have those by the end of the week.

"Hopefully, what they find will confirm that he's just the delivery driver and had no idea about anything else. He'll still have to answer for knowing the AR-15 was in the car and not reporting it. But that's not indicative of a bad kid, just one who made a mistake in judgment. He tried to handle what I think everyone can see as some *unusual* circumstances. Way out of his league."

"What Debra Ann saw, or rather, didn't see, affirms that — no sign of fundamental dishonesty or evil intent, at least around this incident.

"I came back to the squad room to check with Eve. She's helping us look into Aunt Tik's website to see what we're up against. Steve gave us access to his premium account — not sure how long we'll have it before he's booted out, but for now, we've got something we can work with."

"Oh, I meant to tell you," Louis said, "Mondo's been trying to reach you. I think he's got something. Give him a shout-out. Gotta prepare for my meeting — I'll catch you on the flip side."

Paul had been thinking about grabbing a bite to eat, but he was more curious about what Mondo had to say than hungry.

Mondo was unexpectedly apologetic when Paul called after returning to his desk. "Paul, I meant to look into your Aunt Tik's social media project. Louis gave me a heads-up that you could use some help. But the brass wanted Vice to put on a big, showy fentanyl and opioid sweep of all the usual suspects. Election season is coming, and I was already down staff with the flu. But I do have a resource who might help your situation. Do you remember Craig Evert?"

"The parole officer?"

"That's the guy," Mondo answered. "I just chatted with him and mentioned the Aunt Tik's thing. He said, 'Yeah, I have a new parolee, busted as a low-level dealer, college guy. He mentioned an invitation to a game with a name like that.'

"Evert set up a conversation, and I talked to this kid. Andy Pardone's a pleasant enough guy, outgoing, and likes to shoot the breeze. He's no dummy. He seems motivated to start his parole off on the right foot and professes to know quite a bit about Aunt Tik's. You might find him worth talking to. I just e-mailed you his contact info. He'll be waiting for your call."

"Thanks, Mondo," Paul said. "I planned to do some background research today, so this is excellent timing.

"Let's hope he can teach us something that'll break this thing wide open."

THE WRITINGS OF
AVRIL MARIA SERENE

CHAPTER 20

I called the number Mondo gave Paul. When Andy Pardone answered, I identified myself and told him I'd gotten his name and number through his PO.

"Mr. Evert says you can help us understand something we stumbled across in an investigation, an organization named 'Aunt Tik's.' I'm calling to see if you know anything about it and if you have time to get together this afternoon."

"Yes," Andy replied, "I was expecting your call. But I thought you'd be a cop, not a reporter."

"My apologies — reaching out to you through officers' contacts may have given the wrong impression. The police aren't formally investigating Aunt Tik's. They're looking into a case where the subjects they questioned mentioned Aunt Tik's website, something law enforcement and the media hadn't seen before. I'm helping everyone get up to speed by exploring the group's goals, what it does to achieve them, and how things work.

"We know Aunt Tik's is pretty secretive, and my first question is how Mr. Evert learned you're a member."

"I didn't want to screw up my probation when it first started," Andy explained, "and I worried they'd be stricter than what they are. So, I told my parole officer that I was a member of Aunt Tik's to make sure they weren't considered off-limits. He says, 'Why should I care how you waste your time? Just show up for your piss tests and your job — and don't break the law.' So, yeah, I've played around with it, and I know some things."

"Got it. I want to record something we could use as an introduction for officers who run into Aunt Tik's in their investigations. When would you have time to sit for an interview?"

"I have a study period at two-thirty — is that okay?"

"That will work. Where can we meet?"

"There's a Cups Outdoor Café in the UCSD Jacobs School of Engineering courtyard. It's quiet that time of day."

That location was a good fit for the other things I needed to do. I described myself and Paul so that Andy would recognize us.

After hanging up, I called Paul to let him know I'd just booked his time in the afternoon without checking with him first. Fortunately, he answered and didn't give me too much grief — yes, he could make himself available for the interview. If we ran across any helpful information, Paul would be the one to pass it along to others in the squad room.

Paul rode with me out to the coffeehouse. Andy was right — there were just a few customers. He waved as we approached. With his strapping athletic physique, surfer-bleached dark-blond hair, and ready smile, he made me think of late-night TV fitness infomercials.

We introduced ourselves, explaining that although Paul was a Forensics supervisor for the state, he wasn't here in his official capacity. We ordered coffee and juice from the bar, seating ourselves at a small high-top in the back corner. I pulled my digital voice recorder out of my purse, placed it on the table, and turned it on.

I started with some ground rules.

"We're not here as law enforcement, and you're not required to tell us anything. But whatever you *do* tell us or that we say to you must be kept confidential. If you break that confidence — say by going to Aunt Tik's and revealing what we discuss here — the authorities could construe that act as obstruction of justice. You'd have violated your parole, and you could be separately prosecuted, among other things. I'll record this conversation so there'll be no question about what was said. Do you understand and agree to that?"

"If I cooperate with you, you'll tell Mr. Evert that I did the stand-up thing here — that's the deal, right?"

"Yes, we'll see you get credit for helping us," Paul confirmed. "But we can't make any promises beyond that."

"Okay, I get it, and I agree. Have you been on Aunt Tik's website?" Andy seemed anxious to get started.

"Yes, we've signed up for premium accounts," I replied, "so we have full access. We've gone through the member's manual and understand at a high level how the process works."

"Good, then you're familiar with the website's purpose and what it offers."

"To a point. One thing that concerns us is the secrecy around everything. I'm sure that was the first website manual I ever downloaded that self-destructed after a few days. Stunt or not, that's a unique commitment to protecting what should be common knowledge about what people are doing. If nothing else, it sends a message."

"Aunt Tik's is super careful," Andy explained. "Other than the public videos, everything is protected, encrypted, and on a need-to-know basis. One of Aunt Tik's attractions for new members is that it protects them from getting into trouble."

That seems like an odd priority for a game.

"What trouble could they get into?"

"Like being sued if they perform a part in a punk and things go bad. The secrecy helps with that, and it keeps the target of the punk from finding out and getting even before the punk's finished."

"The anonymity of the members is a real issue for us," Paul jumped in. "Our role requires that we determine the specific individuals involved in certain behaviors — not all of them by any means, but such that we can drill down into anything that causes harm."

I picked up where Paul left off. "The bottom line is that we need to understand Aunt Tik's enough to know the weaknesses in their system that someone could exploit to do bad things. And by 'bad,' I mean illegal, outside the publicly stated purpose and intent of the Aunt Tik's organization."

"What kinds of things?" Andy was puzzled.

"It's a fair question," I admitted, "but unfortunately, we can't share that with you right now.

"We're obligated to do no harm if we can avoid it, which also means to Aunt Tik's. We don't want to spread news about what people are getting away with because human nature says others will then try it. And I'm sure you understand that any public suggestion of illegal, or even suspect, activity could cause problems for a business or its patrons, especially if they prove untrue."

"The big question is, should we ever need to participate in the website's activities as part of an investigation," Paul added, "we'd want to understand our own risk of exposure."

"You mean like undercover?"

"I was thinking about asking questions discreetly, but I suppose there's always a possibility of covert engagement."

"Either way, we wouldn't want to be thrashing around like bulls in a china shop," I explained, "showing ourselves as newbies with questionable agendas."

"Yeah, Aunt Tik's is paranoid about things like that." Andy nodded his understanding. "They have ways to check you out."

Now we're getting somewhere.

"We'd like to learn about those," I said.

Andy took command of the conversation.

"Okay, probably the best way to go from here is for you to tell me what you already know. I can fill in the missing pieces."

"That should work," I agreed. "We know the website's purpose is to create and perform tricks and pranks played mostly on nonmembers and that members can elect to play minor roles in the performances. The website draws revenues from membership fees and ads displayed to the general public, who mostly watch punk result videos.

"We don't know a lot of details. I brought my laptop. If you can walk us through the website, that would be helpful."

Andy passed me a slip of notepaper.

"Here's the restaurant's Internet connection name, login, and password."

"Okay, we've got WiFi now, and my browser's pointed to the website."

"May I?" Andy asked.

When I nodded, he turned the laptop to access the keyboard.

"I've logged in using my account. When you first see the website's front page, it seems like you can't do anything other than look at some public videos. You get the marketing department's promos for Aunt Tik's and a count of the members logged in. I take it you've checked out some punk results videos?"

"We've viewed a few of the recent postings, so we have some idea what Aunt Tik's does," Paul offered.

"Then you already know this icon takes you to the results videos webpage. The ones marked 'private' are just for the challenge participants on that punk. But there's a cheat where you can see those, too. The ones marked 'premium members-only' are visible just to paid members. Anyone, including free members and the public, can view the rest."

"There's a cheat to see the private punk results videos?" I asked.

"Yes, this icon gets you to their member messaging center, where you can hook into all kinds of stuff — some crazy shit, oops, sorry, stuff. You can see almost all the punk results, even the private ones, because members include links to their latest punks when they post their 'Hey, look what I did!' messages. Sometimes, there are gaps where a member didn't push out a link to their punk result."

"So, the messages might reveal which members did which challenges for a punk?" Paul asked.

"If you right-click on the icon for the video, you can see that information for the members who want you to know. But yeah, if a member didn't publish their participation on the video, they might say something about it in a message."

I turned the laptop back to face me and began scanning the messages in the forum.

"Scrolling through these, I see what you mean — there's a lot of information here. 'Dismembering' is popular. The user manual definitions say that's not as bad as it sounds."

"Aunt Tik's has some unique terms, and that one means losing your membership. It's still a bad thing in actual practice. For instance, they let out all the information in your membership account that used to be secret."

"I see here that members play their practical jokes on nonmembers. As opposed to playing them on other members of the club?" I asked rhetorically. "That sounds like 'unsuspecting targets who can't fight back,' and that doesn't seem kosher. In the real world, you usually prank people who are part of your little circle."

"You're right," Andy admitted, "big difference. I didn't think about that. They do prank members they are kicking out — that dismemberment thing — but otherwise, no."

"There's a lot of emphasis on the fact that the member identities are protected. Some of these messages take advantage of that, even to the point of abuse…" I started to say, but Andy cut me off.

"Some say that the power and popularity of the Internet comes from the anonymity — it lets people say things to and about others that they couldn't if everyone knew their identities. Aunt Tik's brings that idea to playing jokes on people in the real world, and the 'not knowing who did what' part keeps things anonymous."

"But anonymity plus unsuspecting victims with no recourse makes a recipe for abuse," Paul argued. "No one to hold accountable if they go too far."

Andy agreed. "A lot of wink-wink stuff in the manual isn't enforced. The pranks are portrayed as merely for fun, based on no harm, no foul. But that's not necessarily how it ends up. Here, check this out."

Paul and I read a message Andy highlighted where members swapped wheels and tires from a monster truck and a Mini Cooper, rendering both inoperable.

"So, I guess the prohibition against illegal acts doesn't apply to removing car parts. The messages show some punks do get a little harsh.

Aunt Tik's uses it as a selling point — fun, few limits, and safe, at least for the performers. Splitting up the punk keeps any one person from getting sued by a pissed-off target."

"That they have to worry about getting sued says something in and of itself," I observed. "How do they keep nonmembers from getting hurt or injured if the targets cannot see it coming?"

"They say Aunt Tik's structure protects the public," Andy answered, "because the management decides who can do what. The manual claims they filter members and what members can do."

"The manual also states that a premium member has to vouch for candidate members." Paul turned to me.

"That might be a problem — if we apply under our real names and they know we're law enforcement, we may not get in. Or if we did, we'd be pariahs. If we use an alias, members won't vouch for us because they can't recognize who we are.

"You're a civilian and not involved in any of the crimes we'd be investigating — I'd prefer we not use your premium account to vouch for our officers. If something went wrong and they came after you, you're semi-famous, nowhere to hide…."

I turned back to Andy.

"Assuming we get Mr. Evert to sign off on you helping out, would you be willing to endorse an officer operating undercover?"

"Sure, no problem, as long as it doesn't hurt my parole," Andy replied.

"No promises," I cautioned, "but maybe we can help you, some quid pro quo. Someone vouched for you as a paid member, meaning you can validate new applicants. Still, and no offense intended, if you're on parole and got accepted, that doesn't say much about their filters."

"None taken." Andy smiled. "And I do see your point."

"Can you move around between cells once you're a member — say, if you got transferred on your job?" Paul asked. He turned to me. "I'm wondering if, once Aunt Tik's has accepted one of our applications, we could loan that resource out to other jurisdictions."

I nodded. "That'd be great if Aunt Tik's permits it."

"I honestly don't know," Andy answered. "I don't think membership is all that sophisticated. Here, see this question mark icon? You could post a message on the forum. They're always improving the website. Maybe they'll add a feature for moving between cells if they don't already have it."

He grinned.

"But you probably shouldn't tell them why you want it."

CHAPTER 21

I smiled, waving off the barista/waitress making her rounds through the coffee shop's occupied tables.

"I've got a general idea of how all this works. But the punk master role is something we need to understand fully. Can you walk us through a punk from when it's submitted to the punk result?"

"Sure, no problem," Andy said.

"So, where do these punks come from in the first place?"

"An idea for punking somebody has to come from a paid member. It could be one who's accumulated enough points to submit a punk or from a cell captain or czar.

"It must follow certain rules. For example, it's gotta be constructed as a set of smaller challenges so that different members can perform them. They have to provide a general time frame for performing the punk. The rules are in the manual, and the website does some checks and posts instructions to follow when the punk is submitted."

"I assume somebody approves these things once a member suggests them?" Paul asked.

"The cell czar — the local Aunt Tik's boss — has final approval. He'll assign it to a punk master, usually a cell captain, but sometimes himself. The punk master runs the punk."

"And he does that, how…?" I asked.

"If the creator of the punk didn't submit a target's name, the punk master will stage an election to select one. Once that's settled, the punk master handles the bidding by members to perform the challenges that make up the punk. As the challenges are assigned, the punk master schedules each performance. After they've finished the punk, the punk master's responsible for producing a video of the punk results or getting someone else to do it."

"Can you give us an example of how a punk might go?" Paul asked.

"Sure — let's say there are three parts to the punk. Challenge number one is to saw a tree's main branch halfway through and then fill the cut with brown caulk so it's not visible. Challenge number two is to hang two chains on that branch and attach a swing set seat to the ends of the chains. Challenge three is to get an overweight person, maybe somebody famous, to sit in the swing."

"How do members learn about the challenges?" I asked.

"The challenges for this and all the other punks are mixed up and then posted on the website, categorized by the skills or talents needed to perform them. None of the bidders knows what challenges belong with which punks or in what order the challenges go."

"Got it," Paul said. "Now what?"

"Let's say I like cutting things, so I bid on challenge number one for ten thousand points and list the periods I'm available within the challenge's time frame. If I win the bid, I'll get the ten thousand points added to my account when the punk's complete and successful. Paul, you also like cutting things, so you bid twelve thousand points and list your time availability."

"How do they decide who wins the bid?" I asked.

"Simple. If Paul and I are both available at the precise time the punk master sets for that challenge to begin, I get assigned the task because my bid was lower. All other things being equal, the lowest bid always wins. The manual calls that a 'reverse auction.' The bids are secret; nobody knows who bid what except the punk master. The punk master sends you an encrypted notice when you win the right to do a challenge. Paul, you won't get an acceptance notice for the first challenge, but you can still bid on challenge number two. So, let's say you did that and win it, and Debra Ann bids and wins challenge number three."

"A member can bid on several challenges within a punk?" Paul asked.

"Yes, but the most they'll get assigned is one challenge for each punk to give other members a chance to participate."

"What happens when the members finish bidding on all the challenges for a certain punk?" I asked.

"Then the punk master sets the order and exact timing for performing that punk. He sends out encrypted notifications to successful bidders for each challenge. That's something of an art form. In my example, you'd want to perform challenge number one first. If you do it second, the sawing player would see a swing set seat already there and might have misgivings."

This resonated with me.

"Say that the person doing the next challenge became aware of something like that. Can they back out of doing their challenge?" Turning to Paul, I added, "I'm thinking of Steve's situation."

"I don't think so," Andy replied. "It'd make people angry. The messages say you'd get dismembered. The reason is, some of these punks might have two dozen challenges, so when one person backs out, it screws everybody who bid on the punk."

"That seems a little unfair if there's an obvious issue like that," Paul remarked.

"The punk master would try to alleviate that kind of thing," Andy explained. "He'd have to be sure and add an instruction to challenge player number one to clean up their mess so that whoever does challenge number two doesn't see the sawdust and won't suspect a cut. We don't want that number-two challenge player worried he's doing a bad thing hanging a seat from a branch that's sawn halfway through. And you certainly wouldn't want challenge player number three, or the target, seeing or worrying about the cut.

"So, it's a little more complicated being a punk master than you'd think."

I couldn't argue *that*.

"You said the punk master is responsible for producing a video of the punk results?"

"Yes, the video's the whole point — no sense doing a punk nobody sees. Or one that's boring. In this example, the branch breaking when somebody sat in the swing might not be all that interesting."

"But what can you do about that once the punk's finished?" Paul asked.

"Well, for this one, the punk master would be there for the challenges and film all the steps. In editing, they'd speed up the film that showed the prep, in other words, challenges numbers one and two, so it plays at, say, three times normal speed. Then, they might show the man sitting in the swing and the tree branch breaking at regular speed or even in slow motion, maybe adding music. Then stitch it together and post the video on the punk results page."

"So, the punk master gets to say how the punk plays out, at least as far as what the members see in the results video?"

Paul realized my question was about what controls existed to ensure the published punk results matched the rendered performances, and he nodded.

"Like a director, right?" Paul added, bringing to my mind the material left on the cutting room floor.

"Yes." Andy's face had a quizzical expression — he hadn't understood where I was going. "Ultimately, that's the punk master's job — he decides what people see."

Altering the results had raised another possibility in my mind.

"Let me pose a hypothetical. Suppose the cell czar approves a punk submission and assigns it to a punk master. Could the punk master somehow modify one or more of the challenges?"

"Yes, I suppose. I imagine there'd be times they'd have to if there was a mistake in the submission. Or things change, like if there was a big rain on a day when they scheduled an outdoor part of the challenge."

"So, who else would know if there was a change from the original punk?" I asked.

Andy pondered for a moment.

"Well, the person who did the next challenge might know if the change messed up their part."

"What would that next challenge performer do about it?"

"I imagine they'd try their best to do whatever they were supposed to because they'd want to get their points."

"And if they couldn't, or didn't want to?" I pushed ahead.

Andy furrowed his brow in concentration, and he was biting on one side of his lower lip.

"I guess they'd have to tell somebody, and I suppose the punk would have to be stopped or done over."

"But earlier, didn't you say they'd get in trouble for bailing out of their challenge? Possibly even 'dismembered?'" Paul asked.

The situation Steve faced, I thought.

Andy seemed frustrated that he didn't have a ready answer.

"Well, sure. I mean, that's how Aunt Tik's set it up. I guess the member doing the challenge could tell it to the punk master. But it wouldn't make the punk master very happy, and the other challenge performers who didn't get their points would be pissed. When you bid on the challenge, though, you're supposed to make sure you can do the job, even if things change a little."

Interesting that a member far more experienced than Steve was also struggling for an answer to that question.

"What if they had changed a lot?" Paul asked.

Andy was now obviously disappointed that he didn't have all the answers we wanted.

"I-I-I don't know. I've never really encountered anything like that or heard anyone talk about it on the message forum."

"That's okay, Andy. I was just curious," Paul said graciously.

I wanted to change topics a little.

"Several places in the manual mention the autonomy of the local cell. I'm sure the national Aunt Tik's has to watch out for things that hurt their brand.

"I can't believe there haven't been targets who wanted to sue them out of existence. There must have been situations where cell members have crossed the line legally, maybe broken laws that left the national organization feeling some heat. Have you seen any messages or heard rumors regarding legal issues where the national Aunt Tik's office had to get involved?"

"I haven't, no," Andy answered.

I looked at Paul. I wasn't quite sure how to get at who was legally responsible when things went wrong, and I doubted Andy would know.

"I'll make a note to check with the DA to see who is served with the warrants if we have to go that route," Paul offered, "the local cell or the national office."

"In the meantime," I said, "I'll call the national Aunt Tik's to find out what, if any, legal issues they've addressed at the national level and who owns, or at least controls, their servers.

"Sorry to have interrupted you, Andy. You're doing great. I think we understand the general idea a little better. I wanted to ask how someone could game Aunt Tik's rules. I'm curious whether any shortcuts exist where new members can get promoted to cell captain. That seems like a good place to be if we want to look into what transpires within the organization."

"No. From what I know, it takes a while to become a cell captain because you'd have to do several challenges to get the points you need. Cell captains are assigned based on whoever has earned the most points."

"Can a cell captain ask to be appointed punk master over a specific punk?" Paul asked.

"The cell captains normally take turns being punk masters as new punks are submitted. But it's up to the cell czar. The czar can appoint himself the punk master if he wants, so I suppose he could assign any cell captain he liked if they asked."

"Obvious question: I'm looking for another shortcut here, but do you know who the current cell czar is?" I asked.

"Not in real life, no. Aunt Tik's handles can't be real names, and they don't give up personal things in the messages.

"Whoever it is seems more private than the last guy. The cell czar before this one founded the San Diego cell and was the first cell captain and punk master; he built everything up from nothing. I don't know his real name, though.

"He just disappeared. There were a lot of rumors in the messages. The big one was that the government was after him, and he left the country, like John McAfee. But nobody *really* knows."

"How long has it been since the last time anyone heard from him?" I asked.

"Oh, it's been months."

"Hmmm, *that's* interesting."

I glanced at my watch, and my eyes met Paul's before I turned to Andy. I knew Paul had a meeting with the DA on another case this afternoon, and I was late for a conference with Doug Stein.

"I apologize that the time seems to have flown by. We need to go for now. Paul and I will study the Aunt Tik's manual and explore the website. Andy, we can't thank you enough. You've given us a lot of what we needed. Once we finish our homework, we may want to hit you up for another training session. Would you be okay with that?"

"Absolutely. Just let me know when and where. Oh, yeah, I almost forgot. I was on a dating site and ran across a woman who was a premium member of Aunt Tik's for quite a while. She got dismembered for screwing up a punk. Her real name is Vicky Carlson. She might be a good source for more information about the group and the game. Here, let me write it out for you."

Andy tore a piece of notepaper from a pad in his hip pocket, wrote Carlson's information in neat block lettering, and handed it to me.

"I told her I'd be talking to you today. She'll be expecting your call."

<hr>

Driving to my office to meet Doug, I dialed the number Andy gave me for Carlson. Not getting an answer, I left my name, number, and a message on her voicemail. My Caller ID pushes out the name of our news-gathering service, so I've learned to explain why I'm calling to anyone who doesn't already know me.

I can't imagine why, but some people get nervous about talking to investigative reporters.

Must be that *60 Minutes* thing.

Chapter 22

My work conference with Doug Stein went quickly, a welcome rarity. I wanted to put the spare time I'd gained to good use.

First, I was curious to see where the existing Aunt Tik's affiliates were located, or more precisely, were not. I was surprised that while Los Angeles, San Diego, and San José had Aunt Tik's franchises, California's fourth-largest city did not. Armed with that information, I called the national Aunt Tik's main office under the pretext that I wanted to start a cell in San Francisco.

The Aunt Tik's marketer introduced herself as Vanessa. After listening to her sales pitch, I launched into my spiel, "I've been a member of the San Diego cell for a year — I'm familiar with the operations. I have questions about the management side of things. For example, how much autonomy does the local chapter have? Does the national organization get involved in the day-to-day activities of the franchise?"

"Of course," Vanessa replied. "We have rules you and your members must accept before launching a franchise. Those rules override anything else. So long as you comply with them, we don't usually get involved in the franchisee's operations. In our offices here, we mostly certify the creation of new franchises. We collect membership dues and distribute them back to the franchised cells. And, of course, we provide website templates, logos, other advertising materials, and support."

"Have you ever had to directly intercede with a franchise, say, one that broke the rules or engaged in some other behavior, maybe involving litigation or criminal accusations?"

"Oh, no, nothing like that. As you can imagine from the kinds of activities our members engage in — and as mentioned in our manual and other materials — we have hiccups. There've been unavoidable occasions where a disagreement between a member and the subject of a punk arose. The franchisee or the members involved are responsible for resolving those. We've never had to participate in any of those disputes."

"That's good to know. So, there's never been a situation where a franchisee has come to you and asked for legal advice or help?"

"Not that I know of." Her voice disclosed some unease. "I hope you're not imagining a franchise that would push those boundaries...?"

"Not at all — my attorney expressed concern about potential liability for the practical jokes members play on people."

"Oh, I know it might seem like a problem, but it doesn't come up often. We've engineered our structure to protect members and franchisees from having to take personal responsibility for things they can't control. Our formula's been successfully doing that for almost ten years now. We've modeled ourselves after the NFL — a co-op that serves our member organizations. Just think of 'practical jokes' instead of 'football.' The teams, or in our case, 'cells,' are semi-autonomous."

I snuck in a question for Paul about data access for law enforcement.

"I checked out server storage space and software to house all the data, which gets expensive. Does the national organization help with that equipment? Or is it solely the franchisee's obligation?"

"We audit cell data to manage membership revenue," Vanessa answered, "but the data belongs to the cell. We have two server plans. We offer a lease-to-own option, providing servers while the franchise establishes itself. We also have a licensing program that supplies only the proprietary software for mounting on your servers. Those servers can be any you own or lease from a third party."

That helped — local cell responsibility for its data meant that, from an evidentiary standpoint, any potential investigation of the local Aunt Tik's chapter should be well within SDPD's purview.

Paul e-mailed Lt. Harbin a copy of Aunt Tik's member manual that afternoon, along with a short note. After he'd completed his morning forensic lab duties, Paul dropped by the lieutenant's office to brief Louis on what he'd learned from Andy Pardone.

"This thing has the potential to pose a serious threat," Paul said after filling Louis in, "especially in the hands of the wrong people. They focus primarily on enforcing performance, and there are no guardrails for problems like Steve's. And, if parking an auto-firing AR-15 in front of a judge's residence is any indication, I'd say the San Diego cell is under serious mismanagement."

"Even so," Louis replied, "it's more organized than I'd pictured it."

Paul nodded his agreement.

"Its maturity is part of the issue with this Aunt Tik's thing. It's been running under the radar for quite a while. As law enforcement, we've been entirely in the dark. But I don't see how we can keep the blinders on, knowing what we know today.

"I'm worried if we don't get ahead of this, it'll come back to haunt us. What if a terrorist became a cell czar? Or a Russian national? Perhaps somebody stalking a romantic interest? Imagine the cell czar isn't a real person but, say, a group representing the Chinese or the North Koreans. Not good."

Louis's look was pensive, his smile gone.

"You've sold me. Aunt Tik's is a genuine threat — Steve's story checking out tells us we have a legitimate case. We have at least one active criminal matter occurring in our jurisdiction and committed by Aunt Tik's, a group the feds aren't looking at for anything. The crime occurred when they conspired to commit one or more felonies involving several individuals, creating the basis for Steve's actions.

"However, my first problem is that this conspiracy didn't result in a homicide; an *attempted* murder would go to Major Case. Second, upper brass will likely tell me we have enough work and don't need to look for more.

"I agree we need to build a local investigation around Aunt Tik's organization, and it can be independent of the feds' firearms violations *if* we can resolve my first problem. Having a homicide to investigate also gets me around the second issue."

"Conning teenagers into pointing loaded AR-15s at public officials is fairly evolved," Paul said. "Debra Ann has a theory — for things to have gotten to that point, there had to have been prior criminal behaviors. She's digging through the Internet, trying to find harmful things that happened to people and could be related to Aunt Tik's.

"I want to look back through our unsolved homicide cases to see if I can find an Aunt Tik's angle. If I run across one, it could be our way in. I think Debra Ann's right. The whole AR-15 set-up with remote control over the Internet is just too smooth, too confident — this is somebody who's walked this road before."

Louis pursed his lips, rocking back in his chair.

"I agree; it's worth a shot. Anything you find will strengthen my argument if I take it upstairs. If we can't tie a homicide to Aunt Tik's or its members, we'd have to run it by the chief as-is and see what he'll let us do."

"Also, our CI mentioned Aunt Tik's using encryption everywhere," Paul added, "their website, downloads, messages, and — I'm sure — their server data. It would help to get Capt. Mondo's thoughts, since Vice deals with that all the time.

"Also, I'd like to see if he has any talent in his unit that he'd be willing to loan us off-the-books, people who know encryption and online storage data in the context of social media — someone we could tap if we run into a problem. Access to some of the tools they use would also be nice."

Louis nodded.

"Keep it out of your written reports, and let me know if it begins eating up a lot of work hours. But otherwise, you have my blessing. I'll apologize to Debra Ann for loading you with all these extra chores. Getting stuck with homework is how you know you must be learning something."

He looked up at Paul with a wry smile.

"You mean something other than that homework sucks?" Paul replied with a grin, a chuckle from Louis following him back to his desk.

THE WRITINGS OF
AVRIL MARIA SERENE

CHAPTER 23

Paul settled into his office chair, leaned back, and picked up his desk phone's receiver as he punched in Mondo's interoffice extension.

"Hi, Mondo, it's Paul Castro. Got a few minutes?"

"Sure thing. How did Craig Evert's parolee work out for you?"

"Part of why I am calling is to thank you. The CI gave us everything we needed and more."

"Anytime," Mondo replied. "You said 'part'...."

"The 'more' is the problem. Mondo, I think you'll want your team to know Aunt Tik's is out there and what some of their capabilities are. You know how it goes in law enforcement — good work begets more work. And since you were such a big help with the CI, I wanted to hit you up for another favor. Have you got twenty minutes or so for a download on the Aunt Tik's thing?"

"You're in luck. I'm officially off the clock today; comp time for our overtime last week. I'm checking my messages and touching base with team leads in the office. I talked to Louis earlier; he planted the idea that this Aunt Tik's thing might be a big deal. So, to quote George W., 'Bring it on.'"

While Mondo spoke, Paul sent him a copy of Aunt Tik's member manual.

"I just forwarded you an e-mail that explains some of it."

As Mondo skimmed the manual, Paul recited an abbreviated version of what he'd told Louis about his conversation with Andy Pardone. He explained his plan to look into unsolved cases to see if any fit Aunt Tik's model.

"But even if we don't find any homicides, we've already tripped over other violations by Aunt Tik's members, mostly property crimes. I can't say there are direct connections to things Vice worries about. Still, I *can* see a potential for, say, using innocent people to move drugs around."

Mondo agreed.

"Aunt Tik's could front for many things. My first impression says drugs, yes, but also human trafficking and money laundering. Instead of following something from point A to point B, now you're trying to track a relay team with who knows how many members, none of whom know about the others or believe they're doing anything wrong. Considering how innovative they are, I'd be surprised if someone in Aunt Tik's hasn't thought about what they might get away with. How is it I never heard of these guys?"

"Louis says our highest priority needs to be identifying criminal cases to which we can attach the costs of an investigation. The nature of any we find will determine which unit takes responsibility for running down Aunt Tik's. We've got an attempted murder of a judge for Major Case if we can pry it away from the feds."

"Regardless of where this thing lands," Mondo offered, "we have sharp people in Vice who can help with the Internet and computer forensics. I'd be happy to lend you personnel for decryption, or if you need undercover or decoy help, say that you want to get some of our team into Aunt Tik's as paid members. After speaking with Louis, I mentioned Aunt Tik's to my second-in-command, Bob Strickland, and he volunteered his free time."

"Strickland?"

Paul tried not to sound disappointed. If Mondo were willing to provide someone high up the food chain, he'd much rather have Jeff Bennett, but Paul didn't want to come off as a greedy ingrate by raising the issue.

"You introduced me to him at the Children's Hospital charity ball. Debra Ann and I had a great time that night."

"He should be a good fit," Mondo said. "When Strickland was in San Jose, he worked several Silicon Valley cases against underage sexploitation websites. He knows his way around."

Paul paused a moment.

"He's a newly minted lieutenant, right?"

"A year here at rank and six months before that in San Jose, but yes, fairly new."

"If this Aunt Tik's thing goes anywhere, Detective Robbins would be taking point as far as anything homicide-related. I don't want to look a gift horse in the mouth, but will Strickland be comfortable working in a team situation where he outranks the lead? I'm not sure *I* would…."

"He volunteered, and he's a big boy, so I'd think so. I'll touch base with him and let you know if I see potential concerns."

"Thanks. Having one of yours would be helpful." Paul discarded his misgivings — any assistance would be appreciated. "I'm hoping Detective Byrne and I can identify one or more cases within Homicide's jurisdiction that look like Aunt Tik's handiwork. If we're successful, that'll make Louis's life much easier, and I'll return for more help. Should that happen, it would be official."

"Fair enough," Mondo responded. "In the meantime, I'll ask around — I'm curious if people with boots on the ground daily have heard anything about Aunt Tik's."

"Oh, hey, if I sent you some URLs for Aunt Tik's websites and servers," Paul said, "could you check them out? I wanted to know how tough it would be to navigate the encryption. Nothing specific, just a general idea of its sophistication through professional eyes."

"No problem. That would be a good way to bring Lt. Strickland into the loop," Mondo replied. "I'm intrigued; might have to look over his shoulder for myself."

An hour after I'd hung up my conversation with Aunt Tik's corporate office, Vicky Carlson returned my earlier call.

"Yes, Miss Carlson, thank you for calling me back. I'm sorry to have been so cryptic in the message I left. We don't always know who can access what we leave on the recorder, so we try to be discreet. I understand you're acquainted with Andy Pardone, a student at UCSD?"

"You can call me Vicky, and yes, Andy's a friend," she replied. "He told me you might be calling — something about Aunt Tik's?"

"Yes, we're in the information-gathering phase of an investigation. Andy's been helpful as we learn more about this group. He said that you're familiar with the organization and might be able to tell us more. Would you be willing to answer a few questions?"

I didn't sense any hesitation from Vicky.

"Yes, I used to be a member. I left three months ago. But I don't know if I can offer anything useful."

Vicky hadn't hesitated in her reply.

"We're interested in how members leave Aunt Tik's when they're no longer welcome, something Andy says you've experienced. Are you willing to share the details?"

"One of those things I wish I could forget … But certainly, anything to help," Vicky answered. "Would I need to come to your office?"

"We'd be happy to meet anywhere you'd feel comfortable. It depends on how much you have to say, but I doubt it would take more than half an hour."

"You're welcome to come to my home. I have some time tomorrow morning if that's okay?"

With the arrangements made, my curiosity was growing. As Vicky's personality came through the phone, she didn't fit my mental image of a premium Aunt Tik's member. I was looking forward to hearing her story.

It was time to connect with Paul, to let him know what I'd learned from Aunt Tik's marketing rep and about my upcoming interview with Vicky Carlson.

"Hi, honey," Paul answered from the lab's wall phone. He went silent as he listened carefully to Debra Ann's pass-down.

"That's good to know," Paul said. "I talked to Louis, and our biggest challenge right now is to link the Aunt Tik's information we've gathered to an active case. Eve's been looking through our unsolved and cold cases for something that fits their modus operandi. Let me see how things are going for her. I'll fill you in when I see you and Tommy tonight."

After he and Debra Ann said their goodbyes, Paul dropped by Detective Byrne's desk in the bullpen to check in.

"I've got Aunt Tik's handles for most of their cell captains," Eve reported, "and I'm able to track their activities somewhat through messages in Aunt Tik's user forums, but it's not a complete picture. All we see in the messages are the finished punks. The conversations between challenge participants and the punk master about punks in progress are through direct encrypted Signal messages and e-mails. Google searches access only the Aunt Tik's message forums."

"Some of it's hidden from us, then," Paul mused.

"We're missing a piece," Eve agreed. "There's a non-public server — it might be behind a web service or not on the Internet — that stores data we need. But I'm just getting started. I'll know more by the end of the day."

Paul raised his eyebrows.

"That may be the best problem we could have because help's coming. Mondo's providing us with resources to handle encryption and maybe hack some servers if we treat him right. He's given us a direct contact, his second-in-command, Lt. Bob Strickland. Have you worked with him?"

Eve shook her head no.

"I haven't either." Paul frowned. "I met him at a shindig for the Children's Hospital — a little full of himself, but he seems alright. Strickland has experience dealing with encrypted servers at his previous duty station while investigating underage trafficking. Mondo says we can call on him whenever we need help.

"I'll let Det. Robbins know Louis wants her as the lead on this if and when it becomes a real case — we'll need to loop her in on everything. I assume Marci will want us all to meet soon. It's easier to work together if we can visualize the other faces."

"Should I hit Strickland up for help with Aunt Tik's data servers?"

"Let's see what Marci says. It should be okay to ask for an estimate of how long it might take him and see what he says. The work you're doing mapping Aunt Tik's handles to cell captains, punk masters, and messages is important. Decrypting Aunt Tik's servers will take some work. We need to check with her, but I'm sure Marci won't want us asking too much of another unit's time until we have an actual case. By the way, Debra Ann's got a meeting tomorrow morning with Vicky Carlson, the one Andy Pardone said Aunt Tik's dismembered."

"Do we need to be there?"

"I can wangle us an invitation if you think it's important — I have an in with the reporter." Paul smiled and then grew serious. "But I don't expect a whole lot out of that interview. Probably more useful for you to pull what you can out of Aunt Tik's message forums."

"I'm on a roll, so I'd rather stick it out here anyway and get the first pass on these messages done."

"Oh, my bad. Sorry to have interrupted," Paul apologized. "But I did have another reason. While Marci's tied up with Escalation Management, I thought we could try to dig out from our unsolved cases at least one on which we can hang our investigation. That would grease the wheels to make this official and get you some credit for your work. Since right now, you and I know more than anyone in the department about Aunt Tik's, I thought it would be better if we tackled this as a team."

"I didn't say I couldn't use a *little* break from these messages." Eve grinned. "I'm at a good stopping point now."

"Great. Let's use Interrogation Room A. That'll give us some privacy and whiteboards we can scribble on."

And the other detectives in the squad room won't have to ask themselves what we're doing all up in their cases.

CHAPTER 24

Paul grabbed his laptop and walked across the bullpen to the interrogation room. Eve had beaten him there, and he sat across from her at the stainless-steel table. The soundproofed room, built from concrete block painted off-white, had a massive one-way mirror in one wall so that others could privately watch interviews. Paul liked using the interrogation rooms for meetings because they had digital video cameras. Using the cameras to record the sessions meant people could review them later or share the files with colleagues.

"The first question is, 'How do we identify potential Aunt Tik's cases?'" Paul began. "We'll start with anything classified as a homicide where we don't yet have a strong suspect, especially any stranger-on-stranger cases."

Eve's expression was thoughtful.

"Shouldn't we look at suspicious accidents, too? Drownings, for example?"

"Good point, and for active cases, yes. But let's avoid opening any tagged 'closed,' even if they seem suspect. You know how people get when you reopen their cases. Let's not add that hurdle to the hill we must climb. I suspect you're right, though — once we fully understand this Aunt Tik's can of worms, we'll revisit several things. Our goal now is the low-hanging fruit, if we can find any. If we can't, we'll return to closed cases, including suspicious accidents."

"How far back should we go?"

"Andy Pardone mentioned that the local Aunt Tik's cell recently changed czars. I have a gnawing feeling that all this has to do with whoever took over — maybe they've not learned how to do the job, and someone's taking advantage? Let's start with current cases and go back two years. If that doesn't get us anywhere, we'll add two years to the range and include cold cases."

"So, what exactly are we looking for?"

"We'll have to use our imaginations — anything resulting from an orchestrated chain of separate events. Starting with the newest homicides and working back, let's check the case status. We can toss those with a strong suspect, or where the events are straightforward, or it's a heat-of-passion thing between husband and wife. But if it's more convoluted, where we think the husband might have used a hired killer to stage something that looks like an accident, or the clues to the actual doer don't make sense, *that* would be a strong candidate."

"So, case-by-case, see what the problems with the investigation are and if something Aunt Tik's could have done addresses those issues," Eve summarized.

"Exactly. We shouldn't spend much time making a specific case fit in this first pass. We can always go back later for a deeper dive."

Within thirty minutes, Eve had identified the first candidate.

"Paul, I've got one!"

She seemed surprised and excited, like a child catching their first fish.

"It's a product-tampering case, less than two months old. The victim, Carla Littman, died of a peanut allergy from a box of cereal. It arrived in an Amazon bag, yet Amazon has no delivery record. The purchase was from a local Vons, but they have a private delivery service. On top of that, detectives discovered her EpiPen was compromised.

"What are the odds of two tampered products from different vendors being parts of the same murder?"

"Nice job! The first one's always the hardest." Paul and Eve high-fived.

Eve read off the case number, and Paul looked it up on his laptop. Paul's smile dropped from his face as he reviewed the digital file.

"*Oh, no* … this was the victim they were transporting when the ambulance hit and killed our babysitter."

Paul went quiet, his thoughts elsewhere. Then, taking a deep breath, he returned to their work.

"But this is a good fit. Okay, now that we know our premise works, let's see if we can find others."

He'd just swung back to his laptop screen and finished digging into his next database entry when it was his turn to celebrate.

"I've got one, too, from a few months ago. Somebody dumped several tons of concrete from an end loader on top of a Ford Fiesta, killing the occupants: Marianne Foreman and Gary Barker.

"We know someone stole the end loader and its trailer from the general contractor who rented it, but nobody knows how the machine got to the top of that cliff, how it got loaded with concrete, or who dumped the bucket.

"Cell phone text messages duped the victims into going to that location. They went to look at real estate, yet the realtor knew nothing about it. Let's see if we find any more."

An hour later, Paul struck paydirt again.

"We've got a bizarre case involving two very similar runaway trucks. The vehicles crashed within moments of each other in the same neighborhood, one of them killing a divorce attorney, JoAnne Mabry. This case screams, 'Aunt Tik's did it!'"

Over the next hour and a half, they pulled up several more cases with Aunt Tik's potential, but none as strong as their first three. The San Diego area records around eighty-five homicides a year, on average — a little more than three every two weeks — and they'd scanned through most of the cases for the past year.

"I had no idea we'd find this many potential candidates in a quick search." Paul was impressed. "Some might not be 'Aunt Tik's' cases, and we likely missed a few, but those first three stand out."

"The Mabry runaway truck case has to be their doing," Eve agreed. "What was the requirement you said? 'Convoluted?' And you look at the lead detective's case notes — her list of the various steps somebody took to kill this poor woman — the *only* way it makes sense is Aunt Tik's."

Paul nodded enthusiastically.

"The minute I spotted it, I knew we had our case. Luckily, detectives are already working it as a murder. It's high-profile because of the victim's visibility, and the homicide team assigned to it has stalled. This news will give them and us a new avenue to explore.

"And unlike the Marianne Foreman and Gary Barker rock-crushing or the Carla Littman food-tampering murders, there's no way anyone could argue that the nearly identical behaviors of the two trucks were coincidental or accidental."

Eve nodded, reciting all the suspicious coincidences and complicated steps.

"The odds of all those things happening organically in a coordinated fashion, the way they did, are astronomical."

"And that last entry in the file — Andy Pardone said the punk master needed to post a video, or at least *something*, to commemorate the punk," Paul added. "That squares perfectly with someone taking pictures at the scene with a cell phone and then disappearing. I'd love to find that video on Aunt Tik's punk results site. Can you add that to the research you're doing?"

"That *would* be awesome," Eve replied. "If it's there, I'll find it."

"I'll text Lt. Harbin, flagging all three of these. I'll also let him know there may be more, but the Mabry case gets our vote. He could open an investigation of Aunt Tik's just on his authority based on much less than we have here. Still, he'll want to get the captain involved because they'll need to coordinate the work of several units. He'll have the other two cases in his back pocket if the captain needs more convincing that this Aunt Tik's thing is a serious worry for us."

Eve was still scrolling through the open investigations.

"Hopefully, the lieutenant can get us resources to look for other cases that fit the pattern. But we'll be busy enough chasing down Aunt Tik's connection to the Mabry case, along with any threads that tie it to the other two or Steve's situation. I'm hoping they're all connected. If so, work on one will help solve the others."

Paul was well satisfied with their progress.

"We made it past step one, finding a homicide case to justify an Aunt Tik's investigation. Thanks for helping out — not the most fun thing."

"You're welcome. If it's alright with you, I'll clock out and head home."

"Of course." Paul nodded. "You report to Louis, not me. I'm going to cut out, too. Have a nice evening."

Eve gave Paul a tired smile and waved on her way out of the squad room.

Paul texted Louis with the details of the three cases they'd discovered. His phone pinged as Louis texted him back no more than fifteen minutes later. Paul was still at his desk and hadn't finished the paperwork he wanted to complete before he left.

"Expect a Xmas card from Det. Braxton," the text began. "She'll appreciate the help. They're putting in long hours but struggling. I agree — Mabry's a solid case for opening an official Aunt Tik's investigation. The other 2 illustrate the potential scope of the problem. Nice job.

"BTW, don't be surprised when you get home and see the twins there. Jenny & I've got a date night & Debra Ann volunteered to babysit. See you when we pick them up."

"Perfect," Paul typed back. "We'll feed 'em junk food & make them watch 'Arachnophobia.' They won't sleep for a week!"

"Hi, honey!" I called out when I heard Paul walk in. "Can you do me a favor and grab the deck of cards out of the closet? The girls want you to play them a hand of gin rummy before supper. They've been working on their secret code, so they'll know what to discard. Tommy's in here with me."

"*Uncle Paul!*" Two squeals burst out simultaneously as the twins came running around the corner from the den. They grabbed Paul around the waist and tried their best to pull him down as he marched stiff-legged like Frankenstein toward the hall closet.

After he'd suffered ignominious defeats in two hands of rummy, my announcement that supper was ready granted Paul a reprieve. Once we'd eaten, the girls decided to build a house of cards on the coffee table in the living room as Paul and I relaxed on the couch. Tommy sat to his right, taking in a Blippi video, and my head was on Paul's lap as we watched the construction.

I idly considered how impossible it would be to insert another story between the layers as Ashley, the older twin by eleven minutes, placed the second pair of trusses on the third level.

Somehow, that thought turned into a minor epiphany.

Impossible for a house of cards, yes, but I'd suddenly realized someone could insert a task no one knew about into a punk, maybe even performing it themselves, without telling anyone. The secrecy between challenges would make it very easy to do. Focused on understanding Aunt Tik's processes, I hadn't thought about someone intentionally stepping outside the presumed chain of challenges.

All that was necessary to change Steve's punk from something innocent and fun into a murder attempt was to swap out the paintball gun for an AR-15 then alter its final destination. Anyone could do that — no need for a formal written challenge. By monitoring the progress of the official challenges, they could sneak in any modifications between them. Steve hadn't mentioned the punk tasking anyone to watch that vehicle between challenge steps.

That external manipulator would spend a few seconds using a laptop to edit the GPS coordinates for the delivery. It was a detail nobody'd care about, except when dropping off the car. Anyone performing that task — as it happened, Steve — couldn't have known there'd ever been a different landing spot.

Everyone in my home who loved me surely thought I'd gone bonkers. I'd suddenly jumped off the couch, pumped my fist at empty air, and hissed, "Yes!" through gritted teeth.

Their stunned silence quickly brought me back to reality. All I could do was look sheepishly around the room at the eyes staring back and meekly explain, "Sorry, it's a work thing...."

I crooked a finger at my husband.

"Uhhh, Paul, can I talk to you in the kitchen for a minute?"

AUNT TIK'S: THE KILLER APP

"Uhhh, Paul, can I talk to you in the kitchen for a minute?"

THE WRITINGS OF
AVRIL MARIA SERENE

CHAPTER 25

Paul saw a sticky note from Detective Byrne on the seat of his chair when he arrived at his desk the following morning — it read simply, "Call me! *-E.*" Paul had a meeting outside the building at nine, but exclamation points weren't Eve's usual style, so he cruised over to her desk.

He found her smiling like Tommy had this past Christmas after he'd handed Debra Ann his gift, anxiously waiting for her to open it.

"I got your note — seems you're in a good mood. What's up?"

"My research is beginning to pay off!"

Eve was bubbling over with excitement.

"Those three cases we picked out for the brass to look at as a basis for our Aunt Tik's investigation? I found the punk results for all three!"

"You're kidding…. you're *not* kidding! So, we were right — woohoo, great work!" Paul exclaimed, breaking out into a big smile.

"But here's the kicker: guess who the punk master was for the Foreman and Barker car-crushing *and* the Carla Littman poisoning? A cell captain, the one-and-only 'blotto_bill'!"

Her self-satisfied grin spread ear-to-ear.

"The results video showed the landslide, but he kept the smashed Fiesta out of the picture."

Paul's expression was puzzled.

"Uh, 'blotto bill?' Should I know who that is?"

"It was from a case that Det. Robbins and I caught a little over two months ago — the dead body in a blue Audi alongside the highway? James Marshall III? You were on the scene for the forensics, and I thought …. Sorry, we haven't been copying you in; you couldn't have known.

"Escalation Management turned up a 'blotto_bill' as the social media username of a person of interest in that investigation. We don't know yet who 'blotto_bill' is. Or how a straight-up roadside killing by someone impersonating a traffic officer relates to Aunt Tik's punks. But now we've linked him in some way to four murders."

"Ah, okay, got it. That and finding those videos *is* an impressive morning's work," Paul said, eyebrows raised, eyes wide open, and the corners of his mouth turned way down in respect.

Eve had the triumphant look of a stud poker hand winner getting ready to flip their hole card.

"And it gets better. Everything points to Marshall as the cell czar who started the Aunt Tik's franchise in San Diego. I don't know yet who became czar after Marshall's demise. But after he took over, that czar's generic e-mail account is showing as the punk master for the challenges related to — ready for it? — *both* of the runaway truck punks!"

"Seriously? Wow, you went for the trifecta and pulled it off…."

Paul rocked his head and neck forward and back in approval.

"For the Littman murder, they subbed out the video's ending using a different punk result — one where they'd blurred out the face of a heavyset woman suffering from an overdose of stimulant laxatives. But the girl in an Amazon Prime T-shirt delivering the Fruity Cheerios gave it away.

"For both of the junker flatbed punks, they're displaying the same video, the results of the crash that wasn't fatal."

"No wonder you're so pumped up!" Paul exclaimed in a voice too loud for the bullpen, almost as excited as she was. Eve stood up from her chair, and they fist-bumped. Other officers in the squad room turned away from their work to give the two of them quizzical looks.

"This is starting to come together; no question we're on the right track. That had to take some real digging through all those punk results …. Awesome job, Eve.

"And a great way to start the day!"

I was a bit frazzled and running late — I'd hoped to get an earlier start because I was interviewing Vicky Carlson at her place this morning, and I'd be going with the rush-hour traffic. Still, I got to the Carlson residence right at nine. It was an old walk-up apartment building near the campus of UCSD. I pushed the call button for "V. Carlson" on the panel in the vestibule. A young woman's voice asked who I was, and after I responded, she buzzed me in.

"Hello, Vicky, I'm Debra Ann Wynn," I repeated when a pleasant-looking brunette in her early thirties, wearing dark slacks and a burgundy cable-knit sweater, opened her apartment door.

"We spoke on the phone about your experiences with Aunt Tik's website."

"Of course. Please, come in." Vicky swept one hand in invitation toward an overstuffed, amber-colored chair across from a floral-print couch.

The apartment was small but neat and nicely furnished, with the kind of bric-a-brac and wall hangings that suggested she'd lived there a while. The faint but unmistakable scent of banana nut bread lingered in the air. A large white Persian cat was spread out, lazily cleaning herself, on one end of the couch, seemingly oblivious to my presence.

I sat in the chair as Vicky seated herself on the end of the couch closest to it. She lifted a saucer from the end table.

"Would you like coffee or something else to drink?"

"No, thank you. I hit the Starbucks pretty hard earlier this morning."

"Restroom, then?" she followed up coyly.

I laughed.

"Not at the moment, thanks."

With that, any tension in the room melted away.

"First, let me offer some background on why I wanted to talk to you this morning."

I smiled to help keep her at ease.

"A teenager I know got into serious trouble performing one of the challenges to an Aunt Tik's punk. His mother asked our friend, who's on the force, for help. He wanted someone to look into Aunt Tik's not as a criminal matter, per se, but to understand what it is. I'm a reporter and volunteered — I don't wear a uniform, but I know how to ask the right questions."

Vicky cut right to the heart of it.

"So, you want to know what's going on with Aunt Tik's without making waves. Is that it?"

"Pretty much," I replied. "For now, no one associated with Aunt Tik's is being accused of anything. If there were future allegations of wrongdoing, they wouldn't involve you.

"Your situation is interesting, Vicky — Andy tells me they put you in a unique position. Not only were you once a member, but they've also targeted you as a victim of a malicious punk — he calls it 'dismembering.' I'm here because Andy thought you'd be willing to share your experiences."

Her body language suggested she still had questions, and I addressed those I anticipated.

"Whatever you say today is in confidence. With your permission, I'd like to record our talk. I'll use the recording only for reference later. There's always the possibility that we can't find a secondary source for something you've told us that becomes critical to a formal investigation. In that case, I'll come to you then to discuss the situation."

"I understand." Vicky's voice had softened. "Andy filled me in on the ground rules and his experiences when you spoke with him. I'm unsure how much I know, but I'll try to be helpful."

"That's perfect. I'll be as brief as possible. We'll keep it relaxed and take this at a speed that's comfortable for you. We can begin with how you learned about Aunt Tik's and got caught up in it."

"Of course. My previous boyfriend introduced me to their website. His real name is Jim Detmer. I don't remember his Aunt Tik's handle, but I can get it if needed. He wouldn't let me see his password, so I can't help you there."

"When did you meet Mr. Detmer?"

"Three years ago. Jimmy had just joined Aunt Tik's. He was so gonzo about earning points and wanted to become one of the cell captains. He'd come over, we'd be doing something together, and then suddenly, he'd take off, saying he had a challenge to do. It was like a teenager looking for excuses to drive the family car. It got ridiculous. Eventually, I'd had enough, and we broke up."

"When was that?"

"Three months ago, just before I got dismembered — for failing a punk challenge, not for breaking up with him. Before all that, Jimmy talked me into joining Aunt Tik's. At first, it was fun. I'd go out with him on his challenges most of the time. I didn't bid on many challenges myself."

"And when was it that you joined as a member?"

"About six months after I met him. He had a kind of running punk challenge where he and other members would randomly go to this man's house at maybe three in the morning. The guy had one of those little Smart cars. His garage must have been full because he always parked on the curb or in his driveway.

"Jimmy and the others would lift the car with a floor jack and wheel it over to one of the neighbor's driveways, in somebody's front yard, or down another street. One time, I remember, they put it over a little fountain at the park. Jimmy said it looked like a turtle using a bidet."

She smiled at the recollection.

"They'd dress in wild costumes, and afterward, they'd do what they called a 'touchdown dance' to entertain the Ring doorbells in the neighborhood. Then, someone would take videos the following morning when the poor man tried to find his car. They stitched them all together at double speed. I was so naïve at the time — I thought it was hilarious.

"Finally, the guy wised up and got an alarm system for the car, so the Aunt Tik's punks focused on moving his golf caddy lawn ornament around instead. I thought it was getting a little old, myself."

Vicky sighed, then shrugged as if to say, "But what can you do?"

I needed some context.

"Do you recall when these events happened? Or details that would help us identify the victim or the location?"

"It was so long ago…. It was in the spring, I guess, two years ago. The Smart car was in a nice neighborhood around a golf course. North of the Ted Williams, not too far from the 15.

"Jimmy was driving, and it was in the wee hours. I'm sorry, I don't remember exactly. I'd know the house and the neighborhood if I saw it again."

"The police can search their records," I assured her, "and see if they have any vandalism or trespassing reports around that area at that time."

"It did seem like the punks were getting more mean-spirited, especially after they got this new czar over the San Diego cell."

Vicky frowned.

"One of the punks I was in turned bad, and I felt terrible."

"How so?"

"Somebody got Internet background checks on two neighbors. You know, where you spend like a hundred and twenty dollars, and they give you everything they can find on the Internet for that person? It's scary how much they can turn up. Old phone numbers, e-mail accounts, snail-mail addresses, relatives, jobs, credit, lawsuits or criminal histories, friends, and lovers."

"Internet background checks have caused real problems," I conceded. "Serious crimes like assaults and arson, a lot of them hate-based, are committed against people. Some become victims simply because the background check information is wrong. The attackers read something online that they don't like about somebody. They'll pay for a cheap background check based on the name and then do something to harm the person described in the data dump they get back.

"As often as not, the victim they choose isn't the intended target; they just happen to have a similar name."

Vicky nodded and continued with her story.

"These neighbors were married, not to each other, of course, and they had kids — typical middle-class suburbia. So, the punk challenges were all about writing love letters back and forth between these four people — from the wife of one neighbor to the husband of the other and vice versa.

"We'd send these gushy, sometimes pornographic, messages by e-mail and regular mail. Or tuck them under the windshield wipers of their cars.

We would even send messages to their jobs or have flowers and Hallmark stuff delivered.

"It seemed like a lot of fun because you could get so creative, taking on one role and then the other, playing up these fake relationships. To apply the bellows to the fire, we'd call and hang up when anyone answered."

I wondered if she knew what she was doing was wrong, but I didn't want to put her on the defensive.

"The big reveal for the punk was supposed to be a billboard across the street from them that they could both see, explaining the punk. But that never happened. The wife of the one guy threw him out of the house. They have these three kids around junior high school age, and the man's stuff is in piles all over the front yard — everybody's yelling, screaming, and crying."

The moisture in her eyes bore witness to Vicky's empathy.

"At the same time, somebody — they *had* to be like the world's biggest asshole — filmed it all from across the street and posted it on Aunt Tik's website. Seeing this thing is so upsetting, especially if you know it's all one big punk. Nasty, nasty, nasty."

Vicky gave a scowl that looked unnatural on her otherwise attractive face.

"Do you recall the dates? Or the locations of the residences?"

"Two years ago, in the summer. It was on Barrymore. I'd have to look up the house numbers. Can I e-mail it to the address on your card?"

"Yes, that would be great. Please put 'Aunt Tik's' in caps in the subject line — that helps me keep things organized."

"I will. Jimmy had one where they took the motor out of a guy's new car and put in an audio player that made the noises of an engine: starting, revving up, shifting gears, all that.

"I guess insurance would cover most of it, and maybe for some of these punks, they pay to undo whatever they did. But when they showed the big reveal video for the punk, the guy's wife, girlfriend, or whatever, is pregnant, like eight months. Maybe men don't get it. But as a woman, you freak out when you're that far along, and somebody screws with your transportation, or your finances, or all the things that can go bad."

It was clear from her tone and expression that recalling past Aunt Tik's punks upset Vicky.

"As I'm talking to people," I said, "I'm not hearing much about Aunt Tik's members showing sympathy or support for their victims. I guess that part of it wasn't a great fit for you."

She flashed a cynical smile as if to say, "You think?" Then the corners of her mouth dropped, her eyes softened, and she sighed.

"You start hearing rumors, like the one about smashing somebody's car with rocks and killing the people in it. Or you see something terrible in the paper or on CNN that sounds like one of your cell's punks. At some point, I got scared."

Her eyes went wide as she raised her eyebrows.

"Had you ever considered voluntarily giving up your Aunt Tik's membership?"

"Yes, I wanted out, away from Jimmy, and for things to return to normal. But before I left, I accepted one last challenge to avoid another argument with him. We were going through a rough patch, and I just wanted things to be … easier, you know?"

A hint of a tear showed itself in the corner of her eye.

"I've been there. It can be painful."

"It was. You do your best, but sometimes it just doesn't work. Anyway, I chose the simplest challenge. I was supposed to pick up a package and deliver it to a house.

"When I decrypted the Aunt Tik's message, I misread 'a.m.' as 'p.m.,' so I was twelve hours late delivering the package, and it broke the punk. I mean, I understood that if you did something like that *on purpose,* you could get dismembered, and I knew that getting kicked out was a horrible ordeal. But I thought it had to be for something really bad.

"Aunt Tik's completely trashed my brand-new car for the difference between an 'a' and a 'p.' I worked *so hard* to buy it…."

She seemed defeated; her shoulders sagged forward, her elbows on her knees, and her fingertips pressing her forehead on both sides as she sobbed.

CHAPTER 26

After handing Vicky a box of tissues from her coffee table, I looked around her small apartment to avoid eye contact while she gathered herself. I hated bringing up such bad memories for her.

Still, this was our first opportunity to see a dismemberment from the inside. We needed to understand how Aunt Tik's targeted someone to force them out and how it affected victims since that was the website's big stick to keep members in line. That knowledge could help us mitigate the fear it inspired in Aunt Tik's associates that we might want to flip.

"Can you tell me how they damaged your car?" I pushed forward once she'd regained her composure.

"It's clear now I had no clue what Aunt Tik's was about. I'd just bought this new BMW, a silver X1. I saved for two years to make enough of a down payment that the installments wouldn't be any more than what I was paying for my old car.

"A week and a half after I failed the challenge, I left work and walked out to the parking lot. The entire driver's side of my car, including the wheels and the windows, was painted fluorescent orange. Over that, they'd painted 'punk'd bitch' in big letters in black paint, with a huge arrow pointing at the driver's window."

Déjà vu all over again.

The local Aunt Tik's community can't be that large. Louis told me Steve purchased orange and black paint for a challenge with a credit card he took from his mother, who'd confirmed the incident.

But for now, I wouldn't share my suspicions with Vicky.

"The dealer said the chemical Aunt Tik's used dissolved the clear coat, paint, and weatherstripping around the doors. Aunt Tik's sandpapered the glass and ruined it. The bill to the insurance company was more than eleven thousand dollars. I filed a police report and got my deductible reimbursed, which helped. The dealer gave me a loaner to drive, and they did a great job fixing the car. You can't even tell. But *I* know."

"I don't suppose Aunt Tik's ponied up anything to cover the damages?"

She shook her head, anger flashing across her face.

"It doesn't feel like a new car anymore, and it just makes me sick. It's bad enough they do this and get away with it, but on top of that, people think it's funny. Then you walk around for months thinking, 'What else are they going to do?' — because you know from all the punks you've read that they have no limits, no class, and they couldn't care less." A tear escaped each of her eyes.

I studied my notes for a long moment, allowing her time to dab away the moisture.

"I'm sorry that happened to you, Vicky. I can't pretend to understand what you've gone through. The police believe Aunt Tik's associates may have put others in serious harm's way, including setting up a murder. I'm not telling you that to alarm you any further. But I wanted to let you know that they're looking into other things related to Aunt Tik's punks, including the possibility of capital crimes."

"Will the victims get their voices heard? Or will they be stuck like me, not even having a face to scream at?"

"I'm not at liberty to tell you more than that, but you need to know that the authorities are taking this very seriously."

I felt guilty asking Vicky to focus on a situation that dredged up unresolved and painful feelings for her. I wanted to make amends if I could.

"Look, you've been the victim of illegal acts, and sometimes the feelings of being violated or no longer secure in your own spaces can be incredibly difficult to overcome. That doesn't have to be. Let me give you the name of someone who once helped me."

Marci had referred me to a wonderful woman a couple of years ago, and I wrote her contact information on one of my business cards. Talking to a professional helped me get back to a healthy place after being abducted at knifepoint in a murder case I was investigating.

"Hopefully, we can stop Aunt Tik's involvement in illegal activities so no one else gets hurt."

I handed her my card.

"It seems clear that these cell captains and the cell czar exercise serious power over the members, the punk performances, and the punk challenges. Do you have any information that might help us learn more about the people in those roles?"

"I wasn't in it to be part of the organization. I'd never have gotten involved if it weren't for my relationship with Jimmy. The real names of members and the people who ran things were supposed to be deep, dark secrets, and I wasn't motivated then to find out.

"But I'm pretty sure Jimmy knows members at those higher levels. He was always such a suck-up where Aunt Tik's was concerned, and he wanted to be part of that next layer. There was a long stretch where he did daily challenges to get his points as high as possible."

"Do you think we could persuade him to help us out?"

"I doubt it. Jimmy's so gung-ho about Aunt Tik's. And even if he decided he didn't like them anymore, he'd be afraid of being dismembered."

"Is there anything you know about, something he's done, that might get him dismembered if Aunt Tik's found out?"

I *was* curious. But I was also casting about for any leverage I might need when talking to Jimmy.

"No, dismembering is such a *huge* thing — he wouldn't risk it. Aunt Tik's holds it over everybody's head and never lets you forget about it. That's how they keep everyone toeing the line. They claim members aren't allowed to commit crimes, but I think my situation proves *that* isn't true. They relax those rules a *lot* when it comes to dismembering someone.

"Only the cell czar knows anything about the real people behind their Aunt Tik's handles, and he won't out anyone. That makes whoever does these things a ghost."

I thought for a moment.

"I see your point, but the lieutenant has people who know how to deal with those situations. I want to talk to Jimmy. Would you be willing to give me his contact information?"

"Of course." Vicky reached for her purse on the end table and dug through it for a pen. She wrote on a notepad lying on the end table, passing the top sheet to me.

"Thanks. I won't mention that I spoke to you, but prepare yourself. Jimmy'll probably assume you were the one who gave him up.

"Let me ask you a hypothetical question: Suppose we could manipulate the situation so that Jimmy cooperated with us, possibly without his knowledge. Would you be comfortable interacting with him again? Not romantically, but maybe just calling him up, saying, 'How's the weather? Oh, and by the way, have you done anything interesting lately with Aunt Tik's?' Is that something you could do?"

She shrugged. "If it helps, I could do that. If I asked *too* many questions, Jimmy might get suspicious."

Vicky thought for a moment.

"Still, I left him, not the other way around. And he understands that I know Aunt Tik's is the one thing he's into. So, yes, that would work."

"Okay, good. Once I've spoken to Jimmy, we'll reach out if there's something you could do on that front. You've been truly accommodating, Vicky, and this conversation will help us get a handle on this thing."

She was gracious.

"It's been frustrating, but I'm glad you're looking into this now."

"I'll keep you in the loop as we make progress. In the meantime, my contact info is on the front of the card I gave you. Please let us know if you remember anything that might be helpful or need anything from us related to this investigation. I hope you have a nice day. I can see myself out."

I considered Vicky's situation as I returned to my car.

While I appreciate what Aunt Tik's once set out to do, what they've created is no joke.

THE WRITINGS OF
AVRIL MARIA SERENE

CHAPTER 27

It wasn't until Thursday evening, during our third attempt to catch him at home, that Paul and I finally interviewed Jimmy Detmer. Paul had pulled Detmer's rap sheet beforehand. Though he would never interfere with my work, Paul insisted he go along for this interview, tapping into the personal time off he'd built up on the job. That's how concerned he was about Detmer's character and history.

Detmer lived in a one-story frame home in Clairemont, just south of Balboa, near the 805 interchange. The yard, surrounded by a badly rusted hurricane fence, was unkempt. Trash had filled in any empty spaces, the rest strewn with used automobile parts and a broken-down two-stroke motorcycle missing the gas tank and a front wheel. An old, battered swing set rested against the outside garage wall — chains hanging from it suggested it had served as an engine hoist. Dog feces and decomposing small animal carcasses littered the ground, bare of vegetation save for the occasional dried-up weed. Even in a poorer neighborhood, the residence stood out for its neglected condition.

We could see movement within the house. But before we knocked on the door, I quickly created a high-priority e-mail on my burner phone with the subject, "WATCH OUT FOR POLICE!" I'd be sending it from Steve's premium Aunt Tik's account to Detmer's, which I'd gotten from Vicky. But I didn't hit the Send button yet — I just slid the cell phone back inside my front jacket pocket.

Detmer answered our knock on the dilapidated wooden screen door, wearing a soiled T-shirt and cargo shorts. He kept the door closed as he scowled at Paul and then sneered up and down at me, making it obvious he was undressing me in his mind.

"What do *you* want?" he snarled, condescension dripping from his voice as his eyes returned to meet Paul's.

Paul showed his badge and said in as level a tone as he could muster, "I'm working with the San Diego Police Department, and we have some questions related to your role with an organization known as 'Aunt Tik's.'"

"I haven't done anything," Detmer protested, making no effort to open the door. "I don't have to talk to you — I know my rights!"

I resisted the temptation to roll my eyes. But Detmer's response told me he was worried about something.

"Mr. Detmer, we're here regarding an active murder investigation," Paul said, stretching the truth just a little. "We've come to your residence as a courtesy. You can let us in, and we can have a conversation in the comfort of your home, or we can have that discussion down at the precinct. The choice is yours."

Paul's bluff worked. Something about a perp walk in front of your neighbors — or a landlord to whom you owe two months' back rent — can be very persuasive. Paul's exaggeration was more of timing than outright dishonesty. The department *did* have a relevant open homicide case and was merely waiting for the Aunt Tik's investigation to be officially attached to it.

Though Detmer had to think about it for a moment, he grudgingly opened the screen door. He seemed to go out of his way to avoid acknowledging me. When I offered my business card upon entering and introducing ourselves, he ignored my outstretched hand to take Paul's instead. Paul pulled his back, took my card, and handed it to Detmer, which, for some reason, caused him to snort.

Detmer turned his back on us as he walked into the living room. We followed him inside, and Paul pocketed his badge. We could see into the kitchen, where dirty dishes filled the sink and overflowed onto the counter — beer cans, some half crushed, littered the surfaces and the living room floor. A cockroach skittered along a baseboard. The ragged, worn carpet was threadbare in spots and smelled of pet accidents.

An aging and toothless German Shepherd had taken up most of the sagging and torn pleather couch, and Detmer settled into an old brown vinyl recliner held together with duct tape, leaving no seating options for either of us.

Paul and I looked at one another. Because Detmer had obvious issues dealing with women in positions of authority and we intended to put him under stress, we knew I needed to ask the questions.

"Mr. Detmer," I said, looking down at him once he'd seated himself, "have you ever heard of a social media gaming website called 'Aunt Tik's'?"

"I don't know anything about any damned Aunt Tik's," Detmer said, his upper lip curled into a sneer, "but I know how to deal with punks." Looking straight at Paul, he made it sound vaguely like a threat.

"I don't recall mentioning that Aunt Tik's was associated with punks, Mr. Detmer," I informed him with a forced smile. "So, if I asked you whether you'd performed any challenges for Aunt Tik's punks, I suppose you'd tell me you don't know anything about those either?"

"Damned straight. The only punks I know work for the police department."

Our Mr. Detmer wasn't very quick on the uptake. His intentional misunderstanding of a punk's meaning in this context didn't work the first time he tried it, and repeating it wasn't any more effective.

Detmer was in bantam rooster mode, looking for a fight. As he claimed he knew nothing about Aunt Tik's, punks, or punk challenges, I used my thumb to send my pre-created e-mail from the cell phone inside my jacket pocket. Sure enough, we immediately heard a message notification chiming from the front of Detmer's shorts.

"You might want to get that, Jimmy," I said. "It could be important news from this Aunt Tik's website that you know nothing about. It might even be about our visit tonight."

Detmer wasn't one to resist childish impulses. His expression changed back and forth between the game face meant for us and furtive looks away in nervous curiosity as he worried about the message notification. He kept fingering the phone in his pocket, and as much as he hated to peek, the temptation was too strong.

Finally, shaking his head like a bobblehead, he pulled his phone out of his pocket. His shoulders dropped when he saw the message, and he exhaled heavily, knowing he was outed.

"I only have a free public account because somebody at the gym told me about Aunt Tik's."

"You just lied in front of a law enforcement official," I said, "during an interrogation about matters pertinent to an active murder investigation, Mr. Detmer. That's a felony. You don't want to get in any deeper. Free members don't get Aunt Tik's e-mail and Signal accounts. Would you like to reconsider your answer?"

"Okay, fine. Have it your way," Detmer conceded, ejecting spittle with his words. "But I didn't do any challenges. If you think I did something, prove it."

What possible good does this man think would come from challenging a peace officer to prove something? Detmer's attitude spoke to his intellect, honesty, and awareness.

"Mr. Detmer, can you explain why a homeowner filed multiple complaints against you with the police during April and May two years ago? They've accused you of activities that include the repeated thefts of his Smart car and a cement lawn ornament."

"I don't know anything about that," Detmer said flatly, but his face showed clearly the question rattled him.

"Give us a moment, if you would, Mr. Detmer," I said.

Paul and I stepped back for a quiet conference.

"We got what we came for," I whispered. "We know Detmer's involved up to his eyeballs. If we want to push him any harder, we'll have to invoke something he'll know Vicky gave us. I don't trust him not to go after her."

Paul nodded, and we turned and stepped forward again.

"Mr. Detmer, thank you for seeing us," I said. "We'll be coming back later to ask some additional questions. While we are not here to give you legal advice, it would behoove you to prepare yourself with better answers."

On their face, Detmer's responses were unproductive, but Paul and I felt we'd struck gold. When the time came, we could readily turn a dim-bulb fanatic like Detmer to our advantage. His shallow deceits confirmed what Vicky told us about how deeply he was involved. All we'd need to get real answers was some leverage, and his devotion to Aunt Tik's provided that.

In revealing he'd invested himself sufficiently that he'd lie to authorities, Detmer also told us how susceptible he'd be to the threat of being dismembered. That suggested Vicky was right when she said dismemberment was the one thing that would completely upset his world.

I had some ideas about how to make that threat more immediate with some help from Steve and Vicky.

THE WRITINGS OF
AVRIL MARIA SERENE

CHAPTER 28

When I spoke to Tracy on the phone, she told me it'd taken some time to put up her Temecula home to make Steve's bail.

"The lawyer said California allows substituting real estate equity for cash bail, so I did that. It took three trips to the court and a ton of paperwork, but they finally let Steve out."

I arranged with Tracy to visit them at home the following morning. Eve Byrne had done much of the research to help with Steve's case and was responsible for most of our progress. Still, she hadn't met Steve — it was a meeting long overdue. My call caught her on her way to work, and I picked her up in front of the precinct on the way to the Nielsens' home.

Steve answered the door and invited us in, visibly more at ease than in either jail interview. Tracy was there, as I'd requested. I didn't want to take the chance that the teenager would misconstrue anything we discussed.

"Steve, Tracy, this is Det. Eve Byrne," I said. "She's a good friend and an investigator with the police department. She volunteered to help unofficially with Steve's situation, and she's the one who dug up a lot of the leads we're following now."

Eve nodded, and we shook hands all around.

"Because of that work, it looks like the Aunt Tik's investigation will become official sooner rather than later.

"If there's anything you want to share or questions you need to ask of me, you can also communicate with Eve. I thought it was important to introduce you to each other and that she gets to know everyone. Hopefully, she can catch up with anything I may have forgotten to tell her."

"It's nice to meet you, Detective," Tracy said. "Steve and I appreciate your help."

"Please, just call me Eve, and I am glad to be part of this. I know it's been hard on you, Steve, but I have to say the circumstances are a lot more interesting — and educational — than some other things we get involved in."

Steve had become a little standoffish, saying, "Okay," without making eye contact with her.

He has a little thing for Eve. I smiled to myself.

As Tracy nudged him with her elbow, he added, "Oh, and thanks for everything you're doing for us."

"By the way, Steve, here's your cell phone." This opportunity was the first I'd had to return it since logging onto his Aunt Tik's account using my burner phone.

"Thanks." He brightened. "I could use it now that I'm home again."

"I know you've been through quite a lot, and we're starting to understand more of what you got sucked into," I said to Steve as we moved into the living room. "Given all of that, how have things been going?"

Steve took the coffee-colored fabric-upholstered couch with his knees up and feet on the seat. Tracy offered me the brown faux leather recliner, with Eve taking one of the sylvan-print wingback chairs. Tracy sat on the couch near her son.

"It's okay," Steve replied. "I didn't lose my job. I go back to work this afternoon. My friends ask what's going on, and the lawyer says I can't tell them. He doesn't want the court to use anything I say against me, and he's worried some of my friends might be in Aunt Tik's, too. I'm not allowed to go on Aunt Tik's website, and I haven't. But Mom and I talked about being more responsible and trading that for having the freedom to do other things, so I'm good."

"Speaking of Aunt Tik's website," I said, "we'll need the name of the judge who granted bail and your case number. I'll inform them that you've been a cooperative witness in one of our cases and allowed us to use that account. We don't want any activity we're engaged in to violate your bond."

"I can get that information for you," Tracy offered. "Go ahead with your conversation; it'll take me a few minutes to find it."

"Thank you," Eve said, nodding as Tracy left the room.

"Well, Steve, we've been looking into this Aunt Tik's thing, and I can see how it would be easy to get caught up in it." I wanted him to know I got what had happened — that I wasn't still questioning his motives.

"It's a bigger deal than I thought, especially the dismembering part. As you know, our involvement in this has been unofficial so far as a way to help you and your mom out. But we've learned some things about Aunt Tik's that are very concerning to law enforcement. I can't share everything with you, but you're not the only one fooled into doing things that got people into trouble if that makes you feel any better."

Steve shot me an appreciative look — I suddenly realized he'd been in the dark about what we were doing while incarcerated, other than what his mom might have passed along.

"I guess it makes me think somebody needs to fix this if other people are being messed with, too," he said.

Eve gave him a wry smile.

"Unfortunately, that's a common feeling," she shared, and my mind went to Vicky Carlson. "But there's no 1-800 number hotline yet for people who've been burned by Aunt Tik's."

Steve gave up an ironic grin of his own, seeming more comfortable with Eve.

"There's a pretty good chance that this will become an official investigation," I told him. "If that happens, my situation will change. As a reporter, I can't directly involve myself in police investigations. I don't know yet if they'll assign Eve to the case or her role if they do."

"Since I work for Homicide," Eve stepped in, "it would depend on whether they find direct evidence of a connection between Aunt Tik's and a murder. We've got a case that fits, but nothing's decided yet."

"Murder? Wow, *that's* serious!" Steve sounded surprised. That someone charged with transporting a loaded weapon to a location in front of a judge's home would find the step up to murder remarkable showed that Steve hadn't fully grasped the scope of Aunt Tik's potential.

"There are other cases, many of them property crimes, that Aunt Tik's seems to have a hand in," Eve added. "It looks like a pattern, and *somebody* will investigate it — just a matter of the unit assigned."

Tracy returned, passing me a handwritten note with the name of the judge who'd issued bail and the case number.

"Thanks, Tracy. If you can write down your e-mail address, I'll copy you with my letter to the judge and prosecutor."

Tracy took the note back from me and wrote down the information. "I appreciate this, Debra Ann," she said as she returned it.

I smiled and nodded to say she was welcome. I turned back to face Steve.

"If I'm reading all this right," I said, "and don't take this as making any promises or predicting the future — your part in this situation is small, more of a witness than a criminal. To support that idea, it would help us if you could add to our understanding of Aunt Tik's. Not just getting caught with the gun but also the organization. Would you be willing to answer some questions for me?"

Steve nodded.

"Our lawyer says I am not supposed to tell anybody anything about Aunt Tik's, but he knows you're working on this unofficially, so it should be okay."

"We'll stay away from anything that has to do with your federal charges, and if you or your mom become uncomfortable with anything, just let me know. Eve, if you see a problem, jump right in."

"Will do." Eve looked reassuringly at Steve, who smiled back. The mood in the room lightened a little.

"It looks to us," I continued, "that the problem is bigger than what they tricked you into doing. By the way, we do know they used you. I doubt anyone questions that at this point. I'm not saying the gun thing is no big deal. But it's more that you should have reported it than you having any evil intentions."

Steve swung his legs off the couch and leaned forward, giving me his full attention.

"So, law-enforcement officers have three problems they're responsible for solving here. The first is keeping people from getting duped into doing any part of anything involving an assault rifle and a sitting judge in the same sentence. The second is not allowing a murder, attempted murder, physical harm, destruction of property, or intimidation — anything illegal by anyone, using proxies or not — to go unpunished. The third is stopping anybody from making a game out of capital offenses, or for that matter, any other crime."

"We have to accomplish these things without interfering with people's right to have innocent fun," Eve added.

"I guess law enforcement isn't as simple as it sounds," Steve conceded.

"It can get complicated, that's for sure," I replied. "Steve, what I need from you is anything you can think of regarding names or Aunt Tik's handles for any of the challenges you've done. Member contact info, the cell captain that sent you your challenge, or the cell czar, if you have information on that person, would help, too. Don't worry; nothing you tell me or Eve will get back to the people who charged you with the gun thing. And yes, I have a better picture of your concerns about dismemberment from Aunt Tik's. We've spoken to someone who went through it."

And let's not forget you helped trash that poor woman's car, I thought. But once again, I kept my suspicions to myself — I didn't want to interrupt the rapport we were building with Steve.

"But whatever Aunt Tik's plans to do to you, that ship's already sailed. We're not going to let them know anything about this conversation — we don't need to be giving them excuses to do anything more to you. Are you with me so far?"

"I just wish I knew when and where they were coming after me," Steve said. "Having to worry all the time sucks. I want it to be over with. But it won't change anything they do if I help you. I don't want other people to go through this."

It occurred to me that Steve may have used his recent downtime to think some of these things through for himself.

"We'll try to keep you informed of anything we learn that might affect you," Eve offered.

"As to Aunt Tik's identities," I said, "I'd appreciate any real names you know, but Aunt Tik's handles will work too. The department has some great tech people, and Eve has done a ton of research. We should be able to link those to their real-world identities. First question: do you know the name or Aunt Tik's handle of the cell czar for the San Diego cell?"

"Our cell number is 2763," Steve replied, "and he uses a generic CellCzar2763 at AuntTiks dot-com account. Whoever is the cell czar uses that account, so it's not tied to one person; it goes with their job. But they just made him the czar a couple of months ago. Before that, he was a cell captain — the captains use their regular member e-mail accounts because whoever gets to be a captain changes every month, depending on their scores. I think his Aunt Tik's handle was 'blotto bill,' with an underscore in the middle and some number after it, at AuntTiks dot com.

"I'm sorry, did you say 'blotto_bill — b-l-o-t-t-o, underscore, b-i-l-l'?" I asked incredulously. I looked at Eve, and the expression on her face was as surprised as the one I'm sure was on mine.

"Yeah, that's right, with the number after it. Why? Is that important?"

"It's something we needed to know," I said.

I'd had a printout of the short e-mail from the James Marshall roadside homicide pinned over my desk at the news service for nearly a year, and I saw that name every working day. It seemed this 'blotto_bill' really got around, given Eve's discovery of his connection to punk results that likely ended in murder … and now this.

But I didn't share all of that with Steve.

"I didn't mean to interrupt you. You were on a roll, so please, go ahead."

"I remember because he was the same punk master I had on the first challenge I did. By then, he was the cell czar, but he used his cell captain e-mail account for that challenge. They encipher the messages, and those self-destruct after a while, but the Outlook headers wrapping the e-mails are still in my inbox. They would show the sender's account name, the same as their Aunt Tik's handle."

"Would you mind if Forensics took a look at your laptop? It would be good to copy and back up those e-mails." I saw a look of genuine concern cross Steve's face, and I was sure I knew why. But it wasn't something I could bring up in front of his mother.

"Don't worry, all they'll look at are those e-mails. They won't get into anything else that might be on your computer, and they won't share what they find with me or your mom. They only care about Aunt Tik's communications. If you would like, I'll ask if you can be present when they go through it. If they say no, it's not anything sinister or against you. It's because you're still answerable in the active federal case."

Steve answered carefully, "The lawyer told me they might subpoena my laptop and that I should not erase or change anything."

"He needs his laptop for school and his job," Tracy said. "I'm worried if the federal agents take it, he'll lose his work. Once they have it, it'll be forever before we get it back."

"Don't tell anyone I said this," I replied, "but pay cash for an inexpensive USB drive. Keep it to yourself that you have it, and store it separately from the laptop, maybe in an old backpack you don't use or in the glove compartment of your mom's car. Save all your work on the USB drive occasionally so you won't lose it if they take the laptop.

"Subpoenas can't ask for anything they don't know about or aren't on the premises. There's nothing wrong with using a USB drive, but the feds won't appreciate that I shared that with you. If you have any questions, call your lawyer. Does that help?"

"Yes, it does," Tracy said, smiling thankfully.

Eve's face had a neutral expression. I know her, and that look told me she'd have preferred I not share that with them, and I understood why. But I needed to offer something showing I was on his side to bolster the trust we were building with Steve.

He said hopefully, "They haven't come for my laptop yet, but they have a clone of my cell phone, so maybe they won't need it."

He was still hesitant. I was a teenager once, and I *perfectly* understood that he didn't want his mom finding any links to porn sites on that computer, among other things. Still, he must have realized he couldn't control possession of the machine anyway, saying, "Sure, you can go ahead and take the laptop. I don't need to watch. You'll be there, right?"

I was glad to see the implied trust. "Yes. Either Eve or I will be watching over the process."

"If you let me take it into the precinct this morning," Eve said, "I'll have it back this afternoon. All they need to do is copy out the relevant files. I'll bring it back to you myself."

"Mom, can you get the computer and the power supply from my desk?" Steve asked. "The case for it is on my bookshelf."

"Will you excuse me?" Tracy asked. "Please continue; I'll catch up in a few minutes."

Once she left the room, I leaned toward Steve and said quietly, "Everyone has things on their computer they wouldn't want their parents to know about. We deal with that all the time. Don't worry; it won't ever come up in any reports or file system dumps."

Steve nodded and then, looking down at his socks, quietly said, "Thanks."

From the corner of my eye, I could see Eve winking, one thumb in the air.

CHAPTER 29

I was reviewing my notes when Tracy returned to the living room with the laptop zipped into its case. Finding the entry I wanted, I turned toward Steve.

"Your mom tells me that at some point, you bought a container of paint stripper and black and orange spray paint. I assume for an Aunt Tik's challenge?"

"Yeah, one where I branded a car," Steve answered.

Even though I'd strongly suspected as much, his confirmation that he helped trash Vicky's car was a letdown. The thought brought me back to Earth, reminding me Steve wasn't an innocent victim. I didn't want to interrupt our progress, so I hid my reaction. I saw Eve, way ahead of me in realizing what Steve had done, look down at her fingers intertwined on her lap. I hadn't explicitly mentioned Steve's potential involvement in the BMW vandalism to her. But I'd left her a detailed message from my interview with Vicky Carlson, and Eve had connected the dots.

"How many of these challenges have you performed?"

"I only did those two. I've been on Aunt Tik's website for a year but didn't become a paid member until three months ago when I got my job. The first challenge I bid on was the painting part of the dismemberment branding punk. And you know what happened with the driving challenge."

"Okay, got it — now tell me everything you remember about the branding punk. You said the cell captain was this 'blotto_bill' — the guy with a number after his name, at AuntTiks dot com?"

Steve nodded.

"As I understand it, the cell czar must approve dismembering someone, and then he releases all the ex-member's secret information to use for punking that person. As the challenge performer, do you contact the czar directly to get that information? Or do they post it to everyone, maybe on some forum you go to?"

"No, I never got a message from the czar we had before the new guy, just from the punk master. He was a cell captain. The punk masters know everything about whoever gets dismembered because they write the challenge instructions. They don't usually post private stuff; the information you need is in the challenge notification they send to say your bid won. If the czar is the punk master, then, yeah, you would get the information directly from him. Whoever's doing one of the challenges could spread those personal things around if they wanted to.

"Sometimes that's what the dismemberment punk is, just putting the information out there. Maybe tag the side of a barn or a billboard with something embarrassing about the ex-member — *that* could come from the private info. Or it could be just something like, 'For a good time, call,' and then the dismembered person's cell phone or work number. Or maybe even their mother's, sister's, or daughter's number. Something like that."

"These messages are all encrypted?" Eve asked.

"The Aunt Tik's app takes care of all that, but yes. For the second one I did, the gun, the czar was the punk master. But it wasn't a dismemberment, so there wasn't any member information."

"Okay, got it," I said. "We've confirmed that dismembering somebody is a big deal. But I don't understand why the punk master would assign something that important to someone who'd never done a challenge before. Can you walk me through it?"

"Yes," Steve replied. "It's like a hazing thing — doing a dismembering punk shows everyone you're for real. When you're a free member, they SPAM you a lot about all the fun of doing the punks and seeing the punk results. They pump you up about getting points so you can write punks of your own and collect enough to become a cell captain. They want you to join and pay the membership dues.

"But once you pay, the first thing they hit you with is having to do a dismemberment challenge. My friend's older brother used to be a Marine, and he says it's just like that; they tell you that you'll get to see the world, then right away, when you join, they cut off all your hair, make you march everywhere, and restrict you to the base."

"It's too bad they don't tell you exactly what *part* of the world you are going to see," Eve said, opening a little window into her personal experience in the service. "Trust me; I know."

Steve gave her a sardonic grin and turned back to me. "When you join Aunt Tik's, you get this manual. It tells you that discipline and timing matter. If you don't do your challenge on time, it messes up the challenges for everyone else, and then the punk doesn't go how it should. They say some punks have two dozen challenges, so twenty-four people who don't know each other have to get their act together for it to work. So, be on time and do your challenge right, but as quickly as possible.

"The other big rules are: Don't screw up your challenge or mess up the work anyone else did in the challenges that were ahead of you. Don't get caught, and don't do anything stupid to get anyone else busted.

"That means you're supposed to wear gloves and a mask if you're doing anything where anyone could see you, and cover yourself all over; like, don't wear shorts or a tank top. Wear stuff that blends in, no jewelry, nothing that makes you stand out or can identify you. They have articles on the Aunt Tik's website that tell you how to do some of these things so it's safe and you don't get caught."

"I take it they enforce those rules with the threat of dismemberment?" I asked.

"If you mess any of that up, they can dismember you. They put all the dismemberments right up front on their results page. You're not supposed to commit any crimes when you do a challenge, but I guess that doesn't apply when dismembering somebody. Dismembering is a big deal. Maybe the most important thing, in some ways."

Eve broke in. "We've heard about the 'no-crime' rule several times from different sources. But how is that governed? I get that if somebody does an innocent challenge illegally, maybe shoplifting something they were supposed to buy, they might get dismembered if they get caught.

"For proposed challenges with any upfront illegality to them, I assumed it would be the punk masters who rejected those. But given what happened to you, that can't be true. You accepted a challenge that sounded innocent when you first read it. It wasn't. But the instructions prohibited you from looking — the only way you could have learned it was illegal."

Eve let that sink in, then continued, "Keeping people from discovering something's against the law doesn't sound like 'not committing crimes' to me. That's criminal in and of itself, something we call 'obstruction.'

"Now you're saying there's also a de facto exception to the illegality rule, which applies to dismembering punks. That leaves only one last line of defense in these challenges, as far as breaking the law is concerned. So, here's my question, Steve: Is there anything in the rules where you're allowed to say, 'Hey, I can't do this challenge because it's criminal'?"

He thought a moment.

"No, not really. Everything I know in the rules says they can dismember me for not following the instructions when I looked under the hood. They don't say anything about reporting something illegal."

Pursing her lips, Eve shook her head.

"I was afraid you were going to say that. Any other problematic rules — or lack thereof?"

"Well, another big deal is your first challenge. It's like your initiation. Aunt Tik's hooks you up virtually with another experienced member — kind of a guide — so you can ask questions over e-mail. My guide told me they always use new members for the risky parts of the dismemberment challenges.

"That's mainly because those challenges are the only ones that, supposedly, get close to being illegal. It's partly to make sure the new guys get the message of how important dismemberment is — but also so if they screw up, the only people that get in trouble are the newbies. After you do your first one, you're like, 'in' with the cool guys. Then you can see more challenges to bid on."

The structure of the organization seemed designed to cover someone's ass, but not necessarily those of its members, especially not the new ones.

"Thanks, Steve," I said. "That helps us get a feel for what's going on."

SDPD detectives would want to apply for Aunt Tik's member accounts for investigative purposes. I needed to know what would happen if one of their accounts was exposed. "Suppose you join with someone else, and then one of you gets dismembered. Aunt Tik's wouldn't necessarily know which other members were your friends. Your buddies could get revenge by screwing with the game, maybe hacking a server or something on that order. If Aunt Tik's learns who your friends are, are they dismembered too?"

"They watch out for that. When I got my membership, a bunch of guys who worked together at a Powerhouse gym became paid members. One of them blew off performing their challenge. When he got dismembered, the other trainers who joined when he did bid on his dismemberment punk challenges. They intentionally messed them up so nothing would happen to that first guy.

"Aunt Tik's kicked them all out because they have a rule in the manual: you must tell Aunt Tik's which members you know when you join. If you don't, and they find out, they can dismember everybody in your group. They also go by dates. They know who joins around the same time you do. When they dismember somebody, anyone listed as a friend or who joined when they did sees only the kind of challenges the new members select from. It's like they have to prove themselves all over.

"That makes it even worse when you get dismembered because it screws with the friends you had outside the game, too, and they get pissed off at you. There was a big discussion about all this in the member forum when the Powerhouse trainers were booted out."

"Makes sense they'd have to do that," Eve ventured. "You said earlier that you get your challenge instructions by e-mail from the punk master once you bid on a challenge and win it. In what other ways can members exchange messages? I'm trying to understand how we might get in through the back door."

"Most people use Signal because it's encrypted. But you can also use regular e-mail — the e-mail has a link to the encrypted message, and there's a little utility included with your Aunt Tik's app to decrypt it. If you do it with your phone through their Android app, the e-mail gets encrypted or decrypted automatically."

Steve looked at his mother apologetically. "My mom knew what Signal was because my dad used it to cheat on her with his new girlfriend while they were still married. I didn't want her to find the Signal app on my notebook and think I was doing something to hurt her, too. So, I erased it and always got my messages by e-mail."

Tracy gave a slight cough and looked down, focusing on her fingernails. As a mom myself, I understood her mixed feelings. Her son showed consideration for her, something she could take pride in as a mother; choosing concealment as his means told her she still had more work to do.

CHAPTER 30

The living room went briefly quiet. Steve had just reminded us that the thoughts battling for attention inside his head were complicated, even before considering his relationship with his mom. Still, the problems we were helping him solve were more about his poor choices than his character.

I framed my next question to put him in the driver's seat and back in positive territory. "Tell me everything you can about your first challenge. You bid on it to get points. How does that work, exactly?"

"When you log in, there's a section listing the challenges you're eligible for. Each has a general description, telling you when they posted it, the start time for the punk it's part of, and when the challenge needs to finish. They also tell you the lowest points anyone's bid so far."

Eve had a puzzled look on her face.

"I get the reverse auction concept, but why do they want to lower the bids?"

"It talks about that in Aunt Tik's manual. They choose the cell captains each month based on who has the most points. If they didn't do a reverse auction, people would bid crazy amounts to get promoted after doing only a few challenges. Having the lowest bid win solves that problem."

"Put that way, it makes sense," I acknowledged.

"You can't always bid lower points to get a challenge," Steve continued. "They have ways to limit how low you can bid if you haven't done a lot of challenges or if the punks didn't work on some of the ones you performed. Maybe they only let you bid down to five thousand points on a challenge, something like that. It's a way to keep screwups from bidding if what they messed up before wasn't bad enough to dismember them."

He saw my slightly glazed expression at the tide of information.

"All the rules are in the manual, but it's confusing. If you do the challenges the way you're supposed to, it's no big deal. For brand-new premium members bidding on dismemberment punks, they don't enforce any limits. They don't want to discourage newbies from taking those."

Eve had a talent for getting to the core of things.

"So, that's why you picked the branding challenge. You were new, wanting to prove yourself, and Aunt Tik's only offered you dismemberment punk challenges."

She'd just pointed out that Steve hadn't necessarily *wanted* to destroy Vicky's car; to get the points and recognition he wanted, Steve chose from bad options he didn't control. It's subtle but meaningful when considering Aunt Tik's culpability.

"Yes. The dismemberment punk challenge I won was cut-and-paste: 'Paint the side of somebody's car with spray paint.' There are quite a few like that. Some say to add graffiti, a message, or use specific colors. This one wanted 'punk'd bitch,' black over orange. The last bid was 5,000 points, so I bid 4,999.

"The instructions with the challenge notification letting me know I won my bid had a specific time and location. They described the car and mentioned sanding the windows and applying the paint stripper first. I wasn't sure if I was supposed to do that, too. So, I took some of my dad's sandpaper and bought some stripper when I got the paint."

"The purchases you made with your mom's credit card?" Eve asked.

"Yeah. The time set in the instructions was before my payday."

Steve looked down at his feet, away from his mother.

"When I got paid, I bought replacement paint and stripper and then tried to return that to the store using the first receipt. But they needed the original credit card for the refund, and I'd already put it back in Mom's purse."

Tracy, who'd been quiet most of the discussion, smiled as she spoke. "Steve's got a card in his name now. The interest rate's steep, but he'll have more flexibility to handle budget issues. I'm sure borrowing my card without permission won't be a problem again."

"Thanks, Mom, and I'm sorry." Steve's apology seemed genuine.

I wanted some context for Steve's surprise reveal earlier.

"We didn't intend to make you feel bad; we just needed confirmation. You're doing great. The notification came from 'blotto_bill?' He was just a cell captain?"

Steve shook his head.

"He sent it like he was a cell captain. But he'd been the czar for a month, maybe two, according to the messages in the members' forum. I guess the czars get to keep their member accounts. Maybe he forgot to switch to his new czar e-mail account?"

Learning that our person of interest had two Aunt Tik's user names might be helpful — I pushed forward.

"Okay, good. What happened next?"

"They use GPS coordinates for locations instead of streets and names of things, maybe for security. The car wasn't there when I went where it was supposed to be. I sent a Signal message to my guide and copied the punk master to ask what I should do. It was getting late, and I was about ready to go home; then the punk master called me with the right coordinates."

"He *called* you?" Eve was startled, and I shared her reaction. "Wasn't everything supposed to be encrypted messages, no direct contact between members?"

"Yeah, I'd never heard of them doing that either," Steve said, seeming confused that it was such a big deal to us. "But I'd told them in my message that I couldn't stay where I was very long because it was a bad neighborhood; people were starting to check me out.

"He must have decided it would be better to call me directly so I didn't get beat up or robbed."

I needed clarity.

"But you heard this guy's voice?"

Steve nodded.

"This was 'blotto_bill?' Or was it your guide?"

"The guy who called me back said he was the punk master. So yeah, it was blotto_bill, I suppose."

Eve wanted to be sure.

"Would you recognize the voice if you heard it again?"

"He didn't say much, and it was over a cell phone, but, sure, I think so."

"That's good to know." Eve nodded as she made eye contact with me.

"What happened once you got where you were supposed to be?" I asked.

He paused to recall the scene.

"When I arrived, a tractor-trailer was parked parallel with the BMW on the driver's side, maybe eight feet away. 'Hyundai Leasing' was written in small letters on the side of the trailer — I remember that because it was funny to me. They make these little Korean cars, and here's this big trailer with their name on it.

"A Hummer was parked at one end of the trailer, perpendicular to it across the back of the car. On the other end of the semi was a Transit van parked at a right angle, covering most of the front end of the Beamer. They made this little room to work in, and the whole side of the BMW was like a painting canvas. Nobody could see in unless they walked right up to it."

Eve raised a finger.

"I take it this was in a remote corner of the lot?"

"Yeah, back where the mall employees park. Somebody had already sanded the windows and put some chemicals on the paint. There was sanding dust on the pavement, and some of the paint was gooey, sagging, and dripping on the ground, still wet.

"I sprayed Day-Glo orange all over the car's driver's side, on top of the whole mess. The spray paint started sagging, but mostly just at the bottom. It was dope — looked artistic, like I did it that way on purpose. I had twenty-two cans of orange and two cans of black, and I used up all the orange.

"I tagged the side in big black letters. Then, I got the idea to add an arrow pointing to the driver's window. With it painted orange, I figured she'd have to roll the glass down to see her side mirror — pointing out her profile that way would be awesome."

I wanted to confirm how Steve knew her gender.

"The challenge acceptance notification told you the owner was a woman?"

"Yes. That was pretty much it. I put the empty cans in the box and walked away with them."

"And when was all of this?" Eve asked.

"It was three months ago, maybe a little more," Steve answered, then snorted. "I had orange overspray on my hair and hoodie when I got home. I looked like a pumpkin exploded in front of my face."

"How did I not see you?" Tracy asked.

"You were at work, Mom. I still had the paint thinner, so I used it to get the paint off me and out of my hair. That stuff *stings*. I used the Febreze from the bathroom to cover the smell and threw away my clothes so you wouldn't see them in the wash."

"I remember the house smelling *too* good." Tracy shook her head slightly. "I thought the cat got into the scented candles."

"The next day, a picture of the Beamer was on the Aunt Tik's website without the semi or other cars. It looked sweet, and I had 4,999 points, plus a thousand bonus points for a successful punk, next to my Aunt Tik's handle. I was pretty happy about that."

I made a mental note to talk with Eve later about whether Steve should meet Vicky Carlson. Steve seemed a decent kid at heart, but his priorities and moral compass were more than a little screwed up. It might do him good to face the full consequences of his actions.

For now, I'd plow ahead.

"Do you know who did the other challenges to this punk? And how many do you think there were?"

"No, they're strict about never letting you know who else is in Aunt Tik's. They say it's for your safety so you won't get outed.

"But I think it's more because the other members could be anybody, and you have to be careful because you don't know who might rat you out. It could be your friend, your teacher, or your girlfriend. So, you can't talk about it to anyone else, except if somebody joined when you did, maybe with them. Or I guess the sponsor who vouched for you if you were tight."

"By the way, who sponsored you?" Eve was looking for any other leads to premium Aunt Tik's members.

"I don't know, they never told me."

Eve nodded in acknowledgment, and Steve continued, "My guide explained that they break the punks into as many separate challenges as possible. Say somebody sees you doing one part of it, and you are tall and wearing a gray hoodie. Another guy comes along to do the next challenge, and he's short and wearing a maroon jacket. If there were witnesses for any of the challenges, their stories wouldn't jibe at all. The police aren't going to believe a dozen guys all worked together on this one punk. That wouldn't make any sense to them."

Eve took exception.

"You might want to rethink that, Steve. I'm here, so the department does follow through on some crazy things."

I had to give him some credit — Steve started backpedaling immediately.

"I didn't mean *I* thought that. I meant that Aunt Tik's thinks that because of how they set it up. But I see what you're saying."

Steve gave us his best get-out-of-jail-free-card smile.

"So, the dismembering branding punk I did my challenge for was probably at least eight or nine people.

"I don't know if they changed where the car was; that probably would take one person. Okay, say they didn't move it. So, one member drove the semi in beside the car. Another brought the Transit van in; that's two. A third person parked the Hummer. Somebody else sanded the windows and applied the paint stripper; that's four.

"I do the painting, that's five. Another guy drives the Hummer away, and that makes six. A different member removes the Transit van, seven, and then one returns the semi, that's eight. Some other person, maybe the punk master, takes the picture. That's nine people.

"Who'll believe somebody hired, like, the LA Lakers starters times two just to tag a car?"

I had to admit I was impressed.

"In a way, it's scary smart. A certain amount of evasiveness gets baked in. Could be coincidental, I suppose …."

Eve challenged that thought.

"When we see accountability purposefully stripped from questionable behaviors in law enforcement, words like 'premeditated' come to mind, and we start thinking about intent. Not about anything *you've* done, but the game as a whole."

There was a pause as we considered her point.

"Eve, is there anything else we should ask Steve while we're here?"

"I've got enough to hold me for a while," she replied. "I'll need to take all this in, and I might have more questions later."

I stood.

"Steve, Tracy, I think that's all we have for now, and I'm sure we'll get to chat again. It's been a pleasure, even under what I know are unpleasant circumstances. In the meantime, Steve, keep your head down, stick to your routine, and be sure to call me if you think there's anything unusual going on. You've been a ton of help here today. Hopefully, our team can get ahead of some of this stuff."

I turned to our hostess.

"Thanks, Tracy. I understand how difficult this has been for you, but things are turning around."

"It was good to see you again, and it was nice to meet you, Eve." Tracy reached out to shake Eve's hand.

"Thanks for coming over," Steve said. "I'll be on my best behavior, I promise. Just be careful who you tell. Almost anybody can join Aunt Tik's."

Looking at Steve, I said somberly, "Noted and understood."

I gave him a thumbs-up as I turned to follow Eve out the door and then to our car.

It would take considerable time for me to realize that I hadn't fully understood the implications of what Steve was telling me.

Not in the least.

CHAPTER 31

Paul had left Eve a message asking her to ping him in the lab when she returned to the precinct. After her call, he headed over to her cubicle.

Paul sat in her side chair as Eve related what she'd learned when she and Debra Ann interviewed Tracy and Steve. Both Paul's hands were together in midair, the tips of his thumbs and fingers touching, elbows on the armrests.

"I was thinking about your discovery yesterday of blotto_bill's and Aunt Tik's involvement in all five of these cases, now including Steve's," he said.

"We need to push that tidbit up the chain of command. Louis needs to know the blotto_bill connections to the three cases we sent him and the federal charges. The Escalation Management team handling the James Marshall case will want the information. You know how they are — if they were making any progress, we'd have heard about it. I don't know if they're looking in the right places or for the right things.

"That blotto_bill link to Steve confirms this guy's too involved in all of this. Your interview with Steve and his mother doesn't necessarily add anything to the homicide cases. Still, it supports the general idea that these people are crossing the lines.

"Your work got us blotto_bill as the punk master, so it's your choice: do you want to do the honors and make those calls?"

"Lt. Brooks's team has overheard me chewing them out for showboating." Eve wrinkled her nose. "So we're not exactly BFFs, you know? Why don't *you* talk to them? Toss in my name wherever you think it'll do me some good."

"Okay, fair enough." Paul laughed. "I'll make sure you get the credit you're due."

⊱ ─────── ⊰

Returning to his desk, Paul called Lt. Ezra Brooks. The lieutenant picked up after two rings.

"Lieutenant, glad I caught you — Paul Castro, the criminalist supervisor working with Homicide. Do you have a moment?"

"Sure, Paul, I have ten minutes I can give you. If you think you'll need more, tell me now."

"That should be plenty. It's about the James Marshall roadside homicide from a few months ago. I hadn't heard anything about closing the case, so I wondered if you're still working it."

"We put the word out on the street when it first came to us and several times since, and we've been shaking the trees — you know, the 'usual suspects.' But just between you and me, we haven't caught any breaks yet."

"I'm sorry it's not going better, but I have something that might help. Do you remember when you called Det. Robbins, a couple of weeks into the case, asking her about an e-mail that referenced a 'blotto underscore bill'?"

"Yes, of course; we've been trying to tie that to an e-mail address or Internet user account. No luck so far."

"I just learned of your e-mail. Det. Robbins forwarded it to the other detectives, but there wasn't a Forensics tie-in that would have gone to me. Try 'blotto underscore bill underscore 7492 at AuntTiks dot com.' But if you intend to contact that individual, do me a favor and let me know beforehand.

"We have an unusual situation over here — to save time, I'll skip the finer points — but we're looking into something off-the-books as a side effect of a federal investigation. We turned up an organization called 'Aunt Tik's.' We've tied them to an incident with a remote-controlled AR-15 targeting a judge's residence."

"Yes, we have the same name, 'Aunt Tik's,' a gaming website Marshall ran. We looked but didn't see anything there — certainly, nothing involving guns and judges. That's big-time, but like you said, on the feds' turf."

"When they transferred the Marshall case to you," Paul explained, "the feds were looking at a teenager for transporting the gun in their case. Our investigators had just stumbled across the Aunt Tik's connection; the feds *still* aren't entirely up to speed on that part.

"Our detectives' angle is this Aunt Tik's. The theory is that the local franchisee facilitates some of these bad behaviors. And Det. Byrne turned up none other than your 'blotto_bill' as a person of interest. We show him responsible for the challenge that ordered the delivery of the assembled weapon to the judge's location."

There was a noticeable pause on the line.

"I'll grant you that this blotto_bill deserves more attention…," Brooks hesitantly admitted. Paul remembered something Louis once said about the Escalation Management team's unwillingness to acknowledge ideas they didn't originate. Paul decided to dig in.

"So, here's a thought that occurred to me," Paul continued. "Remember, all this is hypothetical, and I'm way out on a limb here. Before you took over the case, Robbins and Byrne did their preliminaries and knew James Marshall was heavily involved with an online social media gaming website that plays jokes on people, the one we now know as Aunt Tik's," Paul said.

"That much we have," Brooks confirmed.

"Marshal was the founder and head, the 'cell czar,' of the San Diego chapter. As of now, we've learned nothing inherently criminal about the organization itself. But we know aspects of its operations and methods are hackable. We don't know to what extent yet, but at least to the point of aiming a loaded AR-15 with a remote trigger at a judge's house."

"Okay, so you've got blotto_bill as a common denominator. Pretty weak for linking Aunt Tik's and Marshall's murder," Brooks said, not buying into it.

"There's more. None of us likes coincidences; we've got several here. First, we've got the e-mail you found from James Marshall to himself, expressing strong emotions in conjunction with a 'blotto_bill' and a 'tractor.'

"Oddly enough, we've run across a double homicide staged as an Aunt Tik's punk involving an end loader just before the Marshall e-mail. We've since learned 'blotto_bill' was in charge of that punk.

"Three days after the e-mail, James Marshall winds up dead alongside the highway.

"Just days after that, our Aunt Tik's member, blotto_bill, becomes the local Aunt Tik's new cell czar.

"Next up, we've got blotto_bill having that AR-15 delivered.

"Finally, we've got blotto_bill orchestrating two additional punks resulting in odd murders, one from a peanut allergy, another using two old trucks.

"We're just starting, and already, that's a lot of smoke. Enough to start looking for a fire."

Brooks paused.

"I'll need to give this some thought. I see where you're going, and I won't necessarily say it's a stretch. But you must admit, there are a lot of pieces. My first question is whether the 'blotto_bill' account belongs to just one person or several who share it."

"It's interesting that you mentioned 'a lot of pieces,' Lieutenant, because breaking complex tasks into many parts is Aunt Tik's' calling card."

"OK, Paul, I'll look into your idea some more. We'll sync up again and coordinate our resources if there's something to it. But I appreciate that you stayed on that username and got back to me."

"You can thank Eve Byrne. She was the one who burnt the midnight oil to chase it down. Thanks for hearing me out, and I hope it helps."

No one was questioning that the James Marshall case was likely an old-school homicide, and Paul understood why Brooks would have some doubts. Even so, that Marshall's murder was related to Aunt Tik's was clear to Paul, even though it didn't utilize the challenge-punk metaphor. However, Paul's wasn't the opinion that mattered.

Paul's next call went to Louis. He told him everything he'd told Brooks, explaining how the username had come up in Steve's case and tied the Marshall homicide to those he'd sent Louis earlier as potential Aunt Tik's killings — Mabry, Littman, Foreman, and Barker.

There was a moment of silence before Louis responded. "We were looking for just one murder to confirm our theory … Now it seems we've turned up a serial killer, and a prolific one at that."

Days starting with great news had been a rarity since Detective Marci Robbins's assignment to the Escalation Management team; today would be a welcome exception. She learned from the first e-mail she opened that word had come down from above — they now had an official investigation of Aunt Tik's to coordinate with the department's cases around four open homicides.

Both crushed-car deaths, as well as the runaway trucks murder, had been flagged as potential Aunt Tik's homicides. They'd also include the cereal tampering case. However, the Aunt Tik's elements of that killing would wait until the team had resolved the other murders.

Lieutenant Harbin had convinced the brass that the 'tractor' referenced in the 'blotto_bill' e-mail tied to James Marshall's murder was the end loader that dumped the concrete on that Fiesta. Still, the upper ranks had decided the Marshall case would remain with Escalation Management.

Because of the political realities — specifically, pressure on the department from the divorce attorney's law firm — the twin truck collisions would get the initial priority from Lt. Harbin's detectives.

Marci would no longer be assisting Lt. Brooks's team; instead, she'd take the lead in Homicide's new Aunt Tik's case. Eve Byrne would serve as second chair, and Paul Castro would be the Forensics liaison. Lt. Robert Strickland had volunteered his assistance, loaned by the Vice unit for the duration of the Aunt Tik's cases. His role would be to provide investigative experience related to the Internet and the digital realm.

The investigative teams working the four homicides and detectives working the Marshall case for Escalation Management would continue their work, handing off the Aunt Tik's-related elements of those cases to Marci's new squad.

Marci's first step in her latest assignment was to assess status. Several weeks ago, Paul had sent Capt. Cranston a list of URLs and Internet addresses meant for Strickland to explore as he got the time. The request had somehow fallen between the cracks. Paul hadn't followed up — his and Eve's regular work and the informal Aunt Tik's investigation had them swamped. So far, nothing on that list of addresses had stopped either from moving ahead.

Marci suspected that Paul wasn't as enthusiastic about working with Strickland as he'd always been with others in the department. Perhaps it was because there wasn't a pressing or immediate need for Strickland's services. But now that the investigation was official and Strickland was formally part of the team, Marci expected Paul would welcome the man's expertise.

She'd arrange a meeting between the Vice Lieutenant and the rest of the team to kick-start working together. Her first call went out to Strickland, who answered on the first ring.

"Good morning, Lieutenant — Detective Marci Robbins in Homicide. I don't know if you got the news yet — we now have an official investigation of Aunt Tik's that includes four of the active homicide investigations. I'll be leading our efforts. I'm finishing my stint with Escalation Management and wanted to see if you'd gotten the e-mail."

"Hi, Detective, no," Strickland answered after some hesitation, not sounding overly excited, perhaps because he wasn't yet aware he'd have a role in the case. "I just got out of a meeting here in Vice. I hadn't heard."

"I'm calling because the powers that be took you up on your offer to help. You've been assigned to our team until these cases are solved."

Again, Marci noticed a slight pause.

"Good, Detective, that's great. It sounds like an interesting set of cases, and I'm looking forward to helping out." Marci wasn't hearing a lot of energy in his voice, but maybe the meeting he'd just come from had been rough.

"Do you have time for a quick get-together this morning, say ten o'clock, in the homicide conference room? No preparation needed; just introductions and mapping our strategy."

"Yes, no problem. I'll let Capt. Cranston know, and I'll be there."

"Thanks, Lieutenant. See you then."

Marci hung up and looked across the bullpen for Eve. Spotting her at her desk, Marci walked on over. "Capt. Jarvis included you among the recipients of his e-mail. Did you get a chance to see it?"

"Just reading it now," Eve replied. "Hmmm, too bad we didn't get the Marshall case, too. Robert Strickland? I wish they had loaned us Jeff Bennett instead. Strickland never did get back to us on that list of URLs we asked him about."

Great minds do think alike.

Marci smiled to herself — Eve's comment about Bennett mirrored Paul's remarks when Strickland offered his services.

"I know," Marci acknowledged. "I assume they chose Strickland because he volunteered when things were unofficial, and he outranks Jeff. We'll make do. Have time for a quick meeting at ten? I'll be out of my signoff meeting with Brooks by then. I called Strickland, and he'll be there. It'll just be the four of us, but we'll use the conference room anyway."

"That works for me," Eve replied. "The medical examiner's reports came back on that murder/suicide across from Birch Aquarium, and I should have just enough time to close out the case file.

"From what I've seen so far, this Aunt Tik's thing oughta be interesting."

THE WRITINGS OF
AVRIL MARIA SERENE

CHAPTER 32

Promptly at ten, Detectives Marci Robbins and Eve Byrne, Criminalist Supervisor Paul Castro, and Lieutenant Robert Strickland gathered in the conference room outside the bullpen, laptops in tow.

"We're a small team; we'll work closely together," Marci said, "so I think we can drop the formalities of rank inside this room. Does anyone have any objection?"

I need any issues Strickland has out in the open, Marci thought, *and dispense with them constantly resurfacing.*

"Not a problem," Eve said, the other two nodding.

"And you can call me Bob." Despite his offer of informality, the older investigator didn't fit in with the rumples and wrinkles among the others, his expensive suit tailored perfectly to his stocky body, with nary a salt-and-pepper hair out of place.

"Thanks, Bob," Marci replied. "First, some history — Eve and I caught the James Marshall homicide when the body turned up in an Audi alongside the 52. Escalation Management took the case over; before today, I've been providing investigative support to their team.

"The department became aware of a federal case around transporting a loaded AR-15 to park across from Judge Wasserman's residence and, ultimately, the connection to Aunt Tik's online presence. The feds weren't taking the latter seriously, but we were concerned we didn't know what Aunt Tik's was. More importantly, it seemed to have the capacity to do real harm.

"That concern proved prescient. We're now looking at four murders with an Aunt Tik's connection, in addition to Marshall's."

Bob abruptly straightened in his seat, leaning forward with his elbows on the table, his expression concerned as Marci continued.

"We know this because of Eve's off-the-books work, with help from Paul and a local investigative reporter, Debra Ann Wynn. I believe you've met her socially, Bob, but if you weren't aware, Debra Ann is Paul's wife.

"Before the decision came down to make a formal case around Aunt Tik's, Eve and Paul had been working this in the background while keeping Lt. Harbin in the loop."

Bob nodded, a slight frown on his face.

"We sincerely appreciate your volunteering and expertise — welcome to the team, Bob. I'm sorry that we have the momentary advantage regarding the specific details of the Aunt Tik's portion of these cases."

Marci thought she caught a brief smirk from Bob as he shifted in his chair, but she quickly dismissed the idea.

"We'll get you caught up on everything. Since we've not worked together before, let's share some of our careers and credentials."

Marci, Eve, and Paul spoke briefly about themselves and their exploits. Bob then took the floor.

"My given name's Robert Strickland. I've been a police officer for eighteen years, the last nearly two years as a lieutenant. I'm second in command of the Vice unit under Capt. Cranston, better known around here as 'Mondo.'

"Before coming here, I spent seven and a half years working Vice cases in San José. I've become fluent in computer and Internet technologies related to prostitution, child pornography, and sexual exploitation investigations. I've taken courses from Carnegie Mellon University in Silicon Valley. Those primarily dealt with software tools and techniques for locating and deciphering data on the Internet and in databases."

"That experience will help," Eve said. "We've gone as far as we can mining the Aunt Tik's member messages forum. We need access to their encrypted data servers."

"Let me add to that before I forget." Paul jumped in. "We also want to hack the user apps that new Aunt Tik's members download, along with the website and its web services. That might tell us the server addresses and provide clues for data access. Sorry, Bob; please continue."

Bob nodded but took no notes.

"My stint in law enforcement began with academy training here in San Diego. I served here for the first nine years of my career. At that point, my mother became ill. She lived in San José. California's Law Enforcement Mutual Aid Plan helped me land a temporary assignment to the San José Police Department. That became permanent once their Vice unit had an opening.

"My mother's surgery allowed her to care for herself. By that time, I was a newly minted lieutenant. When San Diego's Vice unit posted an opening, I sought a transfer back."

Eve's eyes showed surprise that Bob had served in San Diego previously, and Marci knew why. Typically, a prodigal son's return generates lots of fanfare. Perhaps that had happened within the Vice community, and Homicide missed the celebration.

"Glad to have you on board, Bob," Marci said. "A quick refresher as to how we got here. A little over a month ago, Lt. Harbin was asked by a neighbor, Tracy Nielsen, to look into the arrest of her nineteen-year-old son, Steve, by federal agents. He was the driver of the vehicle transporting the assault rifle."

"I wondered how the department became involved in a federal case," Bob commented. "Still, dangerous business."

"Even so, it wouldn't ordinarily fall in Homicide's lap. But the young man convinced us that he was merely playing a bit part in a social media game, one we now know as 'Aunt Tik's.' When we checked it out, we learned that as off-the-wall as they sounded, his statements turned out to be accurate. I don't believe anything the young man's told us has proven untrue."

Marci looked at Eve for confirmation.

"Not as far as I know," Eve agreed.

"Of course, the vehicle, the loaded assault rifle, its remote operation, the threat, and our judge were quite real. It turned out that transporting the weapon was just one small act, or 'challenge,' in a string of similar challenges assembled into an Aunt Tik's 'punk.' Aunt Tik's describes a punk as ending in a punch line. Someone's perverted this one into an attempted murder.

"To be clear, those performing the challenges know only their part of the punk. They're clueless about the full scope and intent of what they think is a multi-player prank or who's doing the other challenges. They honestly believe their actions are just part of a big joke. Luckily for us, the younger Nielsen violated his challenge instructions by looking at what he was transporting; that tipped the first domino, leading to our involvement.

"Otherwise, the judge would be dead, and we'd be trying to match evidence around her shooting to a single individual who never existed — a ghost."

"But as things stand, it's, at most, attempted murder," Bob noted, "along with weapons charges. There was no killing. How does that fit the Homicide unit's mission?"

"True, we didn't have a deceased body." Marci flashed a wry smile. "But the incident exposed a deadly threat that could easily target someone and end their life, and we'd been oblivious to it.

"Unfortunately, you missed the information dump from Andy Pardone, another Aunt Tik's member. Eve has extensive notes, and I'll get you a recording of the interview if you need it. Eve, could you give Bob a crash course on Aunt Tik's, once we finish here? I know you've got a full plate, but that will help get us to the encrypted data much faster."

"I'd be happy to," Eve replied.

"Thanks. As we learned how Aunt Tik's functioned, we realized our doer co-opted their process for the attempted murder. We also recognized this probably wasn't the first and wouldn't be the last such event. On a hunch, Eve and Paul walked through the department's open cases, identifying four unsolved homicides with all the earmarks of Aunt Tik's involvement.

"There were other candidates, including cold cases, and we'll need to explore them at some point. Eve and Paul submitted three events that caused four killings, along with their field notes and other documentation, in their request for a formal investigation of Aunt Tik's. Upper management reviewed them to determine if an official investigation of Aunt Tik's was warranted — all three passed muster.

"In the meantime, we've had two developments. First, Eve's found punk result videos related to the three cases on Aunt Tik's website."

Bob's frown had deepened.

"Earlier, you said 'doer' in the singular. With all these people involved, what makes you think that?"

"Our second development — we've also established that one individual e-mail address is tied not only to the feds' case and ours but to Escalation Management's investigation of the Marshall murder. We're thinking they're running the show; the rest are patsies. That assessment may change, but even so, they're involved in five murders, four of them firmly in our wheelhouse."

Marci noticed a change in Bob's demeanor – he now seemed genuinely worried.

"Do we create a new case from scratch just on Aunt Tik's, or do we work the Aunt Tik's elements as extensions to the three existing cases?"

"When Eve and Paul started this, they kept a separate case file as though it would someday become a formal investigation. Because we didn't know of any homicides at that point, the case relates primarily to Aunt Tik's and its members. The only piece missing was the case file number, which the brass gave us. We'll keep all Aunt Tik's-specific investigation materials in that file. Eve, Paul, you, and I will become the subject-matter experts on all things Aunt Tik's, and we'll counsel the teams working the three homicide cases."

Bob chewed on his lower lip.

"Are we treating Aunt Tik's as the criminal subjects of this investigation?"

Marci's face bore the hint of a smile.

"A sage man named Louis Harbin once told me we'll have a problem if we approach Aunt Tik's as inherently criminal — they are not. To most people, it's just a social media gaming website where you can have perfectly legal fun. If we went after Aunt Tik's as being the bad guys, we'd get tangled up in free speech issues and a lot of other crap.

"We're assuming one or more individual members of Aunt Tik's have orchestrated bad things; as far as we know now, Aunt Tik's merely provided the structure, methods, and personnel that, although legal, enabled the mastermind.

"It's not too different from perps using burner phones to plan crimes — the fact that the cell phone companies make the secret planning possible doesn't mean we can go after them. Our case file will include those elements of Aunt Tik's that have been used or abused by individuals committing crimes. The criminal activity itself will remain with their current case files."

"So, the result will be adjunct information bundled for merging with criminal cases as the DA sees fit?" Eve displayed her usual grasp of an evolving situation.

"That's the general idea," Marci replied. "Next, we'll develop a specific strategy for proceeding with the Aunt Tik's case. But before we get into that, I wanted to share some thoughts on our approach. Andy did a fantastic job presenting the complexities of Aunt Tik's in a way that helped us understand what's going on with it.

"But as someone who followed the rules in play, he didn't push the corners of the envelope to test the finer points of this thing.

"He didn't have to.

"He doesn't answer to the massive problem we're responsible for solving — the dead bodies of innocent civilians beginning to stack up like cordwood all around this damned thing."

CHAPTER 33

As everyone returned to their seats after a ten-minute break, Marci took the floor.

"Andy Pardone's guidance gave us a running start. We came away with a better idea of how Aunt Tik's intends things to work. But our guy — I'm assuming gender from little things in the case files; still, it's a guess — is not only using Aunt Tik's technology to kill people; he's gotten away with it so far. Several times. That means he's intelligent, knowledgeable, and thinking way outside the box. If we're going to solve these murders, we need to get out there with him.

"Andy explained that no one knows who does the other parts in a punk, where, as a member, you've bid on and won the right to perform a challenge. This intentional ignorance or siloing creates plausible deniability that protects all the members. For example, the fact that we caught Steve doesn't help us determine who performed the other challenges, like the one setting up the remote control on that AR-15. That's the first issue to tackle, as I see it."

"But I think not knowing about the other challenges creates one other, even bigger, problem," Paul warned. "No one would know if the punk master slipped in another challenge, one hidden from everyone else.

"To attract challenge bidders, whoever is manipulating this needs the punk and its other challenges to be public within Aunt Tik's. However, they *can't* include a challenge that calls for murder. So, they create a punk with the elements necessary to achieve a 'normal' result. But it'll be missing one or more steps that accomplish their true goal. Suppose in the original public version of Steve's punk that the weapon *was* a paintball gun, the destination a disgraced celebrity's business. Whoever set up those remote flight controls, and everyone else who'd done a challenge before that, was working with a toy gun. They'd have no reason to believe this was anything but a sophisticated prank."

"So, the punk master," Eve interjected, "not wanting to be seen in the judge's neighborhood, swaps the AR-15 for the paintball gun between the challenge that installed the auto-fire remote control and Steve moving the car. One trigger mechanism isn't all that much different from any other, so it wouldn't be that hard to adapt. The punk master puts a hood over the whole thing, adding an instruction to Steve's challenge notification not to look under that cover."

Marci bought in.

"As a punk master, you could pervert innocent punks into illegal acts by adding secret challenges performed by you or people you trust. Or simply editing one or more items in the downstream instructions. Like, say, changing the GPS coordinates for the delivery."

"But punk masters are cell captains," Bob objected. "They don't have access to private data about members. The cell czar would see what the captain was doing. Too many checks and balances — there's no way a punk master could change a punk after posting with the challenges bid out. Wouldn't work the way you're suggesting."

Bob came up to speed quickly, Marci thought.

Unfazed, Eve ran with the idea.

"Try this on for size: Dozens, maybe hundreds, of these challenges are posted for bidding at any one time, right? For the czar to see what the punk master was doing, he'd have to spot an alteration in a specific challenge, just one of many for the punk, and recall what the original challenge said. GPS coordinates are what, six to eighteen numbers long? Who catches a change that tiny in terabytes of data? Unless the czar was a real micromanager, which seems a little unusual in a gaming scenario. Still, the czar couldn't see a hidden or never-recorded change added to the punk.

"I think it'd be risky, but possible, for a captain who was a punk master to slip changes past the czar."

Bob wasn't going to let go.

"But once caught, the czar knows from then on that punk master doesn't play by the rules and would check up on them."

"That's true," Marci conceded and then thought for a second. "But hold on, that fits perfectly — it *would* explain Marshall's e-mail to himself. Maybe he caught a change he didn't like in the crushed-car homicide punk, hence the word 'tractor' in his message. I agree with Eve; when the captain's the punk master, they'd take chances screwing with the punk, but it's doable."

"However, if the czar were the punk master, there'd be no controls whatsoever," Eve added. "One person, and one person alone, could orchestrate anything they wanted."

"A cell czar can't be a punk master!" Bob protested. "That wouldn't be fair to the cell captains. Why would Aunt Tik's even need them?"

Okay, Bob's not that *far along,* Marci thought. *Otherwise, he'd get that "fair" has little to do with Aunt Tik's punk concepts.*

"Wait, I've got it highlighted." Eve flipped through the pages of the Aunt Tik's manual she'd printed off. She turned the document toward Bob, her forefinger pointing at text describing a czar: "Their roles include all the rights and responsibilities of a cell captain."

"Ah, I see. I missed that," Bob relented with a polite, if insincere, smile.

"We've established a captain acting as a punk master could alter, add, or remove challenges, even invisibly," Marci recapped, "but it would be risky, to Bob's point. However, a punk master who is also a czar has virtually no limits."

"I don't know that changing something between the challenges of a punk has to be done within the challenge-slash-punk framework at all," Paul offered. "Truthfully, I'm not sure you'd have to be an Aunt Tik's member.

"Debra Ann pointed out to me the other night that in the AR-15 punk, there wasn't anyone tasked to watch that stolen car between challenges, much less 24/7.

"It sat there unattended day and night in that empty parking lot — anyone could have changed anything, maybe even swapped out the entire car. The member performing the next challenge has the bare minimum information necessary, so they're in no position to question the details, so long as they can still do their challenge."

"But anyone screwing with the punk stands a big chance of getting caught," Eve pointed out, "if they aren't privy to the time gaps between assigned challenges. And you couldn't be utterly blind to what the punk was about because you'd need some idea of what you could get away with.

"You'd have some reason to make those changes — you'd desire a different outcome than intended for the original punk. So, if you're not the punk master, how do you game that results video?"

"So, we're saying you'd have to have *some* knowledge," Marci summarized, "and either an in with the punk master to post altered results or an ability to hack the server storing the videos. But you wouldn't necessarily have to have any formal relationship with the punk or Aunt Tik's."

Eve and Paul are familiar with this terrain, and Bob would have fresher eyes that might catch something we missed.

Marci paused for a moment and opened the door for Bob's input.

"Bob, feel free to jump in if you have additional thoughts here."

Bob nodded, his brows furrowed. Still, he stayed quiet, one arm across his chest, his chin cupped in his other hand.

"We should talk to Aunt Tik's app developers." Paul took Bob's silence as his opportunity to chime in. "I'd like to know if the captains or czar get a special version of the app, maybe keyed off their account, that lets them modify and edit punks and challenges through its interface. If not, fine; I'm sure an unscrupulous czar with the right skills could hack the changes or have someone under their influence do whatever was needed with no record kept.

"But if the app supports those edits, a trail may be left behind to support an Undo function or transaction tracking. Bob, is interviewing those developers something you could do for us?"

"Sure, I can talk to them and see what they can tell us."

"I'm looking for ways to identify punks gone bad by looking for the ones with midstream changes," Eve said. "The punk master wouldn't have created a written challenge for the gun swap, but he might have added time between challenges to do the additional work he wanted. They'd need to edit the challenge instruction to tell Steve not to look under that hood. He'd also have to change those final destination GPS coordinates to his new target.

"Each record in a runtime database is usually encrypted independently — the encrypted string for a record changes only when the record's contents change. We can locate changes by comparing records to those in a previous backup, even if we had only their encrypted versions."

"I see what you mean," Marci said. "We wouldn't care what the actual record contents *were* on the first pass — just which records changed and approximately when, depending on how often Aunt Tik's backs up their data. Later, we'd concentrate our decryption efforts on only the changed records."

Marci had expected Bob's input here — data extraction was one of the lieutenant's fields of expertise. Still, Bob remained silent, and Marci assumed this was the man's style when things met with his approval.

"I promised you a quick meeting," Marci said. "Let's get back to what we were doing. We'll schedule a general strategy session to map out our approaches to the specific cases. Look for an Outlook calendar item in your inbox. We'll want to button up our other cases or pass them on as necessary. I'm getting an odd feeling that the Aunt Tik's investigation will consume all the resources we can give it.

"Counting Marshall, the five decedents we know of deserve at least that much."

'Six," Paul reminded her. "Were it not for the murder of Carla Littman, Sophia Ferguson would still be alive."

After returning to her desk, Marci checked her messages and found a note from Louis asking her to call.

"Good morning, Lieutenant. What's going on?" Marci asked when he picked up the phone.

"Not a big deal," Louis replied, "but I wanted you to know why we didn't include the James Marshall case in your formal investigation of Aunt Tik's. I don't know what Paul told Lt. Brooks, but the lieutenant's fully on board with your approach."

"That surprises me, to be honest."

"Ezra can be a tough read," Louis admitted, "but he's on our side. He wanted to cooperate with their guys doing the legwork and your team driving the Aunt Tik's part of it. But something else came up … it turns out Lt. Strickland and James Marshall knew each other well. They sat on charity boards together and cochaired some events. Brooks interviewed Strickland as part of the Marshall homicide investigation. Mondo didn't know — Strickland never bothered to tell him.

"They didn't think Strickland was the doer, but still, it wouldn't look right for him to have any role in the same investigation. It came down to taking Strickland off your team or splitting the Marshall case off, and we went the latter route. You'll need the decryption and hacking resources Strickland can provide. Have a sit-down with the man. He has to recuse himself from anything that touches the Marshall case."

"I'll do that today," Marci said.

Damn — I owe it to Bob as a member of our team to find something about him I like, but he keeps making it so … difficult.

"I just wanted you to know that it wasn't a lack of confidence in you or other team members. At all."

"I appreciate that, Lieutenant. Thanks for filling me in. I'll talk to Lt. Strickland."

The news was a development they didn't need, and Marci wasn't happy with Bob's behavior. Still, she'd deal with it and put it behind them.

<hr>

Marci decided it would be best to talk to Bob face-to-face, hoping he wouldn't pull rank and make the conversation difficult. She took the back stairs two flights down to Vice and found the lieutenant at his desk.

"Bob, have you got a moment?"

"Eve gave me a list of partial URLs and IP addresses, and I'm mapping out Aunt Tik's servers," Bob answered. "But I can make the time."

"It looks like Interrogation Room B is open. Let's grab that."

Once seated across from each other at the stainless-steel table, Marci began, "I just spoke to Lt. Harbin, and something's come up. He says Escalation Management interviewed you for the Marshall homicide and that you and Marshall were friends. Is that true?"

Bob's face briefly betrayed an expression of relief as though he was expecting something else.

"Yes, I knew James. I was sorry to learn what happened to him. My parents supported Councilman Scott in his early days of public service. I met James when he ran the councilman's campaign four years ago. Back then, he was single, and I would come down from San José every couple of weeks to manage my parents' properties, and we'd party. After he and Elyssa became an item, that was the end of that."

"Did you continue to interact with him after they got engaged?"

"We stayed friends, and now and again, we'd run into each other on the charity fundraising circuit. It's a small community here in San Diego, so we all know each other."

"We've just formed as a team, and I realize there hasn't been much time to take care of the niceties. However, in the future, when law enforcement interviews you as a subject or a witness related to a felony, you need to communicate that to your superior immediately. When the interview happened, that would have been Capt. Cranston.

"Once you joined our team, you should have informed Lt. Harbin or me. Hearing it from another unit in the same department creates several secondary issues when the person you report to doesn't know."

Marci sat back, studying Bob's face.

"You'll have to advise the team — it's on you to talk to them individually — but we should be okay for now. You need to recuse yourself from anything touching the Marshall case. If in doubt, ask Lt. Harbin, Mondo, or me. We do not want the Aunt Tik's investigation tainted by ethical issues. Are we clear?"

"Absolutely, Detective, and I apologize. It won't happen again. That Marshall interview was short and sweet … honestly, I didn't think about how it might look."

"I get it. As long as we stay on the straight and narrow going forward, it's all good."

They stood and shook hands, then headed back to their desks.

My commitment to embrace Bob as a teammate will take some effort, Marci thought as she returned to her cubicle.

But it's not like I haven't made my fair share of mistakes during my career.

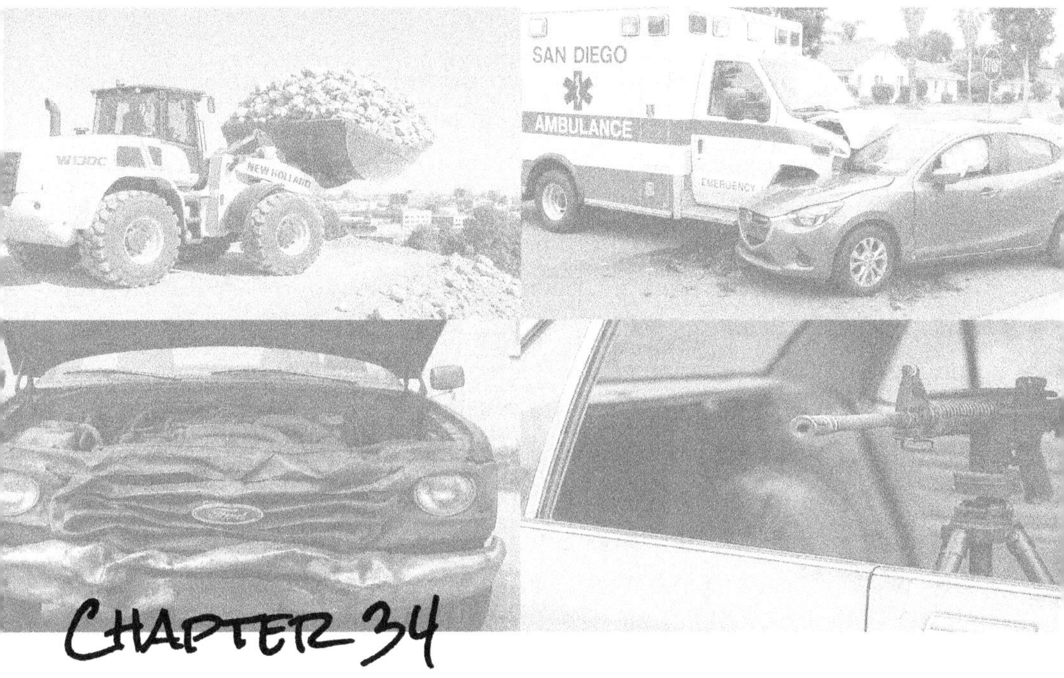

CHAPTER 34

After exchanging e-mails throughout the afternoon, Marci, Paul, Eve, and Bob made themselves available for a case strategy meeting at nine a.m. the following day.

After they'd assembled in the conference room, Marci briefly reviewed the status, history, inventory, and missing elements of the evidence accumulated in the Aunt Tik's investigation. She began the discussion about their master plan for the examination of Aunt Tik's going forward, proposing four simultaneous lines of attack.

"We first want to leverage Vicky Carlson's relationship with Jim Detmer. She's staying in contact with him and monitoring his Aunt Tik's engagements to let us know when he picks up his next punk challenge. Once he does, we'll frustrate his efforts by holding him on misdemeanor charges."

Bob expressed doubts.

"Has the DA signed off on this? Is he comfortable with detaining a private citizen under these circumstances?"

"We have him for lying to a police officer and several property theft charges based on victim complaints. While it's not our regular practice to hold someone on misdemeanors, Detmer has priors — nothing major, but enough to suffice for the purpose. But to your question, yes, the DA has been fully briefed and is on board."

"That should disrupt Detmer's comfort level," Eve added. "We can turn his fear of being dismembered to our advantage. Once we flip him, we can tap into what he knows about the organization, especially other members, captains, and the czar."

"The second approach will be to utilize Steve to daisy-chain a series of new Aunt Tik's premium memberships that we'll control. It depends on Steve not yet being dismembered and still able to vouch for a new application. Once our first member is approved, that member can put a good word in for the next candidate, and so forth.

"We want two accounts scoring points to become cell captains and two accounts free to work challenges for punks that concern us. We can't be sure Aunt Tik's will accept an account's bid for a challenge, nor do we know if an account going for captain might get stalled or outed.

"I'm describing Aunt Tik's member accounts, not the individuals behind them, so one officer can play all four roles. One of Mondo's people working online sex trafficking would be ideal."

"I have someone in mind who'd be good for this," Bob said.

Nice to see some positive input from Bob, Marci thought.

"What happens if we encounter an ethical issue, a challenge that exceeds our boundaries as officers?" Eve asked.

"That's where Vice can help — we deal with that all the time when we're undercover," Bob replied. "Still, it'll have to be navigated situation-by-situation."

"A good problem to have because it means the investigation is on the right track," Marci observed. "Once we have the new Aunt Tik's accounts, we'll bid and perform challenges for punks we want to investigate using those accounts. Once our challenge bid's accepted, we'll perform the task, then use the department's surveillance resources to track all the events and people who perform downstream challenges for the same punk.

"We don't want to be seen by the public dusting for prints or anything on that level because we can't know who's watching. Still, with video, audio, and observation, we'll pick up clues about challenge performers. We can then map out the organization and its members, using the threat of legal jeopardy or dismemberment as leverage to get members to reveal what they know about Aunt Tik's management."

"Fortunately, most Aunt Tik's punks aren't criminal," Paul replied. "There's less pressure to pursue everything that pops up. We can prioritize those punks and challenges that best serve our needs and reassess those priorities as we go along."

"Having choices is so much different than the situation in sexual exploitation cases," Bob noted. "In a sex trafficking investigation, you have to pull on and pursue every thread. Otherwise, you risk the life or freedom of victims.

"Who'll decide which challenges to bid on?"

"We'll make those decisions as a group," Marci answered. "I'll investigate the tie-ins between Aunt Tik's and what the teams working the four homicides turn up. Paul will deal with the forensics, of course. Bob, you'll handle real-time encrypted data, messages, and online activity. Eve will chase down information we need from the decrypted files.

"Besides our primary roles, we'll each take on Aunt Tik's challenge bids that our pseudo-member accounts win. Eve's been at the center of everything, so she'll make the final call if there's an availability issue for performing a challenge.

"Our third approach will be hacking Aunt Tik's servers and apps."

"That'll be my primary function?" Bob asked.

"We'll all work the resulting data together," Marci replied, "but yes, you'll be our lead for extracting it from Aunt Tik's servers. You'll also be our liaison for resources Vice provides for parsing data collected by the website. Vice has a wealth of that kind of experience in pedophilia investigations. We'll gather as much recognizable data as possible, triangulate on select data points, and see how events percolate through their system.

"Our focuses will be the creation of punks and challenges, selecting targets for a punk, bidding for challenges, challenge acceptance notifications, and posting punk results. We'll look for anomalous activity once we understand normal data flows through those servers. Hopefully, we can spot the situation where a captain or czar is intervening abnormally in punks by adding or editing challenge data."

"I know it sounds like a lot of work." Eve, the one person in the room who had experience mining Aunt Tik's data, spoke up. "But once we identify who's causing the changes, we'll narrow our focus to just those individuals, maybe only one, and it'll get exponentially easier."

"The fourth approach," Marci continued, "will be using conventional investigative methods to pursue the four Aunt Tik's–related murders — beginning with the Mabry dual runaway-truck homicide and the falling-concrete murder of the couple in the Fiesta. As time permits, we'll take on the Littman food-tampering anaphylactic shock death.

"The teams already working those murders will continue with the boots-on-the-ground investigative work. Our contribution will be looking for similarities and information gleaned from one case that could apply to the others. We'll take on Aunt Tik's elements of the remote-controlled AR-15 at the judge's residence as opportunities present themselves.

"The feds have the AR-15 case," Eve said. "How will our investigation work around them?"

"The DA is negotiating with them. If the feds don't cooperate, we'll tackle that later, assuming the FBI doesn't fully address Aunt Tik's involvement."

"Attempted murders are in Major Case's wheelhouse, and they'll want their voice heard," Bob ventured.

"Exactly," Marci agreed. "The feds did find traceable physical evidence in the judge's case — the car and the gun — which might be useful when tying Aunt Tik's member identities to real-world actors."

Bob suddenly leaned forward as though something had caught his attention, but he didn't offer anything.

"Having a formal case opens the door to exchanging information with federal investigators," Paul said, "so we might get what we need by simply asking for it."

"Agreed," Marci replied. "Paul, since you still have strong relationships with them, you'll negotiate and coordinate any information-sharing.

"And finally, Escalation Management's working the Marshall homicide, but we have another high-profile case. Since JoAnn Mabry was a prominent local attorney, a crack investigative team's been running down the flatbed trucks case, albeit without knowing Aunt Tik's probable involvement. We'll need to consult with their team immediately and then with detectives assigned to the other homicides. That's all I have for now. Let's open the floor to discussion."

"Wouldn't it be better to announce to the media that we suspect Aunt Tik's in these murders and ask the public for help?" Bob asked.

Marci, Eve, and Paul looked at one another. Marci assumed Bob was eager to show he could contribute and hadn't thought it through.

"Interesting idea," Paul offered diplomatically. "I see how that might work for a pedophile site, where everybody involved is a criminal, and you're just wanting to round up all the actors. Maybe stage something with officers at all the exits, and you catch the rats as they leave a ship you just told them was sinking."

"I need to reiterate," Marci added, "that at least on the surface, Aunt Tik's is not, by its nature, a criminal organization. They have a right to engage in functions that are within the law. My understanding is that would include most of what they do."

"Do we have sufficient information to make any allegation otherwise?" Eve asked.

"No," Marci replied. "Frankly, I doubt we have enough for a search warrant against the physical Aunt Tik's servers. Making a public accusation now would be irresponsible, and we'd be liable for any harm caused to Aunt Tik's. With a probable cause showing of committing a crime, as we have independently with each of the homicides, those problems would go away. But the probable cause we have now points to one or more specific individuals, not Aunt Tik's as a business.

"We can't get out over the tips of our skis alleging things the DA can't charge."

"But we have our CI, Steve, who we can show as an Aunt Tik's member doing crimes as part of a punk," Bob protested.

"He's the only one charged," Marci explained, "and human nature says, 'Of course, he's going to accuse someone else' — you want to run with no more than that? That's pretty weak, but say we publicly accuse Aunt Tik's of that crime. Let's imagine they have ten thousand members and say it turns out we are one hundred percent correct in our theory.

"Even in a worst-case scenario, maybe we can charge ten people. So, we've shut down Aunt Tik's business and denied 9,990 innocent people their right to enjoy Aunt Tik's website for months. People are out of work, and their competition gets a free ride during that time. I can see the lawsuits coming already.

"Worse, we'd forewarn every single member of Aunt Tik's. Those doing bad things would go underground. Even members not involved in crimes but with information useful to us would distance themselves from something we've branded criminal."

"Aunt Tik's would take down their servers and move operations to new locations, IP addresses, and URLs if they tried to return," Paul pointed out. "They'd enhance their encryption and defenses."

"Once we have enough information for a search warrant," Marci added, "we'll need those Aunt Tik's servers to tie everything together. With each punk broken into challenges discreetly performed by different people, that data tells us who did what. Without that information, I don't see how we get a complete picture of all the ongoing activity, especially enough to overcome reasonable doubt.

"If Aunt Tik's folds and destroys the contents of those servers before we obtain a warrant, arresting anyone becomes tougher by an order of magnitude. And how do we prosecute someone without data showing how all this works?"

Bob sighed, his shoulders dropped, and he nodded slightly in resigned acceptance — he'd lost his enthusiasm for this fight.

Paul gave Bob his best trying-to-avoid-public-conflict-here smile, even as he added a parting shot.

"Once all the members are underground, and the server data's vaporized, we can't re-cork that bottle. Do we run ads on every social media site saying, 'Y'all can come back now to playing your games… Oh, and please, do bring your old data with you. We were kidding about that whole 'throwing you in jail for serial murders' thing?'"

Marci recast the issue in gentler terms.

"I think once we can separate the malevolent Aunt Tik's players from the good," Marci said, "maybe we can shake them up with an accusation we can reasonably support, then monitor what happens afterward. But right now, we don't have those monitoring tools in place. And we don't know enough yet to assess what we'd be seeing. So, let's hold off on your idea for the moment, Bob, and keep it in our hip pocket in case we need it later."

Bob nodded his agreement, but his expression betrayed lingering unhappiness. Looking over at Eve as the team heard her phone vibrating, Marci said, "Let's take a short break and meet back here in fifteen minutes."

Before the meeting, Paul had left Assistant District Attorney Art Levine a voicemail, following it up with a detailed e-mail about the potential arrest of Jimmy Detmer.

Once back at his desk, Paul checked his messages and learned that Levine had returned his earlier call.

Paul called the ADA back, hoping they could temporarily keep Detmer from performing future Aunt Tik's challenges. The two men had an enlightening conversation that left Paul feeling good that they were on the right track.

While on the phone with the ADA, Paul heard the double-click of another call coming in but let it go to voicemail. Unfortunately, the discussion with Levine had made Paul late returning to the Aunt Tik's meeting — he needed to hustle back.

He'd recheck his voicemail once the meeting was over.

THE WRITINGS OF
AVRIL MARIA SERENE

CHAPTER 35

After everyone had re-taken their seats, Paul apologized for his tardiness, revealing that the assistant district attorney was ready for Detmer's detention.

The revelation added urgency to Marci's meeting, emphasizing flipping Detmer as priority number one. It was the best option in front of them, offering an immediate shot at not only solving the murders they were facing now but preventing any more by the same killer or killers.

"We opened this meeting with manipulating Jim Detmer as our first of four steps to exploring Aunt Tik's," Marci said. "Why don't you go ahead and fill us in?"

"Let me defer to Eve," Paul replied. "I know she and Debra Ann had a conversation last night regarding Vicky Carlson's participation. That will help set the background for Bob, and then I'll tell you what the ADA had to say."

"Okay, as Paul mentioned, I have good news," Eve began. "Vicky Carlson has been talking to Detmer, keeping an arms-length relationship going so she can tell us when he's doing another Aunt Tik's challenge."

"I'm sorry to interrupt," Bob said, "but her name's come up before — who, exactly, is Vicky Carlson?"

"She's Andy Pardone's friend; Aunt Tik's recently dismembered her," Eve explained. "She's also Detmer's former girlfriend. Because we suspected he's more seriously involved, including, possibly, in these homicides, we've asked Vicky Carlson to help flip him."

"Got it, thanks." Still, Bob's face flashed concern.

"She delivered big time," Eve continued. "She called Debra Ann and told her Detmer wanted to take her on a date; when she suggested Friday, he said no, he had an Aunt Tik's thing then.

"His challenge involves sneaking around private property at night and taking photos. We might want to pick him up as he's doing the challenge on a Peeping Tom complaint. It would be a twofer special: it'd also give us probable cause to search his phone on the pretext of viewing, as evidence, any photos he may have taken. I sent the details to your inboxes.

"That's pretty much exactly what we needed from her."

"I honestly didn't know if she'd come through," Paul admitted. "We'll have to buy her dinner after this is over, or at least give her a Citizen's Award plaque."

"She wants assurances that Detmer won't be available for his date with her," Eve said, "now set for Saturday night. Debra Ann promised we'd make that happen."

"So, what's our plan?" Bob asked.

"The Peeping Tom idea sounds like a winner," Marci said, "but I think Paul's already made some arrangements with the DA. Paul?"

"I spoke to Assistant DA Art Levine," Paul answered, "and it might be best to stay with the original plan — picking him up *before* he performs the challenge, keeping it simple for them.

"They're good with charging Detmer for his past property damage and thefts. They'll book those as felonies for now — they may kick them down to misdemeanors once we've finished with Detmer. That depends on how much the car and lawn ornament were damaged; the ADA's negotiating with the complainant. They'll subpoena that phone to get its GPS data, pinpointing where Detmer's been and when. The ADA will engage Vicky to ensure her safety should Detmer come after her later.

"We'll need to pick him up Friday morning on a forty-eight-hour hold, pending charges. We should be able to sweat him as he sees that Aunt Tik's challenge deadline is approaching. If not, he may cave after the deadline passes, he can't cover for ghosting the gig, and he's about to be dismembered. Either way, Detmer will be tied up until he posts bail after arraignment, and we'll have his full attention for that period.

"With any luck, we'll get out of him what he knows about the higher-ups in Aunt Tik's."

"I'll call Vicky Carlson as soon as I'm back at my desk to keep her in the loop," Eve offered.

"We've still got other investigators looking into the non–Aunt Tik's aspects of these cases," Marci said. "They could trip over Detmer as a suspect through other avenues. Let's get the word out about our intentions — I don't want anyone interviewing Detmer or doing anything else to spook him before we have him in the holding cell.

"I think that means we've finished here. Let's hope the rest of our day goes well."

<hr>

Marci had just gotten back to her desk when Mondo called.

"Hi, Detective. I wanted you to know that at eight this morning, Lt. Strickland presented himself at my office to come clean about being interviewed for the Marshall case.

"Dammit, you'd think a lieutenant would know better. I've talked to Louis about the situation. I know you spoke with Strickland about the circumstances, and you needed to be aware that he followed through."

"Thanks for letting me know he heard me, Captain," Marci replied. "Unfortunate and avoidable, but water over the dam now."

"Sometimes I can't quite figure Strickland out," Mondo said. "He can be a good officer, but keeps tripping over his two left feet. Take this morning. He tells me about being interviewed, apologizes, doesn't try to weasel out, and says it won't happen again. So, at that point, we're good, right?

"But no, he can't let it go at that. He has to invoke Marshall's name to regale me with stories about his glory days when those two used to pal around. Strickland drops the names of everyone he knows and then implies that he was the one who set Marshall up with Councilman Scott's daughter, Elyssa.

"Claims the minute Marshall bought that Triton-blue Audi, Strickland knew they'd get engaged — it wasn't Marshall's style, and the shade was identical to the main color in Elyssa's cosplay costume when they first met. Strickland tried to imply that he and Marshall were tight. My respect for him manning up about the interview changed into 'what an arrogant ass' in two seconds flat."

"*Triton-blue?*" Marci was surprised. "That's how he described the color of the car?"

In her entire life, Marci had heard of someone using the manufacturer's name for a car's paint color in casual conversation twice: once when a uniformed officer told her that the term was used in the 911 call reporting Marshall's car on the shoulder, and just now.

"Yes … you sound like it caught you off-guard," Mondo said.

"Oh, nothing to do with you — a weird coincidence. But I guess it's good to know Lt. Strickland tried to do the right thing, even if he loses style points for execution." Marci chuckled as she and Mondo said their goodbyes.

She didn't know quite what to make of Bob's use of the color name.

It must be a thing among Audi fans and owners, like "candy-apple red" and "Hamm's blue" used to be among street rodders and bikers back in the day.

⁂

As Paul returned to his desk, he remembered receiving another call during his meeting break, one he hadn't been able to take. He dialed into his voicemail.

The message was from Louis.

"Paul, get back to me as soon as you can. Steve Nielsen's missing."

⁂

"Louis, I just got your voicemail," Paul said as soon as the lieutenant picked up. "What did you mean by 'Steve's missing'?"

"I got a call from Tracy earlier this morning," Louis replied, concern evident in his voice. "Steve didn't come home last night. When it got late, she thought, 'Steve has a new girlfriend,' maybe the relationship was further along than Tracy wanted to know. She waited a little longer, ready to read him the riot act when he came through the door. But Steve never showed. She's called everyone they know. No luck."

Louis sighed. "He's still out on bail, so she didn't want to create a situation with his bond. She phoned me, by that point desperate. I gave it to Missing Persons and asked them to prioritize it as a favor for me, but quietly. They have their protocols, and they're chasing down whether he just freaked out over his situation at some point and decided to take off. But his car's still parked in the lot at his job — no obvious indication of a problem. Not promising."

"I'm not sure what we could do." Paul felt helpless.

"I doubt anyone can do much until we learn more. I just wanted to make you and the rest of the team aware of the situation. So, if you happen to hear anything...."

"Do you think this might have something to do with Aunt Tik's?"

"God, I hope not."

Paul knew Louis well enough to recognize the worry in his tone.

Paul's mood was down when he came home. I expected he'd be tired after working three hours past the end of his shift. Even so, Paul was usually upbeat when he walked through the door, welcoming the transition from the job to family. Playing with Tommy on the living room carpet seemed to brighten his spirits. But once we'd put Tommy to bed for the night and had some adult time to ourselves, I could see that something was eating at him.

"I assume you heard about Steve Nielsen?" Paul asked with his head against the couch cushion, staring at the ceiling.

"Marci left me a voicemail." It upset me, but I hadn't wanted to add to everything on Paul's plate. "It was a shock, totally unexpected... Why? And why now? I've tried to call her back, but she's not picking up, which usually means she's busy."

Paul sat up and looked at me.

"Just when it seemed we were getting a handle on this. But it's not the first time. I sometimes think I'm making a mistake by getting myself involved in the street side of these investigations.

"Forensics is straightforward, for the most part. It's all about the intellectual challenge, teasing out the truth, and getting the evidence to tell you the story by following the process. The creative part comes when you have to figure out a scientifically sound approach to expose something you know's in there but impervious to conventional methods."

"Maybe you just need to give yourself a little break and spend more time in the lab?"

"And that's the other side of it. The lab can get boring. It's antiseptic, abstracted from the realities of the crimes. I started involving myself more in what the detectives were doing because it was intellectually stimulating. It mixes things up, and Louis isn't a stickler for job titles — he believes in letting people go where their talents take them, within reason. I think I'm better at my regular duties when I know how the forensics fit in with the fieldwork. I've been dipping in and out of some of the detectives' cases as much as Louis would let me."

"So, what's changed?"

"Now it's official. Louis assigned me to the Aunt Tik's team for the investigative component."

"Oh, I see. You can't just escape to the lab when you need to."

"Exactly. The investigations can be overwhelming at times. Out in the field, there's no discipline to anything. It comes at you in waves of rushed little bunches of stuff, none of it ordered, complete, or identifiable as to what part of the bigger puzzle it fits into. Most of it's irrelevant, but you can't know until you check it out.

"The trained investigators have filters for triaging information as it comes in, but I wouldn't call it 'scientific.' A lot of it's gut instinct or experience calling the shots. They make mistakes that just aren't permitted in my world."

"With your life's work built around the scientific method, I can see how it would drive you crazy...." I struggled to offer something that would make Paul feel better.

Paul paused in meditation.

"When it comes to Aunt Tik's, we can't even tell you which puzzle we're working on. Is it the organization, or just one or more members going off the deep end? Or is someone, maybe a group, manipulating the situation from outside, leveraging a weakness they've discovered?"

He raked a hand through his black curls.

"We can't get the situation to remain stable long enough to get a good look at it. I think that's what tipped me over the edge today. Steve's turning up missing was unexpected, to say the least."

I had questions of my own.

"I deal with the crazy stuff out in the wild daily; even so, I can't make sense of that. If this was Aunt Tik's, for the sake of argument, let's say, blotto_bill, why go after Steve at this late date?"

Maybe if Paul focuses on the problem-solving aspects of the situation, he'll slip out of his funk.

"As far as we know," Paul said, "anything Steve could tell law enforcement has already been said or is available from other sources. There'd have to be something else Steve knows that he hasn't shared or something he said that we didn't hear."

"Or maybe the intention isn't to kill Steve. Could the idea be to keep him from appearing in court so they revoke his bond, and he'll appear more guilty? Or maybe break him down so he'll confess things he didn't do?"

"There'd have to be *some* gain to his kidnapper to justify the risk," Paul agreed. "Stalling for time or muddying up Steve's role in this. Looking at it that way, it screams that we must be closer than we think to something threatening the killer."

And just that quickly, Paul returned to his usual self, ready to rejoin a fight where the team sorely needed him.

THE WRITINGS OF
AVRIL MARIA SERENE

CHAPTER 36

Eve awoke from a vivid dream about choosing her toppings in a brightly lit Baskin-Robbins ice cream shop. Elsie Gonzalez, her wife of five years, was yanking Eve's shoulder. Three months after a successful in vitro procedure, Elsie was subject to intense cravings.

"I'm hungry, Eve, and I can't sleep. Will you go out and get me a veggie burger, *please, please, pretty please?*"

"Honey," Eve replied, not eager to get out of the comfy bed and pawing at the alarm clock to see the time, "it's three in the morning. Nothing's open."

"The Burger King on Bernardo Oaks Drive is open 24 hours, and they have Impossible Whoppers," Elsie pleaded.

"Okay, sweetheart," Eve acquiesced, throwing her covers off and back across Elsie as she climbed out of bed. She dressed quickly and grabbed her purse. Her take-home unmarked was behind Elsie's Mini in the drive, so Eve decided to take her work vehicle for the short trip.

As she headed north up I-15, a call came out over the unit's radio. The dispatcher described a disabled vehicle with an unresponsive driver on the shoulder under the northbound I-15 overpass at Bernardo Center Drive.

Rather than taking the I-15 further north to the Burger King, Eve took the off-ramp. She spotted the bronze Toyota Solara convertible two hundred yards before her. Keying the mike, Eve advised Central that she was on the scene. Eve couldn't get off the road early enough to leave sufficient distance behind the motionless vehicle, so she pulled off onto the shoulder about thirty yards ahead.

Eve focused her unit's driver's side spotlight on the Solara. Grabbing a pair of nitrile gloves from her purse and the flashlight off the dash, she slipped the strap of her bag, sidearm inside, over her shoulder. Shoving the bubble gum light's cord into the cigarette lighter, she stuck its magnetic base to the top of her unmarked.

The detective quickly walked a wide path to the driver's side of the Solara — she didn't want to disturb tire impressions or footwear evidence in the scene ahead of the silent automobile, where a tow or other vehicle might have been during any crime.

The car was well off the road on the generous shoulder, very near the guard rail, engine off. Eve could see the outline of a body hunched over the steering wheel through the windows, misted with early-morning dew. She gloved up as she approached, calling out to the driver. When she got no response, she tested the door latch and found it unlocked.

Eve kept her left hand on the grip of the service weapon inside her purse, and the flashlight clamped between her left shoulder and cheek.

She teased the door open with her right hand.

As she did, the body, unsecured by seat belts, slumped to its right and off the steering wheel toward the center console.

Eve tensed with the unexpected movement, drawing her weapon with her left hand.

She grabbed the flashlight off her shoulder with her right fist, steadying her left arm with the flashlight in one fluid motion.

A quick inspection of the body and the car's interior made it apparent that she was in no danger from the vehicle or any other occupants. The body was cool to the touch and unconscious or, more likely, dead.

A flashlight scan through the back seat and front passenger areas revealed trash everywhere, but no one else was present. The gearshift was in Park with the emergency brake off. Eve returned her service weapon to her purse. To make sure the car was immobile on the downhill slant of the off-ramp, she tried to rock the vehicle backward with her left hand against the doorjamb. It wasn't going anywhere.

The effort made Eve aware of the strong smell of alcohol coming from the vehicle's interior, along with an almost overwhelming body odor.

Eve wedged the flashlight into the space above the upper hinge between the open door and its frame to provide more light. She checked the driver's exposed carotid artery for a pulse. There wasn't one, and he wasn't breathing. She supported the underside of the driver's jaw with her left hand as she pulled his left shoulder upright into the seat with her right hand. Once the seat back supported the driver's weight, she could see it was an early-to-mid-thirties Caucasian male. His clothes were soiled and stained, the undersides of his fingernails caked with grime. There was visible dirt and grease on his forearms like someone might get working on a car's engine.

Eve tilted the man's head into the beam of her flashlight.

Goddammit!

Eve knew him — it was Jimmy Detmer.

She recognized the face from the photos Vicky Carlson had given her and Debra Ann. She was looking at the dead body of the man her team planned to detain and interview in just a few hours.

They weren't catching any breaks; he wouldn't be sharing anything with anyone now.

None of the other first responders had yet arrived on-scene. After opening the Solara's trunk and finding nothing obviously of concern, Eve walked back to her unmarked. She radioed in to advise central dispatch she had a deceased body, then quickly texted Elsie, "Sorry. Burger run on hold, citizen in distress, will text U when done."

Returning to the Solara, Eve closely inspected the occupant and the car's interior.

Her first impression was of a drug overdose. There was a smell of vomit and signs of it on the man's shirt, but not in the car. Detmer's tongue was discolored, the insides of his cheeks were dry and tacky, and there was a telltale bluish-purple tint to his lips.

In Eve's experience, those were the signs of heroin or other opioids. The victim was in a short-sleeved T-shirt, and Eve noted a single injection site on the right arm opposite the wrist on which he wore his watch. That, by itself, set off alarm bells. The watch location suggested Detmer was right-handed, meaning Detmer had used his left hand to shoot up, which would be unusual.

Eve stretched the skin on the inside of both elbows with her thumbs and saw no signs of previous injection sites. Certainly, Detmer could have been shooting up in another part of his body. Still, Eve's experience told her true addicts don't change their habits unless they collapse a vein — and there was no obvious indication of that on what she could see of Detmer's body. Eve also couldn't find the cluster of little figure-eight bruises in the bicep area that junkies who use their arms tend to have from tying themselves off. Eve couldn't recall any mention of drug use from Debra Ann's notes of her interview with Vicky Carlson. Detmer's one-time girlfriend had spoken at length about their other problems, and it seemed odd she'd leave that out.

The coroner would have to perform a complete autopsy with a full toxicology screen to learn more. Still, Eve's instincts told her someone else had to be involved in Detmer's death.

Eve checked Detmer's clothing for personal effects, finding a wallet with credit cards and no cash, a CVS receipt for rubbing alcohol, and nothing else. No cell phone set off more alarms — a guy like Detmer would never be without one for calling someone to post bail, if nothing else. Complicating the scene was that Detmer and his vehicle, including the trunk, were filthy. The phone might be somewhere in the mess. Excluding the area around the gas and brake pedals, garbage and detritus filled the front and rear foot wells, overflowing onto the seats.

The Forensics team would have to bag, tag, and evaluate every item for evidentiary value — they'd spend a lot of time and effort sorting it out.

Satisfied she'd done what she could, Eve closed the Solara's door and returned to her unmarked to call in.

"Dispatch, advise earlier report of a deceased at this location appears to be a homicide. We'll need a patrol unit, a flatbed for vehicle removal, a Forensics team, and the medical examiner. Can you patch me through to Det. Marci Robbins's home phone?"

Though it seemed she'd laid her head on the pillow mere moments ago, Marci was five hours into a sound sleep when the bedroom phone rang. Fighting the covers and trying to catch the phone before it woke Danny, she fumbled for the receiver, answering drowsily, "Hello, this is Marci Robbins."

"Det. Robbins, this is central dispatch with a call from Det. Eve Byrne. Go ahead, Det. Byrne."

"Hey, boss, sorry to wake you. I'm off the I-15 at the northbound Bernardo Center Drive off-ramp. I got a radio call about twenty minutes ago and found Jim Detmer dead in his vehicle on the shoulder. It looks like an apparent heroin overdose, but I'm not buying it. For one thing, there's no sign of car keys anywhere."

Seriously? Shit.

"Okay, Detective, thanks. I'm on my way," Marci said as quietly as she could, yet still be heard over Eve's radio.

Without disturbing Danny, Marci quickly dressed, left him a note, and drove to the crime scene.

When Marci arrived, the forensics team was finishing what work they could do with the vehicle outside their shop. The medical examiner had taken the body, and the tow truck was winching Detmer's convertible onto its bed. Paul Castro had arrived ahead of her, suited up in white forensic coveralls to shepherd the techs. As he spotted Marci, he shook his head and looked down at the ground with pursed lips.

Eve was in her street clothes, arms crossed, leaning against her unmarked unit when Marci found her. Marci walked over to talk to her partner. "How did you get dragged into this at such an hour?"

"Elsie was craving a veggie burger, so I was on a munchie run and happened to be less than a mile from the scene when the call went out. I couldn't shirk my responsibilities when I was that close. The scene reads like a homicide, but we won't know that for sure until the autopsy's complete."

"Who called it in?"

"A freeway passerby was concerned that the vehicle was hazardous to passing traffic. They described it as parked on the shoulder under the overpass with its door swung open out onto the shoulder. The interior lights were on, and he could see the driver had slumped over the wheel. When I arrived a few minutes later, the door was closed but unlocked, and the interior light was off. So, either we have a compromised crime scene, or somebody else is involved — the citizen may have caught them in the middle of whatever they were doing. I'm voting for option number two."

"Where do we stand, then?"

"The ME's already been here and collected the body. The car and the corpse reeked of alcohol. Preliminary indications were a drug overdose, most likely heroin. The question as to whether it was self-administered is yet to be determined. My guess is no — I'd say someone caught Detmer sleeping one off and gave him a hot shot."

Eve and Marci walked around the area where Detmer's Solara had been.

"The car stopped without any noticeable skid marks and parallel to the traffic lanes," Eve said as Marci took stock of the vehicle on the flatbed.

"It was in Park when I found it with the engine off. There was no obvious drug paraphernalia at the scene, and there's the thing about no keys."

"I have to agree; it looks like a murder. Doesn't square with someone dying of a drug overdose while weaving down a freeway."

Eve nodded.

"The perp may have rushed the staging due to the relatively high traffic volume for this time of the morning — too many potential witnesses."

"Or maybe our perp didn't allow themselves enough time to finish laying out the scene," Marci speculated. "Putting the car keys in their pocket is something they'd do instinctively if in a hurry. We'll have to rely on conjecture until the Forensics team completes its examination and report. But this is just too damned convenient. Right before we get him into our interrogation room, *this* happens?"

Eve tilted her head.

"Oh, that reminds me — his cell phone wasn't in his clothing. It could be somewhere in all the crap in that car, but I dialed the number Debra Ann gave us; I didn't hear any ringtones around the car anywhere. You think the doer knew we wanted to look at that phone?"

Marci crossed her arms.

"Somebody out there's toying with us. And killing people is their idea of play."

THE WRITINGS OF
AVRIL MARIA SERENE

CHAPTER 37

At nine a.m. the morning of Detmers' demise, Marci called the Aunt Tik's team to a meeting in the squad room. Bob arrived a little late, looking peaked and complaining of stomach trouble.

"We've had a setback in our investigation of Aunt Tik's," Marci announced. "Earlier this morning, Eve was called to a homicide scene in which Jimmy Detmer was the victim."

There was palpable tension in the complete silence as the team absorbed the news.

"*Crap.* How could something like this happen? We needed him to get us inside Aunt Tik's," Bob lamented.

We deal in murders daily; people get killed because somebody wants them dead, Paul thought before he reconsidered. *Bob isn't a homicide detective and isn't feeling well — my bad for being tired and cranky this morning.*

"The medical examiner's been working this nonstop at my request," Marci continued. "The lab work hasn't come back, and Paul's team hasn't processed all the forensics. But here's what we know so far: Detmer's blood alcohol level was 0.17, twice the legal driving limit.

"The killer injected him with an overdose of heroin shortly after midnight. There were two injection attempts; the first missed the vein and punctured muscle tissue. The ME based the time estimate for the injection on standard tissue repair rates. The toxins in Detmer's system were far more than any addict would use, even if he *wanted* to kill himself. The ME places the time of death between one and one-thirty a.m.

"His car was driven or towed and parked at the crime scene at approximately 2:45 a.m., according to citizen traffic reports of the disabled vehicle. Lividity says the killer then placed his body in the driver's seat. They hastily staged the crime scene, abandoning the Solara in a location that ensured quick discovery.

"The coroner's estimate of the times of injection and then death means he couldn't have driven the car himself to the dump site. For one thing, forensics techs found no car keys."

"Do we know yet how the killer left the scene?" Eve asked.

"Forensics found strap marks on the front wheels and tires," Marci replied. "And markings in the wheel wells and under Detmer's car suggest the killer moved it with a floor jack and a two-wheel tow dolly. That means the doer likely towed the Solara to the scene and left in the tow vehicle.

"Fresh tool marks show someone used a Slim Jim on the driver's door, so the murderer may not have had access to Detmer's keys. We need to check all the rental yards and see who leased a dolly over a period that covers last night and early this morning.

"Let's also check private owners. Those dollies are treated like trailers and are supposed to be registered and plated. But we know that doesn't always happen, so we should also look for dollies registered in the past, even if they aren't now. If there's no record of the dolly, we're out of luck."

"I assume what we're looking for among the private dolly owners are names of individuals or businesses and locations that coincide with information picked up during our investigations?" Paul asked. "We'll have to coordinate closely with the other teams."

"To that end," Marci responded, "I've asked all the teams to scan and OCR their field notes onto our shared server every night. We'll do the same. Finding matches will be a fishing expedition, to be sure, but these things have solved homicides for us in the past.

"There's a high likelihood, given the timing, that Mr. Detmer's murder is related to our investigation of Aunt Tik's. But the final determination hasn't yet been made. There are no indications this homicide was, itself, the result of an Aunt Tik's punk.

"All the necessary steps — gaining access to and control of the victim, injecting the heroin, relocating the car with a dead body, and staging the dump scene — are unquestionably criminal. It would have been dangerous and illogical for the perpetrator to involve that many different people in overtly unlawful acts and not expect word to get out. If this killer *was* involved in our Aunt Tik's homicides, we can assume logic matters — they intelligently planned each stage of the Aunt Tik's–related activities that resulted in death."

"The exception might be the Marshall homicide," Eve pointed out. "That seems more reactive to something that set the killer off at the moment, or maybe opportunistic. Same thing here, maybe? It might be a stretch, but perhaps Steve Nielsen's abduction, too. Our usually methodical perp might be coming apart under the stress of these situations."

"Interesting idea," Marci agreed. "I stand corrected. Let's say our doer seems careful and rational within the context of Aunt Tik's processes but not so much otherwise.

"Running with that idea, the timing of Detmer's murder may help us — it appears the killer didn't complete their work at the dump scene. Trying to make a murder appear to be a heroin overdose but delaying the body staging until it's obvious the victim was too dead to drive wasn't a well-executed, calmly deliberated plan. Sloppy. Hopefully, that'll lead to more mistakes or evidence we can use."

"I read the notes from the interview Paul and Debra Ann had with Detmer," Bob said. "With all due respect to the dead, they suggest he wasn't particularly likable. I know it's hard to dismiss the coincidences with our Aunt Tik's investigation, but can you rule out that this may be unrelated?"

"That's a valid point," Marci responded. "But big coincidences to dismiss. It doesn't hurt us to be aware that Aunt Tik's *may* be involved, including possibly monitoring our activities. We know virtually anyone can be an Aunt Tik's member, and on that note, let's be especially vigilant about who we talk to and what we say.

"If our interviewing of Detmer led to this and represented such a threat to the killer that they needed to act immediately," Paul said, "they wouldn't have had a lot of time for prep or cleanup. That bodes well for what we might find searching Detmer's property."

"Are we going to include the Detmer homicide in the Aunt Tik's cases we're working now?" Eve asked. "Under the assumption it's related?"

"Yes, we'll treat it like we would the murder of a material witness," Marci said, "even though, at this time, the case is not specifically connected to a punk or any of a punk's challenges. Nothing about being included in the Aunt Tik's investigation precludes our standard investigative practices. In the event Detmer's murder is attributed to something else at some point, we'll kick it loose and allow it to stand alone."

"I'll talk to Vicky Carlson later this morning to ask if she knew of Detmer using heroin, either casually or as an addict," Paul offered. "All indications are that he didn't. Out of an abundance of caution, we should provide her protection."

"Eve, would you speak to the uniform division and our witness to arrange that?" Marci asked.

"Sure thing. Did you want a safe house or just armed uniforms and patrols?"

"Let's be flexible," Marci responded. "We'll offer her 24/7 uniforms and a patrol unit every two hours. If she still feels insecure, we can move her into a motel."

"Got it," Eve said before pausing.

"None of this is positive as to whether or not Steve Nielsen is still alive. Should we double up the security detail for Tracy Nielsen as well? Technically, she's not a witness, but they could threaten her to influence Steve if they still have him."

Marci nodded.

"With Detmer dead, we'll have to refocus our energies on the other three legs of our investigative attack. That is, submitting Aunt Tik's membership applications and using Steve Nielsen's account to vouch for them, hacking Aunt Tik's servers, and following the standard investigative protocols for our known cases, with an eye out for any connections to Aunt Tik's. We've applied for two memberships using Steve to vouch for us. That's as far as we want to push that envelope until we get an answer on our applications."

"I'm getting some heat from upstairs on the Mabry case," Marci relayed, turning to Bob.

"That one is more dependent than the others on complex challenges, and I'm crossing my fingers we can resolve most of it from Aunt Tik's data."

"Our computer forensics officers in Vice are working on Aunt Tik's servers," Bob replied, "and we're utilizing all the resources we can swing in that area."

"Good, keep me posted. Okay, that's it for now," Marci said. "We'll keep you updated if anything else turns up. Stay safe out there, and pay attention to your e-mails.

"This thing has many moving parts, and you'll want to keep up."

THE WRITINGS OF
AVRIL MARIA SERENE

CHAPTER 38

Det. Tad Roberts, a homicide detective doubling as an applicant for two new Aunt Tik's memberships, stood alongside Marci's desk when she returned from the meeting.

"Det. Roberts, good morning. What glad tidings have you brought me?" Marci asked.

"I'm sorry, Detective, but the news I have isn't good," Roberts answered. "One of my Aunt Tik's membership applications has been rejected. I printed off the e-mail they sent Steve's account."

He handed Marci a sheet of paper, which she read aloud.

" 'Sponsoring new members requires an Aunt Tik's account in good standing. Please message your cell czar if you have questions,' from a generic 'info@' unmonitored email address. That tells us they've dismembered Steve, but quietly. That's interesting. Thanks for letting me know, Detective."

Marci shared the information about the rejected application with Eve, who needed the login accounts for her research, and Paul, who'd been with Debra Ann when she interviewed Andy Pardone. They didn't want Debra Ann's Aunt Tik's account associated with the department's undercover accounts. If they had to submit new Aunt Tik's account applications under different names, they'd need Andy Pardone to sponsor them.

Marci sent e-mails to Eve, Paul, and Bob that Steve's Aunt Tik's account was no longer active. She added that they hadn't punked him yet, that she knew of — she was assuming his kidnapping wouldn't have been part of a dismemberment, though it was possible. She also texted Tracy Nielsen with the same information in case she wasn't yet aware.

An hour later, Det. Roberts called to inform Marci he'd received a second rejection e-mail, with the same explanation as the first, for their other pseudo-applicant — no surprise, but not a good thing either.

Marci called Paul, telling him neither of their Aunt Tik's member applications had succeeded.

"If you send me the names and backgrounds we've conjured up," Paul said, "I'll call Andy and ask him to sponsor two new applications.

"He's been cooperative, but if there's an issue, I'll ping you."

As it turned out, Andy had no problem helping investigators. But he did have one request — that Paul advise his parole officer what he'd done if things went badly and Andy's name came up in the aftermath. Once he had the go-ahead from Andy, Paul submitted the applications several hours apart, using the information Marci sent him and copying screenshots of the completed forms to Det. Roberts.

When I got home, Tommy was absorbed in building a Magna-Tiles barn for his collection of Joyin vehicles in the middle of the living room floor.

"Hi, Mommy," he said without looking away from his project. Paul, who'd ordinarily be on the floor with him, was on the couch, hands behind his neck, staring intensely but without focus at the living room's far wall.

"Hi, Sprout. Is that a garage you're building?"

Tommy gave a vigorous up-and-down shake of his head, his concentration on his task unwavering.

I kissed the top of his head and moved over to the sofa. Something was eating at Paul. He didn't usually talk about his work when he came home, but it looked like he needed to.

"Care to share?" I asked him after motioning for some space on the couch.

"Please, have a seat. Glad you're home," Paul said, breaking out of his reverie. "I'm sitting here wondering if I might have screwed up at work and put somebody in harm's way."

"How so, honey?"

"You remember Andy Pardone from the interview we did together?"

"Sure. Andy seemed like a good kid. Got us rockin' and rollin' on how Aunt Tik's works, or at least the way it's supposed to."

"The team applied for paid Aunt Tik's memberships using Steve to sponsor us, but they've dismembered him and denied the applications. So, I called Andy to ask if he'd vouch for us, and he agreed. I didn't tell him the last guy we asked to sponsor us has likely been kidnapped and possibly killed. I also didn't mention that the other current Aunt Tik's member the department engaged with is now dead — Jim Detmer."

"They killed Detmer?" I was surprised, but more by the timing than the choice of victims.

"Somebody did. Not yet sure who, but circumstances say it likely had something to do with Aunt Tik's."

"I'm sorry — Vicky Carlson told me about setting Detmer up, so he'd have to reveal everything he knew."

"Unfortunate. After that setback, I knew we needed Andy's help. Telling him about Steve's kidnapping or Detmer's murder wouldn't have made a great sales pitch, so I left them out."

"Yes, honey, I know how you are. Whenever a problem suddenly pops up, you immediately want to fix it. But Vicky's a friend of Andy's — you know he'll find out."

"Yeah, I didn't think it through. And as I came home tonight, it hit me that the repercussions could be bad for Andy. Detmer was vulnerable to Aunt Tik's management because, as a long-term member, everything about him was known to them — his profile, past activities, and with whom he'd done challenges. With Andy also a member for a while, I realized he's in the same boat."

"You're worried about Aunt Tik's retaliating? A dismembering punk, or worse?"

I thought a moment.

"But would they do that to Andy? They didn't punk Steve before his disappearance — unless kidnapping him was part of the dismemberment. But Andy's not like Detmer — he hasn't done any illegal challenges that we know and couldn't tell us much about gaming their system. I don't think Andy would be the threat to the bad actors in Aunt Tik's that Detmer was."

"It isn't just Aunt Tik's. I don't know that the website has strong defenses around vouching for a new member other than requiring the sponsor to be in good standing. We know applicants from the same group often sign up in bunches, with the new members vouching for one another. Sponsoring one of our fake members would be Andy's only real exposure, and even then, only if that member gets caught.

"It's more that I can't shake the feeling someone's watching us, somehow."

"And it's this 'watcher' you're concerned about?"

"Exactly. Killing Detmer hours before we intended to interview the man again, this time with leverage in our pocket, would raise anyone's suspicions. But dismembering Steve without punking him before he turned up missing is more concerning to me. Based on what happened to Vicky, the comments Andy made, and fears Steve expressed, that just isn't how Aunt Tik's operates. For them, dismembering seems to be an opportunity to let loose the hounds, one they welcome.

"If a federal investigation is a deterrent, it wasn't enough to stop Steve's kidnapping or possible murder, or Detmer's homicide, assuming Aunt Tik's was responsible. Maybe the group might tone it down because the feds were lurking about, but no dismemberment punk at all? Just doesn't fit. I'd expect a punk to be *more* likely now, just as an act of defiance to show we're not the boss of them.

"People and organizations suddenly doing things differently under the harsh glare of an investigation is a criminal's biggest tell. And all these behaviors, Steve's being gone, Detmer's murder, and the no-punk, seem to be in direct response to the hand we're holding. We aren't showing anyone those cards — at least, that we know of."

"But we keep hearing that members of Aunt Tik's could be anyone." I tried to fathom how the information would be leaking out. "And didn't

Steve say members join when the people they hang with do? James Marshall was political, and when he was the czar, he would have recruited members who were local politicians or tied to them.

"Perhaps that's why you're having so many problems. Maybe you're looking for someone powerful enough to have eyes and ears in the police department, someone who could push people to do things for them they wouldn't otherwise do."

I paused.

"How about someone like Councilman Sweeney? He first got elected from the retired police ranks during that big law-and-order push a few years ago, and he seems to hate everyone."

"Interesting idea, but officers can't go around investigating a city councilman based on that thought alone."

"Well, who else is hanging around with connections and a bone to pick with the department?"

Paul would share with me later that his thoughts went immediately to Jeff Bennett, and he felt guilty the moment they did. And Bennett *should* be bitter about getting bumped aside for a promotion, though he seemed more disappointed than angry. But again, no one knows who might have a relationship with Aunt Tik's … and the quiet types *are* the ones you worry about.

But Paul shook his head.

"I can't think of anyone."

THE WRITINGS OF
AVRIL MARIA SERENE

CHAPTER 39

Two weeks after Jimmy Detmer's death, the investigation was grinding along but hadn't generated encouraging results. Missing Persons had made no progress in locating Steve. Nothing at Paul's desk inspired him, so he'd make his lab rounds early. But before he did, he walked across the bullpen to Eve's desk.

As he did, Bob Strickland joined him.

"Hey, Paul. I wanted you to know that I talked to Mondo. After Marci mentioned it to me, I informed him that investigators had interviewed me about the Marshall homicide. I apologized for not telling him earlier. I should have told the team, too. I screwed up. I'm sorry for that."

"No apologies necessary, Bob. I'm glad you fixed it, and I'm sure it won't happen again. For my part, I'm aware you're coming from Vice onto a team working murders where everyone else is Homicide — as the only Forensics guy myself among detectives, I understand how things can get awkward, especially for a senior officer."

"I appreciate you saying that. Mondo suggested it might help to socialize outside the workplace occasionally — team-building, those kinds of things. To that end, I thought I'd ask you and Eve to come for dinner tomorrow night. I don't mean to brag, but my housekeeper's a great cook, and it's a comfortable place for conversation."

Paul took the offer as an olive branch of sorts, though he had the brief thought it sounded forced. Still, he *was* curious...

"I haven't talked to Debra Ann about our plans, but I can swing it as far as I know. I was going over to chat with Eve. Why don't we ask her?"

"Good morning, Eve," Paul announced as they arrived at her desk. "I was on my way to see you and ran into Bob."

"Hi, guys, what's up?"

Strickland spoke first. "I'd like to ask you both to join me for dinner at my place — Arlessa, my housekeeper, is a mean chef. It would allow us to get to know each other away from the precinct. Are you available tomorrow night?"

Eve's eyes met Paul's and flicked back to Bob. "That's a tempting offer," she replied with a polite smile, "but my wife and I just got the ultrasounds from the hospital for our little — yes — boy! We're going out for a gender-reveal celebration, just the two of us and a few friends. I am *so* sorry. I would have loved to go."

"Oh, congratulations! Exciting times. No worries, there will be plenty of other opportunities, and family is the most important thing. Paul, I hope you can still make it. Feel free to bring your wife along if she has nothing else going on."

"Yes, of course, I wouldn't miss it. I'll check with Debra Ann and let you know if she can come."

"Good, I'll e-mail you my address. I know you and Eve were working on something, and I need to get back to what I was doing. Again, thanks for sharing the great news about your son. Let me know when you've picked a name so I can send something to welcome him into the world." Bob turned to me. "I'm looking forward to seeing you tomorrow night."

Once Bob was safely away, Paul turned back and grinned at Eve. "So, I assume the gender-reveal party Debra Ann went to last week was for a *different* son? She told me she had a blast."

Eve gave Paul a sideways smirk. "Don't you dare tell a soul I lied," she said with a little laugh.

"He seemed to take that you couldn't make it in stride — kind of odd for a 'team-building' exercise. I'd have expected him to reschedule to include you. I'll go — file it under 'scratching an itch.' Mondo told me at the Rady Children's Ball that Bob has a nice place. I'll fill you in afterward. I'm heading over to talk to Lt. Harbin. Thought I'd check in with you first and see how things are going."

"I'm stymied getting any more out of the public messages on the site." Eve's expression turned serious.

"It seems like someone's purged the messages around the specific cases we're interested in. For example, the dual runaway trucks: absolute silence, except for one post. Super-techie — it's about stepping down currents to control a high-amperage servo motor with a low-voltage radio-controlled airplane slave receiver. The message's subject line is about steering a 'lorry' remotely. I'm guessing whoever removed these postings used search keywords around 'truck' to find the ones they wanted and missed this one. This message has several links to other threads, but what they pointed to is gone.

"I took snapshots of all the message forum subject headers when Andy showed you we could see these posts. I wanted the snapshots as an index, but the messages are disappearing quickly. Still, it shows me there were once several discussions about those challenges. Now that Steve's dismembered and we don't yet have fake member accounts, I'm using the one Debra Ann created. Maybe that has something to do with it."

"What about the punk videos?"

"The links to the results videos for the punks we're investigating are broken, too. But I downloaded each of those videos and still images when I first found them, so we have copies."

"Smart move. Has Bob been able to help you?"

"Maybe I'm just disappointed in how my work is going, but it's been like pulling teeth. I'll ask if Bob can get me access to something, and he'll say, 'Sure, no problem.' Then, after not hearing anything for a few hours, I'll check with him, and now there's an issue. He never lets me know before I have to ask, though. I've been doing workarounds for what I need, but that only takes me so far."

Exasperation was audible in Eve's voice, and a frown creased her forehead. She tossed her head as if to shake it off. "Never mind, forget I said that; I don't like talking behind anybody's back. But it's slower than I thought it would be. Those guys in Vice are pretty sharp; usually, I ask, and ten minutes later, there it is."

"I hear what you're saying. Let me see if I can do anything to speed things up. I'll let you know if there's any news."

Maybe because Paul's frustrations with the case were also growing, he was developing gnawing concerns about the slow progress of the Aunt Tik's server data extraction. Eve was an exceptionally diligent worker, and having her confirm his unease deepened it.

Paul didn't want to be scapegoating anyone on their team, especially not their newest member, who just happened to outrank him — at minimum, bad optics. General dissatisfaction at not solving any of their homicides was normal and probably healthy. If that was behind what Paul and Eve felt, inciting more negative karma within their group wouldn't help. But then again, neither would further delays.

Bouncing ideas off a trusted mentor can help in situations like this. Paul decided to share his concerns with Louis, knowing the lieutenant would put them into their proper perspective. Paul visited Louis's new office for the first time — despite having his rank bumped up months ago, he'd only recently moved into his fancier digs.

"Hey, Lieutenant, do you have a moment?"

"Addressing me as 'Lieutenant' seems pretty formal and suggests that maybe I should *make* some time." Louis looked up with a wry smile. "What's going on?"

"Can I ask you a question I shouldn't be asking about a fellow team member?" Paul began hesitantly.

"I don't know why not. What's on your mind? It must be serious if you think you need permission."

"Thanks, but personnel matters aren't in my job description, so I should tread lightly. These things don't come up all that often in our unit."

Paul paused before continuing.

"Does Lt. Strickland seem a little, well, *off* to you? I mean, he volunteered to be on this investigation. He just returned to the department;

you'd think he'd be anxious to prove himself. But for all of that, he doesn't seem very enthusiastic about getting the work done."

Louis pursed his lips and sat back in his chair. His expression told Paul he was taking the question seriously.

"What are you seeing that raises doubts?"

"I'm a little disappointed he hasn't gotten anywhere with the Aunt Tik's handles. I've seen Mondo wade into those underage pervert servers and have all the users identified in a week. You'd think it wouldn't be that much different on Aunt Tik's servers — same encryption technologies, and the owners would have the same paranoia level due to the risks of litigation or even prosecution if the data falls into the wrong hands."

"If it makes you feel any better, you're not the first to raise the question." Louis frowned. "I'm not sure what to think. Maybe we're spoiled because we've worked so many of our past cases with Mondo. Perhaps the encryption is more sophisticated than anything we've seen before. Bob may have a different work style, or perhaps the way they did things in San José isn't the same as what we do here. But you're right; he hasn't been as productive as we'd hoped."

"Maybe part of it is a rank thing." Paul tried to see both sides. "He comes here as a new lieutenant and has to answer to a detective. That could be tough, I suppose."

"And let's not forget this is Det. Robbins's first solo leadership gig, supervising more than just her partner," Louis pointed out.

"I'm impressed with how she's doing, but she'll need to get used to being tested and others questioning her decisions. The more the detective surrounds herself with competent people with different thinking styles, the stronger her team will be. But that means she'll have to justify her words and deeds — not easy, but it makes her a better leader."

Paul tried to consider things in that context.

"I can see that. Lt. Strickland makes it clear he's got other ideas, but he's not challenging her. Honestly, I think she could deal with him if he did. Instead, he seems to be slow-walking things. But every day we don't find answers is a day we could be facing another homicide. And Steve's situation, whatever it may be, isn't getting better as time passes. I wonder if the feds, with all their resources, couldn't get there faster if we persuaded them to work with us."

"That's valid. But Mondo wouldn't have let Bob assist our team if he didn't think the man could do the job. The captain has a lot of pride in his unit. Let's give Bob a little more time. Maybe we'll sit him down for a talk if things don't pick up. It could be that he needs help and is hesitant to ask. If that doesn't work, the next step is to bring Mondo into the loop."

Paul took a breath and nodded.

"By the way, the lieutenant's invited me to his house tomorrow night. He wants to talk away from the shop. Not sure what that's about, but I'm bringing Debra Ann along, and I'll keep you posted."

"Bon appétit. And don't hesitate to let me know if things don't resolve themselves quickly. I heard what you said regarding time, new homicides, and Steve. I'm seriously considering starting a backchannel conversation with the feds to convince them of the importance of this Aunt Tik's thing. I'd like to see if we can tap into some of their resources."

As Paul returned to his desk from Louis's office, his cell phone buzzed. It was an e-mail from Bob with his home address. Paul couldn't help himself — he had to check it out on Zillow. Once he did, he had to admit that the man had a lovely home. It should be; its last selling price over ten years ago was precisely one hundred times Paul's gross annual salary ... to the penny.

Paul needed to hold his emotions in check. It just wouldn't do for a grown man to walk through the precinct's bullpen, lined with heavy weaponry, crying like a baby. He doubted that spending time in a rubber room wearing one of those heavy canvas jackets with the sleeves tied together in the back would improve his finances much.

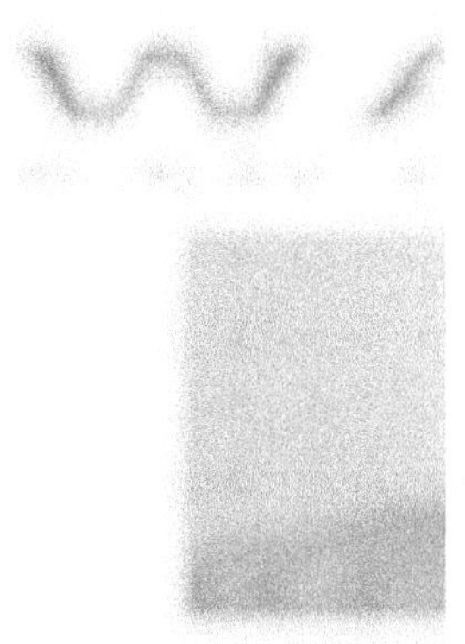

CHAPTER 40

Good news had been hard to come by in this case, and Eve welcomed the e-mail from Bob Strickland that his team had finally decrypted the first significant tranche of Aunt Tik's data. Bob was back on her good side, and Eve knew what she'd go looking for first.

It took her three hours to familiarize herself with the data layout and formats. But once she'd perfected the query to search for "blotto_bill" in all its possible forms, it wasn't long before the results began piling up.

The data doesn't lie, and it pointed to one, and only one, real-world identity inextricably tied to that username. Still, Eve felt compelled to run the query several times. The results were consistent, returning just one member profile using "blotto_bill" as any part of their username.

And yes, that member had been a cell captain for long periods. Most importantly, he'd been the cell czar since just a few days after James Robert Marshall III's murder. According to the data, he'd served as punk master for several punks, including those the team had identified as suspicious.

It was time to pull up this guy's sheet and see if the pieces fit. William Darnell Eastman wasn't hard to find. He'd had a series of run-ins with local authorities over the years; nothing murderous showed up in his record, but he certainly wasn't a law-abiding citizen. The transcript showed his adult crimes began promptly when he turned eighteen; that suggested he'd been in trouble when younger. His juvey records weren't part of his sheet; she'd have to go before a judge and get them unsealed.

What she had now showed Eastman committing his first crime before entering the Navy. He'd joined to escape jail time for joyriding in a stolen car. He received a general, rather than honorable, discharge after serving only fourteen months. While still in, he'd taken rate training after boot camp as an electronics tech, which likely meant he knew his way around a soldering iron, software, and programming. After that, Eastman spent most of his Navy duty undergoing punishments ordered by a series of captain's masts for everything from AWOL to petty theft. The man had severe issues with authority.

Nonetheless, Eastman had been hired and served for a year with the City of Compton police force. His employment was during a long period when Compton accepted anyone who could stand without wobbling and was willing to wear the uniform. After they kicked him loose, the state denied Eastman unemployment, which said a lot about the quality of his service.

Eastman had been in and out of trouble ever since. Domestic abuse, fraud, larceny, theft of services, running a gaming establishment without a license, disorderly conduct, and an assortment of relatively low-level drug charges. Among his arrests and convictions were two connections Eve was looking for. Three years ago, Carla Littman filed for a restraining order against him after a domestic incident following an Internet date that went bad. Eastman had served sixteen months on a stolen weapons charge after breaking into a motor home owned by Gary Barker and taking a handgun.

Identifying Eastman's link to JoAnn Mabry was more challenging. Frustrated with what the department's databases and search tools could tell her, Eve googled the general Internet, throwing in every keyword she could think of. There it was, four items down, on the second page of listings. Before joining her last firm and making partner, Mabry had hung out her law shingle in her name alone. Her firm had been awarded $285,000 from Eastman to settle a civil suit around a Bitcoin scam. That wasn't Eastman's only foray into financial scams. Eve presumed he'd migrated to civil offenses as a less risky way to make his living.

There'd be time to flesh all that out later. What mattered now was that Eve had the son of a bitch in her sights. Now she could let herself revel in that "*holy cow!*" rush she'd been anticipating — from doubting Thomas to a true believer in five seconds flat, a feeling like no other, that version of a sugar high unique to being a cop.

Now the crazy would start: filling in their team and the other squads working the non–Aunt-Tik's parts of their homicide cases and Steve's kidnapping, chasing Eastman to ground, and pulling together all the evidence they could find to build the cases against him. After she'd called Marci, and with her boss's shrill "*woohoo!*" still ringing in her ears, she left "Get back to me as soon as you see this!" messages for Paul and Bob.

Having enjoyed her moment, Eve went back to work. Getting the rest of the data decrypted and analyzed was now more critical than ever. The DA would have to argue much of this case before a jury based on the information contained in those servers.

<hr>

With the first batch of Aunt Tik's data yielding positive results, the prospects for the rest of what they could pull down over the Internet were promising. Bob and his Vice technicians would push forward with downloading and decrypting the rest of the data.

That wouldn't be enough. Once law enforcement found Eastman, prosecuting him would require pristine copies of the original data from Aunt Tik's, preferably from the organization's backup servers. Those would show changes in the data as they occurred over time. The backups would not likely be accessible via the Internet. Typically, archiving software would copy that data over a nonpublic Ethernet backbone to backroom servers. Aunt Tik's would control the physical and digital access to those servers.

Having been several steps behind Eastman for months, the team was eager to get ahead of him — it was time to ask for search warrants. Paul made the call to Assistant DA Levine.

As it happened, the ADA and Lt. Harbin had just finished discussing the same thing, and there was a problem.

"Look, Paul, I sympathize with your situation. I understand your excitement about finding Eastman's name after all these months of hard work. But all you have at the moment is an accusation. I can get any search warrants you need around Eastman and his property. But for third parties that we don't intend to charge? Too soon.

"If Aunt Tik's chooses to fight, we don't have enough. We tried to get some voluntary cooperation from the local Aunt Tik's cell, hoping they'd open a window into their data that would at least address our immediate needs, but no dice. Their position is that if they help us, they risk exposing themselves to litigation in the federal case around the attempted murder of Judge Wasserman. Frankly, they have a valid point.

"Still, we're willing to run it past Judge Stewart. She's as police-friendly as they come, but I can't push it too hard. If she turns us down, I need her on our side when we ask again with more to offer. I asked Lt. Harbin to come to my office yesterday to help my staff draw up a probable cause affidavit.

"But unless Judge Stewart is in a crazy-generous mood, we don't have much of what she'll need. Circumstantially, sure, you and I might believe there's likely one or more Aunt Tik's members up to their eyeballs in your cases. But nothing says Aunt Tik's is sponsoring, supporting, or encouraging them to do bad acts. To be blunt, Paul, with your strongest witness now missing, a participating suspect dead, no forensic evidence against Aunt Tik's as an organization, and your primary suspect not yet apprehended or interviewed, well … let's just say it's going to be a real challenge."

***

Lt. Harbin had been as jubilant as any member of the team when Lt. Robbins called to let him know they'd identified William Eastman as "blotto_bill," the key player and likely serial murderer tied to all the Aunt Tik's cases. Still, Paul Castro's point about the lost productivity when mining that first batch of enciphered server data had hit home — the passing of time translated directly to more suffering and loss of life. Had they obtained that data just a little sooner, Steve Nielsen's kidnapping might not have happened. Without question, Jimmy Detmer would still be alive.

Eastman and any cronies he may have had were still in the wind. With the perpetrators free, able to kill and cause harm, Lt. Harbin wasn't about to let slow data processing add to the damage. Successfully extracting a suspect from that data took the exercise out of the realm of a fishing expedition. Louis was no longer reluctant to ask his good friend Captain Cranston for more help to speed things along.

Louis picked up the phone and, when Mondo answered, informed him that the team had finally identified a suspect from the portion of Aunt Tik's data that Lt. Strickland had turned over to Eve. Mondo didn't hesitate when Louis asked for more data decryption help, but there was a potential complication.

"Louis, I'd like to give you Jeff Bennett. He's the best we have, other than yours truly. Knowing he had some competition might kick Bob in the pants and get him going."

"But there's history there," Louis pointed out. "Aunt Tik's is a small team. If I were Jeff, I'd resent working alongside the guy who pushed me down in the org chart under circumstances that weren't fair. Worse, I've worked with Jeff, and hands down, he's the more productive of the two. If it were me, doing better work while the guy I'm standing beside enjoys all the rewards would get under my skin."

"Jeff's a consummate professional," Mondo argued, "and while those things bother our competitive natures, you might be surprised how Jeff would take it. He's in it for the results, which the man can produce. Why don't I send him up to talk with you? You and he can thrash it out and see how you feel. If it's a fit, a good thing for everyone; otherwise, I'll send you someone else, no harm, no foul."

"That's a deal, Mondo. Let's do that."

"You going to be around a while longer tonight?"

"Yup — Jenny's got class, Austin's at Bible camp, and the twins have a sleepover; they took the mutt with them."

"I'll have a quick chat with Jeff and send him up. I'll be heading home — let me know how everything turns out in the morning."

***

No more than fifteen minutes later, Louis looked up to see Jeff Bennett tapping on the metal frame of his open office door. Bennett was average in height, but his high forehead made him seem taller. The readers he kept riding at the hairline of his graying blonde crewcut made him seem like an academic, in keeping with his calm, considerate demeanor.

Louis stood to shake Bennett's hand, and the Vice investigator spoke first.

"Mondo tells me you could use my help, but the situation might be delicate, and you'd explain."

Bennett's eyes immediately went to the William Eastman rap sheet and other contents of a manila folder lying open on the lieutenant's desk. Spinning the arrest record toward himself, Bennett looked at it momentarily, his expression a half smile, eyebrows knitted together.

"Oh, is *this* what you wanted to speak to me about — you want me to go undercover? I mean, I'm getting a little old for that shit. But hey, if you think it'll help, why not?"

Louis was dumbstruck, pulling his head back with a deep frown, his lips curled downward, looking at Bennett like he'd just described being probed by a UFO.

"Jeff, I've known you for ten years, and you've always been the straightest of shooters — but what the *fuck* are you talking about?"

CHAPTER 41

Paul drove, allowing me to take in the view. It was a gorgeous evening, slightly under seventy degrees, as the sun sank below the tops of the trees. Beautiful orange, red, and yellow highlights formed a mackerel pattern in the clouds flowing from the distant horizon. Paul pulled up to the keypad at the gated entrance to Bob Strickland's exclusive community, and our host buzzed us in.

These were gorgeous homes, each uniquely oriented on their spacious plot of land, rolling hills undulating between them. I didn't see any floor plans that were obviously like the others. The homes I could see looked larger than 5,000 square feet, with four or five bedrooms and a bathroom for each. All featured three- or four-car garages and wide brick, cobblestone, or stained concrete driveways, some with extensions curving up to access the main entrances of the homes. Those featured variations on a similar theme — large vestibules with mostly open glass from the top of the entryway to the roof's peak, revealing expensive ornamental lighting or chandeliers.

Jags, Beamers, Bentleys, Teslas, and the occasional Land Rover dotted the garages and driveways. Every home I looked down on as we crested the top of a hill seemed to have a pool and a hot tub. During my teenage years, summers shadowing my father as he built up his construction business taught me to recognize signs of the occasional sauna, steam room, or other outdoor amenity. The landscaping and lighting were straight from a glossy real estate digest, and some larger corner lots featured English gardens.

Bob's residence was equal to any of the others in the neighborhood. As we topped a slight rise looking down on the Strickland property, I saw the four-bedroom, three-and-a-half bath, two-story residence on an expansive corner lot below me, just as Paul had described it from its Zillow listing. The home had a softly floodlit exterior and a variety of ornately trimmed junipers around the residence and the grounds. The front yard featured a pond with underwater lighting and a backlit waterfall. Sculpted clay tiles formed the broad main walkway, illuminated with low-profile, indirect architectural lighting. As I walked the curving path, I saw that even the bedrooms had designer interior window treatments and sculptured ceilings.

I half expected a butler to answer the door, but Bob performed the honors himself.

"Wow," Paul said after Bob greeted us and led the way inside. "You *do* have a nice home — Eve should have come with us. She'd die to see this place."

We followed Bob into a sunken living room with a twelve-foot-wide fireplace and what looked like actual gaslit sconces on the wall for lighting. The décor must have been professionally designed, with none of the overtly masculine touches you'd expect from a bachelor pad or a man cave. The furnishings in the home were exquisite yet appeared comfortable. The attention-getter was the high glass wall, bracketed by opulent drapes on either side and taking up the entire rear panel of the living room.

The sweeping expanse of glass looked out onto a massive swimming pool. On one side of it stood a sauna, the gorgeous orange cedar panels visible through its glass front. Across from that, on the other side of the pool, was an exercise room with a weight machine and a Peloton bike visible through the glass in its door. Subdued ambient lighting — in the walkways and tucked among the coconut and needle palms and Greco-Roman statuary in the surrounding yard — glinted off the smooth surface of the water.

"Thank you," Bob responded. He then headed off a question he'd anticipated. "Obviously, I couldn't afford anything like this on my lieutenant's wages."

He grinned and ushered us to a couch, adding, "My parents did well and have helped out over the years. I received a pretty nice inheritance when my mother passed. Let me tell Arlessa you're here."

Paul looked at me, his eyes wide, eyebrows arched, and the corners of his mouth turned down in appreciation. I could only nod as my eyes flitted about, taking in the details of our surroundings. We took our seats side by side on the white Italian leather sofa. A large painting of a matronly woman dominated the area above the fireplace. I assumed she was Bob's mother from the period of the clothes she wore for the sitting.

Suddenly, I experienced a mild bout of social anxiety. I wasn't quite sure of the etiquette required if the topic of Bob's mother came up in conversation. He'd just said she'd passed, implying it had been some time ago, certainly enough to get through the probate process. But when he introduced himself to Paul's coworkers, he told them he returned to San Diego because his mother had surgery and was feeling better, in sufficiently good health to live by herself. That would have been just a little over a year ago.

During the introductions at the Rady's Children's Ball, Mondo told Paul he'd visited this home when Lt. Strickland first came back to join his unit in Vice, so Bob already had the house then. I supposed that his parents could have "helped out" some time ago to buy the home, meaning that his inheritance was irrelevant to its purchase.

None of that was any of my business, of course. Still, the subject of family comes up often during conversations in casual home settings. How safe would it be to talk about parents in general if the man might still be grieving for his mother? Or maybe his stepmother, if he had both … that *would* explain the confusion. I'd have to be sure to tread lightly.

A middle-aged woman with a pleasant face, graying hair, and an ample figure arrived from the direction of the dining room.

"Paul, Debra Ann, meet Arlessa, my housekeeper. Ask her for anything you want, and she'll take care of it."

"I'll be in the kitchen," Arlessa said. "Just say, 'Alexa, call Arlessa,' and she will let me know you need me." Arlessa tilted her head downward, then turned to leave the room.

Paul had warned me there might be a lot of talking shop this evening, and the conversation didn't take long to turn that way.

"With my change in residence leaving San José," the lieutenant said, "and then working on loan to your unit rather than Vice, I haven't gotten to know anyone on either of our teams very well. The people who knew me as I worked up the ranks are in San Jose. Coming here as a lieutenant was the first time I'd been in the position of having people under me. Unfortunately, I hadn't worked among them first, so there was no shared history to begin friendships. Asking officers I supervise in my Vice unit to socialize would be, at best, awkward."

Paul nodded slowly.

"I struggled with that, too, but in a different way. When I was younger, I'd always been just 'PJ'" — Paul grinned as he glanced at me — "or 'Paul' to everyone, and I liked it that way. Making rank in the military meant learning to say no and being responsible for what other people do. That was a fundamental change and a big learning curve. Even so, the social aspect wasn't a big part of it – it's the Navy. Very simple: Do what your superiors say. Liking them wasn't necessary or expected, though it helped you get promoted.

"When I became a civilian again and made criminalist supervisor, military training didn't help form relationships with the people who reported to me."

Bob's eyes showed surprise. "I heard that before Louis Harbin took over Homicide, you and he were the gold standard around here as far as detective and Forensics partnerships go. The Batman and Robin of investigative teams. With everyone looking up to you, I wouldn't have thought fraternizing would present any problems."

"Well, if it makes you feel any better," Paul conceded, "Det. Harbin was that 'gold standard' long before I came to work with him. Talk about intimidating — honestly, he wasn't, but his reputation was. When he made lieutenant, they didn't have an administrative slot for him yet, and he wanted to stay in Homicide. Partnering with a detective of lower rank was awkward with the union and everything, and I was still with the state at the time, so the two of us teamed up.

"I would never have admitted it back then, but I was scared to death." Paul looked in my direction.

"You never showed it," I assured him. "Anything I saw, I just attributed to all the changes in our lives. We'd lost Cindy, you switched jobs, we moved in together, getting married...."

"We *were* dealing with a lot of things." Paul smiled gently, pausing before turning back to Bob. "The lieutenant's investigative style was hands-on. He was known to get in a subject's face occasionally. I thought he might put me in situations where he'd get me killed. But it wound up being the best experience I could have had."

"In our unit, Capt. Cranston is the living legend," Bob explained. "Mondo brought Vice out of the Stone Age, from trolling hookers and johns down by the Naval Station into the Internet Age. Almost everything we do now in the vice unit came from systems the captain originated back when there was no model, nothing anyone could copy. Rumors say Mondo was a two-finger typist — some say he still is — and didn't even know how to turn on a computer when he started chasing pedophiles on these websites."

"And look at Vice now," Paul observed. "It takes years to get onto the waiting list for interns wanting to work in your online investigation unit."

"I know. I had to wait until I became a lieutenant in San José before I could pull rank to get one of the open slots in San Diego's vice unit. Now, I need to build a team to create my legacy. I thought I'd start by getting to know the members of the unit I'm working with and go from there."

Paul nodded.

"I think it's a good situation for you. The Aunt Tik's investigation is visible to everyone. We appreciate the skills you have that we don't, and everyone on our team wants you to succeed."

Bob glanced in my direction and changed topics to include me.

"But I'm sure you must be hungry. Arlessa has prepared a couple of meal options. I wasn't sure where your tastes might lie or if you had any dietary restrictions, so she's tried to cover all the bases."

"Thank you, Bob," I said. "You shouldn't have gone to such trouble. Paul and I don't have any issues with food, and we've heard that anything you put in front of us will be excellent."

About that, I was entirely right. I decided on the salmon, thinking that might be the healthier choice. It had a light, sweet glaze, served with charred vegetables and rice pilaf. Paul went with the duck, and when we sampled each other's plates, we realized there was no wrong choice.

The conversation was light; we talked about some of the different personalities we knew between their two units in the department and the world at large. The talk turned to their career opportunities. The department had announced a new program that would cooperate with SDSU to offer discounts on the university's courses. Unlike previous programs, it eliminated most of the limits on officers' class choices. Though Bob had his master's in criminology, he was interested in tune-up courses that would make his education more current and relevant. Paul wanted to learn more about profiling and criminal psychology.

After a very nice Beaujolais and a slice of strawberry-garnished New York–style cheesecake, Paul and I were both ready for our naps.

We adjourned to the living room and continued the small talk that had started during our dinner.

"You have a sweet setup here, Bob," I said. "I'm surprised one of the fine ladies I'm sure you know hasn't staked her claim."

"I do get my share of offers," Bob replied with a sly, almost cocky, grin. "But I've sown enough wild oats for one lifetime, and I'm not eager to get into any situation that isn't right. I was married once, and it didn't end well. When you have money in your family, and she says she does but doesn't, it can get ugly rather quickly. Fortunately, we had no children, and though it took a while, I was able to put all that behind me."

It wasn't in Paul's or my nature to share the circumstances of past relationships in social settings with casual acquaintances, so we kept silent. But I could empathize with some of what Bob said.

Bob had what I must admit was an impressive jazz collection, including some original 78 rpm shellac. He put on an Etta James album at a low volume so we could speak over it comfortably.

Backed by the softened, sultry tones of an early rendition of "At Last," the conversation inevitably turned to the squad room, specifically the Aunt Tik's investigation. With that, I could tell the situation was becoming a little uncomfortable for Paul.

"Even though we now know William Eastman is 'blotto_bill,'" Bob said, "we still have much work to do. The glacial pace of this investigation is maddening. With all these cases having a common element, we keep taking down the trees and not considering the forest."

He was voicing the same frustrations Paul had told me the entire team felt about the tortoise-like pace of the case. But Paul had mentioned other things, and part of me kept wanting to scream, *"Then get off your ass, Bob, and do your damned job!"* I knew that in Paul's mind, the lack of membership and management data from encrypted Aunt Tik's servers held the investigation back the most.

But, of course, neither of us was about to offend our host and turn the otherwise pleasant evening into a disaster. Not only were we firmly on Bob's turf, but I suspected that was the whole point — I felt the current topic had been the planned agenda for our get-together all along.

That reinforced my sense of being manipulated, adding to my other emotions. Still, I politely held my tongue, not wanting to create problems for Paul.

Paul was diplomatic.

"Homicide's a little different from cases you had in Vice, I'd imagine. For most vice crimes, neither the perpetrator nor the victim is going anywhere — plenty of people to talk to, if they're willing — and the primary challenges are sorting out who did what and protecting those at continuing risk during the investigation.

"But in these killings, we lose everything the victims knew and a lot of what they've done because they're gone and can't tell us. Although there can be exceptions when a murderer is on the loose and a threat to others, there's usually no one left to protect. With the Aunt Tik's situation, we have a huge exception — we've got to rescue, or at least recover, Steve.

"But from what I know of the other members, our team is always open to new ideas and perspectives. Keeping the urgency of Steve's situation top of mind, what do you think we should be doing differently?"

Kudos to Paul — his phrasing and tone when he posed the question were genuine and sincere. There were times that Paul exhibited a graciousness that I just wouldn't have been able to pull off myself.

CHAPTER 42

I knew Paul hoped that opening the door to new ideas might lighten the conversation and maybe even allow a novel thought or two to break through. But the tension within me quickly worsened when Bob began not very subtly questioning Marci's decisions and, by extension, her leadership when she wasn't there to defend herself.

"I just don't think that trying to dig out small pieces of the puzzle from all the Aunt Tik's data to fit the working theory is the way to go. We're trying to find out who filled the tractor bucket with the concrete that crushed Marianne Foreman and Gary Barker. Why? Even if we find out, we can't charge them with anything. There's nothing illegal about putting broken concrete in a bucket.

"We know this Eastman likely did it, but he couldn't have pulled it off without Aunt Tik's infrastructure. Instead of digging through servers subject to Aunt Tik's whims, we should put the fear of Jesus into them and make them come to us. We should just say, 'Look, we know you aided and abetted him because he couldn't have done it otherwise. If you don't help us get where we need to go, we'll shut you down.' "

"But Bob, we've had this conversation before," Paul spoke slowly, trying to keep any aggravation out of his voice. "Even if we could make that accusation — and, as I said then, I don't think we can, legally — what's to keep Aunt Tik's from calling our bluff? They could easily say, 'Just try it, we'll see you in court,' knowing they can draw things out for years in civil litigation. Publicly appearing as if they're adversarial to authority only helps their brand. "But for the sake of this discussion, let's say we find a way to ruin their business. People we don't yet know, with resources from a national organization that we can't touch, merely change the website names and URLs, and they're back in business the next day. Or, if not them, a copycat. Everything about the people who committed these murders evaporates, yet the future threat remains."

Bob wasn't about to let this go.

"But they *do* have resources we can access. The servers are physical, and we can get search warrants. Once we have those, we can acquire all of what we need from the data on them, rather than piecemeal."

"Warrants based on *what?*" Paul asked. "Right now, we can't show a single Aunt Tik's member committing a significant crime, except for a guy who hasn't yet given us his statement and a nineteen-year-old kid who just happens to be the Homicide commander's next-door neighbor. How would that look, given that we haven't found either of them?"

Paul tried to get Bob to see his circular logic.

"But say we could show a different member committed another crime — to get a warrant, we'd have to show the evidence is in that data, and going through those data points was the very frustration you were expressing."

Bob had a different point of view.

"But where we're at now proves my point. Great, we have one subject's name, but only bits and pieces of his activities. Nothing yet says he's done anything other than approving some iffy challenges, maybe changing a few data items, and possibly faking some videos. We need a lot more, and getting it through the data we can access via the Internet isn't efficient."

"You're right," Paul conceded, "we've got a long way to go. But the other road isn't any better. We know what happens when we instead use brute force through the courts to get the server data directly. First, we'd need

Aunt Tik's membership list. That's not going to happen *unless* we can show probable cause that at least one person is on the member rolls who committed murder and that the list likely contains more persons of interest.

"Once we have Eastman's statement, we'll be closer to fulfilling that requirement. Still, we're not allowed to go on fishing expeditions. And that will be true for every specialized server they have — we'll have to show probable cause for each. No judge will give us carte blanche to search every server in a private business with more than ten thousand members when there may be just one person solely responsible for all the crimes we're trying to solve."

"But it *couldn't* be just one," Bob persisted, his facial muscles tightening. "We've got at least six murders and five cases, all broken into multiple separate activities."

Bob's beginning to sound like a defense attorney representing the accused. He seems more invested in his arguments than if he were merely playing devil's advocate. I'll have to ask Paul later if this is how investigations usually go.

"That's true," Paul replied, trying to find common ground. "But only a tiny percentage of those activities were crimes. And the evidence is slowly piling up that just one person *could have been* responsible — I'm not saying *was* because we don't know that yet — for the specific parts of these punks that resulted in murders."

"I see where you're going … Still, even if he's solely responsible for the criminal intent, the data won't show Eastman did any of the challenges." Lowering his eyelids, Bob drew a deep breath, followed by a dismissive sigh. He seemed annoyed. "Eastman can just point his finger at the members who did. I don't see how that gets us anywhere if we could never convict the guy because of 'he said, she said.'"

"Our theory is that to make all this work, he has to do the hidden challenges, those with clearly illegal elements, himself." Paul glanced at me. "Once we know which parts Eastman or his cohorts had to do outside Aunt Tik's process, we can get physical evidence to tie him to them. Same as we'd do with any other crime. At that point, we know what we're looking for and can gather evidence in ways that are comfortably within the scope of what we do every day.

"Best case for us is if Eastman needed help for some of that off-the-books work — once we identify who he used, we should be able to get one or more of them to talk by making the consequences personal, raising the stakes, turning one against the other, and including serious jail time in the mix — again, as we'd do anyone else to flip them. I'm pretty sure we had one on the hook in Detmer and didn't realize it — Eastmen had to kill him before we put it together."

"But once we can prove Eastman's role in any one of these crimes, the rest will fall into place."

"I get that Eastman is in the middle of all this," Bob argued. "But I saw his sheet. He doesn't seem like a rocket scientist to me. How do we know he's not loaning out the 'blotto_bill' handle to anyone who needs to use it? If he's just a tool for somebody else or even a group, we're no closer than we were."

"That's also true," Paul responded with confidence, "but when Marshall sent that e-mail to himself, he was cell czar and knew exactly which Aunt Tik's handle went with which real human being, or, to your point, beings. He would have known what they were doing with that handle and their level of responsibility. But he wrote 'ASSHOLE!' in the singular, not the plural. I think we're looking for one individual and male, given he didn't use 'BITCH!' That all squares with Eastman.

"Even if Eastman didn't do these crimes, it's reasonable to believe he knows who did because he assigned the performers, and no one else knew all the challenges to the punk or their order. As the punk master, he's responsible for the punk results video, and we know he gamed those results for the Foreman and Barker car-crushing killings, the Littman Cheerios-tampering homicide, and the Mabry runaway-trucks murder. We have to, at least, know Eastman's intent before we can let him off the hook.

"So, for now, we need anything we can get on just one guy, Eastman. To the extent that finding out about the challenge participants and their activities helps us locate him, and in the absence of anything better we can do, that's fine; let's do that. If there's a shortcut getting to Eastman, we need to follow it, but we can't blow up Aunt Tik's to see where the pieces land as our bypass."

"Well, it certainly wouldn't hurt to locate him," Bob acknowledged, toning down the tension, "for Steve's sake, if nothing else."

Even as he backed down, Bob's voice lacked enthusiasm. He was scowling as he shifted topics slightly.

"The encryption on these Internet-facing servers is a bear. It's not that the enciphering itself is such a big deal; it's the homegrown and nonstandard way they're applying it. The Aunt Tik's server contents are being re-encrypted every night, during the wee hours, with multiple rolling codes, and they force IP address resolution through different DNS servers each day. The levels and number of obfuscations are much greater than we expected."

I couldn't help but wonder. *Had everything we'd heard before this from Bob been a smokescreen to cover the real problem — was he out of his element trying to decipher those servers? Were we finally getting to the real problem?*

Paul frowned, and I got the sense he wasn't buying into any excuses this late in the game.

"I'd hoped the national organization would provide those servers as part of the franchising agreement. I assumed they'd want the membership servers under their control for auditing since the umbrella corporation collects the membership dues and redistributes them back to the franchisees. Surely hiding franchise data from them wouldn't make them happy."

I couldn't tell if Bob didn't know who controlled the data — which made little sense, given he worked with those servers every day — or didn't want Paul to have the answers, which made even less sense.

"I think those servers are leased independently from a national ISP by the local chapter," Bob said.

I knew Paul well enough to realize *that* answer tripped all over his built-in BS detector. They'd been working on this too long to still be at "I think."

"I'd have to ask one of the vice guys working this," Bob continued. "As far as I know, those servers are under the unique control of the local cell czar, and that's why we're dealing with an unusual deployment."

Paul didn't want to challenge Bob's competence directly while in his home, so he asked a different question.

"Is it possible the nonstandard encryption means that Aunt Tik's management is trying deliberately to frustrate our investigation?"

"No," Bob answered, "I don't believe so. Because it's on top of the standard server encryption, I view it as general institutional paranoia from the local Aunt Tik's. Like adding a deadbolt to your front door without rekeying the handle lock — now you have to carry two different keys."

I knew Paul was planning to talk to Bob about this at the precinct, but he broached the subject now.

"Maybe the czar's extracurricular activities are making him insecure. We can get you more resources, and if you need something we can't provide, I know Mondo can get you anything available. Lt. Harbin is considering engaging the feds to see if they'll lend a helping hand."

My tingling spidey sense told me Bob felt trapped by Paul's suggestions; still, I couldn't fathom why. But Bob, somewhat grudgingly, agreed he could use more staff.

"I could split my team to specialize in certain tasks if we had additional resources. There'd be some headwinds from expanding the group, so the results might not be immediate. Any new team members in the digital forensics area would have to stay within the organizational structure under my supervision to keep us from going madly off in all directions."

I attributed all the caveats around taking on more help to professional pride or maybe a macho unwillingness to admit approaching defeat. The latter is rarely helpful to police investigations since those are team efforts — perhaps Bob didn't feel fully integrated into Marci's squad yet.

Bob's cell phone buzzed, and he glanced at the display. He apologized for the distraction, saying he needed to use the restroom and return a call. He invited us to look around and feel at home as he left.

Paul and I took Bob up on his offer. We checked out a wide passageway off the living room. It featured school, family, and event photos, as well as memorabilia, on its walls.

We entertained ourselves by looking over the meaningful moments of Bob's life, happening across an old Lewis and Clark College photo of his rowing team. "Well, *la-de-da*," I said to Paul, who gave out a little snort. Undoubtedly spurred on by pure envy, I'd always associated collegiate lacrosse, sailing, and rowing with prissy Ivy League schools I could never have afforded — even if they would have accepted me, which was doubtful. *"Green monster of jealousy, arise from thy bed!"* I thought, laughing at myself.

As Paul wandered further down the hall, I tried to tell which of the rowers was Bob Strickland, but the resolution in the faded old photo was poor. Curious, I lifted the bottom of the photo frame out and up. Sure enough, there was a label affixed with now-yellowed, cracked, and curling Scotch tape:

COXSWAIN: STEVE ("MIGHTY") MILROY
CALL BOW: BART ("BOATBOY") BEAMAN
BOW SEAT: JAMES ("STEELIE") WILLIS
3 SEAT: MILES ("STANDISH") MCPHEELAN
4 SEAT: MARK ("CATFISH") FISHER
5 SEAT: DAVID ("DEEDEE") DANIELS
6 SEAT: DMITRI ("MAD RUSSIAN") SIDOROV
7 SEAT: BARRY ("BAD ASS"' HINTERSKUL

My heart began racing, and I felt the blood draining from my face. I had to catch my breath as I read the last name:

STROKE SEAT: R. WILLIAM ("BLOTTO BILL") STRICKLAND.

THE WRITINGS OF
AVRIL MARIA SERENE

CHAPTER 43

My fingers trembling, I quickly put the photo back in place.

I pretended to focus on another framed image featuring the Lewis and Clark men's softball team while peeking toward the couch to see where Strickland was.

Not spotting him, I hissed at Paul.

"Paul! *Paul! Get over here!*"

Startled by the command and my tone, Paul turned on his heels and headed back toward me.

"What in the world is going on with *you?*" he asked, almost as though he was going to check my forehead for a fever.

"*Shhh!*" I whispered at the top of my lungs.

"Keep your voice down! Look at the back of the rowing photo, but be casual."

Giving me his "*Are you insane?*" side-eye, Paul pulled the bottom of the frame away from the wall, and after a moment, I saw his jaw drop and his complexion turn ashen.

"*Holy shit!*"

He immediately patted the frame back in place, quickly looking back at the living room.

"*Mother of Mary…* But we already have a 'blotto_bill' — *don't we?*"

Paul put both palms to the upper back part of his skull, his fingers out; he puffed his cheeks and let the air slowly leak out through his lips.

As we stared into each other's wide eyes, I knew we'd both jumped ahead to the same thought — one wrong move now, and we could be signing Steve Nielsen's death warrant if he was still alive.

"Okay," Paul whispered after a second of silence. "You're a better actor than I am. Is your phone powered on? Check it for battery and turn up the ringer volume."

"Got it … My phone's good. What's the plan?"

"Let's go back to the couch. I'll excuse myself to use the restroom and call you from there in a few minutes. Tell Strickland it's your babysitter … *Shit*, here he comes. Just follow my lead."

Paul's eyes went straight to the wall.

At that very moment, Strickland put his hand on my shoulder; I thought I'd have a heart attack right then and there.

He reached between Paul and me to the rowing picture with his other hand and straightened it.

"Ahhh, fond memories. I got promoted to coxswain in my senior year."

Crap, so Strickland knows we were scoping out that photo. Hopefully, he doesn't remember what's behind it and won't check.

Fortunately, Strickland couldn't see my expression directly from where he was.

Paul drew Strickland's attention away from me.

"Looks like you really *did* have some glory days, Bob. What year was that taken?".

Thank God for nonglare glass. The last thing we needed was for him to see the look on my face in the reflections from that wall.

Paul's question bought me enough time to regain some of my composure. But I knew Paul had another reason for asking — we'd need the year to verify the image and his nickname with the school.

Trying as smoothly as he could to turn the conversation in another direction, Paul pointed with his forefinger at a different picture, "I see you were on the softball team. You should join the department's squad. Mostly, it's just for fun, but we play the fire department every year, and that one can get a little intense. How'd your college team do?"

Strickland seemed to accept redirecting the topic to the softball photo. However, I caught him peering back over his shoulder with a concerned expression at the wall of pictures we'd been looking at. Perhaps he just wanted to ensure the rest were still hanging straight, or we hadn't left visible fingerprints.

"We were a small school, Division III." Strickland's tone softened as he reminisced. "We had games against Washington and at Puget Sound, Pacific Lutheran, and Western Intercollegiate. We ended the season with a winning record in my last year, but nothing that made any big headlines in our school paper."

Internally panicking, I was struggling to deal with the sudden revelation that Paul's coworker and fellow peace officer was a brutal multiple murderer — and so goddamned cavalier about it.

I wanted to scream, *"What have you done with Steve?"* and for Paul to place handcuffs on the son of a bitch. But I knew this was not the time for that. Getting this man to face justice would be a process, and each step had to work itself out. My job now was to play a part, keep my wits, and, above all, not reveal to Strickland that we knew anything.

We reclaimed our seats, and the conversation resumed, with Strickland enthusiastically lobbying for his idea from several weeks past to go public with our investigation of Aunt Tik's. Concentrating on his words was hard because I genuinely couldn't have cared less, and his gambit to stall the investigation was now so transparent.

But I did care about Paul getting the chance to do his job well, and that was my motivation to listen intently to what both of them said. As the rationale for revisiting the topic, Strickland used what I now knew was his intentional slow-walking of the computer forensics investigation.

You had to give the man credit for one thing — he had an unbelievable stash of pure chutzpah.

By the time Strickland finished regurgitating the same talking points he'd used earlier, albeit with different phrasing, I badly wanted out of this conversation. Paul needed to be having a meaningful discussion with Louis, Mondo, and the rest of the Aunt Tik's team, not listening to self-serving drivel from this imposter.

But Strickland was an experienced officer and a lieutenant. As a trained interrogator seated only four feet away from us, he could see every microexpression on our faces. Raising his suspicions could be a terrible thing in many different ways. Our successful escape would require a sure yet gentle touch. Paul tried to show genuine sincerity as he promised to take Strickland's position up with Louis in the morning.

Then he asked where the restroom was.

"Down the far hallway, on the right," Strickland answered.

After Paul left, Bob turned his attention to me. He politely apologized that so much of the discussion revolved around work topics; I admit my response was awkward.

Then Paul, now out of Strickland's line of sight, gave me a hand signal to the side of his face with his thumb and pinkie extended, his other fingers tucked, to let me know he was about to telephone me.

As my cell rang a few seconds later, I looked into my purse, making it clear I was checking the phone's Caller ID.

"Oh, I'm so sorry — I need to take this, it's our babysitter," I excused myself, displaying my best "what can you do?" expression.

"Do you need some privacy?"

"Oh, no. I'm sure it won't take but a moment," I replied. "Yes, Chrissy, this is Debra Ann."

"I'm Chrissy, and I'm telling you that Tommy just got tangled up with the neighbor's cat. It's nothing major, but he's bleeding a little and won't stop crying. Break a leg — and say 'hi' to Jody Foster for me when you see her at the Oscars," Paul said, and then he was gone.

"Oh, *no*," I said into the phone. "Tommy knows not to pull its tail. The Band-Aids and the Neosporin are in the cabinet below the sink in our bathroom. Tell him Mommy's on her way; make sure he understands the cat didn't mean it. He can have one of the chocolate ice cream bonbons in the freezer. No, just one; it's too close to his bedtime. We'll be home in a little bit."

I looked up at my host. "Our three-year-old wanted to play with our babysitter's cat, and it took exception," I explained as I put away my phone.

"Is he going to be okay?" Strickland wondered.

"I heard the last part of that — is everything alright?" Paul asked as he returned from the hallway.

"The cat nipped him, and Tommy's got some scratches, but I'm sure he'll be fine. Still, I should get home…," I said, answering both questions.

"Please excuse us, Bob," Paul said apologetically. "Never a dull moment when you have family. We had a wonderful evening. Tell Arlessa that her meals were truly excellent. I also appreciate all the food for thought that you and I shared."

"We'd love to return the favor and have you over at the earliest opportunity," I added, "but don't expect accommodations quite as nice as these!"

Strickland graciously accepted the indefinite commitment and walked us to the door.

Paul and I sat in tense silence as he drove us out of the gated community, almost as though we were holding our breath until we knew we were out of the lieutenant's reach.

But one thing was sure — no way in hell would *that* man ever be welcome in Paul's and my home.

THE WRITINGS OF
AVRIL MARIA SERENE

CHAPTER 44

O nce we were several miles away from Strickland's home — sufficiently distant to at least avoid any accidental sightings by him of us or our vehicle — Paul pulled over so we could exhale and collect our thoughts. I'd never hyperventilated in my life, but I was close.

Paul's first instinct was to figure out what to do next.

His eyes searched mine as he said, "For the moment, we'll have to work on the assumption there are two 'blotto_bill's, crazy as that sounds. I'd be inclined to think the first one must be bullshit, except I've seen the man's rap sheet. My initial, almost overpowering thought is to call Louis immediately, then Marci and Eve.

"But my objectivity is completely shot at this point. Will Louis take the idea of Strickland as a suspect as seriously as we do? Or would he place it under the heading of just another bizarre coincidence? If not, how will Louis react to learning that one of the possible killers is right here among the critical members of our team?"

"I won't be much help as to objectivity," I admitted. "My brain's completely locked into the story I want to write about this — all I can think of is getting to my computer and typing. I don't have to deal with everything this means for you and the department."

"I envy you your focus." Paul's laugh was uneasy. "Thoughts are flying pell-mell through my mind from all directions.

"But Strickland as the doer just … *fits*. 'Triton-blue.' The foot-dragging at decrypting those Aunt Tik's servers or hacking the website and apps, and the classic signs of a traffic stop by an officer at the Marshall homicide scene. And one of the places we specifically hadn't looked for 'blotto_bill' was in the department's human resources files, something we'd have to get special clearance for. Why *would* we, without knowing what we know now?"

I nodded.

"The idea these cases might have been solved — twice in the same day, with two different killers — in such a dramatic fashion is one thing. But juxtaposed against your conversation with Strickland *just twenty minutes ago* about the futility of the team's approach … I mean, it seems *surreal*, almost unbelievable. I'll say this: surreal or not, Bob Strickland is one devious, murderous son of a bitch. I think it's him. I do."

Paul was on the same page but concerned about how he'd share the news.

"That Strickland didn't tell us he once had that nickname after we'd learned how important it was to our cases is inexcusable, whether or not he's *the* 'blotto_bill.' Still, a premature accusation against an investigative team member would be, at best, problematic."

The formality of Paul's word choices told me that his training as a dutiful law-enforcement professional was kicking in.

"Open wounds often linger from Internal Affairs inquiries over those things for years. Whatever I do now will immediately impact everything we were trying to accomplish."

Paul was working it through, out loud, in real-time.

"A false accusation would be destructive, certainly to the team as it stands, and no doubt, to my career. Strickland's a lieutenant, so any decision to address him directly is above my pay grade, even Marci's. Obviously, that's a matter for Louis and Mondo, maybe Internal Affairs."

"I'm nervous, Paul, whether we might have alerted Strickland. You said earlier that blotto_bill's first reaction under stress is to kill somebody. What will he do to Steve?"

Paul drew a deep breath, nodding.

"We'll need to get the wheels turning before the start of regular business tomorrow morning. I can't see how we avoid this turning into a train wreck, but everyone needs to get ahead of it sooner rather than later."

I voiced what Paul already knew.

"Not telling Louis now would violate your friendship and undermine everything you built when you were partners."

"You're right, as usual," Paul conceded with a sad smile. "I'm avoiding telling him because I wanted to spare him that nauseating mule-kick-to-the-gut feeling we all get in law enforcement when one of our own betrays us. I'm feeling it right now.

"And I think it's going to be harder for Louis — he went out of his way to offer Strickland every opportunity to succeed. I'll call Louis at home, and if he answers, good; I'll fill him in. If I don't get him on the line, I'll go to plan B, gathering as much information as possible to back up what we think we know.

"Either way, I'll need to stop by the house to say goodnight to Tommy, and you can start writing. Then, I'll go to the precinct and make some calls. I think you know it'll be a long night, so don't wait up for me."

⁂

As soon as Paul was back on the road, headed to the precinct, he phoned Louis. After three rings, Louis's voicemail announced itself. Paul hesitated — he hadn't thought about what he'd say in a message. He didn't want to accuse the Vice lieutenant in a recording without including what he had to support it, especially given the concerns about Strickland that Paul had expressed to Louis earlier. Rather than complicating things, he'd keep them simple.

"Louis, it's Paul. Call me as soon as you get this. It's important but needs to be kept quiet. Best if we talk before roll call."

Next, Paul pulled over into a 7-Eleven lot to grab some coffee. Before exiting his car, he texted Marci and Eve the same message:

"URGENT that you contact me, but don't share with ANYONE that I reached out to you. I'll explain when we talk."

Coffee in hand, Paul headed to his office. He pulled into the precinct garage and took the stairs two at a time, not wanting to wait on the elevators — he needed to start his research.

It was almost ten-thirty p.m., awfully late to call people at home. But Paul wanted to sneak in at least one attempt. He couldn't say he considered anyone in the Internal Affairs Division a friend. Still, he did know one of the officers, Rod Blakesley, whom he felt he could trust more than most. It just so happened that Rod owed Paul something of a favor. Not a big thing — Paul had been the first outside-the-family Girl Scout cookie customer for Rod's youngest girl. But when a parent has daughters, those things matter.

"Sorry to call you at home so late at night and disturb your family time, Rod, but I think I have a situation here. I need help deciding what I have or maybe don't. I know you've got your rules, but is there anything you can tell me off the record about a relatively new transfer here — a lieutenant by the name of Robert William Strickland?"

There was a pronounced silence on the other end of the phone.

"First," Rod said, "you're getting this only because we've known each other a while, and our understanding going forward is that you haven't heard anything about this from me. Secondly, none of what I'm about to say can appear in writing anywhere — you get my drift? Thirdly, he's a pay grade above you, so be careful whatever you're doing that involves this guy — don't tell me what it is now, or I'll have to open a formal complaint. If he, as the senior officer, says you're instigating things, it'll be *me* having to come after *you*. Fourth, if this involves IAD shit at any point, you come directly to me with it. Got that? No passing 'Go,' no collecting two hundred dollars — straight to my fucking door."

Paul thanked him in advance for his help and agreed to his conditions.

"Odd that you're bringing *that* individual up," Rod started. "He's been the topic of an ongoing conversation around the office. Your boy gamed us, and that's not something we take kindly in IAD. Nine or ten years ago, Strickland was a sergeant going through a nasty divorce — nasty because he *made* it nasty. He wouldn't let it go, got increasingly wound up."

"Any signs of violence?"

"His soon-to-be ex's dad owned a plumbing company, and Strickland would pull over the old man's employees just to fuck with them. We had evidence of him using the department's computer database to hassle people in and around his divorce case. He threatened her old man directly a couple of times. Supposedly, there was a gun drawn at one point. Still, it was he-said, she-said in a domestic legal situation, which ties our hands without something more substantial.

"He was never that great as a cop — average performance reviews or worse — and we started hearing about drinking issues. The dude has money from his family and a fancy suburban home. He gives off this vibe that he doesn't have to work and is doing whatever he does as a favor to the rest of us. The technical term for that is 'arrogant prick.'"

"Yes, the last part, I know. I was just in Strickland's home. I assume keeping that house was one of the reasons he was fighting the divorce so hard."

"I don't *even* want to know what you were doing there," Rod responded. "But yes, he was bound and determined she wasn't going to get a damned thing. At some point, he threw her out. There was some violence on both sides, though I think hers was primarily defensive. We had complaints from his assigned work partner and several people in the squad that he was abusive. But one person's definition of 'abusive' is the next one's idea of 'just having a bad day.'"

"I take it you didn't have enough evidence to move forward?"

"You know how these cases go, Paul." Frustration was detectable in Rod's voice. "We had evidence, and then one day we didn't. Some misguided friend on the force with access to the evidence locker thinks they are 'helping' by making it disappear. People on the street go quiet once they learn the assailant's a police officer. The screaming, terrified victim at the time of the assault apologetically recants in a whisper two days later."

"Recanting witnesses and disappearing evidence in homicides usually means people fear the murderer or their associates, or someone's actively coercing them — I suppose it's the same kind of problem for you." Paul had to admit to some empathy for the difficulty of Rod's role, though the man willingly chose what he wanted to do with his life.

Rod went on, "Then one day he 'accidentally' rammed his then-wife's vehicle with a squad car. She wasn't hurt, but that was the line he couldn't cross with us. We worked up a case against him. He hired this hyper-expensive lawyer, a former cop and union rep, and it devolved into an impasse. We didn't want him on *our* streets anymore, so they worked out a deal where he'd go off to San José on an intercity exchange program to cool his heels — we thought, forever."

"The department booted him but didn't take his badge?" Paul was a little surprised.

"The brass thought the divorce was the main problem, and getting him physically away from the situation would help. I don't know what they saw in this guy that was worth saving. Regardless, once he requested a permanent position in San José, we agreed to expunge anything related to his divorce from his record here, and he gets to walk free.

"We didn't think we'd ever see him again. Guys like that usually get caught doing bad things and wind up eating their gun, anyway — too cowardly to answer fully for what they've done. And you know it's not depression; it's 'fuck you, world!' vengeance. Because right before they do that, the offender goes down to their lawyer's office and writes the people they blame out of their will."

"How'd he get back *here*, then?" Paul was becoming resentful that no one had told his team any of this.

"When we heard he'd snuck back into our Vice unit, it pissed us off. As I said, he gamed the situation. But HR says, 'Hey, he's got a clean sheet, no red flags we knew about.' In the meantime, he's made lieutenant in San José, God knows how, and he's throwing his weight around there. And now, here. We can't actively engage because he hasn't done anything we know about recently. Still, just between you and me, we're watching him."

"I may have something for you, Rod. But first, I need to get everything into one pile to understand better what it looks like. Do you happen to know how to reach his ex?"

"I do. She's remarried, using 'Foreman' as her last name. We checked in on her unofficially when Strickland returned to let her know and see if she was having any issues with him. When we spoke with her, she'd just left her new husband and already had another fiancé. His name was Jerry, or maybe

Gary. Barker, like the old *Price Is Right* guy. She might use his last name if she divorced Foreman and hooked up with Barker."

Paul nearly choked on his coffee. *That evil son of a bitch* — and how is it no one caught that Marianne Foreman was Strickland's ex?

But Paul didn't want to open that can of worms with IAD yet. Before doing anything, he needed to talk to Louis about what was best for all the team's cases, which might not suit IAD's agenda. Internal Affairs had a reputation for being something of a bull in a china shop and for having a singular focus on modifying or terminating the subject's role as a police officer above any other consideration.

Once publicly accused, Strickland would likely lawyer up under the protection of his union rep. Before going through all that, the team needed to discover and explore alternatives that would better serve their homicide cases.

"Thanks, Rod, that helps a ton," Paul said in closing, choosing not to explain Strickland's probable involvement in any of Aunt Tik's homicides. "I'll remember the ground rules.

"I have a feeling we're going to be chatting again and damned soon."

THE WRITINGS OF
AVRIL MARIA SERENE

CHAPTER 45

*T*wo '*blotto_bill's,*' *my ass,* Paul thought. *I don't know how Strickland inserted someone else into this. Still, we finally have him: our czar, our multiple murderer.*

He closed his eyes and took a few moments to strategize. It was almost midnight, and Paul nearly jumped out of his seat when the desktop phone rang, shattering the silence of the squad room.

"Paul, it's Louis. The twins have a sleepover, and Austin's got church camp, so Jenny and I caught a late movie after her class.

"I thought you were out hobnobbing with the rich and famous tonight. I called your cell, but it went to voicemail. Your message sounded like you were in work mode, so I thought I'd try your desk. Listen, I have something urgent I need to talk to you about."

Paul looked at his cell phone sitting on his desk. *Damn*, he'd left the ringer turned off after they left Strickland's home.

"Louis, thanks for calling back. Sorry about the hour. I also have something *you* need to hear, and you won't believe it. But you're the boss; you go first."

"Fair enough. Jeff Bennett stopped by my office late tonight. I'd asked Mondo how thrilled Jeff would be helping us decrypt Aunt Tik's data, given how he'd lost being second-in-command over Vice to Strickland. I thought there could still be hard feelings … maybe the two of them working side-by-side wouldn't be the best arrangement.

"Jeff wasn't in my office five minutes when he spotted William Eastman's rap sheet and file. Jeff asked me if the 'delicate matter' Mondo mentioned was about Jeff going undercover for us. I thought he'd lost his marbles — what the hell did 'undercover' have to do with anything?

"Turns out the joke was on us. The 'William Darnell Eastman' we've got in our sights for the Aunt Tik's killings isn't real — it's an undercover alias like they use in Vice. A piece of software cooks up those identities — creates fake documents and inserts them into the various jurisdictions' systems, makes up Internet postings, and distributes them to social media and servers."

"Wow, this is turning into one screwy night — how did Jeff know so quickly?"

"Mondo hacked that software years ago so that when Vice is out in the field and pulls up somebody's rap sheet during a bust, they can verify if the subject is one of their guys. It's not like their undercovers can carry a badge or say anything about their status in the presence of other suspects. The modification finagles the case and court numbers on the rap sheet so that the first three digits in the number series, added together, match the last three numbers when you add them up.

"William Darnell Eastman doesn't exist. Never did."

"Holy shit," Paul said, surprised and just as suddenly relieved. "But from what Debra Ann and I learned tonight, that makes perfect sense. You'll want to hear what I have to tell you. But it might be best if you're sitting down for this. Seriously."

"I'm in my easy chair; the mangy hound, Rusty, is on my lap. Shoot."

"I didn't know how I would tell you we have another 'blotto_bill' in the mix, but you solved *that* problem. Louis, we've nailed the *real* Aunt Tik's bastard. That's the good news. The bad news is that it's one of our own. Not just a cop but on our team. It's Lt. Strickland, or as he called himself at Lewis and Clarke College, 'R. William Strickland,' also known back then as 'blotto_bill.'"

"Not the best time for a joke, Paul, and not about that…." The information wasn't registering with Louis.

"Louis, Debra Ann and I were just at his home. We — well, *she* — checked out an old rowing team photo he had hanging on his wall from his college days, maybe twenty years ago. It listed his nickname on the back. He called himself 'Blotto Bill.' Strickland must have forgotten the picture had that information taped to it."

The silence on the other end of the phone seemed interminable.

Finally, Louis spoke, every syllable carefully considered.

"Paul, we'll have to cover all our bases here."

He paused again, internalizing the news.

"This is going to create a shitstorm of celestial proportions."

"There's more, Louis. A lot more."

Paul outlined what Rod Blakesley had told him about Strickland.

"But here's the kicker. Remember our victims of the car-crushing homicides? Marianne Foreman and Gary Barker? She'd married once since divorcing Strickland and used 'Foreman' from that last marriage, so no one connected the dots. She'd separated from her latest husband — and Gary Barker was her new boyfriend."

Another brief pause.

"*Goddammit*," Louis said, anger rising in his voice. "I can't say you didn't try to warn me. I should have listened and trusted your instincts. Are you going to be down there for a while?"

"I planned to do an all-nighter; Debra Ann's on board with the idea. I can't sleep, so I thought I'd use my time filling in some holes. You know there'll be plenty of resistance among Strickland's fellow officers at first. We've got to get our act together because until they accept it, they'll be hitting us from all sides."

"Absolutely," Louis agreed. "I'm going to put Jenny to bed and change, and then you're going to have company, like it or not. Give me an hour to get down there."

"I'll take all the help I can get. Thanks, Louis, and do give my apologies to Jenny."

With that, Paul hung up and went back to work. It was too late to be making phone calls to anyone else. Instead, he searched the Internet for everything he could find on Marianne Foreman and Gary Barker. The investigators already had extensive research in the file regarding their murders.

Still, they hadn't looked at them from the perspective of Strickland as a subject other than a phone interview at the time of the killings. That hadn't raised any red flags, so detectives didn't push the information forward about Strickland as the first ex from nearly a decade ago.

Paul used Strickland's collegiate version of his name, "R. William Strickland, " in the search criteria. Paul had never trusted those guys with an initial for their first name — you could never tell what they were hiding.

Another clue leaped from the search result listings displayed on the flatscreen. When Strickland and Marianne Keenan married, it made the society pages because Strickland's parents were wealthy. And there, off to one side of the photo, looking gorgeous as she smiled for the camera in her peach chiffon bridesmaid's dress, was Carla Anderson, the then-new bride's best friend since sixth grade.

Her face was *so* familiar to Paul, but not her name. They did, however, have a 'Carla' as a victim in their Cheerios product-tampering case. Out of curiosity, Paul pulled Carla Littman's photo from their file — it was a match. More digging revealed that Carla Littman, née Anderson, had been Marianne Keenan's maid of honor when Keenan married Strickland. That was the connection and why Strickland killed Littman after he murdered Keenan, by then Foreman.

Paul googled Carla using both last names in the search criteria to ensure he had a paper trail on the name change. And there it was: Carla Anderson had married Wayne Littman, and they'd divorced four years later.

We may have dodged a bullet by not having any allergies to report when Strickland so casually asked us about our food restrictions last night, Paul thought in a flash of macabre humor.

Regardless, poor Carla had been Strickland's third Aunt Tik's murder victim, of those the team knew about.

Paul was developing a clear picture of how the pieces of this gigantic puzzle fit together. He'd have to wait until the courts opened in the morning to research dockets and case assignments. But at this point, he'd have been shocked if the targeted judge in Steve's AR-15 challenge-gone-wrong hadn't presided over the Strickland divorce proceedings. Paul would check with FlytNow in the morning to see if they could trace any remote control flight service subscriptions back to Strickland.

When regular business hours arrived, they'd need to confirm the role played by the fourth homicide victim, JoAnn Mabry, the well-regarded divorce lawyer. Paul was willing to bet his next paycheck that she was the lead attorney for one of the two sides of the Strickland divorce — most probably the ex-wife since Strickland had kept the house and wouldn't, at least on the surface, have any reason to go killing the lawyer representing him.

Paul reviewed the Mabry case file. The investigators had gone through the attorney's client list, but the fact that Strickland's ex-wife was on that list had raised no eyebrows. There was a lot of background noise. Mabry specialized in messy divorces between parties with money, so intense acrimony wouldn't differentiate one case from another. By those standards, the Strickland litigation probably seemed mild compared with Mabry's other dissolutions.

Unfortunately, since Strickland was a cop, any allegations of domestic abuse and the like had probably been swept under the rug, something that should never be but often is. On the surface, Strickland appeared to be a senior police officer in good standing and probably got a free pass from investigators on that alone.

What IAD had on Strickland was never official, and they'd effectively scrubbed his record once he transferred to San José. And, likely *because* he was in San José, there were no more extrajudicial incidents between the ex-spouses. By the time of Mabry's killing, the Strickland divorce was old news — it had been more than eight years since the judge signed off on it.

It was now nearly one-thirty, and Paul felt he was making progress in preparing for what was coming with the morning shift change. There was little more he could do without talking to other people, most of whom were, by now, snoozing soundly. Paul decided to stay in the squad room and catch up on his paperwork. He couldn't sleep anyway, and there was no reason to risk waking Debra Ann, Tommy, and the dog from sound slumber when he was too antsy to join them.

Paul heard the elevator rising from the first floor, and shortly afterward, Louis came to his desk bearing fresh cups of Starbucks. The lieutenant carefully set the coffee on Paul's desk. As he did, he said solemnly, "The tragedy of all of this is, we have six murdered innocents and the very worst of a bad cop. It's no time for high-fives. But you know, what the hell..." He broke into a smile, though subdued, and high-five they did.

"You had some decent moments back when you were my partner," Louis acknowledged, "but this time you outdid yourself, kid."

To a law-enforcement professional, nothing feels better than hearing something like that from someone like Louis.

"The credit should go to Debra Ann, but since she's not here to accept it...," Paul said with a wink.

After taking their victory lap, it was time to look at the harsher realities they were facing. Louis had solid diplomacy skills when negotiating treacherous political waters. Still, there were times when he was unashamed to let it all hang out.

"I can't believe it's Strickland, the same goddamned asswipe who's been stalling our work at every turn ... *that* piece of unholy shit!"

CHAPTER 46

Other officers had begun straggling in and out of the squad room as the night slid further into the wee hours of the morning. It was now close to two a.m. The bars frequented by the homicide witnesses and snitches that detectives were seeking had begun shutting down, and drug and sex trade activity was slowing, so officers were coming in to finish their reports.

Suddenly aware Paul wasn't his only audience, Louis lowered his voice, looking around the room apologetically. But when he turned back, Paul could see the emotions still boiling beneath the surface. *"Un-fucking-believable."*

Louis took a deep breath, and a long pull from his coffee cup seemed to settle him. "Okay, tell me the whole story, and don't leave anything out. I assume you haven't told anyone else?"

"Debra Ann knows, of course, and she's aware of our Aunt Tik's cases, at least the sketchy outlines. But she's the only one privy to who 'blotto_bill' is. Until it becomes public by other means, Debra Ann will clear what she writes with the department before publishing. I've left Marci and

Eve messages that something was up and told them not to engage anyone, but I included no details."

"I'm fine with that," Louis said. "Go ahead; I'm just starting to see how little bits and pieces would fit in with the idea of Strickland as a serial killer. But, wow, it's a lot to grasp. Fill me in on everything."

Paul provided Louis with all the details of his and Debra Ann's evening through the moment they left Strickland's home.

"What was his grand plan in inviting you?" Louis asked. "I mean, now we know he was gaming us, but what was his pretext — you not letting him publicly go after Aunt Tik's because it would force all the players underground? I guess he would have benefitted from no one talking to us."

"My gut says he wanted to accomplish three things, starting with sowing dissension. As soon as we'd eaten, the gloves began coming off, and I felt like he was trying to undermine the team's handling of the Aunt Tik's investigation. He wasn't very subtle about driving a wedge between Detective Robbins and the rest of the team.

"Secondly, Strickland seemed determined to hammer a stake through the heart of the investigation itself. Getting tangled up in First Amendment issues and court intervention would have been the death knell for everything we were trying to do, and Strickland knew it.

"Finally, he needed to buy time. In retrospect, we'd been gradually closing in on him, but we hadn't realized it. He couldn't stall delivering the decrypted server data to us any longer. Either the DA or the feds would get access to those backup servers eventually — no way he could game a dozen terabytes of time-encoded data stretching back eight months or more all by himself and without detection."

"Using the Vice alias was a 'Hail Mary' then," Louis said, "hoping we wouldn't look any deeper into that data."

"That fits."

Louis just sat there, slowly moving his head from side to side as he connected with the bigger picture.

When Paul passed Louis the full version of what Rod Blakesley had told him about Strickland's history with the department, a mixture of anger and disgust clouded Louis's expression. Paul finished with all the links between Strickland and the victims of crimes related to Aunt Tik's.

"So, Strickland's story about coming back here because his sick mother felt better was likely bullshit," Paul added. "He returned to kill anyone, and everyone, connected to his divorce. Along with whatever other wrongs he wanted to right, I'm sure. The divorce was final eight-plus years ago — a long time to hold a grudge, but we do see obsessions like that. The terms of that divorce may contain something that reignited things. Perhaps he learned his ex had moved on to something better, which set him off again. Maybe her engagement to Gary Barker was the trigger?

"Chicken-and-egg question: Did discovering Aunt Tik's as the perfect cover motivate him to fulfill revenge fantasies? Or did he come back from San José already planning to kill, and Aunt Tik's just happened to present itself as the ideal weapon at the right time?"

"My guess?" Louis mused. "That Marshall recruited Strickland into Aunt Tik's as a friend, after which Strickland recognized its potential. We'll never know. Pathological liars get so good at it that the truth becomes irrelevant. Strickland moved back and forth between here and San José fortuitously and timed it well enough by luck or happenstance that his lies slipped through the cracks and never caught up to him."

Paul agreed. "He's gotten so arrogant he doesn't even bother to track his falsehoods. Last night, Strickland insinuated his mother had passed. Yet just a few weeks ago, he claimed instead that she'd gotten better, prompting his return to San Diego. Even sitting here now, I still don't know if Strickland's mother is alive or dead or ever lived in San José, or if there's a stepmother, or what's going on. Whatever her state of health, I doubt she had anything to do with his movements.

"Even so, we would have gotten him eventually. The connections to Aunt Tik's caused us to aggregate all these cases. We were reexamining things for their commonalities. We would have caught on to the Foreman and Littman connection soon enough — someone among their or Barker's families and associates would have mentioned her having an asshole ex on the force. In the context of all these cases, that would have rung a louder bell. From there, the Mabry connection is a no-brainer, and Marshall and Detmer fall into place."

"Yep," Louis said, "and as you mentioned earlier, we didn't know that IAD had a motivated interest and was looking in. Strickland had to have felt the noose tightening around his neck, which in and of itself caused forced errors on his part. The Detmer murder was amateur hour. But we should be grateful we caught this break now because we need to find Steve. Strickland would likely have killed others as we closed in."

"Why kidnap or knock on wood, kill Steve?" Paul cocked his head, his expression one of wonderment. "That's something I just can't figure out...."

"I'm with you, Paul. I don't get it either. But we'll wrestle this thing to the ground and do whatever we can to help Steve, even if it's only to find him to give Tracy closure."

Louis paused, put both elbows on the desktop, clasped his hands together, and rested his chin on his knuckles for several seconds. Sadness and disappointment passed over his face like a cloud blocking the sun.

"It's lamentable that we fed Strickland reasons to murder Detmer. But how could we have known?"

"Once Strickland understood the threat the man represented to him, he must have left our meeting that day burning rubber to get to Detmer." Paul sighed. "Damned shame. Jimmy Detmer was never going to be our friend. But as a crucial witness, if nothing else, he deserved better than that from us. Steve had tried to warn me that Aunt Tik's members could be anyone. I thought I'd listened to him, but clearly, not well enough. We need to make sure we're hearing him now."

"I read your case notes," Louis said. "Steve's friends were all in the game with him, and his story about the Powerhouse gym members suggests that people tend to join in bunches that reflect their social and work circles. I hate to think it, but that means there may be other officers, some in our unit, who are members of Aunt Tik's. If so, would they follow Strickland's lead and exploit opportunities to abuse Aunt Tik's? We know now that a cop's powers combined with the organization's capabilities are formidable."

"And they could promote themselves up Aunt Tik's ladder almost at will," Paul added. "I realized earlier tonight that they could interfere with any competition for cell captain by selectively arresting members before or during challenge performances.

"With what we planned for Detmer to get him to flip, we unintentionally created the model for that."

CHAPTER 47

L ouis unclasped his hands and sat back in his chair with a deep sigh. He then leaned forward and placed the heels of both hands on the edge of Paul's desk.

"Okay, here's what we're going to do."

Louis's tone had shifted; now, he was projecting authority.

"Jump in if you have any thoughts or suggestions. First, at our after-roll-call unit meeting this morning, we don't let on anything to anyone, business as usual. I want you to make a big deal about promoting Strickland's idea to me, the one about going public with Aunt Tik's involvement in these homicides. I'll pretend I'm so frustrated with the progress in our cases that I'm willing to consider it."

Paul had grabbed his notepad and begun scribbling.

"Is there any way we can isolate Strickland without tipping him off? We need him away from our troops and off those Aunt Tik's servers until we can take him down. We still don't know who else could be a member of Aunt Tik's and in league with him."

"Lady Luck has decided to give us a break this time." A crooked smile came to Louis's face.

"I'd already arranged for Strickland to go up to Sacramento tomorrow to talk to the state encryption lab there — I was trying to help him over the hump."

Louis raised his eyebrows and sighed.

"Yeesh … I guess that shows how much he took me in. The good thing is, having him off-campus for the day should keep him from knowing what we're up to back here or that we're onto him."

"Will Sacramento know Strickland's status with us?"

"I'll make a discreet phone call to a guy I know — he'd never join something like Aunt Tik's. If it becomes necessary, he's got the chops to apprehend Strickland on behalf of the state.

"I hear you about not knowing who Aunt Tik's members are, though. So, until we get cuffs on Strickland, use the privacy booths for any telephone discussions about this situation. Let's have our face-to-face conversations about this away from headquarters. Any returned calls must go to personal cells, not your desk phones in the squad room — we don't want anyone else picking up and figuring out what's happening. We'll try to limit the people in the know to as few as possible.

"If word gets out before we're ready, we'll have a morale issue around deceiving our other officers. But, if we do it right and things go smoothly, everyone will understand post facto that we had a rat on our squad, and that's why we couldn't be straight up with everyone."

Paul looked up from his notepad.

"What charges are we going to arrest him on? We haven't had time since learning about Strickland to cross our *t*'s and dot our *i*'s in any of our cases."

"To that end, I'll leave it to you to confirm what we think we know — that the targeted judge had presided over the Strickland divorce and which of the Stricklands Mabry represented. And let's get hold of Strickland's cell phone records to see if we can tie him to the times and locations of the Mabry, Marshall, or Detmer murders. Let's reinterview the Mabry witnesses with an updated photo spread. We might get a hit on Strickland recording that video.

"Meanwhile, take Strickland's prints out of the elimination set for any of these cases. Tell the techs we pulled the print card for the wrong Strickland when we did the first pass. The same goes for Lt. Brooks's team. I want to know if and where Strickland's prints turned up.

"Would you check with the feds, but quietly, to see if they found his prints anywhere around the AR-15 or the stolen car?"

"I'll do that," Paul replied. "And I'll let Marci have my notes from this conversation so she can reallocate the team's workload."

"That's as far as I want to push the envelope over the next 24 hours. I want to avoid advertising Strickland's involvement in anything to the extent possible. I'll chat with the DA to answer your question once we've gathered what we can today."

Louis paused and leaned back in his chair, interlacing his fingers on his head.

"Let's fold the Marshall homicide into our investigations of Aunt Tik's. We'll need to walk softly and not bruise any feelings. I think I know how to mitigate that."

"How so?" Paul was genuinely curious. Navigating dangerous waters like these was one area where Louis held a distinct advantage, and Paul was eager to learn.

"While Strickland's in Sacramento, we can meet and educate everyone about our new situation, then map our path forward. I'm not exactly sure where Escalation Management is with their investigation.

"I'll take Lt. Brooks aside when he arrives this morning. I'll tell him they want to move Strickland to the top of their list of prime suspects but not to engage him directly until after we discuss things in tomorrow's meeting. If I can get the captain to sign off, we'll leave Brooks the public-facing elements of the Marshall case and throw him a bone — we'll let him deal with the press on the Mabry homicide as well. Having a viable suspect for both will make Brooks's job more manageable.

"Marci's team will take over the boots-on-the-ground pieces of Marshall's homicide, and we'll give her some more people. Brooks is a good egg; he'll appreciate the help, even if it comes from another unit. And he'll see we're playing nice, cooling down the hot seat his keester's parked on. In his job, that doesn't happen often…."

"No way in hell I'd want to work those celebrity cases," Paul agreed.

"I'm going with what I think are safe assumptions," Louis continued. "We know that Marshall was the founder and promoter of the local chapter of Aunt Tik's. When Strickland came back from San José and murdered his ex and her new fiancé with tons of concrete, he did it as a cell captain. Marshall had a higher vantage point as the czar and got wise about what was happening. He may have threatened Strickland, or perhaps they had a confrontation, but either way, Strickland killed Marshall.

"We could go with an alternate theory of the case. The second tack says Strickland killed Marshall specifically to gain control of Aunt Tik's. Strickland would have realized from Marshall's questions that he couldn't do what he wanted from the cell captain role."

"Sounds right to me, but everything we've got so far is circumstantial...."

"That'll change quickly now that we have a suspect; we've gained probable cause and a home, an office, a work locker, and vehicles to search. As things stand, the Marshall case is our most solid, and it's a conventional crime — we might get a conviction without invoking much of Aunt Tik's.

"I want to leverage that to rein Strickland in, given the considerable resources he has for fleeing our jurisdiction. We've got enough to detain him as a material witness for the Marshall case. It's a bit of a gamble. But with him as a viable suspect and out of the way for a while, I'm betting our investigators can gather enough evidence to book him for at least that homicide.

"We'll hold off charging Strickland until our evidence is rock solid. Meanwhile, we need his face in all the papers and on every major news website as soon as we make the arrest. Lt. Brooks's team can do that kind of thing in their sleep. Let's let those dogs run ... see how far Strickland thinks he can roam against that publicity. If we have to take the Marshall case away from Lt. Brooks later, he'll have had his day in the sun and no right to complain."

"Sweet. A win-win for everybody." Paul was impressed with Louis's plan.

"We'll wait to tell the feds we've got a suspect until Strickland's in custody," Louis explained. "Otherwise, those people are all so damned political; one of them will want to take credit and spill the beans. They'll try to interview Strickland on the attempted murder beef, and he'll know the jig's up. Then he'll be in the wind with all his money."

"The timing is critical," Paul agreed. "But once Strickland's detained, we'll need to bring the feds up to speed as soon as possible. I wouldn't put it past Strickland to angle for a deal. I can see him offering to flip on Aunt Tik's as though the organization is the problem. And somebody over there's bound to fall for it if we don't salt the earth first."

Louis nodded.

"We can start a conversation between the DA and the feds after the DA is fully informed. I'll reach out to ADA Levine. Separately, I'll call Captain Jarvis. He'll want to be on top of everything as the Investigations II Division head. But I'd rather he get it straight from the horse's mouth. You, Marci, and Eve know Aunt Tik's front to back. I'll set up a private meeting between the captain and the three of you. That should happen today."

Paul frowned.

"I'm not sure what Marci has going on…."

"Let me reach out to her, and I'll copy you and Eve," Louis said. "As to tomorrow's meeting, it'll be discreet and offsite, need-to-know personnel only. We'll book a private conference room at a hotel unless one of our participants has a better idea. You, me, Marci, Eve, Mondo, Brooks, Capt. Jarvis, your IAD guy, Blakesley, the SWAT commander, and a prosecutor from the DA's office. That'll be the best way to see if there's anything we need to do first to help our cases and work out how we'll arrest this asshole."

Paul nodded. "I'll fill Marci and Eve in as soon as they come in or contact me and make sure their calendars are clear for tomorrow. It might be good for one or both to catch a case of the flu. We'll need to reduce the number of people who are at work but not shown available on the same day that Strickland's off to Sacramento. You can't underestimate the rumor mill around here — several people at a clandestine meeting will get people talking. Oh, but before I talk to Marci or Eve, I'd better call Rod Blakesley at IAD to honor my agreement with him."

"Great. Let's stay on good terms with IAD," Louis said. "He'll have some homework to do before our meeting. He'll advise us on the union and policy requirements for Strickland's takedown. I'll make the other calls."

"Mondo needs to know before the meeting — Strickland's his second-in-command, and we wouldn't want him finding out stone-cold in a room full of people. Do you want me to tell him?"

"*Fuck* … This keeps getting better and better." Louis didn't bother to hide his disappointment. "Mondo's going to lose his lunch when he hears about this. No, I have to be the one. Our master manipulator went to Mondo about what Strickland characterized as 'friction' between you and him. Mondo's gotta know right from the start that's not what this is, and that'll come across better if I tell him."

"I didn't realize I made my feelings that obvious. Not very professional of me." Paul was somewhat surprised and chastened at the same time.

"I wouldn't be too hard on yourself, kid." Louis flashed a sideways grin. "After all, you *were* right, at least about anything you shared with me. Don't lord it over anyone, and you'll be fine."

Louis sighed, and his expression changed to one of regret.

"Mondo's going to blame himself. But there's nothing anyone could have done other than what they did. But, yeah, I can't avoid telling him — we need Mondo on board before Strickland goes to Sacramento. We'll want trusted members of his team to get us full control of Aunt Tik's data before Strickland can destroy it or have someone else do the deed."

"How do you think Strickland will react? On the one hand, he's a professional. But from what Blakesley told me about Strickland's divorce, this guy can go off on you."

"Good point," Louis conceded. "Let me inform the captain and make him aware of that aspect. He may have resources and options he can bring to bear or know of someone else who does. Try to keep your crew busy doing things that will be productive, considering what we now know. But concentrate on the evidence-gathering tasks rather than the suspect elements. We can't tell the rest of the world yet that the whodunnit is now a 'hedunnit.'"

"We can't reveal the focus on Strickland, but we can certainly chase blotto_bill," Paul offered. "Eve's been doing most of the drudge work parsing the user messages forum, and she'll know about Strickland; we won't waste any of our time."

"Good." Paul could see Louis was a little distracted, no doubt thinking ahead to what he'd say to Mondo.

"Our list should include working up a plan if we get cut off from the data on those Aunt Tik's servers," Paul said. "We'll want to review all the physical evidence eventually, in light of what we know now, but most of that will have to wait until Strickland's in a holding cell — too much chance of a leak. After you talk to Mondo, I'll ask him for advice on backing up the server data or at least our access to the servers. I'm unsure what Strickland could do, but we'd better prepare for the worst."

"Okay, good." Louis tapped a forefinger on Paul's desk. "Once we've apprehended Strickland, we can focus on supporting whatever the DA will need for prosecution."

"It'll be better once Strickland's behind bars. But I won't feel comfortable until we get Steve back home or at least know what happened to him."

"You and me both, Paul. Meanwhile, try to get some sleep in the officer's lounge. You look like hell."

The conversation with Louis had taken the edge off — the one that was keeping Paul awake — and he could feel a crash coming. It was almost four a.m.

He'd take Louis up on another of his better ideas and headed for the officer's lounge.

THE WRITINGS OF
AVRIL MARIA SERENE

CHAPTER 48

After roll call and the morning team meeting, Lt. Harbin called Capt. Cranston to check whether he was at his desk. He caught Mondo in a jovial mood.

"Louis, how's everything going in your neck of the woods?"

"Better than you'd expect, Mondo, worse than you'd imagine. We had a breakthrough last night with the Aunt Tik's case that your team's helping us with. I wanted to drop by and talk to you about it."

"You're always welcome down here; no need to feel threatened by the flypaper. We're having a rare, slow day. Lt. Strickland said he'd be feeding us work, but it's been hit-or-miss coming to us this past week. I assume he's tied up with other aspects of your case."

I'll bet, Louis thought, but he wouldn't share the story with the captain just yet.

"Perfect, I'm headed your way."

"I'll warn everyone." The lieutenant could hear the smirk in Mondo's voice.

Crap, Louis thought. *The one time I wish I'd caught him in a less ebullient frame of mind.*

The lieutenant took the back stairs down two floors to Mondo's office to avoid elevator chitchat. He didn't want to deal with any casual observations about overstepping the Vice lieutenant working in his unit to visit the Vice captain. As he descended the staircase, Louis pondered how he'd tell his friend and workmate of more than twenty years the bad news. He still wasn't sure as he stepped through Mondo's office door, and the two shook hands.

The captain seemed to know something was wrong upon seeing Louis's face. "I hoped when you called that your major development would be good news; congratulations all 'round, et cetera. I see that isn't the situation. So, what's up?"

"One of those good news, bad news things, Mondo. I take it you haven't spoken to Jeff Bennett yet?"

"He's working second shift this week — I won't see him for another couple of hours. Why do you ask?"

"Jeff helped us see a problem we didn't know we had. Debra Ann and Paul filled in the other parts. Mondo, we know who our doer is, the multiple murderer who's been using Aunt Tik's as his on-demand killing crew. And we have him dead to rights."

"Okay, nothing wrong with that; let's find a corkscrew. What's the downside?"

"The bad news is that it's Lt. Robert William Strickland."

The words fell on disbelieving ears.

"If you're trying to pull my leg, it's not funny." Mondo studied Louis's face for some indication of humor. He wouldn't find any.

"I had the same reaction," Louis admitted, offering nothing further than his grim expression.

"*Jesus*, Louis, are you sure?" Then Mondo's tone sank. "Of course you are. You wouldn't be here if you weren't."

His eyes darted first to the floor and then to the wall. As he sat back heavily in his chair, his eyes returned to Louis's face.

After a few seconds, Mondo asked quietly, "How'd you catch the asshole?"

As Louis sat across from him and started laying out Strickland's history, Mondo's face reddened, and his features grew more rigid.

"Christ, how'd we miss that when he came on board here?"

"Bureaucratic screwups, mostly. Internal Affairs lost interest once Strickland took an interdepartmental transfer to San José. No one thought he'd have the stones to show back up here again. When he did, HR did their checking with San José's IAD, but not ours. It wouldn't have mattered; they expunged Strickland's records here as part of San Diego IAD's original deal to ship him away. For anyone unaware of the truth, Strickland covered his moving around by claiming his mother in San José fell ill, and he left to care for her, returning when her health improved. Paul Castro's convinced Strickland returned solely to avenge his divorce."

"But wait; back up. Strickland's marital situation tells you nothing about his crimes since. How'd you connect Aunt Tik's and Bob Strickland outside his work?" Mondo was missing a link.

"Ezra Brooks takes the Marshall homicide, connecting a 'blotto_bill' via an e-mail. Eve Byrne digs into Aunt Tik's online data, learning 'blotto_bill' is the punk master behind four murders. You know something of my neighbor's son and his involvement with Aunt Tik's, the remote-controlled AR-15, and the judge. The kid says the punk master for that challenge was his old cell captain, known to him as, yup, 'blotto_bill.'

"Strickland invites Paul and Debra Ann over to his house, probably as a countermeasure to muddy the waters. Strickland goes to the restroom, and Debra Ann checks out the photos hanging on a wall in the hall. She's looking at the back of a photo to see which of the men in it was Strickland, and there's his college nickname — 'Blotto Bill.'

"Somehow, our boy Paul scoots out of there without making water in his pants. Having Debra Ann with him helped, no doubt. I'm not sure I could have pulled it off myself. It wouldn't necessarily be Strickland I'd be concerned about … Without any contingency plan for a surprise like that, I'd be worried about screwing up our cases or the recovery of our missing witness by tipping Strickland off. In close quarters, on his home turf, with no quick and plausible escape? Not to mention a strong urge to punch the guy's lights out."

Turning somber, Louis said, "But no one is sorrier than I am that I had to tell you this."

"Thanks for coming to see me personally, Louis." Mondo chewed on his lower lip and nodded in gratitude. "We both take pride in our units, so I know you understand how a betrayal like this feels. And my God, five innocent people dead."

"Six, plus a likely kidnapping victim." Louis's expression was grave. "We're fairly certain Strickland killed Jimmy Detmer, someone he persuaded to do illegal activity for these punks, right after learning in our team meeting that we intended to flip Detmer. And Steve Nielsen, the teenager whose arrest by the feds kicked this off, is missing; we haven't been able to locate him for almost a month."

Pursing his lips, Mondo rocked back and forth in his seat. "In Vice, your unit members, your squad room, that's your safe place." His eyes were unfocused in the general direction of the nameplate on his desk.

"Those are the people who *get* your day-to-day struggle not to burn out, not to become angry, or worse, depressed. You have to trust *somebody*, so you trust them — absolutely."

Louis nodded. Every word meant something to him.

"Sure, vice raids and child pornography website stings do periodically turn up police officers doing bad acts," Mondo said. "Lieutenants, captains, even the occasional chief, but nothing on the level of what Strickland's done, and never from within *your* vice unit. Another jurisdiction's maybe, but not yours."

As Mondo dissected the news and integrated it into his worldview as best he could on short notice, he became more philosophic.

"When Bob came to me complaining about Paul's decisions concerning Aunt Tik's cases, I remember thinking, 'Who in the hell gets in a pissing match with Paul, of all people?' Paul has his faults, but not getting along isn't one of them. I should have listened better to myself."

"Wait, before you take a cat-o-nine-tails off the wall and begin flogging yourself," Louis stepped in, "let's not forget the situation as it stood.

"You didn't have much chance to work with Strickland or understand the man. He snuck into your unit via the back door. He had reasons to keep a low profile, things nobody but IAD knew. He'd gotten himself cleansed by the bureaucracy. Strickland volunteering for Marci's team for reasons that are now obvious didn't give you much one-on-one time with him."

The men went silent.

Mondo spoke first. "Well, I'm grateful for the opportunity to put that sorry asshole away."

"On the positive side," Louis replied, "Strickland's victim choices were all self-serving, centered around his divorce and his station in Aunt Tik's. He probably wasn't conspiring with anyone else in Vice or Homicide. Still, we'll need to watch for signs of Aunt Tik's presence on our teams and fend off their future infiltration into our units. Maybe the brass can work with the union to issue a rule banning membership in Aunt Tik's for all officers.

"Mondo, I hate to ask for anything more from you under these circumstances. But we need your crack computer forensics team to redo any work Strickland was assigned that didn't produce results. It's critical that those Aunt Tik's servers get hacked and their contents downloaded to the extent possible before Strickland discovers we're onto him."

Mondo was all business.

"I agree. We'll need Aunt Tik's server data to ensure his successful prosecution. There's plenty of time to extract it after Strickland's behind bars; my concern is understanding those servers' contents well enough to know if Strickland's modifying them while he's still free. The best-case scenario would be obtaining a copy of the data in its current state that we could work with at our leisure on our in-house hard drives. We'll set that as our goal."

Louis picked up on the thought.

"Now that we have a suspect in multiple homicides and can show the murderer is a principal in the local Aunt Tik's, we can get search warrants. Once we know the physical location of those servers, we can take possession of the data storage and backup drives long enough to make copies. That'll be much easier than streaming the data covertly over the Internet.

"By happy coincidence, we're sending Strickland to Sacramento tomorrow for Internet decryption training, something I'd set up before we knew he was blotto_bill. While he's out, we'll orchestrate his apprehension. We'll need your help."

Mondo nodded in understanding as Louis rose to his feet.

"Okay, I guess that's all. I'm genuinely sorry to deliver this news, Mondo."

"Better you than anyone else, Louis," the captain replied as they shook hands. Then Mondo took a deep breath. He'd absorbed the hit and was back in control of his world.

"Fuck the son of a bitch. Let's go get that jagoff."

CHAPTER 49

To Paul, it seemed he'd just shut his eyes in the officers' lounge when his cell phone rang. But when he looked at the time displayed on its face, it showed 6:55 a.m. — he'd been out almost three hours. More importantly, it was Eve calling, and that conversation would be crucial to their team's activities over the next 48 hours.

"I'm sorry I missed your text last night," she said. "I don't think I've ever seen you use all caps. What's going on that we can't share?"

"If you're driving, pull over," Paul answered. "If you're not sitting down, sit. You may even want to strap yourself in for this one."

"Okay, I'm buckled in, helmet on…." Eve sounded hesitant.

Paul didn't want to tease her anymore.

"Bob Strickland's our killer. He's 'blotto_bill.'"

"Say *what?*" Eve nearly screamed the last word.

"Foreman's his ex-wife. Barker, the fiancé, was in the wrong place at the wrong time, collateral damage, but I doubt Strickland shed any tears for him. Littman was Foreman's best friend, and we think Mabry was Foreman's attorney — could you check on that for us? Marshall was in Strickland's way. Something about that end loader may have exposed Strickland's behaviors to

Marshall. Or, Strickland just wanted the power and freedom that went with being the czar. Doesn't matter, same result."

"You've *got* to be shitting me...." Eve's voice was almost inaudible.

Regret crept into Paul's voice.

"We served Detmer up to Strickland on a silver platter because we had no clue. I'm guessing Detmer knew more than we thought; maybe he did Strickland's dirty work for him. I'm assuming that Judge Wasserman oversaw Strickland's divorce — we'll have to confirm that. Once you know Strickland is the doer, it all falls perfectly into place. Still no clue where Steve's abduction fits in, though."

There was a long silence on the other end of the phone.

"Wow, I wasn't prepared for *that* this early in the morning. I knew Strickland was dragging his ass, but...." Eve's voice trailed off. "Yeah, as soon as you know it's him, it all makes sense. But there's a big part you haven't told me. The last *I* knew, you and Debra Ann were having dinner at his place last night. What happened? Did he meet you at the door in tears and confess?"

Paul couldn't help but chuckle despite the seriousness of the topic. "No, not quite."

He repeated to her everything he'd told Louis. Paul informed her of Louis's plans to have a clandestine, offsite meeting with the brass tomorrow while Strickland was out of town, letting Eve know she'd be an essential part of that. Paul finished by asking a favor.

"Look, I don't know where I'll be this morning or with whom. Marci hasn't returned my call, so she knows nothing about this. Could you do me a favor and tell her what's happened as soon as possible? Text, phone, e-mail, or Pony Express, doesn't matter as long as it's before she talks to Strickland. But remember, we're keeping all of this from anyone else but IAD and the people upstairs, for now."

"Sure, Paul, of course. I'm glad I called you this morning. If I'd learned this last night, I wouldn't have slept. Man, these next couple of days should be *fascinating*."

The next day at 7:15 a.m., just as Strickland would have been removing his breakfast waffle from the grill provided by his motel in Sacramento, Paul received a call from Mondo.

"Good morning, Paul. You'll want to know ahead of the meeting today that we have clones of all the disk drives for Aunt Tik's servers. I couldn't reach Louis to inform him before our meeting — could you let him know? The clones themselves are now in evidence lockup. I'm sitting here looking at two backups being loaded onto server boxes as I speak to you."

"Now, *that's* the way to start this day." Paul welcomed the good news. "We needed something positive; it'll provide the brass with some breathing room. What's the situation with the encryption?"

"Aunt Tik's rented the servers from Cogent One, a cloud service provider downtown. And, get this: Cogent gave us everything we need to unwind their baseline encryption. They're also the department's service provider, so we had some leverage, given how much business we do with them.

"However, nothing prevented Aunt Tik's from adding an encryption layer. So, we've got some homegrown, roll-your-own enciphering around some of these files — likely Strickland's doing. There are two ways this can go. Once we determine the provider, we can extract the data from any added encryption applied using shrink-wrapped software.

"But anything too off the wall would require a court order forcing Strickland to provide keys and methods, assuming we don't find them via search warrants. Fifty-fifty shot. The good news is that not all the files have added encryption layers. We can read files used for day-to-day Aunt Tik's business, meaning the runtime membership data and logs."

"So that's it — we've got at least the minimum of what we needed?" Paul jumped ahead.

"It's a little more complicated than that. Our immediate priority is to terminate Strickland's access to his account. Aunt Tik's' national office wasn't willing to cooperate with anything regarding the local cell's data.

"Still, they agreed to exercise a provision in the cell charter that allows them to remove a czar for their version of moral turpitude. They're willing to make the termination look like a technical problem and not a sudden and complete cutoff. We agreed to let them maintain control of their source code, so we're reliant on them. Our tech will interface with them to manage Strickland's access during his termination.

"We can do anything we wish with the copied data. However, we won't have access to live runtime data without a subpoena. We can't trample on the rights of innocent parties to play the game within the rules.

"The good news is, it doesn't matter if Strickland tries to destroy or modify data we've already copied — it might be disruptive to Aunt Tik's runtime data and operations, but our copies are outside the fray. Fingers crossed that Aunt Tik's keeps up their end of our deal. Once we pull the trigger, Strickland won't be able to do anything on the live Aunt Tik's system."

Despite all Mondo's caveats and cautions, Paul knew things were in good hands now.

"Thanks, Mondo, that should get us through Strickland's apprehension. The meeting today should tell us specifically when to disconnect him. In the meantime, I'll pass your progress on once I see Louis."

"We're not home free," Mondo warned. "We'll still have to determine the nature of the files Strickland encrypted himself and where they fit in the grand scheme. There's a lot of work left to extract everything needed to prosecute and convict Strickland. But yes, we're well on our way. Gotta run; see you at the meeting."

About an hour after Mondo's call, Louis stopped by Paul's desk to see if he wanted a ride to the meeting. Careful not to discuss Strickland's apprehension in the squad room, Paul waited until they were rolling to share his conversation with Mondo about gaining access to the Aunt Tik's servers.

The two men lapsed into silence as they tried to anticipate the unpredictable and prepare for the unusual meeting ahead.

CHAPTER 50

Paul dropped in on me unexpectedly at home a half hour after the Strickland apprehension meeting ended. He wanted to tell me what had happened and that he'd return late this evening after they made the arrest.

"Lt. Harbin ordered everyone working tonight's apprehension of Strickland to get out of the precinct for a few hours and relax. Marci took off to check in on Danny, who'd stayed home from the firehouse today with a twisted ankle. Eve wanted to hang out with her wife and maybe feel the baby kick.

"I planned on sacking out in the precinct's lounge for the next couple of hours, but I wanted to stop by first and let you know the plan we came up with."

Paul had my full attention.

"I *am* curious. For all Strickland's faults — maybe because of them — the man is cagey. If he learns what's up, there's no telling what he might do. So, spill the beans, and don't leave anything out."

Paul came up behind me at the kitchen's center island, giving me a quick neck rub — he knew I tended to spend too much time staring at a computer monitor.

"Before the meeting, Mondo called and told me they had copies of Aunt Tik's server data. The national Aunt Tik's is aware of what's happening and, most importantly, cooperating. I took that as a good sign."

That told me that Strickland had lost much of his leverage.

"Strickland's neutralized as far as doing anything through Aunt Tik's, then. Still, he's pretty devious."

"Have you ever been to the San Diego National Armory?" Paul went to the fridge and threw together a ham and cheese sandwich.

I shook my head no.

"Good place to hold that kind of meeting, no one would suspect; built in the fifties, red brick, old-school, nothing fancy about it. Still, the conference room SDPD reserved was spacious. They'd updated it with all the amenities and electronics.

"Louis, Marci, and Eve were there. Capt. Jarvis, his administrative assistant, and Ezra Brooks. Mondo, Rod Blakesley, SWAT Capt. Allen Bouchard, Amy Armand from Missing Persons, and Deputy District Attorney Pamela Calley — twelve total, counting me. Capt. Jarvis took his seat at the front of the table, and the rest of us sat in the five seats closest to him on either side, by order of rank, except for his admin."

"All the big guns in the department, then," I mused.

"Everyone in management connected to anything Aunt Tik's." Paul reached into his briefcase with his free hand, then plopped a thick manila folder on the dining room table.

"Each of us got one of these. You can peek at mine, but I need it back when I go. It contains copies of Strickland's complete service record across all three periods of his San Diego and San José employment.

"Most of it's summaries of the victims, types of crime, and probable motives associated with the cases the Aunt Tik's team was working. There's a printed version of Aunt Tik's user manual. It also has separate summaries of the James Marshall and Jim Detmer homicides, along with Steve's missing-person case. There's a bulleted list of relevant known circumstantial and evidentiary items, including their status."

"They came to this prepared." I was impressed as I flipped through the pages. "Mind if I take some shots with my cell?"

"I don't think anyone would complain. Much of it's in the public record, though I could see where the department might not like parts of it getting out. Just be careful how you use the information."

I nodded my agreement, and Paul continued.

"Some participants passed out additional materials they put together, and I also tossed those in that folder. Rod Blakesley provided a synopsis of IAD materials expunged from Strickland's service record eight years ago. Eve distributed a document Andy Pardone had sent her elaborating on the practical aspects of Aunt Tik's operations.

"I don't think anyone ever falls asleep at one of Capt. Jarvis's meetings. He's burly and has that booming voice, the James Earl Jones thing. Kind of a walking fire hydrant with a built-in bullhorn."

"I remember from the Children's Ball," I murmured.

"On top of that, you could tell this Strickland thing had him angry. Cap did a good job convincing everyone that time was of the essence. His biggest concern is that once Strickland knows what's happening, Steve's survival would be on the clock if he's still alive. The captain called Strickland out for the danger the man represents to the community and our fellow officers. He listed Strickland's experience, knowledge of police tactics, and access to virtually unlimited personal resources, weaponry, and equipment. He stressed that, based on his track record, Strickland wouldn't hesitate to kill by any means available, including through intermediaries."

Paul took a bite of his sandwich.

"Cap described each of the six homicide victims with a brief synopsis of the details of each murder. He included Steve's abduction and the attempt on Judge Wasserman. He touched briefly on how Aunt Tik's works and Strickland's manipulation of their capabilities. Everyone knew what we were dealing with by the time Cap finished."

I nodded, understanding what Strickland represented.

"The captain's big point was that Strickland's apprehension had to serve the needs and safety of the public as well as preserve any evidence and successfully manage media interaction." Paul winked at me — I took that as my opportunity to ask him something I'd been thinking about since that dinner at Strickland's.

"Speaking of which, honey…," I started.

"Oh, no, whenever you call me that, and the sun's still up, I know trouble's coming." Paul narrowed his eyes, pulling his head back in mock suspicion. Still, he *was* listening attentively.

"I'd like to be in on Strickland's arrest, just as an observer reporting the facts. It would help if someone impartially told the story — the last thing you want is for Strickland's pricey lawyers to leak out insinuations of a coverup or malfeasance … the OJ thing."

I could see in Paul's eyes that I'd have to plead my case.

"Name me another investigative journalist who knows the background of this better. It won't be easy telling Aunt Tik's part in all this without unfairly accusing them and creating legal and other problems for the department. Or, on the other hand, without glorifying them and creating more of these things down the road."

"Jeez, Debra Ann…." Paul's expression told me I'd put him between a rock and a hard place. "I take your point, but the timing sucks for making that kind of request. There are *so* many moving parts to this; I don't think news reporting is the highest priority.

"But Cap *did* mention media coverage, so I'd have a buy-in. And if I'm going to ask the question, it should be now. Let me run it past Louis — he'd be the most sympathetic audience, and having an embedded reporter on the apprehension team *would* help address any questions of transparency."

"Thanks, Paul." I kissed him on the cheek.

"I don't think I had a chance to tell you yet, but Louis sent Strickland to Sacramento this morning for a training seminar with the California Highway Patrol computer crime lab. It was pure dumb luck schedule-wise, but that gave us cover for our meeting. Our brass notified state officials of Strickland's current standing, situation, and pending detention, but on a need-to-know basis only.

"Meanwhile, CHiP gave Mondo's unit hooks into Strickland's access to online resources. They'll monitor and control those while he's on their campus. Capt. Bouchard's SWAT team attached a magnetic GPS tracker to

Strickland's maroon Lexus, parked at the San Diego airport; they've confirmed their tracking capabilities.

"Louis touched on the strengths and weaknesses of the cases for the various homicides. He emphasized they'd only grown stronger in the twenty-four hours since we knew Strickland was our suspect."

"Stronger, how?"

"Yesterday, Escalation Management matched the slug from Marshall's Audi door panel to one removed from the woodwork at a crack house during a Vice raid a year ago — Strickland was the supervising officer. Internal Affairs took a sworn statement from another officer that he witnessed Strickland pocketing that handgun during the raid, stating that 'he needed to replace his throw-down.' It had drilled-out serial numbers — probably why Strickland wanted it. But that particular handgun has a long history, and they can identify it by half a dozen ballistics matches in the same number of crimes — they don't need the serial number.

"They also have a right-hand index and middle fingerprint on the driver's side taillight of Marshall's Audi. The old-timers recalled that back in the day, the department trained rookies to touch the taillights of a car or truck whenever they approached on foot for a traffic stop. The prints proved officer contact with the vehicle if the driver rabbited or the officer became incapacitated. Old-school stuff, a habit that dies hard. I doubt Strickland even remembers doing it.

"Lt. Brooks wasn't sure how Strickland got on the list of elimination prints in the first place for the Marshall killing — he was never officially on the scene as an investigator. His prints popped once they included him among the permitted matches."

"It sounds like they've got this locked down, then."

Paul raised an eyebrow and one side of his smile.

"You'd think — still, it's one of those 'yeah, but…' things because of the Aunt Tik's wild card.

"Cap brought up that Aunt Tik's members would be out there in our audience, in numbers we couldn't know. He wants us to treat Aunt Tik's involvement like we would crowd control — consider any implications for the arrest itself and any post-apprehension blowback.

"For example, could other Aunt Tik's members interfere with or retaliate for a czar's arrest? Or for Strickland's arrest specifically? Or as a broad statement against police intrusion?

"Finally, the scariest possibility is that Steve's still alive … and someone, possibly an Aunt Tik's member, is watching over him with instructions to do Steve harm if anything happens to Strickland."

CHAPTER 51

Paul took a moment to finish his sandwich, chasing it with a half-full glass of milk.

"Louis made the point, and everyone agreed, that our lives would be easier if we avoided tangling up the initial arrest warrant in Aunt Tik's challenge-and-punk complications. By that criterion, the two best homicide candidates would be Marshall and Detmer. We have strong circumstantial and evidentiary cases against Strickland for both murders, along with means, motive, and opportunity. Each killing has a single perpetrator and victim — they all had the same hobby, but otherwise, very little Aunt Tik's involvement to explain to a judge or jury."

Louis's logic made sense.

"I've been writing up these cases for my article series, and I'm learning how tricky it can be explaining a gaming website in the context of real people getting murdered. I can only imagine how rough it might get teaching Aunt Tik's to twelve people in a jury box when opposing counsel is objecting to every other word."

Paul acknowledged my comment with a one-sided grin.

"The Marshall case, especially, touches Aunt Tik's only tangentially, primarily as to motive — Marshall and Strickland both had unpaid employment with Aunt Tik's. It was clashes in their roles and goals that likely incited Strickland to murder Marshall. Nothing about challenges and punks played a direct part. The wrinkle is that Marshall's e-mail to himself *did* indirectly reference the crushed-car punk, implicating Strickland in two additional murders. Captain Jarvis was concerned that the defense could use that link to muddy up the waters of the Marshall case by bringing in the other homicides prematurely.

"To her credit, DDA Calley addressed that worry head-on. She thought a defense introducing Aunt Tik's methods and operations into the Marshall trial would be tantamount to malpractice. The car-crushing case linked to that e-mail is the strongest and simplest of the DA's punk-and-challenge cases. The tie to Strickland's ex is straightforward. The DA's office is willing to accept the risk and stands ready to argue Aunt Tik's issues if necessary. Calley seems eager — like she *wants* Strickland's lawyers to open that door."

"It's good to hear the district attorney's office is on the same page as the department for once."

"With Marshall as a sympathetic victim and all the public pressure to resolve his murder, it was a no-brainer. Louis's suggestion to arrest Strickland with warrants based solely on the Marshall roadside assassination was approved.

"So, with that settled, I thought the meeting was over. Our SWAT team knows what they're doing, and CHiP has eyes on Strickland — how hard could this be?" Paul sighed. "Remind me never again to discount the politics that go with something like this."

"I don't understand — how political could it get? You know who did it, what they did, and why. You arrest the guy, everybody takes a bow...."

Paul shook his head.

"You'd think, but no. Cap was sitting on a proposal that came to him via his back channel with CHiP. Their offer was simply to let them arrest the offender on the CHiP campus in Sacramento. But in exchange, they want to retain Strickland in their custody and prosecute him there."

"Oh, I get it." The lightbulb had gone off. "It's a high-profile case you've already solved, for which the state can take credit, and we're in an election season. I can do *that* math for myself."

"Times like these are when you love working for Louis. He never raised his voice, didn't slam the table, but make no mistake, he gave them both barrels. He started by acknowledging that safety's always paramount, and sure, that's the easy option for our officers here. But we have six homicides, a kidnapping, and an attempted murder of a sitting judge. The likelihood is years of trials, public exposure, and fighting our Aunt Tik's cell. Giving up local control of these cases and surrendering management of the public's view of them over the long term for a short-term gain isn't our best option.

"Louis is savvy, so he sprinkles some sugar on top. He said, 'Let's not deny state officials credit where it's due — we're grateful for CHiP's help. Having the state pick up the tab for the resource allocations and expenses of housing and prosecuting Strickland for the duration of these cases might not seem such a bad thing from a pure law-enforcement perspective.' "

"Okay, so he's making nice…."

"Wait for it." Paul grinned. "Then Louis pointed out that Sacramento is more than five hundred miles, an eight-hour drive, from us. There are serious economic and logistical concerns regarding travel for our personnel and witnesses if Sacramento takes over these cases and the prosecution gets re-centered so far away. Worse, detaining Strickland post-conviction in facilities convenient to Sacramento rather than San Diego causes more hardship to the victims trying to recover from him financially through civil litigation."

"Okay, that's a good point," I acknowledged.

"Hammer's down on the first barrel, one more to go." Paul gave me a sly look. "He goes, 'The Aunt Tik's anonymous membership problem worries me. We're aware of it here now at the highest levels of SDPD.' As he's saying this, he tilts his head toward Capt. Jarvis. 'But determining who among our officers are members, and then convincing them to give it up voluntarily, will be difficult enough. Keeping other officers from joining during their time off is another can of worms.' "

Knowing Louis, I wondered what he was setting up.

"Now, Lt. Harbin is in full stride. 'You may think not knowing who among CHiP personnel or in the prosecutor's office in Sacramento could be Aunt Tik's members isn't a serious issue. Let me remind you that six people are dead that we know of. A young man just starting his life is missing, and there's been another attempted murder. All in just fifteen months, all because we were unaware of just *one* Aunt Tik's membership.'

"Then he pauses for dramatic effect, then starts in again. 'With all deference to the reporter and the Forensics supervisor who made that connection,'" — Paul waggled his eyebrows at me — " 'we got lucky catching onto Strickland when we did. And that singular bit of luck doesn't address the larger problem: we barely know what we might have with Aunt Tik's in San Diego; we have no clue what the extent of this thing is in Sacramento or anywhere else. I'm honestly fearful of what happens once the news gets out — when officers and the public learn the potential and opportunities for doing bad things within Aunt Tik's, their copycats, and future derivatives.' "

"Louis must have rehearsed this … It's too perfect."

"You have no idea," Paul said wryly. "That was just the warm-up. Now he's delivering his pitch. He said, 'Beyond that, elevating all of this to the state level would magnify media attention by a factor of ten. Locally, we'd have no control over what's passed out to the press. Any concerns about Aunt Tik's will amplify from just one rogue cell to all the cells in the state or even wider.

" 'They'd be immediately dumping the same painful learning experiences we're going through here in San Diego around Aunt Tik's on every law-enforcement entity in the state. Large and small, irrespective of their available resources. Think about what Strickland nearly got away with as an example for every disgruntled cop in any jurisdiction having an Aunt Tik's cell. Consider the implications of cops who happen to be Aunt Tik's members looking the other way whenever a czar needs them to.'

"Louis stopped to let it sink in.

"Then he goes, 'Can you say *clusterfuck*?' You could almost hear it echoing through the quiet in the room."

My eyes went wide.

"Remind me not to get on Louis's bad side."

"Then he went for his summation," Paul continued. "He said that while working on this, Det. Robbins's team uncovered several other homicide cases that may also be Aunt Tik's-related but which didn't meet the criteria they'd set at the time. He reminded them we haven't touched the cold cases yet. He asked them, 'Do we want to set the precedent that San Diego Aunt Tik's cases with San Diego victims and San Diego offenders will be tried and prosecuted in Sacramento? And how reliable is the channel back from the capital? Will we be kept in the loop and our voices, or those of our victims, heard as we evaluate new or uncovered Aunt Tik's cases here?'

"That was all it took. Louis's arguments were powerful enough that there was no dissent to Capt. Jarvis's decision. We'll make the arrest here in San Diego after Strickland returns."

"I would have loved to have been a fly on the wall to hear that little speech." I snorted.

"It took all the nonsense out of the discussion, that's for sure. Captain Bouchard of SWAT must have talked to Louis before the meeting. When Bouchard took the podium, he'd pre-planned a San Diego arrest.

"They determined the arrival gate on his flight home presented the best opportunity for apprehending Strickland locally. He won't have any chance to retrieve checked baggage potentially containing firearms.

"The concern is that news media usually have representatives at the airport and would notice SWAT's presence when they assemble at the gate. It's a long path from there to the airport exit. SWAT will have to manage the number of eyes and ears witnessing the event. That includes any airport crowds potentially exposed to violence during the arrest, as well as those perhaps too eager to get their fifteen minutes of fame via the media."

I asked what they'd decided to do.

"They looked at other options and alternatives and went with the arrival-gate arrest."

***

Upon returning to the precinct, Paul delayed his midday nap to honor his promise to Debra Ann. He headed to Lt. Harbin's office, grateful to see him seated at his desk.

"Louis, I have a huge favor to ask on behalf of Debra Ann — I know the ultimate decision has to be made higher in the chain of command, but I wanted to run it by you first. She wants to be at Strickland's arrest and write it up."

"Oh, Paul, that's a tall order." Louis frowned. "I'm not saying she doesn't deserve to be there or that I don't support the idea. It's that the brass has much bigger fish to fry right now. Proposing something that serves the interests of a specific individual might seem … opportunistic. Look, Paul, she's not law enforcement; she's not always on our side, and this is about one of our own gone bad. It's personal, private."

"I understand, and you're right. It feels awkward even asking. Just between the two of us, it's not about making the department look bad, or bragging rights, or any of that crap. For us, this thing became personal with the death of our babysitter, Sophia Ferguson, as collateral damage in the Carla Littman murder. Debra Ann feels obligated to see it through. She's the only reporter out there who knows the whole story and can do it justice, including that the homicide department took a risk investigating all this back when only the feds had any of it."

"Okay, Paul, I hear you," Louis relented. "I can't guarantee anything, and I've no idea how long it'll take to get an answer. But I'll make the request. I can play the trump card that if it weren't for Debra Ann nosing into that rowing photo, we'd still be in the dark and finding more bodies."

"I'd watch over her," Paul offered, "and ensure she doesn't get in anyone's way during the arrest. I can be there in an off-duty capacity, so the department doesn't take any unnecessary hits if things go badly."

The lieutenant hesitated, torn.

"Paul, I don't think you understand. If we were to lose an embedded reporter in a situation this fucked up already, all our careers would be over."

Chapter 52

It wasn't long after Paul closed his eyes for a quick nap that the buzz of a text nudged him toward wakefulness, followed a few minutes later by the relentless dinging of an incoming call. Paul's watch read two-thirty, four hours before Strickland's planned takedown.

It was Marci.

"Louis reached out to me. He needs us in his office as soon as we can get there. You're already in the precinct, and I have to hit the road. Can you find Eve and get her there? Can't tie up the phone, gotta go."

Paul rubbed his eyes as he telephoned Eve.

"Sorry to interrupt what you're doing, but Marci just informed me Louis called us into his office, pronto. No idea what's going on, but given he'd asked us to take things easy, it can't be good."

"Traffic is light this time of day," Eve replied. "I should be there in twenty, twenty-five minutes."

Paul threw on his jacket and headed to Louis's office.

Half the bullpen away from Louis's door, Paul could hear a loud conversation between angry participants — Capt. Jarvis's voice was easily recognizable.

As Paul walked in, he saw the captain standing, both fists clenched at his sides, leaning into the speakerphone on the desk. Louis was propped up against his credenza, looking intensely down at the floor as he listened, his chin resting on his right fist and his left arm across his diaphragm.

Mondo stood near the doorway with a grim look on his face.

He waved Paul over, whispering, "Strickland's on the loose. Or his car's been taken from the airport by someone else, not clear which. A SWAT tech was testing their GPS tracking on Strickland's vehicle ahead of time, their backup plan if Strickland escaped arrest and tried to run. The tech saw the vehicle moving, and everyone freaked. They're still trying to sort it out. They've got multiple lines patched in — on speakerphone, so don't say anything."

"What the *fuck*, Leonard, you had one job! You couldn't keep track of a serial murderer in the goddamn headquarters of the state's largest law-enforcement agency?" Capt. Jarvis's deep voice was so loud it shook the books on the shelves; Paul had never heard him so angry.

"Listen, Jarvis," shouted a voice from the speaker, shrill and irate, "you called me up yesterday on short notice, and you told me you've got a guy who killed six people; he's one of yours. And today, you tell me you don't want *us* to make the arrest? But you *do* want us to babysit this assclown.

"Should we shine your shoes, too, Jarvis?"

Oh, here we go, Paul thought. *It's all about payback.*

"We've got 450 attendees from all over the state at this seminar," the voice continued. "We have dozens of exhibits, vendor stalls, and two hundred people wandering the halls. You told us your guy is here for the day, so we took you at your word. We put a man on him, but you didn't give us any reason to believe he was going anywhere — you haven't sent us *any* paperwork, for God's sake!

"But you say, 'Don't make it obvious we're tailing him; he'll spook.' So, no, we didn't follow him into the can every time he took a leak or got out of his seat.

"We screwed with his phone's WiFi connection, as you requested. So, *of course,* he's moving around, trying to get a better hookup. My officer tells me your guy left for a break around 10:20, and a short time later, someone looking like him takes that seat. What did you want us to do, check his ID every time he got up or sat down?"

"Look, Leonard, this isn't getting us anywhere," Capt. Jarvis replied. "Do you have the exit/entrance surveillance videos yet?"

"Yes, just handed to me now. We have someone who looks like your boy leaving the premises through a side door at 10:27 a.m. Okay, they just told me he boarded a flight back to San Diego at 12:07."

"*Fuck*," Paul heard Louis say, not entirely under his breath.

"It's an hour and thirty-five-minute flight," the other voice said, "puts him back in San Diego at 1:42 p.m. Assuming he checked his firearm, he's out of baggage claim and parking probably 2:05 or 2:10."

"We have his GPS showing his vehicle leaving the parking garage at 2:23 p.m., so that squares," Jarvis confirmed. "We'll take it from here. Have a great afternoon, Leonard." There was a telltale lack of sincerity in his voice as Jarvis punched the speakerphone button and hung up the receiver.

Louis's earlier comment linking "clusterfuck" and Sacramento's involvement in these cases now seemed remarkably prescient.

Once the other party was gone, Capt. Cranston stepped closer to the phone. "Our GPS tracking tech has Strickland's vehicle at 1202 Kettner Boulevard downtown; he's been there about ten minutes. It shows as a health spa, 'DCompress Downtown.' Interesting. I'm starting to think Strickland isn't *trying* to evade apprehension. I believe the arrogant pissant might have just pulled a Ferris Bueller on the department's dime."

Louis eyed Mondo, lips pursed. "So, Strickland shows up at the seminar and signs in. He stays just long enough to be seen. He has no intention of applying anything they're teaching to the Aunt Tik's work anyway, so he bails out for an afternoon at a health spa? If the guy weren't a multiple murderer, it would almost be funny. But he is, and that isn't. So, the question becomes, 'If all that's true, where should we apprehend him?'"

"I just heard, got here as fast as I could," Capt. Bouchard of the SWAT unit announced as he strode through Louis's door. Bouchard's massive frame made the room feel quite a bit more crowded. Marci and Eve were trailing behind and stayed in the doorway, listening in.

There was a burst of crosstalk as each of them updated the others.

Louis summarized, "Option one seems to be apprehending him at the day spa; option two, assume he's playing hooky and heading home when he's finished, meaning we'll arrest him there."

"I'm not comfortable trying to detain him at the spa with no time for us to prepare or plan," Bouchard said. "We don't know the layout; we've got no eyes or ears. It's in a public area with an unknown number of guests. We have no idea how competent, cooperative, or discreet the staff might be, and we don't know how long he'll be there. From the standpoint of potentially having at least a little time to prepare, I'd prefer arresting him at home."

A quick scan through the room revealed no disagreement. "We explored that possibility in preparation for the earlier meeting today. Strickland lives in a gated community with a single point of egress, which makes it workable for the apprehension location from a security and safety perspective. The GPS tracker will tell us when he's leaving the spa and how much time we have. We'll get the housekeeper out of the home, by pretext, if necessary, before the arrest and evacuate the immediate neighbors."

"Do we have the floor plans yet for the residence?" Eve asked.

"Yes, Daniels printed off the blueprints," Bouchard replied. "Anyone who needs one can grab it off the table in Interrogation Room B."

"Are we controlling access to those?" Capt. Jarvis asked.

"Daniels is watching over them, so nothing gets out to the wrong people." Bouchard continued, "We'll need to coordinate the timing of Mondo's team severing Strickland's connections to Aunt Tik's website so we don't forewarn him. Before the arrest, Strickland will be allowed access to the Aunt Tik's site. However, Mondo's team arranged modifications to generate 404-page errors and other streaming issues. Those will keep him from doing anything without cutting him off completely. Hopefully, his spa activities and driving won't permit him much online time anyway. By the time he's back in his home, the arrest will come soon enough that any connection issues he experiences will become moot.

"Once Strickland has passed through the subdivision gate, we'll post an officer there to control other traffic coming or going. Mondo, Louis, Paul, and two senior members of Mondo's vice unit will lead the approach team. SWAT officers in full engagement gear will back them. The idea here is that the presence of familiar faces will help mitigate any thoughts of rash action

Strickland might have. It would be nice to have Det. Robbins's knowledge of Strickland and Det. Byrne's tactical skills on the approach team, but the offender has known issues with strong females, issues which lean toward violence."

"Thanks for including me in that discussion on the walkover, Captain," Eve said. "I appreciate it, I do. But I also understand that it's just one of Strickland's many flaws, and there's no sense in aggravating the situation. I'll be glad to help out supporting the SWAT team."

"So, Det. Robbins will consult with SWAT leadership and Det. Byrne will be with the SWAT members, backing up the approach team. These houses are aligned differently on their lots. The only nearby rooftop with the desired line of sight is across the street. That location would expose our officers to view from Strickland's front windows. Instead, we'll have officers on the ground monitoring each window and any secondary entrances."

Bouchard closed his metal notebook case with a quick flip of his wrist.

"Are there any questions?"

Marci spoke up from the doorway. "Do we have a contingency plan if Strickland doesn't return home?"

"We'll have units running parallel to his path once he's away from the spa facilities," Bouchard answered, "and if he deviates from the routes we're allowing him, those units will determine an apprehension location and make contact."

Jarvis was listening as he leaned against the credenza, and Louis asked, "Does the new plan work for you, Captain?"

"Yes, I think it's as good as any on short notice. Carry on. I've got to run, and you'll be fighting the clock, too. I'll leave the rest of this in your capable hands. Best of luck to you, and stay safe, everyone."

"Okay, people, we've got too many bodies in this little space," Louis said. "Let's move to the big conference room where we can spread out, write on the whiteboards, and use the flatscreen. Paul, do you have a minute?"

As everyone cleared out, Paul and Louis moved to either side of the lieutenant's desk.

"I ran your request to allow Debra Ann to witness Strickland's apprehension up the flagpole and got the green light from upstairs. I'll need to reconfirm now that the arrest scenario has changed, but they took my question more positively than I thought they might. So, unless you hear otherwise from me, she's good to go."

"Thanks, Louis; we both appreciate it."

"Don't thank me yet." Louis's expression was stern and unsmiling. "She wears a Kevlar helmet and a bulletproof vest at all times. She goes where SWAT tells her to go, with no exceptions. That's not coming from upstairs; that's coming from me. If I catch either of you taking shortcuts or breaking my rules, I'll throw you both out of there myself. *Are we clear?*"

"Perfectly," Paul said somberly, even as he anticipated Debra Ann's excitement at hearing the news.

As they left Louis's office together, Paul realized how far the goalposts had moved. They'd once planned to arrest a man coming unarmed off a plane through a controlled gateway with which he was unfamiliar.

Now, they'd be trying to apprehend a likely armed law enforcement professional with significant resources available to him in the familiarity of his own home.

CHAPTER 53

The apprehension team waited in vehicles scattered alongside the curbs of quiet side streets outside Strickland's gated community. With on-screen maps broadcast to their notebooks, they watched the GPS tracking app as Strickland left the day spa at 6:05 p.m. and wound his way home. I looked over Paul's shoulder in the communications truck while he followed along.

Strickland pulled briefly into a Stop-N-Go, just long enough to gas up and grab something from inside the mini-mart.

"He's carrying a small sack and a large to-go drink," one of the officers announced quietly into the radio.

But when Strickland got back into his car, he turned left instead of right at the next light, opposite the straightest route toward his home, though his pace was leisurely.

Lt. Harbin was inside the comms van with us. As his cell phone rang, he checked its display. "It's Capt. Bouchard," he said in Paul's direction before answering.

"Yes, Captain. No, I don't know where he might be going."

Louis listened a moment.

"Yes, Captain, I understand. But if you're OK waiting before the traffic units intercept him, I'd like to see where he might be going. He doesn't seem to be in any hurry, certainly nothing that indicates panicked or erratic behavior."

Louis paused again.

"So far, neither our plan nor the public is at risk. If the sirens and lights set Strickland off for some reason, then we're dealing with a potential high-speed chase — the guy's got a fast car and a full gas tank. I'm not saying he can escape us, but it does mean he could wreak a lot of havoc against innocent souls. I don't think he's given us reason yet to take that chance."

Louis listened for a moment.

"Okay, Captain, will do. We'll stay with the plan so long as he remains reasonably close to the speed limit and doesn't look like he's leaving our jurisdiction."

Hanging up, Louis announced to the rest of the van's occupants, "We're still a go — the original approach, for now."

Strickland had turned into a downscale residential neighborhood in the Clairemont community of San Diego. He stopped unexpectedly in front of a house well off the main thoroughfare, parking at the curb rather than turning into its driveway.

"The subject has entered the residence, carrying the bag and the drink from the mini-mart," the radio announced, the voice subdued.

Ten minutes later, just as we'd begun wondering if SWAT might engage him there, Strickland was back on the move, empty-handed. He was now following a path that would bring him straight to us.

Why then, I'll never know, but as Strickland was leaving the Clairemont address, I suddenly had a flash of insight — all the pieces of the puzzle had crisply fallen into their rightful places for me. Once they did, the clarity was astounding.

Still, I'd have to convince Louis in a hurry for the revelation to mean anything.

I touched the lieutenant on his shoulder.

Intensely focused and immersed in thought, Louis was startled and uncharacteristically irritated for a split second.

He immediately returned to his professional demeanor as he tilted his head back to look at me, his body still facing the comms console.

"Louis, I know I'm out of line here, and this will sound insane. But you've got to send police officers back to the house Strickland just left."

"I'm listening, Debra Ann. Make it quick, though. You know we have a lot on our plate right now."

"I think I know what's going on."

It was all tumbling out of me now, tripping over itself as it left my lips.

"We couldn't figure out what threat Steve posed to Aunt Tik's that would get him abducted. I know why — *please*, just hear me out.

"When Eve and I interviewed Steve at home, Steve had just made bail after being locked up. During that interview, Steve told us about painting Vicky's car. When he started that challenge, it had the wrong GPS coordinates, and the punk master called Steve while he was in his car to give him the right ones. That punk master was blotto_bill — in other words, Steve heard Strickland's voice."

Louis was paying close attention.

"I didn't realize Steve could identify blotto_bill…."

"Eve made notes, but the knowledge wasn't helpful without a suspect. Still, once you had someone for a voice lineup, Steve could verify whether they were blotto_bill, something of an ace up your sleeve. I think that's why Strickland faked the Eastman persona instead of framing someone else — he must have read Eve's notes and realized an actual human couldn't pass the voice test.

"Paul told me you formed Marci's official team around the Aunt Tik's investigation a few days later, including Strickland. With Steve free and Strickland working Aunt Tik's cases every day, it was just a matter of time until Steve and Strickland were in the same place at the same time. If Steve recognized Strickland's voice, it was all over. I think that's why he had to kidnap Steve.

"I assume he planned to have Steve killed, maybe by Detmer, but certainly with Detmer taking the blame. Then he'd get rid of Detmer; problem solved."

Paul understood where I was heading and jumped in to let me catch my breath.

"But we screwed up his plan when he found out we were about to flip Detmer. He had to kill Detmer immediately. Let's assume neither Detmer nor Strickland had yet murdered Steve. If that's so, Strickland's stuck with a kidnapping victim he can't get rid of until he sets up somebody else for Steve's death or comes up with a different plan.

"That's tagged gang turf over there — crack houses, bars on the windows and doors — transients in and out at all hours. Nobody snitches if they see something strange. Perfect place to stash somebody."

I took over. "Steve's still alive! And he's at the house Strickland just left. Being gone all day meant Strickland had to feed Steve and provide him water — he couldn't afford to let Steve die on him now. There've been too many bodies; nobody else left to take the heat. That's why he stopped at that mini-mart; he had to pick up a sandwich and something to drink for Steve. I know this sounds so frigging crazy, but it works — I *know* he's there."

Louis gave me a sidelong glance, and then his eyes flicked over to meet Paul's as he chewed on his upper lip.

"I don't think Strickland would've killed Steve once he couldn't hang the homicide on Detmer," Paul added. "Murdering Detmer was an act of desperation; Strickland had to know the walls were closing in. Without Detmer available as the fall guy for Steve's murder, I think Strickland would keep Steve alive to use as leverage if he ever needed it. For one thing, Steve isn't a physical threat and wouldn't be baiting Strickland with what he knew, unlike Detmer. There wouldn't be the provocation that Strickland apparently can't handle."

His eyes still fixed on Paul, Louis reached for the mike of the radio tuned to the uniformed officers' frequency.

"This is Lt. Louis Harbin. Let the subject get another mile down the road so we know he won't double back. Then I need the last tailing unit to peel off and return to that Clairemont address. The officers are to make entry under exigent circumstances on my authority. You're looking for a nineteen-year-old Caucasian male named Steve Nielsen — maybe in a locked room, a crawlspace, or the attic or basement. He's a hostage, not a perp. Treat him accordingly. Radio back your status once you've made contact or completed your search."

Louis turned to glance at me and then said to Paul. "If this goes south and Steve's not there, cross your fingers we get a judge with a lenient definition of exigent circumstances."

A little over ten minutes later, a call crackled over the radio.

"Lieutenant, we've got your kidnap victim."

My hands went straight up in the air as I let out a rebel yell. Louis and Paul fist-bumped and grinned at one another.

"He's conversant and ambulatory," the officer continued, "no obvious injuries other than a contusion in the back of his head. We've got a bus on the way. He's asking for his mother. Please advise the family that they'll be transporting him to Sharp Trauma Center II if they want to meet him there."

Beaming from ear to ear, Louis asked, "Debra Ann, can you call Tracy and let her know?"

"Oh, absolutely!" I exclaimed, happy to have been given the joyful task. Tracy's shrieking into my ear as she took in the news made it even sweeter.

It wasn't long before the raspy rattle of radio traffic reminded us of the gravity of the situation holding us captive in that van. The celebration quieted as everyone returned to the solemn task before them. Still, the positivity remained, with Steve's safe recovery serving as a good omen.

A few moments after they'd gotten the word about Steve, Louis spun around in his seat, a forefinger to the earpiece of his headset.

"Capt. Bouchard just updated us. Strickland entered the community gates at 7:35 p.m., drove straight to his home, and parked in the garage. We need to move our van inside the gates. We'll fall in twenty yards behind SWAT.

"This is it. *Showtime, people.*"

THE WRITINGS OF
AVRIL MARIA SERENE

CHAPTER 54

Four neighboring families, three of whom had property abutting Bob Strickland's, and one across the street from him, had been temporarily relocated earlier in the evening. The arrest team was in place, with some members secreted behind plants and the neighbors' buildings.

Dusk was now slipping into nightfall, and the SWAT van moved into position in front of the house two doors west of Strickland's home. Louis and Paul volunteered, with Mondo taking the lead, to make initial contact as a group. They were wearing Kevlar helmets, goggles, and bulletproof vests as they prepared to approach the front door, surrounded by Eve and SWAT team members crouched behind them, weapons at the ready.

The rest of us had assembled behind the SWAT van, nervously watching the scene, fingers crossed.

But it didn't happen. Just as the initial contact group was forming up to cross the yard, Ken Benson, a technician in the comms van, ran across the street and addressed Lt. Sanders, the SWAT commander on scene.

"The parabolic mike picked up two voices inside the residence; the other participant sounds like a young Latina," Benson said.

"We thought it was a conversation over speakerphone, but the infrared scanner shows two mobile heat sources in the area of the den."

Sanders asked in surprise, "How did we miss that?"

Benson replied, "The second heat source came from that back bedroom. When we scanned this afternoon, we detected a low-grade reading at the location, but it wasn't mobile or dynamic. It read out as a small appliance or aquarium. Before this conversation, we had no glass vibrations to indicate human presence. I'd guess she has a small build, was sleeping under covers in the fetal position, and doesn't snore."

"Guessing won't cut it here, Benson," Sanders replied. "Get back to the van and make sure there's nothing else we've missed."

"Dammit, this isn't good," Mondo said. "It's on me. I waved off executing the search warrants for his house or his locker at the station until we had Strickland in custody. We assumed the house was unoccupied — no evidence of the housekeeper or anyone answering their landline. I didn't want us tripping any residence alarms or a 'helpful' passing neighbor getting curious about the activity and tipping Strickland off."

Mondo's cell phone rang; its Caller ID showed Robert Strickland's department-issued mobile number. Stabbing the speakerphone icon with his forefinger, Mondo answered as we gathered around, "This is Capt. Edmond Cranston."

"My security drone tells me that I have uninvited guests on my property," Strickland complained. "It's truly a pity you couldn't have called ahead — I would have told you not to waste your time. I would also have informed you that a young lady is staying with me. She was napping in the back. She's awake now, and all your creeping about has gotten her quite upset. I believe you understand how your presence here creates a situation for me. And, especially, for her."

"*Fuck.*" Louis spoke for all of us. Everyone around the SWAT van recognized our new problem and the danger posed to the woman. Their expressions told the story: we hadn't prepared for a hostage situation that no one had anticipated. I don't think any of us doubted for a moment that Strickland — now facing six first-degree murder charges and answerable to a kidnapping and felony attempted murder, all premeditated — would kill another to evade capture. The questions on my lips were, "Who is this woman? Does she have any influence over Strickland?" and "Can she defend herself?"

Mondo muted the conversation as Sanders whispered over Mondo's shoulder, "We're going to cut off the power, water, cable, and phone lines. If Strickland's using VoIP or a landline, it may break your connection."

"He's on his work cell. Do what you need to do," Mondo said with a nod.

He unmuted the call and said into the cell phone, "Lt. Strickland, you and I know you're in an untenable position. We have a warrant to detain you as a material witness in the murder of James Marshall III. We have a sworn duty to execute that warrant. Committing additional crimes by interfering with that woman's free will, causing her injury, or putting her in harm's way will not serve your best interests. You need to surrender her, any weapons you have, and yourself to us immediately to preserve your opportunities in the legal system."

The house went dark, and there was a brief silence from Strickland. Then, suddenly, he was back on the line, the anger rising in his voice, apparent even over a cell phone on loudspeaker.

"Let's set something straight here, Mondo." Strickland had added a sarcastic and mocking lilt to Mondo's name. "You're in no position to tell me what to do. You want to serve me with a warrant? Fine. Get me my union rep, and we can discuss that at the station tomorrow. But I'm on my own time, and you will *not* come onto *my* property with stormtroopers and try to tell *me* what to do when I'm off duty."

His vehemence bordered on maniacal. It was clear he was escalating.

"Now, get those goddamned people out of my yard and quit trying to put on a show for the fucking neighbors. I'm holding all the cards here, so get those damned SWAT assholes off my lawn *now*. I can *see* you jagoffs, so *move* it!"

Mondo muted his cell, and he, Louis, and Sanders conferred briefly while Marci, Eve, and I listened in.

"I see a Ring security drone making its rounds on the right side of the house at roof gutter level," the SWAT commander said. "It's on battery power and won't be able to recharge. Shouldn't last too long. I'd guess Strickland's seeing the drone videos over his cell connection."

"If we destroy it now," Louis said, "we risk infuriating Strickland further and increasing the possibility of harm to the woman."

"We need to defuse the situation as much as possible," Mondo agreed.

"I can back out our officers for now," Sanders offered. "That should reduce his stress level a little."

Mondo nodded, and Marci and Louis left us to go with the SWAT commander. Mondo called out into the speakerphone after unmuting it.

"Okay, Bob, we're pulling back the SWAT team, so they'll be off your property for now. But we're not going away. You know we have to execute the arrest warrant. You've been in this situation from our side; you know how this works. Before proceeding, we must confirm that the woman in your home is alive and well."

There was a moment of silence, and a young woman's frightened voice came over the cell phone. "I am Christina. I don't understand what's going on here."

The woman broke into sobs.

"I am just Bob's friend. He asked me to watch his home and care for his fish. I didn't *do* anything."

Her sobbing grew more intense.

"He'll shoot me if I don't do what he says. Please go away and leave us alone."

"Christina?" I quietly asked Mondo as I leaned into his left ear. Besides Paul, he was the only one standing with us who'd also attended the gala event. "Wasn't she Strickland's companion at the Children's Hospital charity ball?"

Mondo nodded and gave me a thumbs-up.

Strickland came back on the line. "Okay, you got your damned proof of life. But you're on the clock here. I want the SWAT vehicles and anything with a gumball or a siren off the street. *Now!*"

"Bob, you know that's not how this works," Mondo spoke into the phone. "We took our officers off your lawn. That's one thing. But we're not leaving because that won't resolve this problem. You need to surrender to us *immediately.*"

"Fuck you, Mondo." Strickland's voice again had a derisive tone. "This negotiating bullshit won't work with me. You're on my turf, and here we do things *my* way.

"Now get those goddamned vehicles off my street!"

Everyone on the Strickland apprehension team paused briefly to assess the seriousness of their unexpected situation. Mondo and Paul took a moment aside to discuss Strickland's hostage. "If this is the same Christina, she goes maybe ninety-five pounds soaking wet. She's — what, twenty-seven, twenty-eight? And didn't look to me like she came from the ranks of law enforcement."

"The voice sounds right," Mondo agreed. "I don't think she will be much help to us or herself. That may be a good thing; she's less likely to do something unexpected, and dealing with her fear and hesitation may slow Strickland down."

"He needs her at the moment," Louis said. "That may help keep her alive. You never want to put a hostage at further risk, and having only one gives Strickland very little real bargaining power. Abusing his victim would increase the probability of an all-out SWAT assault. And the size of Strickland's home now works against him — there are too many entry points to defend. He effectively imprisons himself if he has a safe room and goes to it. It becomes a siege, and we wait him out. Killing his hostage leaves Strickland with no leverage or protection whatsoever if he wants to leave that house."

Mondo made Strickland aware that he knew all this by leaving the other vehicle group, now grown to include a fire rescue unit, an ambulance, and two patrol cruisers, right where they were — a visible reminder to Strickland of his relative impotence. But SWAT did move their van from its place two doors to the west to a position right at the eastern edge of Strickland's property.

Startled by sudden, strange noises coming through the cell phone and from the closed garage, the officers around the patrol unit realized they were hearing the sound of a circular saw ripping through wood. There'd been no tell-tale yammering from a generator, so it had to be battery-powered.

"What's going on there, Bob? " Mondo asked tersely into the phone. "Now's not the time to build anything, and if you're causing any harm to that young lady, we'll have to come in. You know that."

Strickland replied dismissively. "Don't get your pantyhose into an uproar, Mondo. I told you — you're not in charge here; I am. One way or the other, I'm leaving here, and the young lady is coming with me. There isn't a goddamned thing you can do about it. Christina, tell this so-called man you're fine."

The lameness of Strickland's insults revealed the weakness of his position. In some ways, that made him more dangerous, like a cornered dog suffering from an injury.

The young woman's halting voice came over the phone. "I am okay; he is not hurting me."

Then Strickland came back on. "Listen, asshole; this is the way it's going to be. You'll clear the path up my driveway, and Christina and I are driving out of here. If you get in our way, I cannot guarantee her safety, as they say, and you'll force me to take out a few of you as well. Are we clear? Let's get this damned show on the road." The officers heard a clang of what sounded like a hammer on steel coming over the phone and, again, from the garage.

Mondo muted the cell phone as Sanders approached him. "That driveway gives us about twenty yards to work with. I need a few minutes with my team to prep the equipment we'll need," Sanders said. "Can you buy us a little time?"

Mondo spoke into the phone once again. "Okay, Bob. We can do this your way, but we need some time to get our people moved off the drive and on the same page so we can keep everyone safe. Give us ten minutes."

Sanders left for the SWAT van. Mondo muted the phone again as he saw the SWAT lieutenant returning a few minutes later. "Okay, Mondo, we're good to go. Our goals are to keep the hostage alive and our officers out of danger. The worst-case scenario is Strickland making it out of the gated community. Even so, we've got that GPS tracker on the Lexus and chase teams waiting outside the gate."

"Thank you, Lieutenant." Mondo turned and asked, "Does everyone understand their role in what we're about to do? Any questions?" Seeing nodding heads and no responses, Mondo said, "SWAT has this covered. My concern is that all our officers know their escape routes once that garage door begins opening. We don't want anyone left exposed to any line of fire simply because they ran into one another. Okay, let's do this."

Mondo unmuted the cell phone. "Okay, Bob, we've cleared a path for you. As long as you don't cause harm to our officers or the young woman, you'll be allowed to back out of the driveway and follow the street to the main gate. From there, you may pass through the gate onto the street outside. Are we in agreement on this?"

I couldn't help but think that if Strickland had any natural talents as a police officer, he would have known this was *too* easy. But I'm sure we were all counting on Strickland's arrogance, narcissism, and years of having things go how he wanted.

Sure enough, Strickland fired back over the cell, "Okay, asshole, just remember this — if anything goes hinky, what happens after that's on you. Play it straight if everyone wants to go home to their beds tonight."

Mondo raised an eyebrow at Paul as he uttered a flat one-word response, "Understood."

The dice had been cast.

THE WRITINGS OF
AVRIL MARIA SERENE

CHAPTER 55

As I cleaned the ballistic goggles SWAT provided me, I could see two snipers kneeling behind shrubbery that flanked the drive where it intersected the sidewalk. Two more, each with a helper, crouched as they hugged the wall on either side of the garage door. I'd taken cover with the other officers at the Strickland apprehension site behind the large SWAT van. We fell into two groups — some paced to and fro beside the vehicle; most of us stood or took a knee, staring around the front fender at the scene in anticipation and suspense.

With a slight creaking, the garage door began to open, a single panel pivoting as an unbending wooden slab, the bottom edge swinging out as it rose.

Not a leaf was rustling nor a blade of grass moving, and it seemed that no one on our team was breathing.

The tension was palpable and magnified what little sound there was, including the soft *sproinngg* made by the door's springs expanding and collapsing.

Barely audible, I heard a *pfffft*, quickly followed by another, to my right as a SWAT sniper behind the corner of the truck took out the Ring drone with silenced .22 rounds.

And now, the first puff of condensation from the car's exhaust escaped into the night air from under the slowly rising garage door.

At the same time, black-clad figures in the shadows on either side of the door silently placed the snipers' elevated shooting platforms on their sides of the driveway, one directly across from the other, allowing enough space between them for the car to pass.

As the helpers slipped silently into the darkness at each side of the garage, a sniper mounted each platform without a sound and rested his rifle's handguard on the platform's built-in support.

The Lexus inched backward, at first haltingly, out of the garage.

Its brake lights flashed quickly on, off, and back on again before it began rolling more confidently.

There was a slight squeaking of tire rubber on the coated garage floor as the car backed out, the Lexus's engine purring evenly, not another sound disturbing the night.

I marveled at the split-screen moment — on the one side, the odd serenity of the scene; on the other, the hammering of my heart against the wall of my chest.

Then suddenly, the first staccato *"pap-pap-pap-pap,"* starbursts of muzzle flash, and an explosion of shattering glass startled me.

Milliseconds later, a second burst from the AR-15 on the passenger side of the car, a screech of torn sheet metal, and the *clang-clang-clang* of something striking hardened steel.

No more than two seconds later, another round of gunshots. These were slower, more deliberate, and closer to us from behind bushes where the sidewalk crossed the drive. The Lexus's tires were deflating one by one as we crowded against the side of the SWAT van, peering around its nose.

With the car's windows gone, Christina's screams reverberated through the night air, punctuated with Strickland's yells of *"Drive! Go! Go!"*

Wisps of blue-gray smoke curled from the snipers' positions — a few seconds later, I caught the slightly acrid smell of freshly burned gunpowder wafting through the air.

The Lexus continued backing out of the driveway, more quickly now. The flattened tires flopped, waddled, and crunched through the tiny sharp squares of safety glass as the car passed through the SWAT gauntlet.

One or more rounds had gone through the floorboard and pierced the tailpipe ahead of the muffler, adding a harsh sputter and rattle to the sounds of the engine.

The vehicle backed onto the street with a quarter-circle turn. As it stopped and the driver shifted gears, the car bounced slightly on its springs. The Lexus began pulling forward, heading west onto the street with a chirp and a quick squeal of what remained of the front tires. The squeaking and grinding sounds grew louder as the bare metal of the wheels sparked more frequently against the pavement.

SWAT's snipers had run from their platforms and reported to Sanders, standing beside us.

"Lieutenant, couldn't get a clear line of sight," the shooter who'd been on the passenger side of the vehicle announced. "He's got metal plating on the driver's side of the rear footwells and wooden panels covering him on the other side. I think I got a couple of good hits, but I can't confirm any damage. I heard a male voice, indicating the target is still alive and coherent."

"*Dammit* … I don't mean you," Sanders quickly apologized to the young sniper. "The execution looked flawless from here; thought maybe we'd gotten the SOB. The good news is, they can't get far on those tires."

Almost on cue, the front wheels of the Lexus began spitting chunks of rubber off to the sides. The intermittent squalling of the wheels became more insistent as they spun inside the tires' sidewall beads.

Then, after two hundred yards of slow and erratic travel, meandering over the centerline and back, the Lexus's brake lights brightened, the right turn signal flashed, and the vehicle pulled over to the curb. The blinkers told us the young woman was still alive and driving, a positive sign; I couldn't imagine anyone but a terrified victim signaling their intentions in those circumstances.

But why pull over? The possibilities raced through my mind. *Was Strickland going to take over the driving now? Wishful thinking, maybe, but would he release the hostage? Or would he use her to negotiate a replacement vehicle?*

At a half crouch, SWAT officers approached the vehicle's rear from behind shields, bobbing up for glances through the missing windows and then back down to safety, trying to determine Christina's and Strickland's positions inside.

We could hear Christina sobbing in fits and starts but little else.

After an excruciatingly long three minutes, the rear passenger door swung open. Strickland crawled out on his belly, dragging himself forward with his elbows and falling onto the grassy easement face-first.

Dark red stains marked the flow of bodily fluids from his right shoulder and left forearm. His right leg spurted blood in weak pulses. He'd wrapped his leather belt around it but had lacked the strength to pull it tight enough to stop the bleeding.

We split into two teams. I followed Marci, Eve, and Paul to the driver's side of the Lexus to tend to Christina. Dropping their shields, the SWAT team led Louis, Mondo, and the other officers as they ran to the passenger side, weapons drawn, to deal with Strickland.

The four of us had bent over slightly. Marci, Eve, and Paul had their firearms ready as they approached. Crouching further to stay below the window frame, Marci reached out and pulled the door handle with her left hand.

The door swung open effortlessly, revealing Christina frozen in fear. Eyes wide with terror, mouth open, and lower lip quivering, her face was ghostly pale. The girl's arms were rigid, her hands white from gripping the steering wheel as hard as they could. Tremors wracked Christina's body as she saw the guns pointed in her direction. Releasing the wheel, she held her shaking hands up to the car's roof, palms out, in a gesture of surrender. She was unrecognizable as the composed and demure woman I'd met at the children's benefit gala.

Seeing no threat, Paul, Marci, and the other officers holstered their weapons. Marci leaned across Christina's lap, punching the Start button to turn off the vehicle. "Are you hurt anywhere?" she asked, and Christina frantically shook her head no.

Reaching across Christina's abdomen, Marci released the young woman's seatbelt. Christina threw both her hands around Marci's neck as though she were drowning and let out a loud sob. Lifting her out of the car,

Marci transferred her to Paul's waiting arms. She was light enough that Paul could easily carry her, still crying, to the sidewalk opposite where SWAT was holding Strickland. One of the SWAT team members had thoughtfully brought a folding lawn chair from Strickland's open garage, and Paul sat her carefully in it.

Eve quietly began comforting her. "Hi, Christina, my name is Eve. I'm so sorry for what you've been through, but we're here to help. An ambulance is on its way for you. Are you sure you're not feeling any pain?"

"Thank you," Christina whispered, the look on her face beseeching. Tears trickled down her cheeks, and her hands were still shaking slightly, but her voice no longer betrayed sheer panic. "I think I'm okay. Can you tell me what will happen now? Am I in trouble?"

"Oh, heavens no, sweetheart. You just got caught up in a bad situation. The man you were housesitting for, Robert Strickland, has been accused of some pretty horrific things, and we've arrested him.

"The paramedics will take you to the hospital to check your physical health. What you've been through is a terrible thing to happen to anyone, and we want you to have the right care for your emotional and mental wellness, too. Someone will talk to you about that. We'll put you in touch with Victims' Services, and they'll help you over the long term. Is there anyone we can call to be with you right now?"

"Yes, my brother," Christina answered. "But my phone and my purse are back inside the house. Bob wouldn't let me bring them."

Eve turned to a nearby uniform. "Officer, can you help get Christina's belongings out of the house?"

"It's a black purse with a letter *C* on the front — it's on the kitchen counter," Christina said. The officer dipped his head and turned toward Strickland's residence.

"I see your ambulance is here, Christina," Eve said. "Let me talk to them briefly, and I'll be right back. Will you be okay?" Christina nodded yes.

As Eve was about to leave, a young black patrol officer wearing a ready smile and a stethoscope and carrying a blood pressure cuff appeared beside Christina. "This officer's name is Julia," Eve said, "and she'll stay with you. She's here to help you with anything you need."

The disco-ball effect of red, blue, white, and yellow spears of light from gumballs, light bars, the rear panels of ambulances, taillights, and headlights now danced across the entire neighborhood. With Eve responsible for Christina's care, I joined the team members encircling Strickland.

Peering into the back seat of Strickland's vehicle through the open door, I saw a large section of heavy deck plate on the far side and splintered plywood panels on the cushions. On top were three bulletproof vests, one bloodied. Spotting the blued butt of a handgun in the far footwell, I called it out to Paul.

Paul waved over one of the uniforms from the street. "Officer, we have an unsecured handgun in the rear driver's side footwell. I need you to stand watch until someone from Forensics can secure, bag, and tag the weapon."

While the team I'd been with extricated Christina from the car, SWAT officers flex-cuffed Strickland, turned him over so that he was face-up, and patted him down for weapons. The two keeping Strickland in the crosshairs of their assault rifles had lowered their weapons. Paramedics were applying a tourniquet to his leg wound and a pressure bandage to his shoulder.

I could see Strickland's face was bloodied and creased with agony, pierced every few seconds with grimaces of what had to be excruciating pain.

Mondo was standing near Strickland's feet. Two uniforms had just handed him a white Tyvek envelope as Louis walked up from behind. "Louis, change of plans from Captain Jarvis," Mondo said. "We're going to forego the material witness warrant. We just received an arrest warrant for the Marshall homicide. We'll be taking this man into custody on the second warrant."

"I think you should have the honor," Louis replied.

Nodding his thanks, Mondo moved behind Strickland's head and Mirandaized him, relishing every word: "Robert William Strickland, you are being placed under arrest for the first-degree murder of James Marshall III. You have the right to remain silent. Anything you say can and will be used against you in court. You have a right to an attorney. If you cannot afford an attorney, one will be appointed for you. Do you understand these rights?"

Strickland raised his eyes to Mondo, saying, "Yes," through gritted teeth. I'd stood there studying Strickland's expressions as shock dulled his suffering. His thought process was easy to read. First, the possibility that he would survive this, then the reality of his detention, and finally, resignation to his fate passed across Strickland's face in waves, settling on a whitish shade of defeat.

In the meantime, Paul and Marci had joined the group standing around Strickland. Paramedics had placed a collapsible gurney alongside the injured man lying in the grass, prepping for his transport to the hospital. Paul stepped a few feet to my left, next to Mondo.

As Paul stood over Strickland, he couldn't help but smile, nodding slightly, satisfied with the outcome. Strickland glared at Paul and tried to spit to one side. But he was facing upward, and his effort was weak. The blood-tainted spittle came back into his face, splattering on his cheek. Strickland averted his face, unwilling to make further eye contact.

Paul squatted down, just above the bullet wound in Strickland's right shoulder, and said, "Bob, tomorrow for lunch, our detention facility will feature chopped-up moldy whitefish. It's pressure-formed into small squares, battered with corn flour and mouse droppings, and deep-fat-fried in rancid oil that they haven't changed in a week.

"I know it's fish … well, technically. But instead of a white wine, ask our sommelier for a rosé of Pinot Noir — it will go nicely with that." Paul patted Strickland's injured shoulder twice — quickly but very firmly — as he arose to wink at me.

A second group of paramedics soon arrived. I watched as their ambulance left to transport Strickland, accompanied by two armed officers, to the hospital. As they departed, the HAZMAT team arrived to deal with Strickland's Lexus, which had begun leaking automotive fluids, including gasoline, onto the street.

With Strickland safely carted away by the EMTs, my helmet, goggles, and Kevlar vest surrendered to their SWAT lenders, and my heart rate and breathing returned to normal, I could join the celebration. Not only had the apprehension succeeded despite its setbacks, but now we could fully enjoy Steve's safe recovery.

I decided to stay at the scene as long as Paul had work to do. The SWAT team closed up shop, the Forensics team taking control of Strickland's vehicle and property to begin their work. SDPD officers graciously thanked neighboring residents for their trouble and sacrifices as they returned home. I suspected the day's events would feed the subdivision's rumor mill for years.

Louis, Marci, Eve, and Paul agreed to finish their reports in the morning. I looked forward to our living room and spending quality time with Paul and Tommy. But before enjoying our evening together, we'd visit Steve at the hospital.

Though it certainly had its white-knuckle moments, the day had ended as well as it possibly could under the circumstances, with no one but the bad guy suffering significant injury.

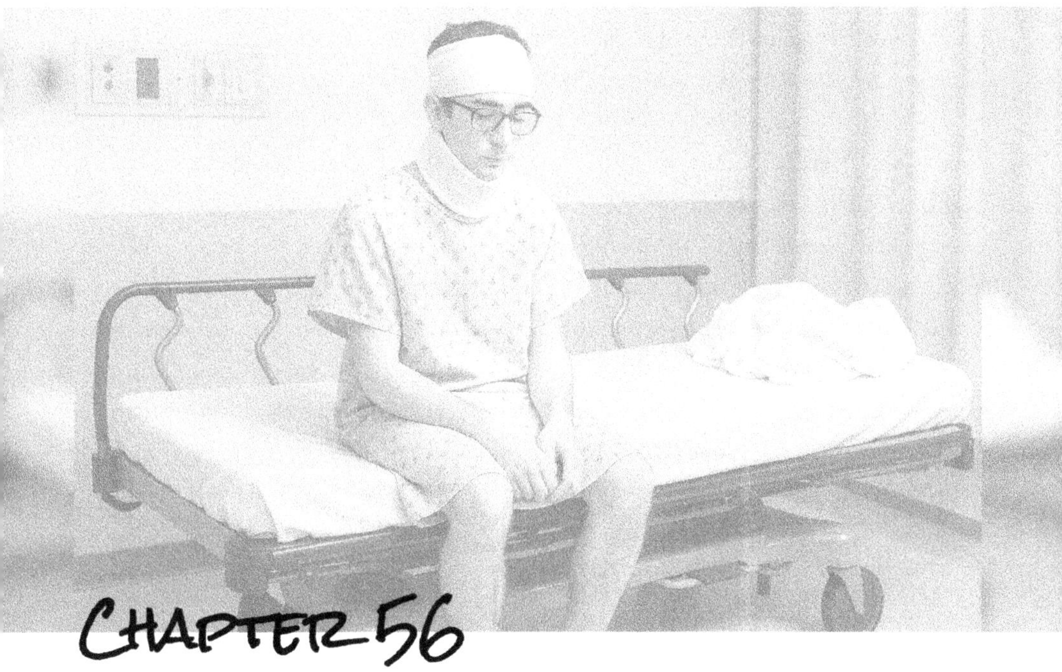

CHAPTER 56

Steve was in an examination room when we saw him for the first time in five weeks. As he sat on the edge of a gurney in a hospital gown and neck brace, his bandaged head was down and tilted to the side. Steve was swinging his legs back and forth, listening to the conversation between his mother and the doctor.

A middle-aged nurse with a pleasant smile quietly intercepted Paul and me outside Steve's room. "I'm sorry, visiting hours are over."

Tracy turned her head toward us when she heard the gentle admonition.

"It's alright; they're family friends." Tracy waved us over with one hand.

The doctor peered over his reading glasses and gave the nurse a curt nod of approval. I walked over to hug Tracy while Paul shook hands with Steve.

"You have no idea how glad we are to see you, Steve," Paul said. "How are you feeling?"

"I'm good — a lot better than I was." Steve's grin was lopsided. "I'm really glad they found me. I was kinda worried they wouldn't …" As Tracy raised an eyebrow, Steve rephrased, "Well, OK, a *lot* worried."

After giving everyone a few moments to exchange greetings, the doctor shepherded Tracy into a corner for some privacy to discuss Steve's health.

He then turned to Paul and me to share the rest of the news. "We've run the preliminary tests to catch any urgent issues. Other than dehydration and a bump on the head, we haven't seen anything causing us additional concerns. We'll hold Steve for twenty-four hours of observation. In the morning, we'll run a few more tests to be thorough. As things stand now, I don't see any problems with his prognosis, and barring any surprises, he can return home tomorrow evening. But let's see that he gets a good night's sleep. Try to avoid anything that might be upsetting."

Turning to me, the doctor said, "I'll ask the nurse to let you have thirty minutes longer. I'm sorry we can't give you more, but it's getting late, and we must consider our other patients."

"Thank you, Doctor," I said. "We won't overstay our welcome, I promise."

The physician turned to Steve. "Get some rest, young man, and I'll see you in the morning."

With a smile for Tracy and a nod to the rest of us, he and his clipboard left to tend to other patients.

"Steve, you've been through such a traumatic experience," I said softly. "I can't imagine what it'd be like to be locked for five weeks in a place like that. I know the police have been asking about everything, and you must be exhausted. I'm curious to hear how it all happened. But it can wait for another day if you'd rather…."

"Oh, no, I don't mind." Steve seemed eager. "Telling *them* made me nervous, but you don't."

"Okay, Steve. But I know it's stressful for you." Tracy flashed an apologetic smile to Paul and me. "You heard what the doctor said. So, try to keep it short, okay?"

"Okay, Mom." I detected a touch of impatience in Steve's voice.

I don't think Steve minds a little attention, and I can't blame him. He paid dearly to have his moment.

"Did you see anyone when they took you?" I asked.

Steve shook his head. "I never saw who grabbed me. It could've been just one person because nobody else said anything. After they taped me up, I heard them get into the driver's seat and start whatever I was in."

"Where were you when he jumped you?"

Paul must be assuming the abduction was Strickland's doing, therefore the "he."

"I'd just left my car in the parking lot and was walking into work when somebody threw a blanket over my head. They hit me from behind on my neck. They pushed me into the back of maybe a truck and wrapped tape all around the blanket. Somebody pulled my hand out from under it and stuck my arm with something sharp."

"When I first woke up, I couldn't see anything, but I could tell from the rattling sounds and feeling the walls that I was in an old van or maybe a pickup with a camper shell. It smelled like burning oil and wet dog. The floor was hard and cold — there wasn't any carpet."

"Did he say anything? Play the radio or talk on the phone?" I asked.

"I don't think so — I fell back asleep right away. The next thing I knew, I was in that locked room with tape over my eyes. I had wire ties around my hands and feet."

"This was at the house where we found you?" Paul asked.

"Yes, they didn't move me again after that."

"Who fed you?" I felt sympathy pangs in my stomach.

"I got the tape off my eyes, but it was dark, and they made me wear a bag over my head before they'd give me any food or water. They'd shine this little LED light in my eyes. Still, I could tell it was the same guy all the time. Older, but not like an old man. He had some gray hair in the back. He wasn't fat or anything, maybe taller than me."

"If you saw him again, would you recognize him?" Paul asked.

"I don't think so. Before the man would bring me food or water or empty the bucket they gave me for a toilet, he'd wear a Hallowe'en mask and put a black hood over my head. I couldn't see while he was in the room. Even if they didn't do that, I'd be afraid to look right at their face. Most of what I saw was the back of him when he was leaving."

"Was someone else in the house all the time?" I wanted to know if Strickland could have done this by himself.

"I don't think so. I'd wait until everything was quiet and see if I could find a way out. I yelled and yelled to check if they were listening, but I guess they couldn't hear me — no one ever came. Once in a while, they'd bring me a sandwich and a bottle of water and dump the bucket. There was this hard mattress they tied to the floor with eyebolts. One light in the ceiling stayed on, except when they came in to feed me. There was a speaker, a microphone, and a webcam up in the corner by the ceiling and three more cameras in the other corners. I figured they were watching and listening to me over the Internet.

"I couldn't tell what time it was, but I knew when it was morning from the light coming in through where the tape was loose on the window. So, I could count how many days I was there."

"Did he ever talk to you? Did you recognize his voice?" Paul was looking for the blotto_bill connection.

"Once, I tipped the bucket over after he'd emptied it and left. I stood up on it to see if I could get to the speaker and maybe take some of the wires. He yelled at me through the speaker. I got scared and fell off the bucket. I could tell he used an electronic device to alter his voice. The speakers were too high for me to reach anyway.

"I was scared shitless —sorry, Mom — when the police broke in. Their flashlights were in my eyes, and I couldn't tell who they were. I thought maybe the guy keeping me prisoner sent them to kill me. I was so happy when the one in front called out my name and said they were rescuing me. But then I thought, 'Are they trying to trick me?' When you're by yourself, you think about all these bad things, and it gets hard to tell what's real."

⋯⋈⋯

Over the next few weeks, I wrote a series based on Aunt Tik's and Strickland's crimes. Louis and Paul followed through on the one crucial chore left — to close the loop on what they'd set out to do at the start of the Aunt Tik's investigation. They had to extricate Steve Nielsen and, by extension, his mother from the investigation surrounding the attempted murder of Judge

Silvia Wasserman. Fortunately for them, the entire department was on board to get that done.

Once Robert Strickland had been arrested and hospitalized under armed guard, there was a lengthy and somewhat combative exchange between the heads of SDPD and the federal agents investigating the firearms charges emanating from the attempted murder.

Politics and bureaucracy in federal law enforcement can encourage agents and their supervisors to adhere to invalid beliefs. The idea that a web-based social media game couldn't possibly drive an assassination attempt had become locked into their thought processes — institutionalization and our tax dollars hard at work. Having a rock-solid case demonstrating how far off-track the feds were did not make correcting them any easier. SDPD detectives had to avoid publicly making fools, accidentally or intentionally, out of senior federal agents who, just a few days ago, were openly insinuating that local investigators were the dunces. There were times Louis and Paul found themselves on tricky footing.

It took several weeks to traverse these minefields. Finally, on a Tuesday, four weeks after Strickland's arrest, federal prosecutors officially dropped all charges against Steve Nielsen.

On Thursday of the same week, Steve appeared in court to face state charges. His mother was with him to provide emotional support. Louis, Paul, and I met them on the courthouse steps — the three of us had petitioned for permission to speak to the court on Steve's behalf before his sentencing.

The judge sentenced Steve to time served and ninety days' probation. He also ordered Steve to perform forty hours of community service and to avoid any association with Aunt Tik's or any of its known members.

Steve politely and sincerely thanked the Court.

His final experience at the courthouse as a charged offender ended with the judge wishing him well from the bench.

THE WRITINGS OF
AVRIL MARIA SERENE

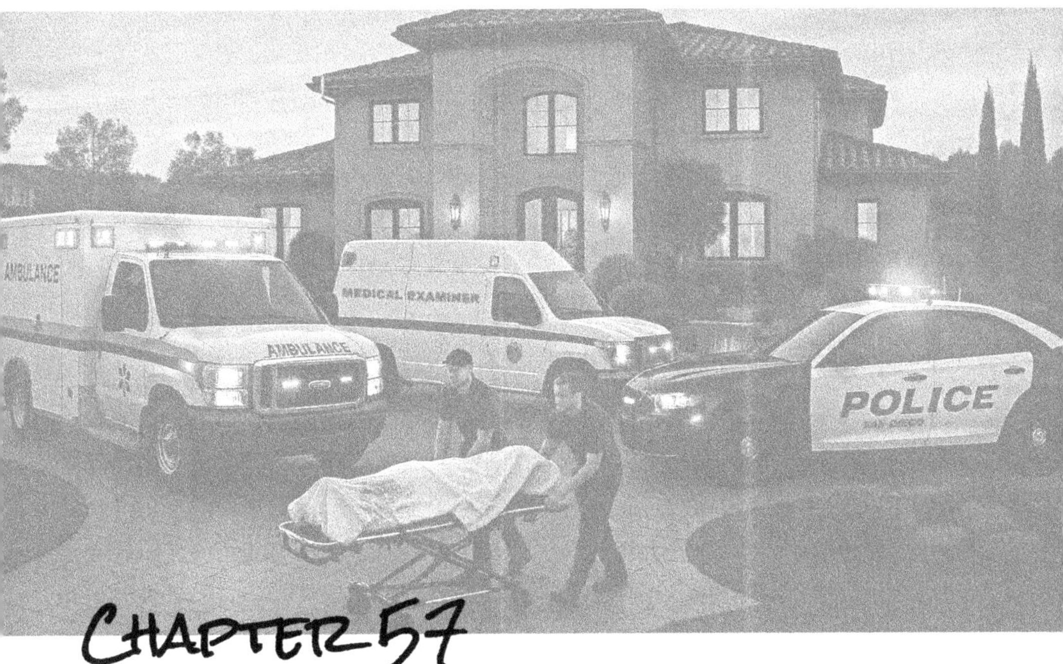

CHAPTER 57

O nce I'd finished my series on Strickland's crimes, I'd write an occasional follow-up on his prosecution as events warranted. After a month of legal wrangling, the court set Strickland's bail at two million dollars, with the conditions that he must wear an electronic monitoring bracelet, not leave the immediate vicinity of his home other than for approved medical care, and surrender any passports he had in his possession.

The court also ordered that he restrict all Internet activity to computers monitored and controlled by the San Diego Police Department or his attorneys, for which they would be held accountable. He was expressly ordered not to log onto or otherwise access any Aunt Tik's–related website or server. He agreed to have the Court monitor his cell phone activity. He was not to have contact with the media or any witnesses in this case other than through his and their attorneys.

Strickland was on unpaid suspension from the department; his superiors had confiscated his known weapons, badge, identification, uniforms, and protective equipment.

While obtaining bail may have gone well for him, preparing for trial would prove to be something else entirely. Strickland's expensive lawyers put up a spirited fight in the pretrial motions, but it proved a monumental task. Not only was their client a disgraced police officer who had tried to murder a judge, but he'd done much of it electronically. That meant he'd left a bright neon digital trail on top of the abundant circumstantial evidence law enforcement had collected.

The data painted a crystal-clear picture of how Strickland had manipulated Aunt Tik's game from the moment he first became a cell captain. The server contents also exposed the laser-like focus with which Strickland had targeted anyone tied to his divorce. Strickland's attorneys had no wiggle room whatsoever to argue against premeditation in any of the homicides, the abduction of the witness, or the attempted murder.

Surprising for a police officer familiar with computer forensics procedures, Strickland had made no effort to conceal his comings and goings within Aunt Tik's data. He'd wrongly assumed the encryption protecting the database and its items would be unbreakable.

Once Mondo's team deciphered sufficient files and folders on Aunt Tik's servers, they had a stash of digital signatures and foreign keys that matched only one person, Strickland. These signatures were, in turn, linked to every activity Strickland was involved in during his membership in Aunt Tik's.

Once a jury understands it, such a clear digital trail is impossible to dispute, just like DNA is in most circumstances. But no one had to take Mondo's word for it. They could take Strickland's instead because the man would soon make it evident that he believed in the strength of the department's case.

At 9:53 p.m. on a Thursday nine weeks after his arrest, Robert William Strickland placed the barrel of a .40 caliber S&W Model 610 with drilled-out serial numbers, a throwdown he'd hidden in his yard and detectives had presumed destroyed, between his lips.

He pointed it at the roof of his mouth and pulled the trigger.

EPILOGUE

The new cell czar settled into his plush, high-backed office chair in the condo bedroom he'd converted to work from home. Scanning the laptop screen before him, he'd looked forward to spending this evening on his computer. Tonight, he'd get his first opportunity to take the power of his recent promotion out for a spin — he'd be surveying the domain that was now his.

Acquiring the role hadn't been difficult. A few quick hacks to the servers, a couple of little adjustments to previous challenge histories, and *voilà!* — he had the points total he needed to declare himself the new czar. His predecessor had voluntarily surrendered his existence on the planet; no one else had the standing to oppose him.

It wasn't like he had to kill anyone.

He allowed himself a smirk at the irony of the inside joke. He had every right to be in a good mood – for one thing, he'd been lucky. He'd inherited a cell that was in surprisingly good shape. The legal affairs of the old czar had thus far not resulted in any negative publicity or accountability for Aunt Tik's as an organization. The man's prosecution had ended with his suicide, and his crimes would never go to trial.

With the finality of that resolution, life had moved on. Articles published when the serial killer was a threat had become old news. Any lingering street chatter focused on the previous czar as a single individual choosing to do bad things.

And so, there'd be no salacious public discussion about the dangers inherent to Aunt Tik's challenges and punks. Administrators had tabled any consideration of public policy changes toward Aunt Tik's. No new legislation waited in the wings to deal with a problem that few people believed still existed.

Best of all, Aunt Tik's membership applications were way up, fueled by curious onlookers drawn in by all the recent attention.

All good. The czar was looking forward to a long and productive reign. But first things first — a personal matter had come to his attention; he'd need to resolve it before it attracted anyone else's.

Rumors persisted among the locals, including the employees of the car wash next door, that the strip mall development company had gone bankrupt. Still, after months of inactivity, a twenty-foot-long concrete block wall was being built on the southern edge of the property, right next to the bus stop.

One of the car wash attendants taking a smoke break snorted, unimpressed with the quality of the work.

"If we get a stiff wind, that whole damn thing will blow over."

His co-worker took exception. "LaMar, you don't know what you're talking about – it's made of concrete blocks, man!"

"I used to work construction, and I'm telling you, they fucked it up. They didn't anchor that bottom row of blocks. But they mortared the rows above it. They reinforced them up and down with rebar threaded through the holes in the blocks, and then they poured concrete through the holes. You got a solid concrete slab balancing itself on that loose bottom row of blocks."

The next day, LaMar got in his "I told you so." To stabilize it, workers had to fasten long two-by-twelves and footers to each end of the wall on the parking lot side. The braces were weighted with several dozen sandbags to anchor the wall, now six feet tall.

Two days later, the wall was nearly twelve feet high, yet almost all the sandbags had gone missing and hadn't been replaced. LaMar was finishing the wipe-down of a now-shiny, new black Mercedes when a tow truck in the neighboring lot caught his attention. The wrecker backed toward the wall from the parking lot side, its hook boom fully extended. The driver seemed unaware of how close he'd gotten to those concrete blocks.

Car wash employees stared, mesmerized, as the boom struck the top of the wall. The barrier teetered momentarily and then suddenly broke free from its base as it leaned toward the street outside the lot. It collapsed as a single concrete panel, smashing onto the sidewalk with a mighty *ker-whoosh,* ejecting dense brown clouds of dust and debris to the sides and top. As it landed, the wall shattered into thousands of broken pieces, scattering into the street.

Hearing what he thought was a scream, LaMar immediately abandoned his post. As his buddy called 911, he helped dig through the rubble until the emergency crews arrived. When first responders were finally able to clear the broken concrete, they discovered a woman's body. Relegated to standing among the crowd observing from the yard across the street, LaMar listened in as onlookers engaged in rabid speculation rife with scraps of information and conjecture.

Her name was Yi Jian. Her cell phone showed she'd been lured to that location by text messages from a burner phone. She was waiting at the bus stop for someone named "Jr.," who'd promised to pick her up and take her shopping.

She was six months pregnant when she was crushed to death. First responders, opening the clasp of a new locket on a delicate gold chain around her neck, found a tightly folded copy of a sonogram.

Someone had doodled hearts and flowers on the back in colored pencil, mixed with several girls' first names.

The punk ending in what appeared to be an unfortunate accident gave the cell czar the excuse he needed to avoid posting a results video. He wiped all evidence of the punk and its related challenges from Aunt Tik's website. The only indication it had ever existed was a short, plain-text message saying, "Aunt Tik's management has canceled punk #AE64-27-8873-2463 due to unforeseen circumstances."

The cell czar grinned. With the afternoon's work complete, he was pleased with himself.

He reflected upon that moment just a few months ago when the real power of Aunt Tik's had revealed itself. He'd figured it out the morning he trekked up Heartvine Circle, and that dually flatbed passed him. There was only one scenario in which having two nearly identical punks so close together in time and space made sense. The fatality that resulted from the first had to be intentional, and the second's only logical purpose was to create confusion and cover.

The new czar had to admit that the staging and execution of the twin punks was pretty clever. Still, the previous czar got caught for being arrogant and getting greedy — *come on, six murders? And going for a seventh?*

The new czar would not make that mistake. He'd do just the one … *that* he could get away with. He just had to be careful and stay sharp. Easy-peasy.

Junior pondered that thought for several moments, drumming his fingers on the desktop.

Well, okay. Maybe two….

<hr>

"Hi, sweetheart." Paul walked into our home office and peeked over my shoulder as I worked on my latest article. Gently placing a hand on each of my shoulders, he kissed the top of my head. Putting my right hand over the top of his left, I leaned back in my chair and looked up to see his face.

Paul asked me about a text I'd sent him earlier.

"Tommy's gone to his first outdoor campout?"

"Terry across the street gave Markie a tent for his birthday. Markie pitched it in their backyard and wanted Tommy to spend the night … or however long they can hold out against all the scary noises. I donated a couple of our flashlights and some extra batteries to their little adventure."

"Oh, boy — we'll get an earful in the morning…."

"Tommy kept bouncing off the walls all afternoon, begging to go early."

"I see you're busy — anything interesting?"

"More of a human interest piece, not that big a deal, but something I wanted to do. I've been thinking about Sophia Ferguson. It's always bothered me that the victims and the other people who get hurt seem to fade away from public consciousness so quickly. I wanted to follow up on all the people impacted by Robert Strickland's crimes, the ones who weren't criminals. I'm happy with how it's turning out – it almost writes itself. These things have been on my mind long enough to give themselves a voice."

A wry smile had come to Paul's face.

"Interesting that you bring up Strickland. The medical examiner looks at all deaths in the county, even if they're not homicides. She and I were chatting about one of our murder cases yesterday when she mentioned another death that's bothering her. It was supposed to have been an accident — a wall got knocked over onto a poor woman waiting at a bus stop. As the ME explained what happened, I got this sense of having been here before — all the odd events and coincidences brought Aunt Tik's to mind.

"I checked out the Internet and local papers for any reports on the incident. The tow truck driver who knocked that partition over is long gone; investigators can't locate him. The development company that owned the lot was in receivership; no work had been authorized by anyone connected to it, certainly not for building a standalone wall.

"She was pregnant, but the ME couldn't determine the father — no male DNA in the system produced a viable paternal test match to the fetus."

"Okay, that *is* just a little too weird," I admitted. "Hmmm, fascinating…. It won't make you mad if I stay up a little longer and look into it after I finish this?"

"Oh, heck no," Paul replied with a quick shake of his head. "Full disclosure: I asked Eve to check it out before I came home. She was on board — the story didn't sit right with her, either. She didn't see anything obvious in a quick scan through Aunt Tik's website, but she wants to do another search when she has more time tomorrow. So, no worries, we're on the same page."

"He was such an asshole," I mused. "I'll probably be seeing the ghost of Robert Strickland in every dark nook and cranny for months before my brain will let it go and accept that he's finally gone.

"Still, I'll sleep better tonight if I take a quick gander...."

Did you enjoy reading *Aunt Tik's: The Killer App*? Would you be willing to leave a review?

Honest reviews from you and others who have read my work help me write the kinds of books you will enjoy. I write to earn kudos from my readers, and your comments keep me on the right track – I appreciate your input more than you know. Your reviews also help new readers find quality books they will like. Please follow this link to leave your review:

https://www.amazon.com/review/create-review/?ie=UTF8&channel=glance-detail&asin=[NEW ASIN GOES HERE]
ADD REVIEW QR CODE HERE

Thank you,

Avril Maria Serene

THE WRITINGS OF
AVRIL MARIA SERENE

MEMBER MANUAL

AUNT TIK'S JAPE JUICE AND DIDO DISPENSARY™

INTRODUCTION

A heartfelt shout-out to our new members! Without you, we don't exist, and our world would be far more boring.

Whether you join as a free or a premium member, you will find this manual helpful. We aim to provide the most enjoyable experience possible for everyone on our website. Ours is the world's first social media and gaming website dedicated to practical jokes as performance art. As such, some of the things we do, how we do them, and the terms we use may be unfamiliar.

This manual contains the information you'll need to enjoy your time spent on our website and participating in our activities while ensuring that your rights, and those of every one of our members, are respected. Our paramount concern is for all members' safety. This manual outlines the simple rules everyone must follow to benefit you, other members, our staff, and Aunt Tik's™ websites and proprietary technology.

Happy punk'ing!

The staff and management of Aunt Tik's Jape Juice and Dido Dispensary

P.S.: One of the protections we offer our members is secrecy, which extends to our rules and practices. We distribute this manual as a secure PDF file to protect your privacy and ours. Ten days after you download this file, you'll no longer be able to read it. To reference the manual after the ten days have expired, you can print the sections you need before file access terminates. Please be respectful of our members and our organization — do not print out more than one copy and destroy that copy securely when done with it. You can also download a fresh PDF file copy by going to your user account settings in the Aunt Tik's™ app and selecting "Download user manual."

DEFINITIONS

App (also "Aunt Tik's app" or "Aunt Tik's application")

We provide access to download the Aunt Tik's mobile or desktop app to accepted candidates for free or premium Aunt Tik's memberships. You can use that app to explore Aunt Tik's website. The Aunt Tik's app includes an embedded version of the Signal secure messaging utility used internally for all messaging. Aunt Tik's app also includes hands-free automatic encryption and decryption tools to protect member communications for other messages, file uploads, and downloads. You can also use the encryption and decryption features manually to encrypt and decrypt third-party files and e-mail messages for sharing with other Aunt Tik's members.

With the Aunt Tik's app, you can monitor your user account, view Aunt Tik's punk results, participate in the messages forum, and encrypt and decrypt uploads, downloads, and messages. Free members can use the app to upgrade to a premium Aunt Tik's membership anytime.

Through the app, **premium Aunt Tik's members** can monitor their challenge point totals, view punk challenges still available for bidding, and bid on one or more of those challenges, in addition to the features made available to free members. Premium members with sufficient challenge points can use the app to enter targets and target lists for punks, submit their new punk ideas with challenge components, vouch for member candidates, and communicate with support staff and the Aunt Tik's czar, as necessary to report Aunt Tik's app, website, or member issues.

Cell captains can use the app to vote in cell czar elections and removals, submit proposed charter changes, and vote on those changes, along with all the capabilities accessible to premium members.

Punk masters have access to all app features available to cell captains. They can also use the app to review and select successful challenge bidders, send out challenge notifications, and publish punk results.

Cell czars can use the app for punk master selection, dismemberment management (including member contact details extraction), implementing national-organization-approved charter changes, and expense preauthorization and reimbursement. They can also access all the functionality available to cell captains.

The capabilities and features available are subject to change periodically as improvements are made to the app and may differ from those described here.

Aunt Tik's™

"Aunt Tik's" is the popular nickname for the Aunt Tik's™ organization, holdings, and affiliates. The nickname can also refer to Aunt Tik's™ intellectual property, including trademarks and its websites, data, members, management, documentation, and real property.

Aunt Tik's handle

Your Aunt Tik's username also serves as your "Aunt Tik's handle."

Bids and bidding (also "challenge bids" and "challenge bidding"):

Punks approved for member participation will have their challenges published to premium members so that those members can compete in a reverse auction for the rights to perform those challenges. The process by which members announce their interest in carrying out a given challenge is known as "bidding." A punk challenge posted for bidding will provide all the details necessary to perform the challenge. It will also include a date and time range for the bidder to accomplish the challenge. A premium member includes with their bid the number of challenge points they expect to earn for performing the challenge. Sometimes, the bidding member may not be available for the entire time range specified for the challenge. In that situation, the bidder must indicate their available times within that range. The member may optionally include their particular skills or experience with the bid if well-suited to the challenge. Of course, members may not bid on challenges associated with their dismemberment.

The punk master is responsible for selecting which of the members' bids will be accepted if there is more than one bid for a challenge. By preference, this will generally be the member who bids the lowest number of challenge points to do the challenge. This rule prevents members who compete for selection each month as one of the monthly cell captains from cheating by bidding an extremely high number of challenge points for easy challenges to pad their point totals. However, in the case where the lowest bidder's time availability or skill set doesn't meet the needs of the challenge, the punk master has the option to choose the next lowest bidder whose bid satisfies all the requirements of the challenge or whose optional arguments for having special qualifications are sufficiently convincing.

A punk is ready for play once the punk master has chosen a bidder for each challenge associated with that punk. The punk master will notify all successful challenge bidders, informing them when to perform their challenges and providing any other details they may need.

Bonus points (also "Challenge bonus points"):

With the selection of the cell captains at the beginning of every month, each captain receives an allocation of challenge bonus points (the cell charter sets the number of points in the monthly per-captain bonus pool). The distribution of bonus points to challenge performers is at the cell captain's discretion. They may use them as they see fit across those punks and challenges for which they are the designated punk master. However, any bonus points awarded must be divided uniformly among all of a punk's challenge participants, with one exception: the cell captain or cell czar who serves as the punk master may not award bonus points to themselves.

Candidate (also "Member candidate"):

Visitors to Aunt Tik's website who are not already Aunt Tik's members can apply to join us. "Candidates" are those who have applied for membership. Candidates must be validated by a premium member in good standing and approved by the cell czar to become members. If not approved within the period defined in the cell charter, Aunt Tik's will remove the candidate from the candidate list.

Anyone previously dismembered may not apply as a candidate — Aunt Tik's will reject the application without notice under those circumstances.

Note that at the time of their application for candidacy, visitors must reveal any other known Aunt Tik's members with whom they have a relationship of any kind. This rule is necessary to avoid selecting members of the same social or work group as challenge participants, exposing that group to potential retaliation and defeating the general Aunt Tik's goals for anonymity. Maintaining secrecy and protecting members and management are essential to Aunt Tik's business model. Aunt Tik's cell management must be fully aware of those cases where secrecy is not possible due to prior existing relationships. A prior relationship with one or more Aunt Tik's members in good standing is not a barrier to membership, so long as the candidate reveals those relationships in good faith.

Captain (also "Cell captain"):

An Aunt Tik's cell captain represents the middle layer of the local cell management team. Cell captains are selected monthly from premium members in good standing based on their accumulated challenge point totals. The middle management layer is a meritocracy to the extent that point totals represent accomplishment and experience. The local cell's charter sets the number of cell captains chosen; that number of members with the highest total accumulated points at the beginning of the calendar month become cell captains.

Cell captains have all the rights and responsibilities allocated to premium members, in addition to some that are specific to cell captains. Cell captains vote for the cell czar based on a simple majority at the end of the previous occupant's term in office. The cell's charter determines the length of a czar's term. Cell captains may also vote to remove a czar based on the approval of two-thirds or more of the cell captains, subject to any rules and conditions specified in the cell's charter. Cell captains can nominate themselves as candidates to become czar.

Cell captains may propose cell charter changes and vote, along with the cell czar, upon any proposed changes.

Cell captains also serve as the punk masters for individual punks as new punks are submitted and approved. Punk master assignments are usually round-robin to each cell captain, in descending order of their accumulated point totals. However, the cell czar can override any assignment and select themselves or another cell captain as punk master over a given punk. A cell captain having a higher accumulated point total may also request that the cell czar assign them as a punk master over a cell captain who has a lower accumulated point total.

Cell (also "Aunt Tik's cell"):

An Aunt Tik's cell is the local chapter, or franchise, of the Aunt Tik's™ organization. The cell represents a geographic area such as a zip code, area code, district, city, parish, or county. The affinity to a given area ensures that all cell members have access to the same resources and targets associated with the challenges of a punk. When members join Aunt Tik's, the system automatically assigns them to the cell closest to the home address they provided in their member application. During the application process, they can request a different cell location, such as one close to their work address. An applicant can be a member of only one cell at a time.

A cell is a semiautonomous unit of the national Aunt Tik's organization. It follows the national Aunt Tik's rules and bylaws and the directives established by the cell's franchise agreement. The national organization collects membership fees for premium members and redistributes a percentage back to the individual cells. Cells use websites, website templates, trademarks, logos, and other materials the national organization provides under license. Cells may also optionally use servers and other data storage resources the national organization supplies under separate agreements. In all other respects, cells are self-governing. Matters the local cell presides over include:

The selection and term of the cell czar	The selection and number of cell captains
The selection of punk masters	The administration of punks
The bidding process for challenges	The monthly bonus challenge points pool allocations for cell captains
The expiration period for unapproved candidate submissions	The awarding of challenges between multiple bidders
The operations budget	The dollar amount kept in the potential litigation and mitigation account

<table>
<tr><td>The dollar amount kept in the expense petty cash fund</td><td>The notification process for awarded challenges</td></tr>
<tr><td>The awarding of points for completed challenges</td><td>The posting of punk results</td></tr>
<tr><td>Disciplinary procedures for membership violations</td><td></td></tr>
</table>

Note that cell charter changes require approval of the national Aunt Tik's organization. For most day-to-day operations, Aunt Tik's functions around punks and challenges are the cell's responsibility. The national organization can guide cell management in these areas and optionally supply training under separate agreements.

Challenge (also "Punk challenge"):

A challenge is one of the subordinate tasks that together comprise a punk. By breaking a more complicated punk into its basic units of work, i.e., challenges, several good things happen:

- The individual challenges become simple enough that almost anyone can perform them;
- many members can form a team together around the challenges in a punk; and
- if the punk target is unhappy with the results, the separation of work protects member participants who did the individual challenges from reprisals through anonymity and plausible deniability.

Beyond that, watching a punk come together through the performance of a bunch of separate challenges is fun for the performers and the audience … and often impressive!

Premium members bid on challenges, and Aunt Tik's bases the performer selected on a reverse auction of expected points, unique skills, experience, or resources of the bidder, and time availability required by the challenge. Awarded challenges that are successfully performed reward the winning bidder with challenge points they can use to propose new punks and challenges, submit targets for punks, or save to build a campaign to become a cell captain. Some completed punks and their challenges are even eligible for bonus points at the behest of the punk master, which can significantly boost a member's point totals. And every member who completes a challenge to a punk can revel in seeing the published punk results, a source of pride and bragging rights for everyone who participated.

Some restrictions apply to the permitted challenges to a punk: Aunt Tik's does not allow challenges that may involve illegal behaviors or pose a health or safety risk to the challenge performer or the target. Challenge participants must avoid any potential permanent damage to a target's property if foreseeable. The challenge criteria must specify any identifiable potential for harm or damage to a target's property and arrange, before the challenge performance, for adequate compensation or correction should injury or loss occur.

Charter (also "Cell charter"):

Each cell has a local cell charter, which contains rules and bylaws for the cell that are unspecified in the terms and conditions of their franchise agreement with the national Aunt Tik's organization. A cell proposes its charter and has it approved by Aunt Tik's — that negotiation occurs before signing the cell's franchise agreement.

Cells may modify their charters from time to time. Cell captains or the cell czar propose charter modifications. It is a requirement that all cell captains and the cell czar vote on proposed charter changes, which must pass unanimously. Once passed, the cell czar submits the changes to the national Aunt Tik's organization for final approval.

Czar (also "Cell czar"):

The cell czar is the sole principal administrative officer of the local cell and must be a premium member in good standing who has most recently served as a cell captain. Their roles include all the rights and responsibilities of a cell captain and to:

- Supervise the cell captains

- Set up and administer the automated punk master selection process for punks

- Manually override punk master selections when appropriate, including appointing themselves as punk master

- Resolve disputes between any members, including cell captains

- Filter and approve sponsored membership applications

- Submit to the national Aunt Tik's organization an annual operating budget for approval

- Oversee operating budget disbursements and collections

- Approve the submission of punks and their challenges

- Oversee the orderly processing of punks

- Help resolve disputes between members and nonmembers (or punk targets)

- Provide for litigation and mitigation support and resources when necessary

- Preapprove and submit expenses for punks

- Propose cell charter changes and vote, along with the cell captains, on any charter changes proposed

- Approve member discipline requests

- Retrieve detailed member contact information to support a request for administering discipline

Note that access to detailed member contact information is restricted solely to the cell czar and can be retrieved only on a member-by-member basis. National Aunt Tik's organization rules do not permit downloading or other access to partial or complete lists of members at the cell level.

Dismembering/dismemberment:

Dismembering is the highest level of discipline a cell can administer to a member (point penalties are the other recourse for punishment). It is the only means by which the cell can authorize a punk on an Aunt Tik's member (free or premium). As such, the cell czar must approve dismemberment requests, and only the cell czar can access the subject's detailed contact information necessary for dismemberment.

Dismembering has two elements to it. The first element is canceling the subject's Aunt Tik's membership and permanently blocking the subject from any form of future membership.

The second element is optional and consists of one or more dismemberment punks. The number and nature of the dismemberment punks are at the sole discretion of the cell czar.

Encryption/decryption (also "enciphering/deciphering"):

For the safety of our members, resources, and organization, Aunt Tik's requires encryption of all communications between members and between members and management. The mobile and desktop Aunt Tik's apps contain an embedded version of the Signal app that will automatically encrypt and decrypt Aunt Tik's messages, as appropriate. Members can also use the standalone version of the Signal app for communications if they know the Aunt Tik's handle of the member with whom they want to communicate. The Aunt Tik's app also contains proprietary encryption and decryption methods that will automatically encrypt and decrypt any files uploaded or downloaded using the app. The app's built-in encryption and decryption utilities can also encrypt and decrypt third-party files and e-mail contents if a member uses an independent e-mail or messaging application to send messages and files to Aunt Tik's members.

The sender must encrypt all transferred digital materials using the Aunt Tik's app, and the recipient must use the Aunt Tik's app to decrypt all digital materials received. Any violation of this rule is grounds for dismemberment.

Expenses (also "Challenge expenses"):

Occasionally, one or more challenges associated with a punk will require cash expenditures. These include vehicle or equipment rentals, facility or tool rentals, supplies, and construction material purchases. When known beforehand, the punk master will estimate the anticipated cost and get approval from the cell czar for reimbursement from the cell's petty cash fund. It is the responsibility of the successful bidder to advance these costs from their own pocket to complete their challenge. Once they've completed their challenge as intended, the member can apply to the cell czar for reimbursement. Reimbursement for preapproved expenses falling within the designated limit is automatic for successful challenges.

Occasionally, unexpected expenses may arise during the performance of a challenge. Unless extraordinary or unreasonable, Aunt Tik's expects the challenge performer to pay these and submit the costs to the cell czar for approval and reimbursement. **Reimbursement of expenses that were not preapproved is not guaranteed.**

Free member:

A free member is a registered member who has been vouched for by a premium member, approved by the cell czar, and has access to Aunt Tik's mobile or desktop app but is not paying membership dues. Free members comprise most of the nonparticipating audience for cell punk results. They can view all results that are not marked "private" or "premium members only." Free members can participate in the member message forums (as opposed to nonmember visitors, who can only see punk results specifically deemed "public" and who cannot contribute to the member message forums). Free members are subject to discipline by the cell czar, up to and including dismemberment, if they violate Aunt Tik's rules. Free members cannot accumulate points or bid on challenges.

Message forum (also "Member messages"):

The member message forum is a gathering place accessible through Aunt Tik's mobile or desktop app for exchanging secure (encrypted) messages and digital files between members. All members, free or premium, can participate, with the restrictions being that no member other than the specific sender and recipient can see a message exchange marked "private," and free members cannot see messages flagged for "premium members only."

Visitors (nonmembers) cannot see or participate in the member messages forum.

Notification (also "Challenge notification"):

When members have bid on all the challenges to a punk and the successful bidders are selected, the punk is in play. At that point, the punk master will ascertain the proper time (within the successful bidder's stated availability limitations) to perform the first challenge (and, for some punks, the timing of other challenges further down the line). At this point, the punk master will notify the winner of the first challenge bid. A notification contains a precise date and time for performing the challenge and any other previously undisclosed details needed for completion.

Notifications are sent out no less than 24 hours ahead of the required performance time for the challenge they reference.

Penalties (also "Challenge point penalties"):

As an alternative to dismemberment, a cell czar can impose a penalty on a premium member, requiring the surrender of challenge points from the member's challenge point total. The number of points surrendered is at the discretion of the cell czar. If the member is also a cell captain and the member's resulting point total is below the current point total of the lowest serving cell captain, the czar will immediately remove the penalized member as a cell captain. In the penalized member's stead, the czar will promote that premium member with the highest challenge point total, and not already a captain, to cell captain. The new captain will take over all the previous captain's ongoing duties and responsibilities.

Points (also "challenge points"):

Premium members (and only premium members) earn points as a reward for successfully performing punk challenges. They can also earn bonus points when the entire punk is successful — bonus points are awarded solely at the discretion of the punk master for the punk.

A premium member can accumulate points to earn or retain a cell captaincy. Cell czars appoint cell captains on the first of every month from the premium members with the most accumulated points. Premium members can also spend their points to nominate punk targets or to submit new punks and the challenges associated with those punks.

A member's points can be reduced or removed entirely as a disciplinary measure by the cell czar as punishment for breaking cell rules.

Premium member:

A premium member is a registered member who has been vouched for by another premium member and approved by the cell czar, has access to the Aunt Tik's mobile or desktop app, and has paid their membership dues through at least the end of the current month. Premium members accumulate points for successfully performing challenges they've bid on. Premium members can see all punk results except those marked "private" or "participants only," in which they did not perform a challenge. Premium members can participate in the member message forums and are eligible for selection as cell captains if they have accumulated sufficient challenge points. Premium members with enough points can submit punk targets, new punks, and the new punk's associated challenges.

Premium members are subject to discipline by the cell czar, up to and including dismemberment, if they violate Aunt Tik's rules.

Punk (also "Aunt Tik's punk"):

A punk is a practical joke, stunt, or performance art broken into smaller work units or challenges to be performed by various Aunt Tik's premium members. A punk will usually (but not always) include identifying a target person or group that is the subject of the punk (an Aunt Tik's member in good standing cannot be the target — a member can be a target only when the punk is for dismembering that individual).

Premium members bid on the right to perform the challenges associated with the punk.

The goal or purpose of a punk is a punk result, usually a presentation of a video, audio, a collection of still images, or a mainstream news article. The punk author or master can make punk results private (shared with no one). Or, they can flag a pun for sharing only with the participants, only with premium members, with all members, or they can include the general public.

Punk results have traditionally been humorous, especially practical jokes, but they need not be. They can be performance art to support humanitarian causes, for example. The only qualifications are that the punk result must be enjoyable to the intended audience in some fashion and not engage in illegal behaviors.

Punk master:

The punk master is the cell captain or czar assigned to monitor and manage the execution of a specific punk to completion, including all the challenge performances that comprise the punk. The punk master is responsible for identifying or selecting the appropriate target, if any, and selecting the successful challenge bidders.

Once the punk master has accepted bids and selected winners for all challenges, the punk master sends out notifications to at least the first challenge's successful bidder. The punk master may also notify the successful bidders of subsequent challenges as appropriate. For some punks, the challenges occur in straightforward linear progression timewise, making the notification order and timing obvious. For other punks, one or more challenges within the punk may depend upon exactly when a performer completes a previous challenge. For example, the next challenge in artwork creation may have to wait for an adhesive or layer of paint applied in an earlier challenge to dry. In those situations, it may not be possible to know in advance when to send a notification. The notification contains the precise time to perform the challenge, along with any other details the performer might reasonably need.

The punk master monitors progress through the challenges, timing the next challenge performance through notifications as necessary. The punk master is responsible for producing the punk results. See *"Punk results"* below.

Punk results:

The output of a punk is its punk result, often created with the performance of the last challenge. The punk master is responsible for producing the results for a punk, usually a video, audio, collection of still images, or a news article. The punk master publishes those results on Aunt Tik's punk results web page. The punk master can set the visibility of a punk result to private, challenge participants only, premium members only, members only, or public (everyone, including visitors, can see the punk results), as warranted by the original punk specification's display setting.

Punk submission (also "Punk and challenge submission"):

A punk submission consists of all the fully described challenges (including timing ranges) necessary to carry out the punk, a unique title, and a general description. The submission includes several settings for the timing and intended visibility of the punk result and, optionally, a target or target list. Cell captains and czars can submit punks at no cost. Other premium members can also submit punks — the punk master deducts a specified number of challenge points (as set in the cell charter) from their accounts for each accepted punk submission. Punk submissions are reviewed and approved by the cell czar. The punk author, cell czar, or punk master edits the punk before publishing the challenges in the punk for bidding. Before the challenge bidding begins, punk masters must conduct a member election for punks submitted without a specific target but with a target suggestion list. If the punk author provided no target or target list and the punk requires a target, the punk master must elicit target submissions from the members.

Signal (also "Signal app"):

The Signal messaging app is a secure (encrypted) third-party tool embedded into the Aunt Tik's app and used internally for Aunt Tik's messaging. The standalone version of Signal, downloadable from Aunt Tik's website, is compatible with the latest version of the Aunt Tik's app. Members can use the standalone Signal app to send and receive Aunt Tik's messages. (Note that members wishing to use the standalone version of Signal must know the intended recipient's Aunt Tik's handle.)

Target (or "Punk target"):

Most (but not all) punks have an intended target (the person or organization that is the punk's focus). Some, such as those punks devoted to performance art, do not. For those that do, sometimes it is the very nature of a punk that determines who the target is. For example, a punk might focus on a vehicle in, or added to, a car collection, where the celebrity owner is the intended victim. Other types of punk may be more flexible. In those situations, the punk author may include the target's name with the punk submission or leave it open so other members can submit a potential target. Another option allows submitting a target list to be included with the punk or added by another member. In the case of a target list, the punk author submits several potential targets at one time, tagging the list with a note that the final target selection is to be voted on by all members, by cell captains only, or chosen from the list by the punk master. In all cases, the punk master has the final say in determining who a punk's target is.

Note that when a punk is part of a dismemberment, the target must be the dismembered Aunt Tik's member. In no other situation can an Aunt Tik's member be submitted as a target, nor can any group known to contain an Aunt Tik's member (the punk master will run a search against the member database to determine whether any members have stated they belong to the proposed target group).

Target submission (or "Punk target submission"):

When the punk author has submitted neither a target nor a target list with a punk submission, and the punk is flexible enough to be performed on various subjects, any premium member can submit potential targets or target lists. Submitting a target list to be voted on by members or cell captains does not cost the premium member points. To submit a specific target, a premium member must have at least 1,000 points in their challenge points total. If the punk master selects the submitted target for the punk, Aunt Tik's will deduct 1,000 points from the submitting member's challenge point total.

The submitter can designate targets and target lists as applying to a specific punk, or they can be marked for consideration in any suitable punk without a specified target.

Targets and target list submissions are not acceptable for dismembering punks.

Visitor (or "Public viewer"):

A visitor is anyone coming to Aunt Tik's website representing the general public who is not an Aunt Tik's free or premium member. A visitor is unregistered and untracked and has no rights within Aunt Tik's ecosphere other than to see public punk results and public forum messages, post membership candidate requests, and view general information about Aunt Tik's.

Vouching (or "Candidate vouching"):

Vouching is the process by which a premium member in good standing can speak to the quality of a visitor who has posted their contact information on a list of candidates for membership. Candidate applications for candidates not previously dismembered and vouched for by a premium member go to the cell czar for approval. Once approved, the candidate becomes a free member and can promote themselves to a premium membership at any time by paying the membership fee, which qualifies the premium member to bid on challenges and accrue challenge points.

OUR HISTORY AND PURPOSE

First, you might want to know that "Aunt Tik's" is a homophone for "antics." That might give you a little clue as to what we're about.

Aunt Tik's started more than ten years ago with an idea. Our founder, a practical joker by nature and software engineer by trade, wanted to create an audience-participation website dedicated to (safely) playing pranks on celebrities and well-known institutions.

After some experimentation, they developed a mashup of elements from the television shows and movies *Jackass*, *Borat*, and *Punk'd*. Inspiration also came from flash mobs (in which groups of people meet at the same place simultaneously, sometimes gaming the participants with a bit of trickery to increase attendance). Throw in some "Mr. Mayhem" from the Allstate™ commercials, then add a little Facebook for the audience and sharing opportunities.

The result is a game engaging many random individuals who contribute to jokes recorded for others to see, in which the only harm might be to someone's pride. The game, in a nutshell, involves secret members of a clandestine club, most of whom don't know each other, performing bit parts of an overall punk played on unsuspecting people, all while protecting themselves and the targets from any actual harm through filters, anonymity, plausible deniability, and light-touch governance.

Finally, Aunt Tik's gaming is a way for the common man and woman to get their shots in against a world filled with pompous asses! The whole point is to produce something that will make people laugh, which members can take credit for and be proud of.

Little changed from the original vision, Aunt Tik's has exploded in popularity, bringing fun, laughter, and the occasional incredulous gasp to members worldwide. It is the only social media and gaming website that plays practical jokes.

HOW TO PARTICIPATE IN PUNKS AND THEIR CHALLENGES

Once you've become a new premium member, you'll want to share in the fun. Premium members can view all the punk results, which are entertaining in and of themselves, and they can fully participate in the member forums, where they will find acceptance within the Aunt Tik's community.

But most new members join to be part of it all — they want to participate and watch the results video from punks they have contributed to! And we've made that easy. In your Aunt Tik's app's "Your account" menu, look for the item "Bid on challenges." When you click on that menu item, a dropdown list of all the punks that have challenges left to bid on will appear, sorted by name. Here, you can view a description of the punk, the submitting member's Aunt Tik's handle, the date they submitted it, and a list of the challenges for that punk that are still open for member bidding. The app sorts these by name and date range.

Clicking on each challenge item will provide a detailed description of everything you need to know to perform the task that comprises the challenge. If you see a challenge matching your skills and interests, click the "Bid" button.

Note that your available challenges list may be limited if you've never been awarded and successfully performed a punk challenge. Generally speaking, the app will restrict a new member's first challenge opportunities to those associated with dismembering punks (if a sufficient number of unawarded dismembering punk challenges are available — if not, the first-time member will see the complete list of all available challenges). Dismembering punks are overseen by the cell czar and the punk master, providing additional resources to new members who may need help performing their first challenge.

Once you've chosen to bid on a challenge, a dialog box will appear in which you can enter the number of points you want to bid on the challenge. Remember, the punk master will generally, though not always, award the challenge to the member bidding the lowest number of points to perform it. However, being awarded and completing challenges where you bid more points will allow you to accumulate points faster. Wisely choosing the number of points to bid is one of the skills you will develop with experience. The app sets the default bid for you at 10,000 points.

[Note: The scoring rules are updated occasionally to ensure maximum fairness and enjoyment for our premium members. There are also advanced rules covering scoring and bidding in select situations. You can find the updated complete set of rules at *Manual.AuntTiks.com*.]

Each challenge will display a date and time range when the bidder must perform the challenge. Though not intended to be precise, the punk author or master provides the window so that bidders can assess their likely availability to perform the challenge. If you cannot meet the date and time range specifications, you can suggest one or more time frames within the challenge time window that you *will* be available.

In the text box provided, you can enter information about any unique qualifications, such as education, skills, experience, tools, or other resources applicable to the task. When finished, click the "submit" button, and that's it. If the punk master accepts your bid for the challenge, they will notify you. The notification will contain the exact time you must perform the challenge and any other detailed information you need.

CAUTION: Remember to be on time when selected to perform a challenge. Discipline and coordination are necessary for a successful punk. If one challenge performance doesn't happen when planned, all the challenges after it are affected, and the punk may fail. Because of this requirement, while we understand that unexpected things can happen that might not be your fault, failure to perform a challenge on time may be grounds for penalties, including dismemberment. Bidding on a challenge is a commitment you must take seriously, even when the desired result is laughter.

For everyone's protection, challenge performances are on a need-to-know basis. This policy means that when performing a challenge, you are likely unaware of who is performing the other challenges in the punk or how many unique challenges there are (sophisticated punks can require two dozen or more challenges, all precisely timed). Everyone performing a punk challenge depends on everyone else performing challenges for that punk to do their task well and on time.

But you can take comfort in knowing that, perhaps surprisingly, most of Aunt Tik's punks go off without a hitch.

Good luck with your first challenge. We hope you enjoy performing it and seeing the result!

LEGALITY OF CHALLENGES AND PUNKS

Aunt Tik's built its business and reputation on two concepts: having fun and not hurting anyone (other than perhaps a subject's pride, and then only temporarily). Yes, we may occasionally push the envelope of good taste in pursuing the former. However, implicit in the latter is the idea that we do not violate the law or ask members to break the law. The cell czar reviews our punks and all the challenges comprising each punk for legality, safety, and propriety. The punk master again examines those elements before assigning challenge performers and taking responsibility for the challenge timing and notifications.

We also filter the quality of our members by requiring that a premium member in good standing vouches for all membership applicants. Additionally, we require that the cell czar, the highest officer in the cell, review all candidate applications.

We retain member contact information stored in encrypted form after a membership has terminated. We do not sell or allow anyone outside the Aunt Tik's organization access to your private data, which we retain to contact past members and protect other members, past and present. The ability to contact past members ensures that we can maintain the informational integrity critical to our operations and the safety and security of everyone involved. For example, current members should not be concerned that past members could reveal their membership.

HANDLING DISPUTES WITH NONMEMBERS

Due to the nature of our members' activities, and as we mention in our franchise information and other materials, disagreements between one or more members and the subject of a punk may occasionally arise. The cell czar, as the designated representative of involved members, and the franchisee organization are responsible for resolving these conflicts. The national Aunt Tik's bylaws require setting aside budget allocations at the cell level for arbitration, litigation, and other legal conflict-resolution tools and resources.

Aunt Tik's does not condone violent confrontation between members and nonmembers. Sometimes, during the performance of a challenge, conflict is unavoidable. **In the event of a possible conflict, walk away. If the other party does not disengage, call 911 and get help from law enforcement.** Aunt Tik's will not punish members for nonperformance of a challenge if the nonperformance was to avoid or terminate imminent violence.

If the performance of a challenge results in an intervention from law enforcement, always stop whatever you are doing relative to the challenge and cooperate fully with the officers.

If litigation related to the performance of a punk challenge becomes unavoidable, contact your cell czar to see what resources and support may be available from your local cell.

WOULD YOU LIKE TO START YOUR OWN AUNT TIK'S CELL?

While you can undoubtedly perform practical jokes without the security and camaraderie of an Aunt Tik's cell, our structure offers several benefits. We engineer our membership rules and punk performances to highlight the fun and facilitate participation for everyone. The volume of exciting punk results we make available assures a ready audience for the next one. And, the Aunt Tik's approach protects members and franchisees from personal responsibility for circumstances they can't control. We've been successfully doing that for almost ten years now. We are the only website supporting online practical joking worldwide; our popularity speaks for itself.

Our national leadership structure models itself after the proven approach taken by the National Football League — think "practical jokes" instead of "football." The teams, or in our case, cells, are semiautonomous. That allows our members the freedom to be creative and grow under the protective umbrella of a safe, secure, and proven system. We provide prospective franchise information at Aunt Tik's website (AuntTiks.com).

WANT TO TALK? HERE'S HOW TO REACH US

The Aunt Tik's mobile desktop app addresses the most common requests from members for resources and information. The app can determine your location and provide information and assistance specific to your local Aunt Tik's cell. The app offers help and other menus, access to the Aunt Tik's member messages forum, and the capability to send Signal messages to the local Aunt Tik's cell management team.

You can find other resources on the national website at AuntTiks.com.

You may also reach Aunt Tik's employees by mail or telephone via the address and number shown below (mail or telephone messages not directed to a specific employee by name cannot be delivered):

Aunt Tik's Jape Juice and Dido Dispensary
National Headquarters
P.O. Box 158465
Elkhart, Indiana 46516-8465
To the attention of [EMPLOYEE'S NAME GOES HERE]

**Telephone: 574.268.8300 [you will be asked for
the employee's extension or a name for lookup]**

THE WRITINGS OF
AVRIL MARIA SERENE